Signy Wealda

in

An Impression of Boots

By the same author

Memories of a Fading Empire
Journeys Through a Fading Empire
In the Shadow of a Fading Empire
On the Frontier of a Fading Empire

Signy Wealda
in
An Impression of Boots

J Leslie Evenden

Philadelphia, Pennsylvania, October 2024

ISBN 979-8-218-52493-7

FICTION/Historical/Ancient
Keywords: Gaul, Roman Empire, Visigoths, Dark Ages

Published by WiltonLogic LLC
Philadelphia, Pennsylvania, USA

Map 1: Kingdom of the Visigoths, showing principal towns, roads and waterways.

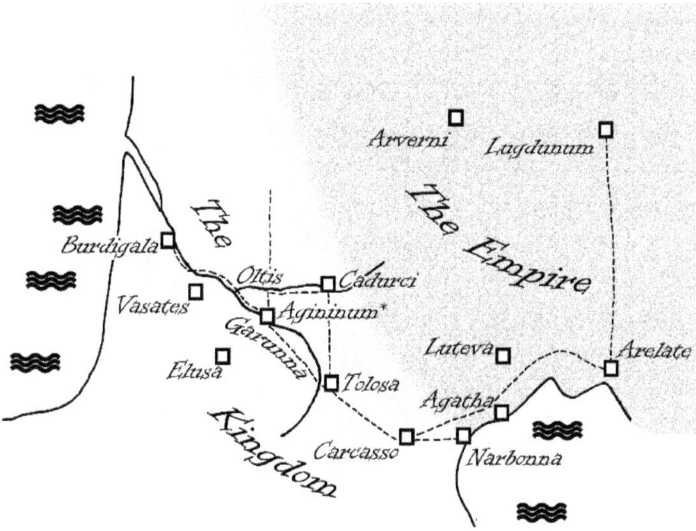

*Agininum is the fictional home of the characters in this story. Its location coincides with the historical city of Aginnum, modern Agen. The names used in this map are taken from the map "La Gaule administrative au Ve siècle" from *La France avant la France*, Bührer-Thierry and Mériaux, Belin, 2014, p.23.

Distances:		
	Burdigala to Agininum:	95 Roman miles
	Agininum to Tolosa	80 Roman miles
	Tolosa to Agatha	140 Roman miles
	Tolosa to Cadurci	90 Roman miles
	Tolosa to Arelate	265 Roman miles

Map 2: The town of Aginum, showing places of interest, antique and modern, and omitting those of none.

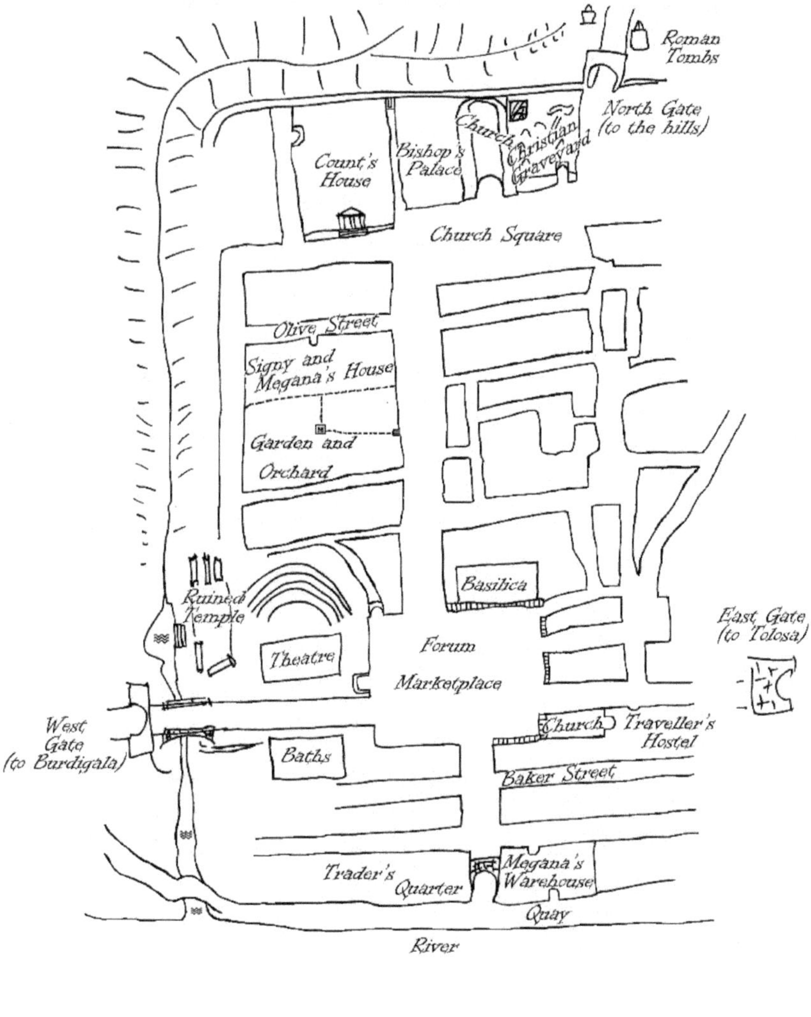

☙ Prologue ❧

The Year of Our Lord, 440

In the Visigoth Kingdom of Tolosa

The hut provided shelter from the rain and wind, shelter for a small fire and for the shepherd and his dog. The man stared out, across the flat grass, faintly illuminated by a sliver of moon peeping through the broken clouds. Here and there he could make out the shape of one of his flock, a darker shadow against the dark grass. In a moment, he would roll up his cape, stuff it under his head and catch some sleep.

His thoughts were interrupted by the dog, slowly uncurling and rising to her feet. She extended her back, first to the front and then to the rear, and after stretching stood still, her ears cocked. Then she growled softly.

How tiresome, thought the shepherd. What can be out there in the darkness? A fox passing by, not a wolf surely, because then the sheep, too, would have been alerted, would be on their feet, bells tinkling, warning the predator it had been spotted?

The dog growled again.

The shepherd stood, reached for his staff and took a couple of paces out of the protection of the hut. The night breeze was almost still. He heard a voice, carried from far off across the valley, but that was not what had alerted the dog. He, the man, could hear nothing suspicious, but the dog had heard something.

Suddenly, she was gone, loping away, not across the grass to where the flock lay, to where a hungry sheep hunter might be lurking, but off behind the hut, towards where a small stream had cut a gully, filled with scrubby trees, the remnants of the forest that had once covered these hills, so he had been told in his youth by his grandfather.

He could hear the dog barking as she vanished down the slope and disappeared. He followed slowly after, gripping his staff firmly. A wolf or stray bear could be sheltering in the gully, and he did not want to be taken by surprise. He followed the footpath, worn in the turf by the feet of thirsty beasts, himself included, which led down to the stream. He could still hear the dog, a little way off, threading her way through the trees. She had passed by the watering place and continued along the bank. Further down, he knew there was a track which crossed the stream at a shallow ford. Well, a sort of track, because he had never known anyone use it. It led from nowhere to nowhere… now. Probably, when people first came to these parts, it had some importance, a shortcut over the hills, perhaps from one settlement to another, but these days the track was more or less just a shading in the grass, a long thin clearing between the trees, only of any use to the forest animals.

The dog stopped barking. Judging from her last sound she must have reached the ford. He expected her to return, trotting along the path, her curiosity satisfied. He continued, taking care with his footing as he navigated tree roots and exposed stones, until he reached the point where the old track cut through the trees and stopped. There was something different, he thought, difficult to make out precisely in the thin beams of moonlight that penetrated the net of branches. He would come back in daylight and check again, but there was definitely something different about the ford than last time he had been here.

Above his head, above the trees, the clouds parted and the moonlight shone a little brighter. Then he caught sight of the dog. She was lying a little way up the track, off to the side.

That's odd, he thought. What's the matter with her? Has she hurt herself?

A few steps brought him closer, close enough to see that the dog had not hurt herself. She had been hurt by something, some animal probably, judging by the stain of blood on her side. He looked around, but could make out no sign of an attacker. He took another couple of steps forward, then dropped to one knee to examine his injured companion. The wound was deep, a gash that could not have come from a sharp stone or the broken end of a branch. A claw, teeth, maybe, or…but that was unlikely. Who would be wandering around on the empty hills at this time of the night?

As he began to rise, the answer came in the form of a blow to his head. As he fell beside the dog, he was dimly aware of a shape standing behind him – not a wolf, not a bear, but a man.

--oo0Ooo--

It was close to dawn when the shepherd came to. He pushed himself to a half-sitting position. Now he could see the dog clearly. She was dead, no doubt. Was he dead himself, he wondered, condemned to wander the world as a spectre, unburied as he seemed to be? He ran his hand down his body, his thigh. He certainly felt solid enough. His staff still lay beside him, and with its help, he managed to get to his feet. There was something he tried to remember, something he had noticed before he had fallen. He rubbed his hand across his head, winced, and then looked at it, now smeared with half-crusted blood. Had he been hit, or had he simply tripped in the dark? But the dog was dead. And the track, that was it, there was something odd about the track. Surely it had not been as broad as this last time he had been here. Then it had just been a thin strip of earth and stones where nothing grew. Now you could almost drive a cart between the trees.

He shook his head. There was something odd with him, too, as if the world was not quite as it should be. He looked down at the dog. He would have to bury her, but first he had to get something to eat and drink to dispel this odd, dizzy feeling. He shook his head again, trying to shake the feeling away, and as he did so, his eye caught an impression in the earth by the path, and a second a little further along. Boot prints.

Boot prints?

That jogged his memory a little more, the shadow that he thought he had seen behind him – a man, a man who could quite easily have hit him, could quite easily have intended to kill him, had perhaps killed the dog already, and who had left his traces in the earth.

He could not make sense of the situation. The man must have been a robber, but a robber of what? Of his sheep probably, but when, with an effort, he reached the side of the gully, the sheep were grazing peacefully in the first rays of the sun. His hut was untouched, not that there was anything there worth stealing.

He began to feel anxious. He could not manage the flock without the dog, without help. The dizziness would not go away. He would have to go for help. He could find help at the monastery, a long trudge across the hills, but they would know what to do. He would tell them what had happened. A strange tension began to take hold of him. He had to tell them what had happened, he felt. He *had* to tell them, before it was too late. He broke into a run, his feet pounding over the turf, his heart beating fit to burst.

The journey seemed effortless, almost as if he was running in a dream, his feet barely touching the ground, until at last the horizon was broken by the dark outline of the monastery buildings, picked out against the sky, growing larger and larger before his eyes. Just a little while longer and he would be hammering at the door, shouting for them to let him in. Then he felt that his legs were no longer obeying him, that they were becoming enormously heavy, that they were becoming tangled, that he was pitching forward. He hit the turf with a thud, and lay still, still, still, until he heard his Maker speaking to him.

↜ Chapter 1 ↝
Burdigala, Aquitania

The bishop was seated in a carved chair, one of his deacons standing beside him. He had a sheet in his hand, her petition, probably. His eyes rose from the sheet and met hers.

"There is only one 'l' in 'episcopal'," he said, with a smile. "You should employ a better-qualified scribe."

Megana Fabiana bowed her head slightly in acknowledgement, in a simulacrum of humble correction. She was her own scribe and had, of course, written episcopal with two l's quite deliberately, to see if the man would notice and react. In fact, she had employed this childish trick because she had a pretty good idea beforehand that he would not be able to resist the temptation to criticise her work. *Nothing gets past him*, Master Lanius had said. Well, that was evident, not even one small spelling error! But the fact he had chosen to mention the mistake, and the tone of voice he used, revealed he was not just a man with an eye for details, but one who was greatly pleased with himself, and only too willing to point out the faults of others.

She had first visited the palace, had approached his clerks asking for an interview weeks ago, but their bland pleasantries had led nowhere. She had visited the church and caught one of his assistants in an unguarded moment, in a place where lying would be sinful.

"You should write a petition," the man had said.

One glance around the church, however, had told her she was unlikely to get very far with her petition. The building might look plain outside, but inside it was like a jewel box, with stained glass, mosaics, paintings, images of the saints in stucco arranged in niches along the walls. Uniformed deacons and other hangers-on had been seated on a horseshoe of benches in the apse at the far end during the service and, to one side, on a splendid throne, the bishop had presided, more finely dressed than a king or emperor.

There was nothing, absolutely nothing, that a merchant, especially a female merchant newly arrived from Britannia, could offer to an organisation like the Church of Burdigala. But it was not the church she had in mind as she stood, gazing at the riches around her.

You have to go through the bishop, Lanius had told her. If she wanted to establish herself as a merchant in the city, not just as an assistant to Master Lanius, not just as her father's pretty daughter, but as a merchant in her own right, she would have to trade with the landowners of Aquitania, buy the produce of their estates, their fields, their orchards and vineyards, and in return sell them the materials they needed to maintain their lifestyles.

Megana was an outsider, but Lanius had lived in Burdigala almost all his life, ever since he had been apprenticed to a merchant and married his daughter, so he should know. But Megana did not really need a lesson, her companion's friendly advice. She had visited the city before, sent by her father to spend a year learning the trade route and the commodities which could be exchanged between Britannia and Aquitania. She had learned that the property and riches around Burdigala were in the hands of the Roman elite, *still* in the hands of the Roman elite, would be a better way of putting it, despite the fading of the Empire. Once the governor and his magistrates, sent out from Rome, would have transmitted the demands of the emperor to the provincial landowners; the desires of his immensely wealthy allies in the Senate, the needs of his army, and the thousands and thousands of poor artisans and slaves who teemed his capital city. Then the landowners, many of whom were absentees, often those self-same senators, would have harvested, been taxed or appropriated, if necessary, and delivered the produce and goods to meet those needs and desires. Now, in the span of a few years, all that organisation had evaporated. New rulers had arrived, the Goths, "Our Men", they called themselves, allies, so it was said, of the emperor, though more like ruffians who needed to be bought off, pacified, until…well, until the emperor sorted himself out and put them in their place: back across the Rhine, under the lash, six feet below the ground, the future would tell. In the meantime, the Roman elite stuck together, defending their dwindling interests, and since the governor had been replaced by a barbarian king, they took their cue from the only symbol of Roman rule who remained: the bishop. And because they, the elite, took their cue from the bishop, then so did everyone else, especially those who feared for their life and livelihood in the present, and their eternal souls in the hereafter. With a good word from the bishop, both body and soul would be redeemed.

The bishop, quite naturally, hated the new rulers, hated the barbarians, not only because they were barbarians, but because they worshipped Christ in the wrong way, so they were damned to hell, and if they were damned to hell in the next life, in the bishop's eyes, they could be damned to hell in this one, too. And the barbarians returned the sentiment. The bishop and his Roman friends and allies were rich, and the barbarians had once been poor, but they did not intend to remain poor. Once their fathers and grandfathers had sacked and pillaged in Italia. The city of Rome itself had been forced to buy them off. As a result, they had been bribed by lands in Aquitania and the Narbonensis, confiscated or, in the most favourable circumstances, bought cheaply from the very same Roman elite. Now they were in charge, officially in charge, with a nice treaty saying so, all signed and sealed by the man at the top.

That was bad luck for the bishop and his friends, and it left them resentful and scheming.

Megana Fabiana was also resentful and scheming. She was resentful due to her current circumstances, a stranger in a strange land, but she had learned to be scheming from infancy. She had learned to be scheming as a woman in a world dominated by men, as a trader in a world where trade was considered beneath contempt, improper, a form of exploitation, practised against dignified worthies and the impoverished alike.

She had to be especially scheming now if she was going to succeed in her new life. She had managed to assemble a considerable quantity of silver before she was compelled to leave. But a hoard of silver, however large, could not provide housing, food and drink for her and her retainers for a lifetime. A hoard of silver could not provide the excitement of the chase for a bargain, the pursuit of a customer, the thrill of the deal. The silver had to be put to work, buying and selling. That was the occupation she knew, and she was good at it, but in Burdigala there were already plenty of traders, traders with good connections. Master Lanius, her father's partner, and now after him her own companion in business, was one of them, and he had advised that there was only one way forward for a newcomer to Burdigala, and that was through Bishop Bartolomeus. With a good word from the bishop, doors would open, barns and storehouses would open, purses would open.

And to gain access to the bishop, Lanius carefully explained, Megana would have to be noticed.

She was a good-looking woman with her clothes on, so people told her, and with her clothes off, she often told herself. She had strolled through the town, discreetly primped, tastefully bejewelled, shopped in the market with a posse of servants, visited the baths and attended the cathedral. Lanius and his clerks spread benign gossip that she was newly widowed in Britannia – to explain her baby daughter, Sophia – but that her husband had died suddenly of the murrain – murrain could kill cows and sheep, so why not husbands? – to explain the absence of the baby's father. She had accompanied Lanius on several expeditions to nearby estates, been seen to gently persuade him to purchase wine and agricultural goods that the merchant did not need for slightly inflated prices.

"Lanius, dear cousin," she had said – his sister was married to her brother – when he had complained of her poor bargaining, "if we can't sell the wine, I'll drink it myself."

There were days when she felt like swallowing an entire barrel, like diving in and drowning herself, but she had managed to offload the wine upcountry for a tolerable loss. *You have to spend money to gain money*, she said to herself. That was an unavoidable aspect of being a merchant. The skill was in knowing when and how much to spend and calculating the likely outcome before you started.

Finally, she had managed to attract enough attention, and that had led to the interview with the bishop.

"A woman's place is not in the market," the bishop declared, preaching to his audience of one, "unless she is a cook or a kitchen maid, of course," he added with a smile. "A woman's place is to create a godly household, to support her husband with a well-run home. A young, wealthy and attractive widow, as you undoubtedly appear to be, Mistress Fabiana, should have no difficulty in finding a partner. I would be quite willing to make introductions of that nature," the bishop concluded.

Megana's mouth smiled. Megana's lips responded dutifully to the bishop's comments with modest acceptance and provided suitable answers to his further questions.

Then an inflexion in the prelate's intonation indicated that the interview had come to an end, a gesture to his deacon that she was dismissed, to be escorted from his presence. She rose, thanking the bishop for his time, promising to donate to the Easter celebrations. She would keep her promise, she reflected, not because she felt a need to mollify the bishop, but because keeping on the right side of the local gods was a sound investment for a trader.

She slowly made her way out of his palace, past the cathedral and into the market square, towards the house Lanius had obtained on her behalf. Once the property of a minor landowner, it was situated in a quiet side street, in easy strolling distance of the quayside. Paulinus, the previous owner, had ingratiated himself with the new rulers at first, and then betrayed them. His house had been looted, and the man had been forced to seek refuge in a neighbouring town. The Roman had been happy to sell the semi-derelict buildings to Merchant Lanius, and finally scuttle away across the frontier, into the remaining domains of the Empire, with the little he had received. He had, apparently, written a poem, bemoaning his fate, but only his friends had read the work. More than likely the bishop was already aware of the real identity of the new owner of Paulinus' neat little residence.

--oo0oo--

"How did your interview with the bishop go?" asked Lanius, later in the evening.

"He kept his hands off you, I hope," added Vespa, Lanius' wife.

"It was a waste of time before I even began," Megana said, sighing. "The man had his mind made up…no, let's say he is so imbued with principles to which he is an unthinking prisoner, it's useless even contemplating engaging his mind."

"That sounds very harsh," said Lanius.

"That's because you are easily contained within the circumference of his principles," replied Megana, "whereas I remain outside."

"Better that way," added Vespa. "He may be a married man but…" The trader's wife sipped at her wine.

Megana frowned. Should she acknowledge an additional insult since the bishop had not stroked her knee or fondled her breast as he patronised her? It would not have been the first time a man had tried those negotiating tactics, she grimly recalled.

"My future isn't here in Burdigala," she said. "That became quite evident from my meeting with the bishop."

"But there's no return to Britannia," murmured Lanius.

"No, there's not, and I'm not going to abandon Burdigala entirely. I know that crucial trade passes through the city. Our fleet's criss-crossing Oceanus, river to river, port to port, from the Garunna to the Liger, and Vigo to Puttby. But despite that, I think I must till other vineyards, so to speak. The Goths are constructing a new capital for their kingdom, a palace, churches, baths, inns and residences, in the city of Tolosa. Every one of those needs filling with goods, furniture, pottery, silver. Every inhabitant requires food and drink, and as their surroundings grow more luxurious, so do their tastes. I've a feeling I might fit in better amongst the barbarians than the fine folk of Burdigala."

Her cousin grimaced.

"I wouldn't say we're so fine."

"I didn't mean you. I meant the landowners and wealthy imperial families who still control this area. No, I'll be visiting on a regular basis, don't worry. Your men have laboured through the winter to patch up the house for me, and the work'll have to be completed because I still intend to stay there when I visit."

"But you'll trade out of Tolosa…or perhaps Aginimum since the city is conveniently about halfway between Burdigala and Tolosa?" Vespa, of course, had read her mind.

"I've already found a house in Aginnum. You know the one, Lanius?"

"That house in Olive Street that's been abandoned for years – ever since I was a child – almost a ruin?" Lanius replied. "It'll need a lot of fixing up, more so than the Paulinus house."

"And your friend will join you," enquired Vespa, still a little unsure of the relationship between Megana and the woman she had described as her blood sister.

"Signy's already there, with some of her retainers. Renovating the buildings will provide them with a project. They've done that type of work before."

All three fell silent for a moment. In Burdigala, it had not helped that her friend looked so much like one of the new rulers, Megana recalled, with her light-coloured hair and blue eyes. It had not helped that Signy spoke Latin with a heavy accent and her grammar was frequently inaccurate. The ordinary townspeople had been suspicious, and the local dignitaries, when they deigned even to notice her, had been downright hostile. Signy had been out of place, ill at ease, ever since they had arrived in Aquitania. She was intelligent, brave, fun to be around, and above all she was not the slightest bit interested in trading. If only Signy was a man, Megana reflected, she would be the ideal husband that everyone wished she would find. Instead, they had sworn an oath, to support one another come what may. She turned her hand to look at the white mark that cut across the pad of her thumb and felt a warm smile spreading across her face. She held up the scarred digit towards Lanius and Vespa.

"To hell with the bishop, to hell with all bishops," she said. "My sister and I'll stick together and defy them all," she continued, with a nod towards Vespa. Then she turned to the merchant. "Tomorrow, Lanius, the packhorses will be loaded, the carts stacked with goods, and this time *I'll* lead the next convoy upriver and to Aginínum, to Tolosa. Just give me your seal and some letters of introduction and see what I can accomplish."

--oo0Ooo--

Vespa raised her glass with a laugh, and slowly Lanius raised his, too. He still wasn't quite sure how this excitable young woman would cope in the southlands, but Vespa's family and Megana's had been trading companions for generations. His own sister had married Alexander, Megana's half-brother – he had introduced the pair himself. Sometimes you just had to go with the flow.

"To your success," he toasted.

"To all our success," Megana replied.

ೞ Chapter 2 ೫
Tolosa, Capital City of the Visigoths

There was a burst of laughter from just outside the arched entrance to the audience chamber. Conversation ceased and all heads turned in that direction. The king, Theodoric, entered the room, his attention at that moment occupied by a heavy-set bearded man of around his own age. He was wily enough, however, to drop the evidently amusing conversation and shift his eyes and smile to the men waiting in the room.

"Thormond!" He held out his arms in greeting. The man addressed stepped forward and shared the embrace. "We'll not be needing your army for a good while, I hope!"

The king's bearded companion gave Thormond an ill-disguised sneer.

"Sismond, my old friend!" The king thumped the next man in line on the shoulder. "We've not seen you at court for a while! How's business in Agininum?"

"All well, my lord," replied Sismond, count of that city, but the king had already passed on to his neighbours.

"Rodmer! Meltris! My old friends!"

Sismond exchanged a glance with Thormond, his cousin, as the king continued his progress down the line, giving out hugs, pats, even a kiss on the cheek, as he made his way to the dais at the far end of the room.

"He seems exceedingly jaunty!" the Count of Agininum commented.

Thormond merely grunted, then added, "The king or Ludiger?"

"Theo, of course."

"Let's hear what he has to say," muttered Thormond, as the king mounted the couple of steps to the platform and turned to face his audience.

"Friends, friends, I have excellent, wonderful news. As you can see, our honoured duke, Ludiger, has returned from Arelate and brought with him a treaty, stamped and sealed by the *magister militum*, General Aetius, confirming a recognition of our right to our lands and promising an end to the hostilities."

The king's bearded companion, Duke Ludiger, swept his eyes over the gathering with a trace of a smile.

"Aetius had already recognised our right to our lands, why does he have to do it again?" muttered Thormond. "It didn't stop him attacking us before," he continued under his breath. "The Empire will never accept our right, and that's that, no matter how many seals and pieces of parchment Ludiger carries back from Aetius."

A glance from Theodoric in his direction put an end to Thormond's whispers.

"General Thormond, you need only muster our cavalry. Thanks to Duke Ludiger, our farmers may remain with their wives this year."

"Shouldn't be any shortage of additional volunteers in that case," came one merry voice.

"And a big boost to our families next spring," came a second, to guffaws around the room.

"I'm glad everyone appreciates what our duke has accomplished," said the king, raising his hand, "and to show my gratitude, tomorrow I'll be holding a feast in his honour."

The expression on his face was all that was needed to ensure the assembly understood that attendance was compulsory.

--oo0Ooo--

Thormond and Sismond had been at the back of the room and were among the first to leave when the meeting broke up. They said nothing while strapping on their swords, which had been stacked in the entry way to the audience chamber while they were in the presence of the king, and maintained their silence until they were crossing the outer court towards the gate.

"I didn't like the look on Ludiger's face," said Thormond at last. "I don't give much for his so-called treaty, but there's no doubt he has managed to ingratiate himself even more with Theodoric."

"They go back years, you know that," replied Sismond. "His father fought with Theo's father in Hispania. We're comparative newcomers."

"And you know that my status, my position in court, is tied to the army. If the army's kept home, I might as well sit in Carcasso and watch my grapes grow."

"Wouldn't do you any harm."

"What? And let Ludiger and his sons spin more lies for the king?"

Sismond laughed.

"You worry too much, cousin."

"And you don't worry enough, cousin," replied the general. "Yes, we're newcomers, and we'd be – our family would be – complete nonentities if I didn't worry, if I didn't sweat the details and make sure Our Men are kept on their toes and don't become just another bunch of dupes of the Empire."

He stopped in the street and turned to his cousin.

"One miss, one sign of weakness, and they'll be on us. You know perfectly well that every son-of-a-bitch Roman in our lands is only waiting for the moment to slit our throats and take back what we've won from them."

Sismond held up his hands.

"Cousin, I'm Count of Agininum. I don't need a sermon from you. I deal with those sons of bitches, as you call them, every day. In my parish, they're quiet as lambs, and I intend to keep it that way."

Thormond snorted.

"You have the luxury of a county that doesn't border the Empire, Sismond. I do not. I don't intend to drop my guard."

There was a shout from further down the street, and they could see two men hurrying from the direction of the palace.

"I'll leave you to your lambs," muttered Thormond, and with a curt wave at the approaching figures, turned up a side street.

"What's got into him?" gasped Rodmer.

Sismond shook his head.

"He's worried Ludiger's rise means his fall."

"I blame the king, Theo himself, with all this talk about maintaining a balance," said Meltris.

"Thormond has a point, though," said Sismond. "He and his men would be first in line if there was treachery from the Empire's side, whereas we, especially you, Meltris, tucked away in Vasates, are well out of arrow range."

"Well, we all know whose arrow he's in range of just now," laughed Meltris. "Cupid's!" Thormond's outline rounded a corner and vanished from sight. "That's just typical of him, that he's pointing fingers at us, and off he sneaks to his girlfriend while his family's down in Carcasso."

"Hardly sneaking," chuckled Rodmer. "Everyone knows about Thormond and Xancha. They're more of a faithful pair than most married couples."

Sismond said nothing. His cousin's relationship with Xancha, the Syrian former dancer, was a source of more than a little bitterness.

"Let's head up to the Fox Tavern," he proposed, forcing himself to sound jolly. "There'll be some fun to be had, and good wine. After all," he added, adopting a groaning voice, "tomorrow we're going to have to sit through half a day of praise for Ludiger."

His companions laughed, and the three men set off along the street, unspokenly taking a different route through the town to the one just taken by General Thormond.

"You don't think much of this treaty, then?" said Rodmer.

"Never trust a damned Roman," answered Sismond. "There've been plenty of treaties before, and they've broken every one, just as soon as it suits them. They don't want us here, and they'll never give up trying to get rid of us, one way or another."

Meltris sighed.

"I suppose that's why there's the rule against intermarriage."

"You sound like you take that personally," Sismond observed.

"You could say that," grumbled Meltris. "After Henna died, I had my eyes on a widow, with a good bit of land just south of Vasates. 'Refused', that's what I got from the court. And she was willing."

"But we're in the minority, dear Meltris," said Sismond, sighing. "It's not you and I…we know what we're doing, but supposing the Romans began demanding to marry *our* daughters. In a generation or two Our Men would be wiped out, and they'd be back in control that way."

"By making love, not war," laughed Rodmer.

Meltris snorted.

"But, Meltris," Rodmer continued, "didn't I hear that you've shacked up with your widow anyway, and to hell with the legal niceties?"

"It's not the same," muttered the Count of Vasates. "I wanted to make an honest woman of her."

"Listen, Meltris," chuckled Rodmer, "you can be honest with us…we know you were really just interested in getting control of her land, and for that you need to marry her."

"Hey, come off it! Apollonia and I get along real well. There's even a kiddie on the way."

"Congratulations, Meltris," said Sismond, thumping his friend on the back, "though I wouldn't say that too loud near my cousin, that you're expecting a little half-Roman addition to the family. You should stick to slave girls in the future, like I do."

Sismond and his companions had arrived at a crossroads, where they almost collided with a figure hurrying across their path.

"Hallo!" called Sismond, reaching out for the man. "Can't you watch where you are going?"

"I'm most sorry," replied the other.

"Neighbour!" Sismond exclaimed. "Bishop, what are you doing here?"

"Oh, I'm sorry, Count Sismond, I didn't recognise you in the dark."

"I don't think you saw me at all, Anastasius," laughed the count, "or any of us," he added, indicating his companions. "May I present my neighbour, Bishop Anastasius of Agininum, and these rogues are Count Rodmer of Elusa and Count Meltris of Vasates."

The bishop bowed his head to the counts.

"What are you doing in Agininum, Anastasius? Not straying from the path, I hope?" Sismond said, to chuckles from his friends.

"I was in Arelate…on church business…and I heard that Duke Ludiger and his party would be travelling to Tolosa, so I joined them. Safety in numbers, you know. And now I must be on my way, duty calls…" And with a wave of his hand, the bishop vanished into the dark of the alley.

"I could swear you'll soon find him in the arms of one of Xancha's beauties," commented Rodmer as the trio set off once again. "It's in the nature of bishops."

"Not Anastasius, I think," Sismond said, smiling. "I'm sure I saw a book under his arm."

"You sound like you get on well with your bishop, Sismond?" grumbled Meltris. "I'm surprised. Mine hates me."

"Maybe you've stolen his girlfriend," chuckled Rodmer. "He probably had his own eyes on her land!"

"Fornication, he called it," muttered Meltris.

"Anastasius is not a bad fellow for a Roman bishop," said Sismond, before his friends could begin to quarrel in earnest. "Doesn't cause any trouble, not too greedy and not too holy."

"Doesn't quarrel with you on account of your lifestyle?" asked Meltris.

"He keeps his opinions to himself," said Sismond, "and besides, he's a great friend of Thormond's sister, Hildefrith, and her companion. I suppose he's learned not to be too censorious. I wouldn't be surprised if his book wasn't a gift for the holy house."

Meltris grunted.

"They should all stick to books. They'd be a damn sight less trouble that way."

Ahead, the Fox Tavern was a welcoming sight, lit up by blazing torches, and with men of all ranks spilling out into the street. The crowd parted deferentially to allow the three counts to enter, and with a wave to the host, they clattered up the stairs to one of the private rooms.

✿ Chapter 3 ✿
Agininum, a Small Town

Signy let the horse find her own pace, cantering over the sheep-nibbled grass of the green way. She loved this ride, loved being out of the town, loved the open country. Even in Juteland she had never dared to let her horse loose in this way, but up on the hills there was no one to pass judgement save a few men tending their flocks, only worried that their dogs would get restless and want to run alongside her. Once or twice, flushed and excited by the speed, she stopped by a shepherd and exchanged a few words to polish up her patois, accepted his offer to share a bite to eat, and then trotted away, sedately down the hill, returning to town as demurely as she could dissemble. She was trying hard to pass as a lady in a society where anyone with fair hair and blue eyes was assumed to be a ruffian, if not worse.

Maybe the displacement to Agininum was going to work, she reflected. Most of the house on Olive Street that Megana had bought was in a terrible state. The accommodation was better than the boat that had brought her and her companions over the ocean, but not a lot better. Just now the whole household was squeezed into the few rooms that had been occupied by the watchman and his family during the years of abandonment. It was just as well that they had all experienced hard lives in earlier times. The men had made some emergency repairs, but sagging roofs and rotten floors still needed fixing.

Much though she missed her son, Einar, and her friend, Megana, that they had remained in Burdigala was for the best. Megana was altogether too used to a materially comfortable life, and the house on Olive Street was still no place for a toddler. However, this situation could not last much longer, Signy reflected. Megana had already written of her frustrations with the authorities in Burdigala. Soon, not only would they need space in the house in Olive Street for herself and her friend, but also quarters for their children, Einar and Megana's daughter, the infant Sophia, and their maids and cooks. And the stables needed fixing up, and chambers for the retainers constructed above. And the garden, which was completely overgrown – there would be space for her herbs and medicinal plants. And the fountain – she would have to get that flowing again. Oddly, she had always dreamed of having a garden with a fountain at the centre.

A grey shadow appeared on the horizon, the outline of the monastery of Mons Agininum against the sky. As yet, she had not dared to ride up to the door and ask permission to look inside. I am, let's face it, she thought, a heathen, with the mark of a sister of Freya tattooed on my shoulder. How welcome would a representative of a pagan religion be in a house of Christian women? She took a tighter grip of the reins, a reminder to the horse that it would soon be time to slow the pace, to pass the monastery in a dignified manner, just in case someone noticed her.

The horse, however, began to slow of her own accord, and Signy could soon see why. A group of people were standing, huddled not far from the track. As she drew nearer, she realised that they were examining a dark heap on the ground. She pulled the horse to a walk, slipped her leg over her back and dropped down. A couple of heads turned at her approach, and then returned to the body, because the heap was the body of a man.

"Let me through," said Signy, elbows separating the crowd. "I was a healer in my own land."

A well-dressed older woman, tall and severe, turned towards her. Her eyes met Signy's, and in an instant they seemed to have taken measure of one another.

"I fear you are a little late," said the woman, "if you were planning on healing him."

Signy only half heard the comment, dropping to her knees, her hand seeking the wrist of the supine man, a countryman by his dress, pitched forward and lying on his belly, his face resting against the turf. There were signs of blood on the dirty and ill-trimmed hair at the back of his head, but it was not recent, and no great damage was apparent.

There was no movement in the wrist. The well-dressed woman was right. The man was beyond her help.

"He's dead," she said, beginning to rise to her feet.

"We didn't need a healer to tell us that. But how," the woman asked, her gaze on Signy rather than the corpse, "would you judge he had died had you been in your own land?"

There were no signs of wounds to his back, no blood on his tunic.

"Can you help me turn him over?" Signy begged, looking up at the curious faces. A couple of the crowd members bent down and heaved at the body.

"No signs of wounds on his body, either," she muttered, mainly to herself, and the only abrasions to his face were where he had fallen.

"His heart, perhaps, has given out," she said, but then something popped into her mind. "Though there's blood on the back of his head. Perhaps he hit his head. Perhaps he fell, tripped in the dark."

"But he couldn't have fallen here, or tripped," said the severe woman.

That was true…unless he had fallen over his own feet. The grass was flat and even, and there were no obstacles. Even a blind person could have run and scampered without fear of falling.

"Perhaps he was struck down by God?" muttered one of the onlookers. There's always one, thought Signy.

"I've seen," said Signy, "a case like this, once before in Britannia. A man fell from his horse while riding home. He came into his house, told his wife what had happened, and moments later he dropped down dead."

She looked around the circle.

"People said that was a punishment from God," she added.

"Amen," murmured several voices from among the crowd.

"And why?" asked the older woman.

"He had been visiting his mistress. Half the neighbourhood knew about the relationship, and they were quite content to spread such gossip."

"You sound sceptical?"

"I would guess," said Signy, "that if you were to cut open this man's head, you would find it full of blood."

"Because you did that, cut open the man's head, on that previous occasion?" The scepticism had vanished from the woman's voice, replaced by a tone more like astonishment.

"Because the man's wife didn't believe the rumours, and because I found damage on the side of the man's head, similar to what we can all see here."

There was no point in admitting she had done exactly what the woman suggested, and sliced open the victim's skull. Astonishment could easily turn to disgust and hostility. Nevertheless, Signy would have been willing to place silver that this man would have a similar blood clot inside his head, perhaps even fresh blood, if the injury was recent. However, she had an inkling that placing bets on the cause of death, and the necessity to cut open a body to confirm the cause, would be frowned on by the severe-looking woman and the people clustered around the corpse.

"He hit his head," Signy said firmly, "and if he didn't do it here, he must have done it somewhere else. Who is he, by the way?"

"Ah, yes," said the woman, "I didn't say. It's our shepherd, Xeno."

"Then where are his sheep?" asked Signy.

The woman's eyebrows slowly arched and she pursed her lips.

"That, my dear, is a very good question."

--oo00oo--

It was a question, however, that had a very simple answer.

"He was here three days ago," said one of the onlookers. "He said he was taking the sheep over towards Ager's stream."

“Then you might want to gather them in,” said another, “otherwise you’ll be losing more than the shepherd. Unguarded sheep…either the wolves will take them or the bandits, depending on who gets there first.”

“Then we had better get there first,” said the older woman, suddenly decisive. “You, sir, since you are being so helpful,” she said to the onlooker, “you shall assist my man to carry the body into the house, and then we had better go and gather in these sheep. Do you fancy another ride, my dear?” she added, turning to Signy.

“And who will I be riding with?”

“Ah yes, you’re a stranger, one of the women who have occupied the house in Olive Street, if my guess is correct. My name is Hildefrith, and for my sins, which are many, I’ve been placed in charge of this monastery.”

Master Lanius had grown up in these parts, Signy recalled, and Sister Hildefrith was one of the people he had mentioned. Sister Hildefrith was of Visigoth stock, he had recounted, and related to the local count and various other important men in Tolosa. Hildefrith must have been practically born on a horse, she thought, although that would have been a fair few years ago.

“My situation here does not present many opportunities for riding, and even more rarely, for a good gallop across the hills,” the abbess continued. “You may bring your horse to the yard, Miss Healer-in-My-Own-Land,” she went on. “My stablemaster, Petrus, will find some refreshment for you and your mount, while I dress more appropriately for a ride. Petrus,” she added, turning to the stablemaster, “don’t you dare leave without me.”

☙ Chapter 4 ❧ Agininum

Signy was already dressed for riding, in clothing much as a man would wear: loose trousers, and a tunic tied in at the waist. Sister Hildefrith was forced to improvise. She returned almost before the stable hands had prepared her horse. Hitching up her long gown, with a heave up from one of the boys, she threw her leg over the animal's back, revealing grey woollen hose and a good stretch of pale bare leg.

"What are we waiting for?" she called to Signy and Petrus and one of his assistants, who were preoccupied exchanging amused smiles, and urged her mount out of the yard. Petrus whistled for his dog, a long-legged hunting hound, and they followed the women.

The four galloped a mile or two, the dog loping easily beside them, before Sister Hildefrith eased up, and then they continued at a gentle trot, the two women now trailing Petrus and his assistant, who knew the hills when they did not.

"Over there, another mile or so," the stablemaster said, pointing into the distance. "Xeno must have come all this way in the night. What on earth could have happened to him to make him do that?"

As they approached the site of the shepherd's last day in life, they were met by an unexpected sight. Sheep, peacefully grazing, quite undisturbed. It was enough to make Petrus rein in his horse and wait until the women had come up alongside.

"This is odd," observed the stablemaster. "If Xeno had been attacked by bandits, I would've expected them to have driven off the sheep, and as for wolves, well, there should be at least one or two carcasses lying around, but I can't see any."

"Wolves might have chased after a running man," observed Signy.

"But they would've returned for their meal," replied the stablemaster.

"Maybe he was spooked," Petrus' assistant began. "I remember a story—"

"Enough of that," snapped Hildefrith, and the man fell silent.

The dog had run on ahead, its nose close to the ground, and finally vanished down a slope into a tree-filled ravine.

"There's a hut by the edge of the trees," said Petrus, "where the shepherds can shelter in bad weather. I'll wager that's where the dog is heading."

They set the horses in motion again, on the trail of the dog.

All at once there came the sound of barking, from out of sight over the brow, down among the vegetation.

"Stay here," said the stablemaster, dismounting and drawing a short sword. He gestured to his assistant to follow him. Ahead, the women could see the hut, so instead of accompanying the men in the direction of the barking dog, they took a sheep-trodden track towards the shelter, merely three low wattle walls and a roof. Signy pulled out her knife, a foot of glinting steel, drawing a quick expression of approval from the abbess. The door was open, and when they looked inside, though the fire was dead, there was no sign of a struggle, and the few, poor objects, a couple of pots, a metal vessel to hang over the fire for cooking purposes, a rough bed covered by a blanket, were undisturbed. The shepherd's jacket lay on the ground.

Just then there was a shout from outside, so they turned, standing blinking for a moment in the daylight. The shout came again, from the direction that Petrus had taken, not a cry for help, but to attract their attention.

A narrow path led from the hut down to the stream, presumably the path taken by the shepherds to collect water. The women followed it, Signy in the lead, still holding her dagger. Petrus was standing about one hundred feet downstream, where a footpath descended the bank, crossed the stream through a shallow ford and disappeared among the trees on the other side. The dog stood whining by his side. When they reached him, they found the source of the dog's disquiet. A shaggy heap, the remains of the shepherd's guard dog, lay by the path.

"Take a look at the wound," said Petrus.

Signy bent over the corpse. While the fur of the dog partially concealed the injury, by running her fingers through the hairs, Signy recognised the similarity to all too many wounds she had seen before, all too many with the same result as had befallen the dog.

She straightened up again.

"A stab to the heart," she confirmed.

"That was no accident and no wolf," said Hildefrith, "and I think we should assume that Xeno must have discovered whoever did it."

"But who could have been wandering out here?" asked Petrus.

"Someone, a man, who didn't like being disturbed," said Hildefrith, "who didn't like others knowing what he was up to."

Motioning his dog to remain, the stablemaster took a few steps forward, peering down at the ground, at the point where the muddy path met the stream.

"Boot prints," he said, "come, look."

The two women cautiously walked forward, their eyes on the earth. The dog, too, silently rose to its feet and padded after them.

"See, there," said Petrus, pointing. Signy crouched down, now seeing the outline of a boot, a pattern of deeper impressions, where hobnails had sunk into the mud.

"Does this tell you anything?" asked Hildefrith, with a note of anxiety. She seemed to be beginning to realise this might not be a good situation for a middle-aged woman.

Petrus sniffed.

"Any other time, I would have said a boot like that would have belonged to a Roman soldier."

"Any other time," echoed Signy.

"Well, Mistress, since our new masters arrived – begging your pardon, Mistress – we've seen precious few soldiers, and those we have seen haven't been the types to be wearing standard-issue military boots."

"And what types would those have been?" asked Signy.

Petrus shrugged.

"Rough ones, auxiliaries, irregular cavalry…" He suddenly pointed. "Look, there are hoof prints…someone must've been riding a horse with them."

"Couldn't that be older?" asked the abbess. "Someone else using the track?"

The stablemaster shook his head.

"Look, here the hoof prints pass over the boots, and here, you can see boots disturbing the hoof prints, almost as if there was a group of booted men, and one – more perhaps – on horseback."

"I don't like this," said Hildefrith, suddenly. Petrus looked up, and saw her face was pale and tight.

"I'm sorry, my lady, you're right. I think it's best we return."

The four of them clambered back up the slope, away from the stream and into the fresh air.

"It's strange," muttered the stablemaster, as they negotiated the rough path, "but I've known that track for years, and no one has ever used it much. Odd that it's got so busy all of a sudden."

Signy, her thoughts on the dead dog and the boot prints, felt her foot slip on a damp stone. She teetered for a moment before Petrus' stable hand, walking behind her, caught her waist.

"Thanks," she said with a smile. "I should have taken more care. There are plenty of places here where you could trip and fall."

"Especially in the dark," said Petrus. "Perhaps the same thing happened to old Xeno."

"It must have been quite a shock," said Hildefrith, "finding his faithful friend dead like that."

When they reached the flat land again, the horses were grazing peacefully, and the sheep, too.

"What about our flock?" asked Hildefrith. "We can't leave the sheep here unguarded. Even if the mysterious dog murderer did not take them, with no shepherd, they'll soon become victims of the next passing thief."

"Or the next passing wolf, maybe," said Petrus. "Can you help me round them up? You see that sheep there," he added, with a glance at Signy and pointing, "the one with the bell, if we can get her moving towards home, the others will follow along."

The stable hand had already ridden off, in a wide circle to the left of Petrus, to help drive the flock together. Signy noticed that Hildefrith had no hesitation in kicking her horse into motion in the opposite direction. For a woman of God, she seemed to have surprising practical skills. Signy herself had never herded sheep and decided to remain close to Petrus and avoid disturbing the work of those with the appropriate experience. The sheep began to look up, anxious, disturbed, first edging and then walking, and then hurrying away from the approaching riders. In a short while, Hildefrith and the stable hand had them converging on the spot where the old sheep with the bell was slowly but surely gaining motion in the direction of the far-off monastery, gently encouraged by the dog.

A yelp from Petrus, and the dog made a curious run, back and forth. The old sheep took one look and lumbered off, followed by the rest of the flock.

It was nightfall before anxious faces peering into the dark saw them approaching, before the sisters could make out the form of their abbess in the gloom, before they had the sheep penned up in the monastery yard, before Signy could set off, a little nervously, into the rapidly darkening southern night, on her way back to town.

"You must come back under more welcoming circumstances," said the abbess, smiling. "We'd be interested to hear your story."

What was the abbess's story? wondered Signy, taking care to follow the road towards Agininum. Lanius had simply mentioned she was friends with his mother, though, now when she thought carefully, the trader had then abruptly changed the subject. And the dead shepherd, were there really murderers wandering the hills, where she had been riding so blithely, alone? She shook her head. No, she mustn't frighten herself with such thoughts. Even an innocent traveller would feel justified defending himself if he was attacked in the dark by a guard dog. But the boots? Petrus had seemed quite surprised to find the traces of soldiers' boots on the track. Were *they* the innocent travellers, and if so, where were they coming from and going to, high in the hills during a summer night?

☙ Chapter 5 ❧
Tolosa

They were lounging on a pile of cushions in a private room, at the rear of a house that had once been the home of a wealthy Roman official. In the recent past, the building had fallen somewhat from grace. Two extra storeys had been added, small rooms clustered around flights of stairs providing lodgings for those in need of discretion. The private room, however, belonged to the original house, and the walls were dark painted, the trace of the fashion when they had last been decorated. Nymphs and sea creatures filled lighter areas, because the house was far from the ocean, and date palms and a lion, though no palm trees and, most probably, no lions had ever roamed the city of Tolosa.

The loungers were two women, one a little older than the other, but both, a cynical observer might have remarked, making an effort to appear younger than they were. Whether by an endowment of nature or their maids' hard work, they would have turned men's heads in the forum had they been seen dressed as they now were, with their cloaks and headscarves put to one side.

A servant cut up meat, placing it on platters arranged on a low table before them. A second carried in a broad dish containing a stew of vegetables, fruit, nuts and spices, silver serving spoons and flat bread. A third poured wine, and then they all retired in discreet silence. Neither woman had spoken while the servants were in the room. This was a measure, perhaps, of their own uncertain status. Neither of them was so high born that they could simply ignore the slaves, as if they were animals or statues, possessed of no faculties worth considering. At the same time, they were wary of too much familiarity with the staff, at least in front of one another, strangers as they were.

Once the servants had departed, the older woman made a gesture, indicating that the younger was welcome to take the food. She herself began to spoon stew onto a piece of bread.

"You invited me," said the younger, Megana Fabiana, finally breaking the silence as she followed suit. "Perhaps you can start by explaining why."

"You know who I am, I suppose," said the older, "my reputation?"

"I know you are Mistress Xancha," said the younger, with a slight smile – her name, of course, had been inscribed on the invitation – "and as for your reputation, I've never felt it worthwhile paying much attention to others' gossip."

They spoke in Greek: Xancha in the language of her birthplace in the east, and Megana since it was her mother's tongue. The instant that Xancha had greeted her in Latin, Megana had recognised the familiar accent of a migrant from Syria or Judea. She had taken the risk of replying in Greek, a risk that had obviously flattered the older woman.

Megana might not pay much attention to gossip, but she was always ready to take good advice.

"You'll have to make the acquaintance of Mistress Xancha," Lanius had said, "when you visit Tolosa. She and I have exchanged plenty of favours over the years."

"What sort of favours?" Megana had asked, thinking of the manoeuvres that are an inevitable and necessary accompaniment to trouble-free dealing. She had been surprised when Lanius had avoided her gaze, only answering furtively, "Various kinds."

When Lanius had started out as a young apprentice, he had spent a good deal of time on the road between the two seas. No doubt, thought Megana, helping herself to more food, tempted by the pleasures along the way, perhaps including the company of her present hostess. Now, since his wife's father had withdrawn from trading, Lanius rarely travelled upriver to Tolosa. Managing the sea routes took most of his time. That was one reason she had suggested taking on the supervision of the land route, the warehouses and relay stations, between Burdigala and Tolosa, the growing capital of the Visigoth Kingdom. She would become a critical link in the chain between the ocean and the Middle Sea. The other end of the chain, on the coast at the port town of Agatha, was in the hands of Lanius' sister and her husband, Megana's half-brother, Alexander.

The older woman took a bite of her rolled-up flatbread before saying more.

"You speak excellent Greek," she said, "for someone from the islands."

"My mother was from the east," replied Megana, "a slave woman, bought by a merchant in Britannia. He treated her as if she was his wife and brought me up as his daughter."

"I doubt he brought you up as his daughter," said Xancha, "because if he had, you would have been married off to some fat, moustachioed potentate, more beef than soul. From what I've heard, and unlike you, Mistress Megana, I'm a great believer in gossip, suitably corroborated, I would say, that you might be fairer to your progenitor if you said he brought you up as if you were his son. Unless I'm much mistaken you visited Burdigala for a short while, what, four or five years ago?"

Megana smiled. The infamous Xancha had clearly managed to pick up the essential details about her before sending the invitation, and was obviously skilled enough to have already extracted more before even the first glass of wine had been emptied. Now was the time, she thought, for her hostess to offer some information about herself in return. Xancha, clearly understanding the game, took a slow drink from her wine glass, and then replaced it gently on the table.

"Had I been five years younger," she said, "I might have travelled on the same boat as your mother, though fortunately not in the slave pen" – she paused momentarily, glancing at Megana – "though I doubt, judging from the daughter, that your mother travelled in that lowly accommodation either." Megana made no response, so she continued. "In those days I was a dancer, a very good one, bare-breasted and in a leopard skin, at least at the start of my act, and I'd earned enough to ensure my freedom." She paused again, reaching for the wine. "Some on my back, I'm not ashamed to admit. What should a girl do if she has nothing but her looks and her body?"

"Use her reason?" suggested Megana.

"Of course," replied her host, "but how far can a woman come with only her intelligence if she has no money? I wasn't born with a bag of silver in my hand."

Ouch, a well-aimed blow, thought Megana. I'm neatly and expertly skewered. There was nothing to be gained by competing in childhood stories of hard luck, she reflected. She had none. She had received the best education available in the province of Britannia Prima. She had sat beside her father and learned the art of trading. She had travelled alone to Burdigala, as Xancha had discovered, and to the East Sea to join one of her father's companions on a journey into the northern lands. But she had never had to earn her living with her body, not even with her hands. As for men, though she had been threatened with marriage on several occasions, she had had the luxury of choosing who she wished to be intimate with, and there were very few who had measured up to her standard.

Enough, she thought, let's get down to business, because that's surely what all this is about.

"I'm impressed, Mistress Xancha, that you've come from such humble beginnings to such a prominent position in Tolosa, but I don't think you invited me here to discuss the past."

"A prominent position, you say, despite all my effort to remain in the shadows."

"Sometimes the figure half-hidden in the shadows occupies more of men's thoughts than the one in full daylight," said Megana.

"I invited you here to see who you were, to size you up," said Xancha, with a sudden switch to a harder, decisive tone, "to see if you lived up to the rumours. You've popped up from beyond the seas. No one here knows anything about you, and yet I find my old friend Lanius has placed his business in Tolosa in your hands. And then I hear another rumour, that Lanius the merchant has suddenly taken to buying land along the Garunna valley, or at least, his seal is on the charters."

Two and two make four, never three and never five, in whichever trade you ply, thought Megana before replying.

"The senatorial families are broken, after the Sack, after the..." Megana had to choose her words carefully; you never knew who was listening, and the one who was had the ear of the most powerful men in the kingdom, so rumour told. "...occupation of Italia. There's still cheap land to be had along the Garunna, and in the other river valleys. There are opportunities for trade for someone who has no axe to grind with the new masters, and who is not embarrassed that their taxes are paid to Tolosa rather than Rome."

"The old masters valued land," said the former dancer. "They collected a whole empire until they were forced to abandon it. Why fall into the same trap? I prefer to keep my riches in an easily transportable form."

"Such riches can easily be transported away by someone else," Megana said, smiling, "someone with a weapon, or greater power. The Huns, I've heard, have a liking for silver and gold."

"Jewels and furs, yes, and women, too, even ones my age," said Xancha, "but if you're not tied to the land, you can stay one step, one galloping horse, ahead of the Huns."

That would entail moving fast, thought Megana, faster than she could manage and probably Xancha, too.

The women's plates were almost empty of meat, and the bread had come to an end. Xancha clapped her hands and called out, and the trio of servants reappeared, hastily gathering the remnants.

"Some dessert, light dessert," said Xancha. "We women must consider our figures. In my dancing days I always swore I would never become as fat as the wealthy women who lounged around the couches watching us. I concluded their corpulence was probably why their husbands invited me and my companions to their beds rather than their own wives. Of course, in those days I often went hungry between performances, so there was little danger of losing my figure, but now, with all to eat that I could want, I have to be careful."

The servants entered carrying a curious mound in yellow and pink. Xancha scooped a portion into a bowl and handed it to Megana. Once Xancha had her own food, Megana took a spoon, filled it from the bowl and placed it in her mouth. In an instant, she began to cough and splutter, only with difficulty managing to restrain herself from spitting out the contents.

"It's freezing cold!" she gasped.

"Have you never had sherbet?" asked Xancha with a laugh. "It's a little luxury I picked up long ago, an indulgence I learned at rich men's tables…to have ice carried down from the mountains in winter and stored in a straw-lined pit so that they can have frozen desserts all year round."

"My guess is that the techniques to make chilled desserts were not the only skills you picked up at rich men's houses," said Megana, sampling the dessert again, this time more cautiously.

"No," said Xancha. "I learned that drunk men thinking of sex can be indiscreet, and that gossip has value. I learned that fat wives and, perhaps more so, their yet-to-be fat daughters craved advice on cosmetics and jewellery from a woman who clearly knew how to deploy them."

"And you also found that the same cosmetics and jewellery could make country girls desirable to your clients' husbands."

Xancha laughed softly.

"So people say."

"And what can I contribute? I don't want your advice on cosmetics and jewellery…" said Megana.

"You hardly need it."

"…thank you…and I've no desire for a quick fuck with a stranger…"

"Oh?"

"…so I don't need one of your handsome young men for an hour."

"That's a little unfair." Xancha held up her hand with an expression of amusement. "Mistress Megana, that wasn't at all why I wanted to meet you. Did dear Lanius not explain?"

"He avoided providing me an explanation."

"Ah, yes, well, we were younger when we began to work together, and I…I found it helped if I made myself available to friends. But that's beside the point. I was one of the first here, you know, in Tolosa, in the time of Wallia. I was one of the few who saw that there were other possibilities to become wealthy than taking other people's stuff for yourself. I helped Merchant Vipso to make contacts in the court in the early days, with the duke and many of the leading counts. Lanius was one of the go-betweens. Then when Lanius married Vipso's daughter…well, let's just say that those contacts have contributed as much to my fortune, especially as I've got older and fashions have changed, as the business my reputation assigns to me, and…"

"And you want to make sure I don't interfere?" said Megana.

"It would be unfortunate if you did…for both of us. Mistress Megana, this kingdom depends on a delicate balance, between those who still think of themselves as Romans and the Goths, between the followers of the Roman Church and those whose beliefs differ…"

"Pagans, you mean?"

Xancha laughed. "If only I did, life would be very much simpler. It would take me all night to explain the quarrels amongst the Christians, not least because I have had to spend nights listening to them when I would have liked to be doing something much more pleasurable."

A smile and a gesture from Megana indicated that an explanation would not be necessary, today, at least.

"You've quite knocked me off my path," murmured Xancha. "Yes, between those living in the lands still loyal to the Empire, and those who look to our king, Theodoric, as their leader, between those who fought their way to prominence among Our Men from the early days and those who joined later and, some say, took advantage, men and women, old and young, in other words, the myriad competing interests of a land in flux. All of them pass through my hands…well, not literally, of course…but those of my girls and boys, who offer pleasure and relaxation, flattery and praise, and listen carefully, as I learned to do."

Megana reflected for a moment, observing the woman sitting across from her. There was something attractively roguish in her. She could understand how men had fallen for her, probably still did. She rose to her feet, crossed to where Xancha was seated, bent down and wrapped her arms around her.

"I shall confine myself to trading goods, not influence," she said. "I promise."

"I thought you might," said Xancha, glancing up at Megana from under her long and evidently artificial lashes. "I thought we could be friends."

Megana took a step back, and as she did so, Xancha clapped her hands once again.

"And now some entertainment…"

Half a dozen bare-chested men and women ran into the room, followed by a couple of musicians.

"They're from Bithynia," said Xancha, "hoping for an engagement at the court. Tell me what you think, and if you change your mind, and decide you want company in bed for the night, you only have to say. When you get to my age, it's better to be adaptable."

With that, she clapped her hands again, the musicians took up their instruments, and with a glance towards the dancers, began to play.

ᏨᏕ Chapter 6 ᏕᏨ
In the Hills Above Aginінum

The weather remained dry and fine, too lovely to remain in the midst of the dust and noise of the building work in Olive Street, so Signy resolved to take up the invitation to visit the monastery before she was forgotten. As her horse crested a rise not far from where the dead man had been lying, Signy remembered the first time she had ridden over the hills, a few days after she had arrived in Agininum, when she had noticed the buildings in the distance, perhaps the country villa of a rich landowner. She had been intrigued and turned her horse in that direction. As she had come nearer, she had seen men and women working in a field, so she had stopped to ask them the name of the owner. As with most of the people she came across on her rides, they were nervous at first to see a horseman dismount and approach them. Signy had a habit of wearing men's clothing while she was out riding, and men often meant trouble, especially men with long fair hair. Their surprise and relief when they realised a woman was addressing them was a reassurance to her, too. She was a woman, after all, despite her outer appearance, and disliked being mistakenly judged. She had no desire to threaten people, to scare them, and was herself nervous about speaking to country people. She had still not mastered their dialect.

"That's no landowner's house," a labourer had informed her. "That's the monastery."

"Christian women," said a second.

"Sister Hildefrith's in charge."

A memory had stirred in Signy's mind. Lanius the trader had mentioned that his mother lived in a monastery, high in the hills above Agininum. He had grown up there, she recalled. Could this be the place? she wondered.

"The monastery of Mons Agininum?" she asked.

"Yes, that's what they call it," said the labourer.

She had thanked the peasants and returned to the horse. The mare was used to her rider's habits of jumping on and off, and had remained quietly waiting for Signy's return. Instead of mounting, she had taken the reins and led the animal along the road. She had been intrigued by the monastery. She had heard about such institutions, but never visited one.

She had come to a path which led up to a narrow gate set into the wall which surrounded the buildings. She had followed the path to the gate and peered in. There was a garden laid out on the other side of the wall, blocks of grey-green plants set around with gravel. She could smell the scent – lavender, probably. She was intrigued but had not dared try the gate. Instead, she had turned and ridden home.

Now, she was responding to an invitation that the abbess, the Hildefrith the countrypeople had named, had called out to her as she had ridden away after their ride across the hills to investigate the death of the shepherd. Signy first thought to continue to the main entrance further along the road, but her curiosity about the garden got the better of her. She pulled up by the opening and dismounted. When she pushed at the gate, it swung open. She hesitated for a moment, quickly tied the horse to the gate post and stepped inside. She was in a familiar world: a herb garden. She let her eyes wander over the carefully spaced beds, recognising some of the plants arranged in front of her, but also seeing that there were many she did not know. She heard steps on the gravel, and turned to see a woman approaching her, an anxious look on her face.

"Can I help you?" asked the woman cautiously, unsure what type of figure had just intruded on their peace. Long, light hair was no signal of femininity among the new overlords, and again the masculine clothing clearly made her nervous.

"My name is Signy," Signy answered, trying to reassure the woman. "I'm a stranger here. Abbess Hildefrith invited me to visit. I know I should have come to the main gate, but what a beautiful garden you have! I used to have a herb garden myself in my old home, and I'm planning to lay one out in my house down in the town."

The woman examined her in silence, trying to make her out, noticing the horse nosing at the gate, as if it also wanted to explore the garden. Her expression was clear. Who was this strange person who had just appeared from nowhere?

Signy squatted down to examine the plants in front of her.

"I suppose these herb plants can survive all winter here so they can grow so large. In the north they usually die when the frost comes, and we have to plant them fresh each spring."

"Some winters we also have frost, and I'm always fearful the plants will die," replied the woman, caught for a moment by Signy's obvious interest. "I'm Sister Agatha. Did you say you are a herbalist, too?"

Her voice still sounded anxious. Her eye seemed to linger on the jewelled brooch holding Signy's cloak in place. It's true, thought Signy, I probably don't look much like a gardener.

"My mother was a midwife and a medicine woman," she started to explain, "and I've followed her. I grew up in the northlands, beyond the frontier. Your plants in the south are different from ours. It would be wonderful to learn more about their properties."

The sister was still cautious.

"Do you know this one?" she asked, almost as if she was testing the intruder.

"Lavender, yes. We didn't have it in the village where I grew up, but in Britannia, in the gardens…"

"You're from Britannia?" asked the sister, sounding confused.

"I'm sorry," said Signy. "I lived in Britannia for a while…"

"I see," said the sister, as if her mind was on another matter.

"It's good for people who have difficulty sleeping," said Signy, returning to the subject of lavender.

"I put bunches in our guest rooms," said the sister, suddenly more friendly. "Would you like to see?"

"I would," said Signy, "very much, but I can't leave my horse alone in the road."

The sister once again looked doubtful, as if she was unsure how to accommodate the horse, as if, perhaps, she was being fooled by a person of ill will. A herbalist should self-evidently walk, thought Signy, taking a step towards the gate. How could she spot useful plants by the wayside from astride a horse? Sister Agatha followed her, some paces behind. The horse was standing peacefully just outside. Signy patted her on the nose. She was a good horse, so patient with her.

"I'm sure you can leave your horse with the stable hands, like other visitors," Agatha suggested, her tone still doubtful.

"She will know Master Petrus from our previous visit."

For a moment, puzzlement filled the sister's face, and then she brightened.

"Oh, you're the young woman who rode with the abbess to fetch old Xeno's sheep. I didn't recognise you immediately." Her voice was filled with relief. "It was such a shock, him dying like that, just by our door. Now I remember there was a woman who said she was a healer."

Signy and Agatha walked together beside the wall, Signy leading the horse, until they came to the larger gate which led into the stable yard.

"Come, Mistress, I'll take you in," said the sister, and called as they entered, "Petrus, we have a visitor…with a horse."

The stablemaster bustled out from a doorway, touched his forehead, said, "Morning, Mistress, good to see you again," and took the horse.

"Thank you, Master Petrus," Signy said, smiling.

Sister Agatha led the way out of the yard and into the heart of the buildings. Signy gazed around as she walked. Now she was inside, she could see that the monastery really was an old villa, immense and well cared for. Whoever built this house and lived here in the old times must have been unbelievably rich, she thought.

"Here are our guest rooms, one for women and one for men, unless you're a special guest of Sister Hildefrith, of course, and then you would have a room to yourself."

The rooms, for the public and the special guests, were wonderfully clean and smelled so fresh.

"I shall have to tell Victoria to do the same," said Signy, thinking of the housekeeper she had just employed, "once we have our rooms prepared as beautifully as you have."

"Oh, you know Mistress Victoria? You're one of the ladies who have taken the house in Olive Street," said Agatha, as if this had resolved some of the questions that had remained. "Fagius, the carter, came by and told us that some foreigners had taken the house; a trader and her companion."

"Yes, that would be my friend, Megana Fabiana, who is the trader," said Signy. "I'm the companion."

The sister hesitated for a moment, as if wondering what to do next with this stranger.

"Would you like me to show you the library?" she asked. "We have many books on medicine there. Do you read?"

"I do," Signy replied, while trying to preserve an appearance of modesty.

As they walked along, Signy could see other women crossing here and there, some of them calling out a greeting to Agatha, and casting curious glances at the ambiguous figure pacing beside her. They walked under an archway into a dark and cool corridor. Sister Agatha tapped on a wooden door, and then opened it carefully. Signy gasped as she entered a high room, flooded with light, and with books and scrolls on shelves and in cupboards, more than she had ever seen. A woman, grey-haired, wearing a simple gown and bent over a writing table, looked up as they came in.

"Sister Ophelia," said Agatha. "I've brought you a visitor, the young lady Hildefrith was telling us about. I found her wandering in the herb garden. She told me she once lived in Britannia. May I leave her here while I run to find our abbess?"

The older woman stood up and came towards them. Her eyes met Signy's. She held out her hand, stained black with ink, and Signy took it. Faint imprints of fingers were left on Signy's own hand when she withdrew it.

"My name is Signy. I rode up from Aginnum," she said. Agatha had spoken in Latin, not patois, to Ophelia, so Signy followed suit. The older woman smiled.

"Aha, you're one of those women my son has been worrying over. We may be far away up here, but we're not entirely out of touch with the world, and when Hildefrith mentioned a curious foreigner…Welcome."

Signy felt a wave of relaxation through her body. So this was Lanius' mother.

The woman continued. "Lanius wrote that you have travelled from Britannia, you and your friend."

"From Corinium," said Signy, and noticed the older woman's gaze drift away, as if distracted for a moment.

"So long ago, another life," said Ophelia, making an obvious attempt to pull herself together. "Are you interested in the library, in books?" she asked.

"Very much," said Signy.

"Then come and look at what I'm working on. Sister Hildefrith has been so fortunate to borrow a copy of the holy Augustine's work, the *City of God*, the first ten books. Bishop Anastasius found them in Arelate, and I'm making copies for our library. Do you know the work of Augustine of Hippo?"

"I'm afraid I don't," said Signy. "Is he a Christian writer? We had very few Christian books in Britannia."

"We were not all pagans," said the older woman, "even in my youth."

What could Signy say? That time had moved on. That the books of Ophelia's childhood had been passed from hand to hand and worn out. That unbelievers had used them to light fires or worse.

"There are Christians in Britannia still, many of them, but the books…"

As she spoke, they heard the door open behind them, and Sister Hildefrith came in, not dressed for riding this time. With her long light hair, tinged now with silver, her sharp nose, her blue eyes, many women would have died to have half her dignity and elegance. A fitting leader for the house, Signy thought.

"My dear Mistress Signy," she said. They might have been herding sheep together just a couple of days before, but Signy had the quick sense to take the offered hand with a kiss, as the woman fixed her with her gaze, examining her.

"I was about to show Mistress Signy our copy of *City of God*, Hildefrith. It seems the word of our holy Augustine has not reached the shores of Britannia."

"His word had not reached *me*," said Signy, as a way to get off this awkward subject. "That's quite another matter. I'm afraid in recent times I've had to spend my effort on geometry, not the scriptures."

Hildefrith gave her a look which would have pierced her through if it had been a spear.

"Geometry! Really, you study geometry? That's a strange occupation for a woman."

Before Signy could reply, the abbess turned and disappeared behind one of the shelves. A moment later, she returned bearing a scroll of papyrus. She brushed the dust off and rolled the sheet out a short way. The material crackled as she did so, obviously dry and unopened for a long time.

"Do you tell me you can understand this stuff?"

Signy looked over her shoulder at the contents of the scroll. Another test, she thought, stretching out a hand to hold the roll in place.

"Why, yes, that's Euclid's fifth book, on the proportions of magnitudes. We only had a poor copy, made by someone who did not really understand it, Deacon Baxter and I."

Hildefrith rolled up the scroll again.

"You read Greek, too, I see," she said before pausing in thought. "Yes, there are plenty of people who can gossip in Greek – on the dockside and other such places – but very few who can read Greek in these parts, and even fewer of them are women. Fewer still who can keep up with me on a horse," the abbess added, with a smile. "Welcome, Mistress Signy, welcome to our little world."

It was Signy's turn to feel relief. She had to admit that ignorant curiosity had led her to their door, mere wanting to find out what lay beyond. It was more than she could have hoped that these wise and elegant women would offer her a welcome. She would have to show she was worth their respect, but how? Not by bluffing with half-learned and half-forgotten memories of lessons in Greek and geometry. No, she would never be accepted on those grounds. What other skills could she use to show she was more than just a barely trained Saxon peasant girl before their welcome turned to the same scorn she had faced in Burdigala?

☙ Chapter 7 ❧
Agininum

Megana had arrived, on her way back from Tolosa, when Signy returned from the monastery. They had taken glasses and a flagon of wine, intending to share their news. The courtyard, with its shady tree, was filled with wooden beams, stacks of tiles and a vile barrel for mixing mortar, so they walked out into the garden, down the gravel path to the stone bench overlooking the remains of the fountain.

"You think we can get that fixed?" asked Signy, glancing at the dried-out stone bowl and its chipped faun.

"There's a man in Burdigala who repaired the fountain in my…our house there," said Megana. "I can send him up."

"Please do, Megana. It would make such a difference to the garden if the fountain worked."

"You have made a good start, I see, with the plants."

Signy sighed. When they had first moved into the house in Olive Street, the garden had been completely overgrown. A man hired from the town had started to clear away brush, revealing the outline of a formal design sloping down from the house and merging, about halfway, into a grove of fruit trees. In the autumn she would see which of those were worth keeping, but just now Signy was focussed on clearing a few of the beds so she could get as many as possible of the seeds and plantlets of the medicinal herbs she had brought from Britannia into the ground before they finally succumbed to the stress of too-long overwintering and travel. It would be difficult enough finding the right replacements for the wild plants needed to make up her potions and salves in this unfamiliar climate, but if she lost the ones she could cultivate, she would have to start again from nothing.

Signy sat quietly while Megana narrated the story of her meeting with the notorious Xancha and then, when it was evident that Megana and the ageing dancer had hit it off, she began to tell her friend about the dead shepherd and the ride upcountry with the abbess and her servants.

"Someone had stabbed the dog," she said. "A person, not a beast."

Megana was puzzled by her mention of boots.

"I don't think the so-called Romans I've met would be seen dead in boots. Golden sandals seem to be more their style."

"I haven't heard that there are many who still claim to be Romans near Aginnum…the bishop maybe and the *notarius*?"

Megana sighed, recalling her meeting with the Bishop of Burdigala with distaste. "I suppose I'll be forced to crawl to our local bishop before long."

Signy was not going to be drawn into that discussion – again.

"I wonder where that path leads," she said. "The tracks…the prints…were pointing north."

"Towards the border with the disputed lands," Megana filled in for her friend.

"What do you mean, the disputed lands?"

"The land north of the River Oltis was not part of the original agreement between the Empire and Our Men, but they took it anyway," said Megana. "I've heard that General Aetius sends out patrols now and then just to remind the Count of Cadurci of that fact."

"So the footprints could have been made by one of the governor's patrols," mused Signy. "But we're south of the river, so why would he send a patrol over our hills? Why do you think a group of Romans would be sneaking around so close to Aginnum?"

"Who said they were sneaking?" said Megana. "Maybe they'd been paying a visit to Aginnum. They could have been retainers of some local bigwig or maybe they were deserters or bandits. Deserters would be wearing boots, and bandits could steal them."

That was true, of course, thought Signy, sipping her wine, and didn't make matters better, considering she had been riding around in the hills on her own. An outlaw who could stab a dog might easily stab a woman, once he'd had his way with her.

"Megana, give me some credit. I recognise sneaking when I see it…in the dead of night, by remote tracks. That was the tactic we used in Britannia."

"Dear Signy, you were very careful never to tell me what you did."

"Besides, if they were deserters, you would surely expect them to be travelling in the opposite direction, from the Roman lands into ours," Signy continued, now feeling defensive. "But I wonder where that track leads. There are no towns in that direction, so Victoria told me."

"The road to Cadurci crosses those hills."

"That's true. If we could follow the tracks—"

"Why, Signy? They aren't bothering us," Megana broke in.

"I don't like that the dog was killed and the old man died, even if it was a mishap. They were harmless enough. How would you like to be a shepherd after what happened to Xeno?" Signy said with a sigh. She didn't want to admit to Megana that she was worried that whoever killed the dog might progress to other victims. "And besides, I'm bored. I need more to do."

"You've got the garden to fix up," grumbled Megana in a manner which suggested she was aware that Signy was being evasive.

"Oh, Megana, for the Christ's sake. You've just got in from Tolosa, and dining with an infamous courtesan. Tomorrow you're going on to Burdigala and you'll leave me here."

"But you were bored in Burdigala?"

"I was bored out of my mind, I agree, and it's definitely better here, but still…I'm sorry, that wasn't necessary, but I would like to get out and explore a little and finding out where that track leads would give me a good excuse."

And perhaps, if she could find out who had been responsible for Xeno's death, she could show her new friends at the monastery what she could accomplish, a solution to their mystery, a removal of the threat to their servants and perhaps to themselves.

"Supposing the booted strangers are deserters or bandits, lying in wait?" Megana insisted.

"I'll take care…I'll take Grunwald with me, and Hrasmus can come, too."

Grunwald and Hrasmus were two warriors from Juteland, survivors of the raid that had brought Signy to Britannia. They had been injured and captured in the battle in which her husband, their leader, had been killed. Signy, after being taken prisoner herself, had treated their wounds and saved them from being sold as slaves, and they remained loyal to their dead chief's wife.

"You'd better take Henrik to be on the safe side," said Megana, referring to her stablemaster. "You don't know who's sneaking around in the hills. You know I'm just thinking of what's best for you."

"If I can borrow Henrik from the building work."

Signy had little doubt that Henrik would be glad to have a break from his toil with repairing the roof to go out for a ride, especially if his labourers had already been requisitioned.

☙ Chapter 8 ❧ Agininum

Signy and the three men took the road up past the women's holy house early the following day. They did not call in. Signy was worried that her new friends might try to dissuade her from riding on. Instead, they circled the monastery and set off across the hills in the direction that she had taken with Petrus and Hildefrith a few days before. None of them were familiar with this part of the country, but they were experienced riders and had no concerns about navigating the terrain.

It was still well before midday when they reached the shepherd's hut. It remained undisturbed, no signs of bandits or wild animals. The body of the dog, however, had gone. Only a few tufts of fur showed where it had lain. The boot prints and the hoof prints that had accompanied them had faded away, though they were still clear in Signy's mind.

Grunwald laughed seeing the track.

"This would have counted as a major road in Juteland," he commented, seeing the well-trodden trail between the trees.

"Like the green roads made by the old people," said Henrik, "the people who lived in Britain before the Romans."

"Very well, Chief," said Grunwald, peering up between the trees, trying to get a fix on the sun, then turning to Signy, "which way do you want us to go?"

The path led up from the south-west, almost from the direction of Agininum, and pointed towards the north-east. The trail of the boots led in that direction.

"Over the stream," Signy said, "up the bank, and we'll follow the path as far as we can."

"If it's anything like the green roads in Britannia, it could stretch over the hills for miles, nowhere near any modern towns," said Henrik, but despite his doubts, he kicked his horse into motion to follow Grunwald and Signy, who were already urging their mounts through the ford and up the opposite bank. Once there, they were on open land again and could see the path stretching ahead of them, almost as straight as a Roman road. Signy was tempted to push her horse into a canter, but good sense held her back. She did not know the path, and an accident up here, far from help, would be a catastrophe.

They rode on at an easy pace, mile after mile, as the sun slowly descended the blue dome of the sky. Only a few clouds gave them the occasional shade.

The sense they were pursuing a mystery filled Signy with excitement, the first real excitement she had felt since they had arrived in the southlands. She wasn't used to towns. In towns there were too many people watching you, looking at you, passing judgement on you.

"We're not returning this evening, I take it," said Henrik. "Then we must look for somewhere to rest up, and water and grass for the horses."

Now they were on a mission, she thought, with an added hint of danger, though she trusted that the men with her and, if the worst came to the worst, their horses would keep them out of any serious trouble.

Just then the path took a gentle turn downhill. Perhaps that was what had prompted Henrik to call out his warning. A few trees began to populate the slope, and in a little while they entered a small valley similar to the one sheltering the shepherd's hut.

Grunwald raised his hand.

"Hold on, folks! Let's pull up before we disturb the track ourselves and see if we can spot any of the prints Signy described."

They tethered the horses and ambled down the final section of path towards the stream they could hear tinkling through the trees.

"Here," shouted Hrasmus, suddenly, from where he had been scouring the earth to one side of the track. Sure enough, undisturbed beneath the fronds of a fern was the print of a hobnail boot, toe pointing resolutely in their direction of travel.

Now knowing what to look for, the men continued along the track, splashing through the stream and up the other bank. In a little while, they returned.

"There are prints all the way across, here and there in places sheltered from the weather. No people have been this way in the last couple of days, though it looks like animals use this path."

"Can you estimate how many men in the group?" asked Signy.

Grunwald shook his head.

"The prints are too sparse, and I can't see any signs of a horseman, either. He must have kept to the middle of the track where it's more stony."

They filled their waterskins and allowed their horses to drink, and then returned a short distance until they were on the edge of the trees. There they made a fire of dry wood, cooked a meal and, after agreeing turns to keep watch, finally fell asleep.

--oo00oo--

It was chilly in the morning when Signy awoke, though Henrik was already blowing life into the fire.

"I've been thinking," said Signy. "There should be a road up here before long, I mean a real Roman road – Megana said so – one that leads from the junction beyond the monastery over towards Cadurci."

"If we continue, we should reach the river, surely," said Henrik. "What's it called, the Oltis?"

"Very well, let's say this," said Signy, "we won't ride further than the river, and if we haven't found our booted men by then, we'll turn back."

"My bet is the soldiers, if that is what they are, went up the road to Cadurci," said Henrik.

They had come to the conclusion from the number and regularity of the tracks that the group must have been well-organised, probably soldiers.

"Perhaps the Count of Cadurci's men," suggested Hrasmus.

It still doesn't explain where they were coming from, or what they were doing there, thought Signy, or why they killed the shepherd's dog, but perhaps we'll never get an answer to those questions. Maybe it'll be enough to know they've gone away and won't be coming back, though that would be a bit of a disappointment.

Sure enough, before long they reached the road, where they could see the track continuing on the other side.

"Shall we go on? I can see the trace of the river towards the horizon," Signy said.

Henrik shook his head. Grunwald and Hrasmus exchanged glances.

"It won't take long," Signy insisted, and before the men could dissuade her, she had crossed the road and was trotting down the track.

On the far side of the road, the track began to curve to the east, and then to the north, as if it was aiming for a particular point. Then it began to descend into the valley. At the bottom, the river spread out, broad and seemingly deep.

"It doesn't make any sense that it comes to an abrupt halt at the river," said Signy, seeing the track descend to the water side. "There must be a ford here."

Without hesitation, she urged her horse forward, into the river.

"Where are you going?" shouted Grunwald.

"Stop," called Henrik, "we said we would go no further than the river."

"There are prints here," said Hrasmus, jumping from his horse and squatting by the bank.

"They must have had a boat," said Henrik, though by then Signy was well out into the river, the horse splashing comfortably through the water. She looked back at them.

"Wait there, I'll just ride as far as I can, to see if I can reach the other side, and then I'll turn back."

The horse splashed on, the water becoming deeper as they approached the middle of the river.

Signy could feel the current pulling at the animal's legs, all the more as the water rushed over the ridge created by the ford. Then the far bank began to get temptingly near, the water became shallower, and in a moment, she was splashing up the last few yards to the shore. She turned to wave to her three companions, barely visible on the far side.

Enough, she thought, dismounting. The trees were thicker on this side of the river, and shadier. "I'll just check if I can see any boot prints," she said to herself, "and then I'll turn the horse and we'll go back." She bent down and started to scrutinise the track where it emerged from the ford. By the river the marks were a mess. The bank had been well trampled. This was obviously a place where animals came down to drink, and their feet had disturbed any traces of men. Maybe further up, away from the bank, she would be able to make out if there were any signs of the men in boots. She took the horse by the bridle and began to lead it up the path and into the trees. A little way up the slope, half-hidden by the bushes, she saw the dark outline of a shallow, flat-bottom boat.

"Stop, right there," came a voice in rough Latin. "Keep your hands up, and don't make any sudden moves!"

Signy froze. She would have frozen at the sound of a voice without any command to do so.

"Stay where you are," came the voice again, now accompanied by the noise of breaking twigs and trampling through leaves. Two men stepped into the path. Even in the shadow of the trees she could see that they bore uniforms, not the classic military uniforms of the sculptures and statues, but uniforms, nonetheless. Almost involuntarily, she glanced at their feet. They were obviously the owners of the boots.

☙ Chapter 9 ❧
Beyond the Oltis River

One of the soldiers stepped towards her, his short sword levelled.

"Don't give us any trouble, boy."

The second rounded her cautiously to take hold of the horse.

"Up the path, and no funny business, friend," the soldier continued.

It took Signy a moment to realise they had called her "boy" and used the masculine gender in Latin. It was on her tongue to correct them, thinking that might protect her, when second and better thoughts prevailed. As "boy" she was a prisoner, as "girl" she could easily become a victim.

She was greatly tempted to glance back as she mounted the rise and came out from among the trees to try to look across the river for Grunwald, Henrik and Hrasmus, but even the slightest movement of her head resulted in a grunt from the man behind her.

They had not walked far before an extraordinary sight spread out before her: a ditch and bank with a wooden fence running along the ridge. The path ran up to a gap in the bank, closed by a gate. As they approached the gate she saw a group of men digging in one of the ditches, and now and then a shovelful of earth would fly up onto the bank. She could almost have laughed. It was a Roman camp, just as described in the field manual she and Deacon Baxter had used in her studies of practical geometry. She had assumed that such constructions had been abandoned long ago, just as they had in Britannia.

It was no joke, however, when the soldiers marched her along the path towards the camp, while the men in the trench rested their shovels and stared as the three of them passed by.

The gate swung open, revealing four neat rows of tents. The path continued straight between the tents. About halfway along was an open space, a mini-forum, with a couple of larger tents and a pair of crudely constructed wooden huts. They reached the square and came to a halt. A squad of troops had been formed up on the parade ground, perhaps ready to go out on patrol. A patrol like that could have made the boot prints, Signy quickly concluded, and would have no hesitation to kill a dog that got in their way. What might such men do to a prisoner? A quick end with a sword might be one of the better outcomes. Her decision to cross the river was beginning to look very foolish. And yet…she had lived in a camp like this before. She had lived among men like these before. She had a pretty good idea how they thought and behaved. The three friends she had left on the far bank were fighters, probably little different from those formed up on the parade ground. If only she had luck with her…

There was an exchange in Latin behind her, and the man who had been leading her horse came up. Signy was ordered to stand, guarded by the remaining soldier, while the other disappeared inside one of the larger tents. She tried to observe the camp while moving as little as possible. She could make out curious glances wherever she shifted her gaze. A moment later, the soldier who had left stuck his head out of the tent and called. There was a grunt from behind her, and she felt the push of a stiff arm against her back.

The first thing that struck her was that the inside of the tent was as neat as the camp outside: squared-off camp bed, clean and ordered, a wooden chest, with a pair of boots arranged exactly beside it. A grey-haired officer, sitting at a portable desk, turned to look at her as she came in.

"Is this the prisoner?" he enquired of the man behind her. "A tribesman?"

"Yes, sir. We caught him crossing the river."

"Looks like one of these Goths to me," said the officer. "That's Captain Junius' responsibility, since he understands their gabble. Take him away and hand him over to the captain."

There was a hand on her arm, but before the soldier could take hold of her, the officer spoke again.

"Have you searched him for weapons?"

Even Signy could detect a note of embarrassment in the voice of the soldier behind her as he admitted his fault. He came round and parted her cloak. His hand closed around the sheath of the dagger, which lay snug against her body, and had not been evident from the outside. The soldier fumbled at the buckle, freeing the dagger and her belt. The officer stood up and took the weapon from him.

"How many times do I have to tell you?" he said, sliding the dagger from the sheath, turning it to catch the light. "Do you want me to end up like Centurion Lavinius? These men are always carrying weapons."

"Good quality," he added, turning to look at Signy. "I haven't seen one like this since I was…on the Lower Rhine." He turned back to the soldier. "Have you searched him properly now?"

The soldier ran his hands round Signy's waist and down her legs. When he stood up, he had a curious questioning expression on his face.

"Nothing more, sir…nothing at all."

"Very well, now take him away to the captain, and thank your lucky stars Junius wasn't on the end of this," he added, sliding Signy's dagger back into its cover and placing it on his table.

The soldier seized her arm once more and she was half drawn, half pushed out of the tent.

"Move," said the soldier, not caring whether she understood Latin or not, and directing her across the parade ground towards one of the tents planted on the opposite side. As they approached, the soldier called out and received a brief reply from within, with the result that when Signy was propelled in through the tent flap, she almost collided with a man who was on the point of coming out. The man jumped hastily back with a curse, and Signy could get a good look at him, and what a good look it was. His hair was dark, and trimmed short but still wavy, his features clean cut, his eyes dark, taking her in. He was wearing a short summer tunic, his legs bare below it, his feet encased in sandals.

"Prisoner, Captain, young Goth came over the river. His companions stayed on the other side, so begging your pardon, sir, but I must go and set a fresh picket."

"Has he been searched for weapons?"

There was a hesitation in the soldier's voice, as if there was something on his mind that might be worth mentioning, before he grunted.

"Yes, sir, his knife is with the centurion."

There was a nod from the captain, and the soldier retreated.

"So you came over the river, young man. That was rather foolhardy. Why did you do that?"

The captain spoke in Gothic, precisely and exactly, but with a light Latin accent, better than Signy could, in fact, since she had had little to do with the new masters, and when she did try to speak their tongue she still struggled with Saxon or Jutish words slipping into her speech.

"I *can* speak Latin," she said.

The man examined her carefully, weighing her up. She decided to take a risk and confess.

"And I'm not a young man, I'm a woman, *femina*."

The captain pursed his lips doubtfully.

"I find it hard to believe that a woman would be so foolish to venture alone across the Oltis into the disputed territories, but a young man wishing to show off his daring, that would be another matter."

"Do I have to prove it to you?" said Signy, inwardly cursing to herself. She undid the clasp of her cloak, slipped it from her shoulders and held it out.

"Take this, Captain," she said.

The moment he had hold of the cloak, she undid the upper hook of her tunic, shook it free and let it fall down her torso. She heard the captain take a sharp intake of breath.

"Are you satisfied?"

He took a step forward, his eyes focussed not as she expected on her breasts, but up and a little to the left. He shifted the cloak to his left hand and then slowly reached out and touched her tattoo, the lynx head pricked into her left shoulder.

"What does that signify?" he asked, his eyes looking directly into hers for a moment.

"It signifies I'm a medicine woman, a healer. Perhaps you could say, Captain, if it's not offensive to you, in my home country I might be considered a priestess, an apprentice, anyway, and a sister of Freya."

"A pagan priestess, huh," said the captain, circling her, "well, that's something new, though I suppose they must still remain in remoter parts, despite the best efforts of our bishops…Ah, I see you have another here." She felt his finger again, against her lower spine. There was something gentle, exploratory in his touch. It had been a long while since she had been touched like that and it began to have a peculiar effect on her, along with the faint odour of sandalwood he must employ as perfume.

She could feel his hand sliding across her rear, and then he came round to face her again. She glanced down at the fringe of his tunic. He was obviously interested in more than just her marks.

"I think you should cover yourself up," he said abruptly, turning his back to her. "You've proved your point well enough, but this is a camp full of men. My *optio* could come in any moment, and I wouldn't wish the rumour to spread that there's a woman in camp…" He turned back to her, a smile on his face. "…even if she is under my protection. In any case," he added, "while some might delight in the prospect, I feel some difficulty in having to interrogate a half-naked woman."

He moved to his desk and sat down, turning away from her.

"We've established beyond doubt that you *are* a woman," he said slowly, scratching away at a sheet stretched out on his desk, "but I shall leave that out of my report. Now, why did you cross the river? Don't you know the Oltis forms the boundary between the administration of the Empire and the lands granted to Wallia and his descendants?"

She sighed…so quickly back to business. He really was quite attractive, and she had not lain with a man for almost a year.

"I'm new to the area," she said.

"Where do you live?" came the next question.

"In Aginінum, on Olive Street." There was more scratching from the desk.

"I don't think I ever got your name. I can hardly write 'lynx-priestess' or 'Freya's sister'."

Why not, thought Signy, since that was what seemed to interest you, but she answered, "Signy." She watched him dip his pen into his ink and scribble across a sheet of parchment.

"Ha, you're from the north, from beyond the *limes*, I would guess," he said, again half turning towards her.

"The Saxon lands," she confirmed, "but I came to the Narbonensis from Britannia. My husband died and left me alone with a child."

"That would explain your accent," he murmured, before continuing, "So you have no husband, no betrothed, no… protector?" She thought she detected a note of hope in his voice.

"No, but I'm a friend of the trader, Master Lanius of Burdigala, and his companions."

The officer fell silent for a moment as if he was sorting through a sheaf of notes in his head. Apparently satisfied, he spoke again.

"But then, how do you maintain yourself?"

A good question, she thought. I'm beginning to wonder myself how I'll ever do that.

"I'm a medicine woman, a midwife…like my mother before me. I told you so."

"I'd forgotten," he said. "I was distracted."

"I share a house with the merchant, Megana Fabiana."

"A woman trader?" Megana evidently did not feature on the list in his head.

"A widow, like me." It was the story they had agreed on to explain their children.

He turned away and made another note, glanced quickly towards her and then sat still for a moment, staring at the wall of his tent. He seemed to have gathered the information he needed and turned to face her.

"You've never explained," he began, "why you rode all the way here, many miles from Agininum. You were accompanied by three men, the patrolman said, yet only *you* crossed the Oltis. There are no pregnant women in this camp, I can assure you."

"Curiosity," she replied, "and compassion. I'm a friend of the women of the monastery of Mons Agininum. Their shepherd was found dead, collapsed close to the monastery. His dog was still with the sheep – stabbed. I hoped to discover who had done that, who might be responsible for the shepherd's accident."

"Ah," he said, and put his pen down.

"We followed the tracks, the boot prints, my servants and I, and they led to the river. Made by your men, I presume?"

"Centurion Maxus' men," he said quickly. "I'm merely attached to the expedition." He frowned. "Yes, the dog…it attacked our patrol, so I heard. The *optio*…he had to defend himself."

"And the shepherd?"

"I don't know of any shepherd. I certainly saw no shepherd."

"He had an injury to his head."

Junius shrugged. "He must have fallen. It was muddy and steep, poor light in the evening. That's how the dog took us by surprise."

Their eyes met for a moment.

"Look, Signy," he said, "I accept your explanation, though I think your actions have been extraordinarily foolish. You can see how an accident might so easily happen out in the hills, rough terrain, poor tracks, unfortunate outcome. I'm sorry the man died. I'll tell you what. You said he was a shepherd, right? I'll apply to the quartermaster…for compensation. You can take the sum to the monastery, as a token of our goodwill. The sisters can ensure it goes to his family, I'm sure."

He got to his feet.

"I can't see any reason to detain you in the camp, though it will soon be evening, and it would not be safe to try to cross the river in poor light. Better to return in the morning, once I've squeezed the money man a little. Your friends won't try anything foolish, I hope, not against a whole camp full of soldiers?"

He glanced around his tent, then shook his head. There was a tinge of regret in his voice when he spoke.

"I can't keep you here in my tent. Once perhaps there would have been tolerance for that, even if you were a boy, but now…" He shook his head, evidently with regret. "In the meantime, it's best you're treated as a prisoner, best to place you somewhere secure, away from prying eyes."

You could still find me, she thought, if you wanted to.

"It would be bad for discipline if the men found out there was a woman in the camp," he went on, "and that I was hiding her, however chastely, in my tent. In the morning your horse and your weapon will be returned, and I'll personally escort you to the ford."

Not so chastely, if I had my way, she thought again, but her thoughts were wasted as he stood up and crossed to the tent opening, before calling outside. A soldier appeared and glanced quickly around in a suspicious manner.

"Take the prisoner, this boy, to the storehouse and close him up." Junius had switched to Latin to give his orders. "No one is to approach except with his meals."

The soldier acknowledged the order in silence by an inclination of his head and beckoned Signy to follow him.

"No tricks, boy," called Junius from the tent.

She followed the soldier, her eyes on the ground, the man's feet lifting and falling on the edge of her vision, leaving a trail of prints in the dirt of the parade ground. It was then she noticed with a shock a distinctive pattern in the print left by the man's boot, the sign of a poor-quality repair that had left a ripple in the leather and a misalignment in the hobnails. She had seen that print before, by the carcass of the dead dog. More than likely, the man leading her to her confinement was the *optio* who had killed the dog, the man Junius admitted was his assistant. It was a sobering reminder of the dangers of her situation worth more than any of Junius' words of warning.

☙ Chapter 10 ❧ Beyond the Oltis River

The storehouse was one of the wooden buildings hastily raised on several large stones along one side of the parade ground. The soldier gesticulated. Signy did not need telling that she should climb the step and enter. He closed the door behind her, and she heard a bar being drawn across. A few thin streams of light broke the darkness, sufficient for her to see that there were several sacks, probably of corn, stacked along one wall and a couple of sides of meat hanging from the ceiling. They were protected by nets, but that did not stop optimistic flies from buzzing around them. Probably the stones were not enough to keep the rats out, either, she thought.

She pulled one of the sacks into a horizontal position and sat down, letting out a deep breath. What shit I've got myself into, she said to herself. She had not had much time to think since she had ridden her horse into the river, but now she had plenty, all the time until she was set free. She only had the officer Junius' word that she would be allowed out, and if his assistant had killed the dog, how far could she trust the master? How in Hel's name had she let herself do this, she wondered, crossing the river alone without a care? And then she had practically stripped naked in front of him. Had it been merely tiredness and lack of thought after a long day in the saddle, or a desperate hope that he would spare her worse if she made herself vulnerable? But then his touch had been so soft, his look so inquisitive. It had been so long since a man had touched her that way. She cursed to herself; just a soft touch from a man, and she had been ready to give herself to him. Was she such a fool? Of course, there was also the risk that the truth would leak out, and half a dozen men would break into the hut during the night. She could be raped and murdered, and no one would give a damn. She was sure the soldier who searched her suspected the truth, and the *optio* had given her a very careful examination. Maybe the rumour was circulating already that the pretty boy that Junius had been interviewing was no boy at all. Maybe Junius himself would pass the word around to men he favoured. That spurred her to her feet, gave her the strength to drag one of the grain sacks across the floor and lay it against the door. Get that open, brothers, she thought. Two can set about barring doors.

Her actions had set her mind down a new track, towards a feeling that had come over her earlier, before the soldiers had stepped out of the trees. It had come over her the moment she had urged her horse into the river when her companions had held back. She had returned to a world she knew. The countryside, the path through the woods, the river, even; far from towns, far from straight paved roads, from water fenced in by docks and quays, from the never-ending ocean. She had felt the river was a friend. She had grown up by a river. A river had carried her away from the humdrum existence as a farm girl to new lands, new friends, a husband, a lover, a child, not always good experiences, but her luck had held. Until last year that was. Then she had been forced to concede that her luck had run out, that her *hamingja*, the component of her spirit which ensured that sticky situations could be turned to her advantage, had abandoned her. Something she had done in Britannia, become too proud, perhaps, considered herself more clever and more cunning than others, had turned her luck, and she had had to be taught a lesson. She had become dependent on Megana, on Lanius, on the sailors, even on Grunwald and the other Jutes. She was grateful, of course, to Megana for her care and support, but the house, the money, even the servants belonged to her friend. It wasn't fair, she knew, but sometimes she felt she had become a slave to her situation, almost that she belonged to Megana, too, like a Barbary ape, a kind of fancy pet, as she had belonged to the man who had become her husband when he had first purchased her in Juteland. But the moment her horse stepped into the river she had begun to feel that she had command of the situation once more, that she was whole once again, that her *hamingja* had returned. By crossing the river, the cleansing, flowing water, she had put her past behind her. She had dared to climb the other side, into the unknown, and after that she had made the right choices, however foolish they might have seemed to an outsider. He had reacted, the officer, as she had wished, as she had desired, as men had responded to her before, when she had her luck with her. He had told her that she would be set free, to return to Grunwald and Hrasmus and Henrik, but she would not return as the person who had left them, but as a whole person, the four parts of her being once more united in harmony. And she would return with the knowledge of who had killed the dog and why, and perhaps with the Romans' gold as evidence.

She must not get carried away, she reflected. There was still something out of joint with her thinking – too much passion and not enough reasoning. Junius might be a good-looking man, interested in her as a woman, but he was still an officer of the Empire and had accused her, several times, of crossing the river from the lands of the Visigoths into theirs, as if there was something wrong with that. In her homeland, the Empire had been the subject of stories told around the fire by men who returned from far-off adventures with scars and gold: in Britannia in the memories of grandfathers recalling what they had been told in their youth. But in this land, she was beginning to realise, the Romans were still a force to be reckoned with. Megana had already described how the Bishop of Burdigala counted himself as a Roman and despised Our Men. He wasn't alone, as she herself had felt hatred and bitterness as she walked the streets and markets of the port city, just because she was mistaken for one of the newcomers, the men who had burned buildings, ripped apart families and stolen land. There were many, and not just rich landowners, who thought of the Romans with admiration and fondness. And unlike in Britannia, the Empire was not far off across the sea, but evidently just on the other side of the river. Or maybe even nearer, she suddenly reflected. Junius might claim the land on this side of the river for the Empire, but he and his men had been far, far inside the Visigoth lands when they killed the dog, and they were on their way back from somewhere even further from the camp. Captain Junius had admitted as much, but he looked nice and he smelled nice and he had caressed her nicely, and because of that she had let him get away without explaining himself. Did *they* have a right to cross the frontier in a way which *she* could not? And beyond that, what were they doing here anyway? Even if the lands on the far side of the Oltis were claimed by both the Empire and Our Men, this was not a patrol, such as Megana had mentioned. This was a camp, and they looked like they were planning to stay.

She heard the bar on the outside of the door being drawn back, reminding her that she was Junius' prisoner. He was not hers.

"What the fuck…" came a voice from outside.

"Just a moment," she said, deepening her voice a shade. "The door's stuck." She shifted the sack a short way from the entrance.

"I've got your fucking dinner here, even if you don't deserve any, you Goth bastard."

A bowl and a wooden spoon were shoved through the gap, and as she took them the door was pulled shut and the bar slammed across.

Thank the gods for some food, she thought. She had always felt it was a good strategy to ensure your stomach was full if you found yourself in a tight situation. If anything, she was relieved by the man's evil temper and bad attitude. So long as she remained a "Goth bastard" she was unlikely to be assaulted during the night, though what might happen in the morning was another matter.

--oo00oo--

Hammering at the door woke her. Another angry voice.

"Hey, you miserable shithead, the captain wants to speak to you."

Signy's heart took a leap as she saw Junius waiting for her outside his tent. He was no longer dressed informally but in his officer's uniform. There was no doubt he was a good-looking man, seemed intelligent, too, she had concluded, pondering on the matter during the loneliness of the night.

"Master Goth," he said, speaking their language, "for want of a better name. It's time I sent you on your way. There's an opinion in the camp that you're a spy and should be hanged, or at the very least bound and thrown in the river. Fortunately, Centurion Maxus favours order and discipline and not mob rule. However, even his reasoning might run awry if the truth came out."

He crossed the parade ground in the direction of his tent. She followed and the irritated guard brought up the rear. He held the tent flap and motioned her to go inside.

"You can tell Centurion Maxus," he said, turning to the guard and switching to Latin, "that I'll escort the Goth prisoner to the river and ensure that he crosses to the other side."

He waited for a moment, watching the man leave, before letting the tent flap drop.

"Thank you for not giving me away," she said.

Before he could react, she lifted herself on her toes and pressed her lips to his.

"I half expected you last night."

"I thought about it, believe me, but the risk would have been too great," he said, turning away from her, "but listen, I'm planning to pay a short visit to Agininum…not soon, but when our work here is complete. Will a message to the house on Olive Street reach you?"

"There's only one such house," she said, "and I live there."

There was a scraping sound from beyond the tent, and after a moment the flap was raised and the *optio* from the day before appeared.

"The escort's ready, Captain."

"Very well, *optio.* I have all the information I need for the moment," he added, once more speaking in Latin for the benefit of the soldier.

He picked up a small leather purse and held it out to Signy.

"I obtained these coins, a goodwill gesture to the local populace for the tragic accident with the shepherd."

With that he ushered her out of his tent, where the *optio* and another pair of soldiers were waiting.

"Now, let's make our way down to the river. My men report there has been a fire burning on the other side all night, so I hope your companions have been patient enough to wait for you. Here comes your horse and…"

There was movement from across the parade ground, and the neat centurion came hurrying.

"I hope your stay was comfortable," he said, handing over her belt and dagger. "I hope Captain Junius took care of you. We've no wish to upset the local population."

"Very well, sir," she said. "I have nothing to complain of in that regard, sir."

"Have a safe journey back then. May the gods…I mean, may the Christ…be with you."

She buckled the dagger around her waist, cautiously, conscious that she was being watched, and desirous to maintain the fiction of her boyhood.

"Let's go, then," she said.

They walked together, side by side, back the way she had been marched the previous day.

"So, Captain…"

"Junius, please?"

Yes, she could manage that now.

"So, Junius, you never explained to me what your soldiers were doing in the Visigoth lands."

He laughed.

"Ah, yes…we're tracking bandits. This whole camp, the century, have been deployed on an anti-bandit campaign, and bandits are no respecters of boundaries, any more than curious lynxes and the sisters of Freya."

They had reached the bank. He held out his hand. She took it to hoist herself back on her horse.

"I expect to be visiting Aginnum shortly," he said, loudly enough to be heard by his companions. "Incognito, of course," he added *sotto voce*. "I'm well aware that not everyone in the Visigoth lands loves Romans, but perhaps we'll meet again."

"In more propitious circumstances," she replied, using Latin in turn, while urging her horse down the last few steps towards the flowing water. She wished she could have kissed him one more time, but that would have given the game away.

Grunwald and Henrik were waiting when she splashed ashore on the far bank.

"Where in Hel have you been?" asked Grunwald.

"We saw you escorted away, outlined against the sky," said Henrik. "We thought we would never see you again."

"I was a guest," she said, "a prisoner of the Empire, for one night only."

"Thank the gods you're safe," said Grunwald. "We sent Hrasmus along the road, to the Christian men's house, the monastery by the bridge, to fetch the holy brothers. We thought they could intercede to get you back."

"Thank you, Henrik, thank you, Grunwald, with all my heart. Perhaps we should return to the road ourselves, and make for the monastery and save them the journey."

As they rode she provided them with a version of her capture, interrogation and imprisonment. She supplied no description of the officer and made no mention of the feelings he had aroused in her. Why bother! She would probably never see him again in any case, she thought.

☙ Chapter 11 ❧
Burdigala

Lanius poured wine for himself and for Megana. He added a good helping of water to his glass and handed the pitcher to his companion. She hesitated for a moment then topped up her glass. Now, sitting in the counting room, it was time for business. Later she could enjoy her wine undiluted, in the barbarian manner.

"You've had no problems?" she asked.

"So long as I conduct all the transactions in my name, no one asks any questions. They know my reputation, and in these times they're not going to turn away silver."

"I'm sorry to put you to the trouble, but no one likes newcomers buying up the best properties, and even though I'm designated as a widow, and legally permitted to carry out my own business…"

"I understand," replied Lanius.

"Half of these farms have been abandoned since the Vandals came through, in '06, correct?"

"It was before my time, Megana," said the merchant with a smile. That was obvious; the man might be balding, but he was barely older than she was.

"But your wife's father remembers?"

"Vipso remembers only too well. It was Vipso who hammered into me that we should rely on trade, not on land."

"I can't see that there's much difference between risking your wealth on the sea or the land."

"You can always run from a storm. It's a lot harder to uproot your vines or corn if there's a horde of raiders coming over the horizon."

"A storm can sink your ship. I've never known land sinking beneath the waves, unless you count Atlantis. Though I'll concede, Lanius, it's not easy either way, even though people always think we're rolling in riches."

The merchant shook his head at the folly of such "people" and took a sip from his glass.

"I'm doing my best," he continued, "but I told you, I've not invested in land before, and I don't want to arouse suspicions."

"But you've seen for yourself," said Megana, "the trade with Britannia is drying up. That was always the basis of Vipso's partnership with my father. Now we have to find other means to maintain the business." She sipped her wine. "What did you get this time when the boat from the islands came in?"

"Lead," said Lanius, "tin, and some salt."

"No slaves?"

"I'm expecting Osmo from Hibernia. He should have slaves…and hides."

"The hides you can keep here in Burdigala, but the lead and the slaves I need to move up to Tolosa before the winter sets in."

"I'm with you there. I don't want to have to feed them all winter. But are you willing to wait, or do you think you can make it to Tolosa and back here before the end of summer?"

"You tell me, Lanius. I've only done the trip a couple of times before."

"I wouldn't like to be caught out on the road with a convoy of slaves if a storm came in."

"Then I suppose I shall have to wait then, until Osmo's boat arrives."

"Before then I should have a cargo from Olisippo, oil and wine…nuts."

Megana shook her head. "Alexander is sending those from Agatha."

Lanius nodded. Megana's half-brother and his wife, their companions located on the shores of the Middle Sea, had convenient access to such products and a shorter distance to reach Tolosa.

"Well, in any case, Megana, I bought two farms along the Oltis, and they're assigned to our partnership under your name. I had my eye on a third, but the owner wished to donate to the church."

"Two's enough for now. I have to build up the contacts to sell the produce. People're hesitant. They don't always trust a new trader, especially a woman, and I'm not going back grovelling to Bishop Bartolomeus again."

"I understand, Megana, but you do use my name?"

"I do." The name Lanius of Burdigala opened doors, but she wanted people to remember her own name, Megana Fabiana. "And you took Signy's money and bought the mill?"

The merchant nodded.

"My name's on the contract, as we agreed, but in our own records it's listed for Mistress Signy."

"The rent and the tithes from the mill should provide her a steady income."

"If there are no floods or pestilence."

"Pestilence…then we'll have more to worry about than Signy's mill, and in any case," said Megana, laughing, "if there is pestilence, she'll be able to earn a good living by treating the sick."

"Yes…you said she has skills as a medicine woman, but the pestilence…there's no cure but repentance and to trust in God."

Megana merely grunted. She was unsure about Signy's skills against the pestilence, but she had seen her friend save many a patient who others had given up for dead.

"You spoke to Mistress Xancha?" Lanius asked.

"I did." Megana gave the merchant a hard look. "I don't understand how you got along with that woman, not that I didn't like her, but she didn't strike me as your type."

Lanius chuckled, glancing around.

"I was younger then, Megana, and hungrier – not for women, you understand, but for trade. Vipso had concentrated on supplying the Romans, but when the new masters arrived, what was the value in those contracts? I was newly married, of course, but I was away for months on end, in Agininum, Carcasso and Tolosa."

"You're not going to tell me you slept with Xancha."

The merchant looked away.

"No…but I stayed at the Fox Tavern. It was a popular meeting place for men, and for men and girls. I gave her a deal, a very generous deal."

"And she gave you a good deal in return?" asked Megana, still with a mischievous expression.

The merchant glanced around nervously again. He lived in rooms across the yard, but there was no telling when his wife might visit the storerooms, especially if she knew Megana was in town.

"Alright, Lanius, you don't need to tell me."

"She helped me…a great deal," Lanius continued. "Xancha got me supplying the palace, several of the leading families. It was a big step up for us then. Vipso profited…your own father profited, too, indirectly."

"We always did well from working with you and Vipso, and I'm grateful that you took me in when I decided to leave Britannia. I think we can use my treasure much better here than in West Britain."

"You've no thought of getting married?" The merchant had been planning his revenge for Megana's impudent enquiries about his own past with a twinkle in his eye. "You're a pretty woman, Megana. There are plenty of men who would take you as a wife."

"Don't let Vespa hear you say that." Megana raised a finger and wagged it in Lanius' direction. "And, honestly, I suspect there are all too many men with thoughts of becoming my husband, but they have eyes on my purse rather than on me. You don't know how many proposals I had to refuse or force my father to refuse in Britannia. But if I were to marry, my husband would take over my fortune, and I and my property would become his property, and I won't accept that. I know I can't hide from you that I've never been married, that it's a story Signy and

I've agreed on to explain away Sophia. I've managed so far without a husband," she said, "though I do get lonely at times."

"And since you've been here?" said the merchant, pursing his lips.

Megana laughed again, though with a tinge of bitterness. "It's early days, but they'll show up, I'm sure, though that doesn't make any difference. The answer's no." She sipped at her wine. "Now, Lanius, let's get back to business. You want me to go and speak to the Bishop of Aginnum? You know how I flopped with the man here in Burdigala."

"That was unfortunate," murmured Lanius, "but Bartolomeus is a little on the traditional side. There's no avoiding bishops, though. They've been forced to take on the role of officials since the Empire has withdrawn. The king has appointed his own people, the duke and the counts, but they simply don't have the local knowledge and experience of administration that the churchmen have. Some of the newcomers can't even read and write. Bishop Anastasius is a decent fellow. I've known him since I was a child."

"But he still needs a bribe to be sure he won't ruin my reputation before I've even had a chance to ruin it myself?"

"Let's not call it a bribe," said Lanius. "Look at it as doing good for the Church, and doing good for the Roman Church will put you on good terms with everyone associated with the institution. And if there are contracts, timber, stone, for example, for building projects, you'll need him on your side. One moment…" The merchant leaned over and picked up a scroll. "I've been checking this list. It's the parcels of land we picked up when we bought Paulinus' house. It had a small estate attached, nothing very much and spread out all over the region. I don't know how Paulinus managed to keep track of it. Probably there are squatters on the land. I've not had a chance to check."

Megana made a mental note to have a copy made of the list. If there were squatters on the farmland, they would be given a brusque reminder: pay up or move on.

Lanius tapped the sheet.

"As I thought, there's a small piece here which I happen to know lies adjacent to some land the bishop owns, or the bishopric, I should say."

"You're talking about Agininum, I suppose."

"Of course. I'm sure Anastasius would be happy to expand the lands of the church in such a convenient manner, and then once the other landowners and their tenants know you're friends with the bishop…"

"And this is not a first-rate vineyard or a hundred *juger* of best wheatland."

"Not at all, just a scrap."

Megana shook her head, wondering what kind of bishop would be satisfied with a scrap if he had a court like that of Bishop Bartolomeus to support. She did not want to imply any mistrust of Lanius, but she would certainly make sure to ride over and check the property herself before it was "donated". She would also take care to check the bishop before she did any "donating".

☙ Chapter 12 ❧ Aginінum

Autumn had come, and Signy had given up any expectation of meeting Junius again. She had spent days at a time at the monastery. She was accepted as Hildefrith's special guest and allowed a room of her own and then, when he joined her in Agininum, to bring Einar with her, to be fussed over and spoiled by the sisters. The death of the shepherd was accepted as being an accident, one of those mysteries with no solution. The coins Junius had given her had been handed over to Hildefrith, who had made arrangements to take care of the shepherd's widow, with enough left over to buy some additional sheep for his son and a cow for his daughter. In troubled times, that was as much as anyone could expect in this life.

Perhaps Junius tried to find me while I was away, Signy reflected. If so, that was a pity, but then the gods had not meant us to meet again.

In that she was wrong. The message arrived at Olive Street one morning, carried by one of the boys who ran errands for the shopkeepers. Junius would be waiting for her that evening in the house with the red door in Baker Street. She knew the street. It was one of the cross streets, beyond the marketplace, that she passed on the way down to Lanius' riverside warehouse – Megana's warehouse now. When she arrived, Junius was standing in the doorway. If she had passed him in the street, she would not have recognised him. Gone were the trappings of the Roman soldier. He was wearing a hooded tunic and leggings, like any other townsman, any other visitor to the town. Beyond the change of clothing, even his appearance was different. He had grown a beard and moustache, neatly trimmed it was true, but he looked more like a packman than a soldier.

For a moment, there was a little awkwardness, neither of them quite sure how to pick up from where they left off, given the circumstances were so different. It's strange, she thought, it's almost like we have exchanged roles. Now I'm the well-dressed lady, and he the traveller far from home.

"Maxus is packing up his tents, and he's almost ready to leave," Junius said, by way of explanation. "I must leave with him."

"You won't stay here?" It was hard to hide her disappointment.

"No," he said, "orders are orders, so we must enjoy what little time we have together."

"Shall we take a walk?" she said, considering it was better not to move too fast. "I can show you the town."

"That would be wonderful," he replied. "I have to be careful not to arouse suspicion or even hostility," he added, gesticulating towards his clothing. "Hence the informality."

"I'll take care of you," she said.

They crossed the forum taking West Street. After a short while, they came to the ruined theatre, with its bank of stone benches carved into the hillside. Signy took a small track that led round to the front of the stage. Junius followed slowly after.

"It must have been wonderful in the old days," said Signy, "but now it's mainly the place where young lovers come to get a bit of peace, a kiss and a cuddle in the shelter of the tumbled stones. One time I persuaded a pair of them to climb up to the top row and I recited a few verses of the *Aeneid* from down here, from the stage. I don't think they understood a word, but they waved enthusiastically, so I suppose they could hear me."

"You don't want to give it another try, see if I can hear you?" he asked, and before she could reply, he bounded up the steps, two at a time.

Signy laughed and shook her head.

"Come on," he shouted from the rim of the bowl.

She took a deep breath.

"Friends, Romans, countrymen, lend me your ears; I come to bury Caesar, not to praise him. The evil that men do lives after them; the good is oft interred with their bones; so let it be with Caesar."

She could hear him laughing.

"Where did you get that from? I never heard that speech before," he called, coming down the steps.

"I had a dream, once," she said, taking him by the hand, "and I heard a man declaiming these words from a stage. That's why they came to mind."

"Your dream man was a fine poet, unlike me, a mere army officer, if he was really a man and not a spirit."

"He was a spirit, unlike you," she said, leading him away from the theatre. "Here's the old temple of Jupiter," she continued, showing him a jumble of fallen columns. "The Christians took most of the shaped blocks to build the church."

Junius let go of her hand and began to thread his way among the stones.

"A stream," he observed, reaching the far side of the temple site.

"Yes," said Signy, following after him. "I think the Romans must have built their temple in a place that was holy before they came."

"Where does it come from?" asked Junius, peering up the hill.

"It flows down this valley, from round behind the town. I've been searching there, behind the bishop's residence and the Christian church, to see what kind of plants grow in the damp places."

"The medicine woman, Freya's sister," he said, smiling. "Do you mean there's a path?"

"Oh, no, not really. I had to scramble over the rocks and even wade in the stream a couple of times."

Junius picked up a pebble and tossed it into the water. There was a deep plop as it disappeared beneath the surface.

"Seems pretty deep just there," he said.

"The children were swimming in that pool earlier in the summer," she said. "There are steps you can use to get down to the water."

Junius turned and made his way alongside the stream and back to the road. She caught up with him again, and once more took his hand in hers. How wonderful to be able to walk through the town with a handsome man beside her.

They turned right and crossed the stream by taking the bridge which led to the west gate. Beyond the gate the road stretched off into the distance, a straight line contrasting with the meandering course of the river. They walked along the outside of the town wall until they reached the quayside between the fortification and the Garunna. There was a paved track that the merchants used to reach their warehouses without their pack animals or carts having to come into the town or, when the state of the river allowed, to offload cargoes that arrived by boat.

As they walked along beside the water, she put her arm around him and laid her head against his shoulder. She felt his hand on her waist.

"Which is your friend's warehouse?" he asked.

She pointed to a pair of stout wooden doors, now closed firmly since no deliveries were expected.

"It's the town rules," she said, "that the doors should be kept closed. We don't want thieves getting in."

"God forbid," he laughed. "And these?" He pointed to another set of doors a few yards further along.

"Oh, that's Merchant Tazzius' store, and that" – she turned and pointed back along the quay – "belongs to Caiphas. They're all merchants in the town."

They finally reached the far end of the quay and turned back towards the road and in through the east gate.

"Charming," he said, "almost enough to distract me from you, my dear companion. It'll soon be dark, and I'm beginning to feel hungry. Let's stop by one of the stalls and buy some food we can take back to the house. I think it's best to avoid the taverns."

Signy was careful not to sound overenthusiastic. Getting him into privacy was exactly what she wanted.

They carried their purchases back to the house he had rented. There was a small yard at the rear and a stable where he had his horse. He had left his *optio* at the camp. They sat on the steps, the food and wine between them, chit-chatting about this and that. She was a widow, she told him. Her husband, who she had married in Juteland, had been killed in a battle in Britannia, and she had been lucky to join Megana's household and become her friend. He was unmarried, he said, committed to his work with the army, regretfully never in one place long enough to put down roots and build a family.

"Even now I have to leave, early in the morning, to return to the camp, before Maxus and his troops set off for winter quarters. That's why I was so keen to come here, to see you again, and to hope that you might wait for me, that you might still be here in the spring."

"I had a feeling when we met that you might be interested in more than just a tour round Agininum and a bite to eat."

"I was intrigued by your marks," he answered. "I had read about them. I assumed it was only warriors who were tattooed. I never expected to see one exposed on such a beautiful woman. It took me quite by surprise."

She felt a sudden urge, a desire, to cut through the barrier between them even if her honour took a little damage in doing so. What was the worst that could happen, that he rejected her? Then she would be no worse off than she was already.

"Junius," she said, standing up, taking a step towards him. "I don't want to sound pushy, but I'm a widow. I'm the mother of a child. I've been without a man for a long time, since my husband died. I can see you…find me attractive. Do I have to wait all winter?"

She reached out, reached behind him, sliding her hands under the tunic and up the muscles of his back. She excited him, that was obvious, and he had the same effect on her.

"Can't we go inside?"

Perhaps she was risking her reputation acting this way. Perhaps he would simply think she was a quick lay, a whore, even. He would be gone, he had said, and he might never come back, so was his opinion so important?

--oo0Ooo--

When she woke – recovered might be a better word – he was already up, dressed once more. She watched him for a moment, seated on a stool writing. He must have heard a movement, because he turned and caught her eye.

"Signy, my nymph, it's morning, and I have to leave. The centurion will be expecting me."

She would have liked to continue lying where she was, naked and stretched out on the bed, savouring what she had experienced, but he was right. Not only was his centurion expecting him, but her household might be concerned where she had gone. She curled round, sat up and reached for her clothes.

"You'll be back?" she asked as she left him, her hood well pulled up to disguise her features. It was probably best she was not spotted leaving a strange house at this time of the morning. She might not be well known in the town, but her own house servants might be up and about.

"I hope so," he said. "That's the plan."

"And will your plan include me?"

"Undoubtedly," he replied, placing his lips against hers.

☙ Chapter 13 ❧
By the Oltis

Megana was irritated with herself. This seemed to be a fool's errand. Why hadn't she just gone to the bishop and offered him the land? It might have been mildly humiliating, but simple, clear and businesslike, characteristics on which she always prided herself.

Drizzle fell steadily. She sat hunched on the *cisium*, the light two-wheeled carriage, her hooded cloak pulled tightly around her. She was not even driving as she preferred. That was the responsibility of Thaddeus, a local man she had hired to assist Henrik with the horses. He said he knew his way around the region. He said that the tracks away from the main roads could be difficult, even dangerous for someone who did not know them. He was right. The *cisium* lurched and shook as the iron-bound wheels clattered over furrows and rocks and tree roots. Grunwald was riding in front and Asser, another of the Jutes, behind. The stories Signy had been telling about the meeting with the Roman bandit hunters had disturbed her. She was not sure whether she was more concerned about encountering bandits or soldiers. Signy had pointed out that the soldiers had probably retired to their winter quarters, though how she had become such an expert was unclear. In turn, Thaddeus had laughed, and said that he had never heard of bandits around Aginnum. On the contrary, he had said, the signs pointed to a longer spell of rainy weather, and that would keep all kinds of miscreants close to home.

Megana wished *she* had stayed close to home. The track they were following curved alongside the river. Somewhere down to the right rushed the Oltis, hidden by scrubby thickets, which also stretched away on the right. No doubt in the past these lands had been farmed, but now they seemed almost worthless. It made no sense that an aristocrat like Paulinus had retained a small section of riverbank in his hands, when other, less scrupulous landowners had donated this land of no value to the church. No doubt such gifts looked good, sitting in a counting house in Burdigala, but up close they seemed more like a swindle. Had she been swindled, too, in a minor way, drawn on an uncomfortable three-days' journey, not counting the travel back, for no good reason?

All the more irritating that she could catch glimpses of the north bank of the river, a succession of vineyards and fruit orchards, only interrupted by pleasant villas and prosperous-looking farmsteads.

"Are you sure this is the right route?" she asked Thaddeus, not for the first time.

"Yes, my lady," the man replied.

"And how much further do we have to go?"

"If the description you gave me's correct, then another mile or so. Master Henrik and I did go and check with the notary before we set out."

Of course they had, because she had sent them.

The road, such as it was, began to curve, with the result that the runnels cut by water flowing down to the river followed the track rather than crossing it. The bumping was replaced by lurching as the wheels of the *cisium* caught first in one rut and then another. The hindquarters of Grunwald's horse and the back of the man himself could be seen through the rain, perhaps ten yards in front.

Just then, there was a break in the clouds, and a single beam of sunshine burst from the sky and lit up a particularly attractive-looking villa across the river. Well, that wasn't hers, not yet, thought Megana, but perhaps the situation was taking a turn for the better.

The road took another dip, and a turn, and suddenly the trees fell away, and the group of travellers were confronted with a stretch of flat land where the river had carved out a bow.

"I think this must be the place, my lady," said Thaddeus, slowing the horse that had almost collided with Grunwald's mount which had come to a halt, probably from surprise, almost as soon as they had cleared the edge of the woods.

"Are you sure?"

Thaddeus jumped down and began to search along the side of the track. Suddenly, he called out.

"Here, my lady, the marker you spoke of."

"Does it say 'boundary marker, Paulinus made this'?" she said, still hunched on the carriage.

"You'll have to come down and see for yourself, my lady."

Naturally, the man was illiterate, she thought with a half-suppressed groan. What more could she expect? She stepped to the ground and crossed the track, her boots splashing in the streamlets that still trickled around her feet. At least the rain was thinning out, she reflected, as she paddled over to where Thaddeus was dragging at the undergrowth obscuring the stone marker.

Grunwald had joined him, but she knew the Jute's literacy skills were barely better than the Gaul's.

She crouched down to scrutinise the small stone, about two feet high, a little to the side of the track. "PA FCT" was all that was carved into one face, but that was good enough. Why else would a stone with just that inscription have been placed just here by an isolated track if it did not mark the boundary to Paulinus' land, or rather the land that formerly belonged to Paulinus?

She stood up straight and stretched her back. Now the situation began to make sense. When this side of the river had been cultivated, this tongue of land would have been a natural place to consolidate the produce from the fields around, and to extract a tithe.

"Is that a building I can see over there?" Megana asked Grunwald. She had a little trouble in making out distant objects, the result of too many hours studying documents by the light of flickering candles or smoky oil lamps. The Jute, on the other hand, had eyes like an eagle.

"Yes, Mistress," he answered, "a couple of stone outhouses and some form of cottage. I can see smoke rising from the roof ridge."

"Squatters," she muttered to herself. "Let's go and check them," she said aloud.

Now they proceeded on foot, Grunwald and Asser leading their mounts and Thaddeus with his hand on the bridle of the horse pulling the *cisium*. Megana had shaken off her gloom and was surveying the land around her. The track was raised and even roughly paved down here where there was less damage from the run-off. There were ditches along either side, and she guessed that it probably cut across the corner until it met the curve of the river again, and then resumed being the bumpy nightmare they had just been traversing. The flat area between the track and the river was be covered by reeds and the remnants of uncut summer grasses. The little she could see resembled more a swamp than cultivated land. Here and there ditches departed at right angles to the road, and these were mostly remarkable for the fine stands of rushes which choked them.

As they approached the smudge on the horizon, even Megana began to make out the forms of several buildings, one of which was inhabited according to Grunwald's judgement, and as further evidence for that, the road was now bordered by thin strips of tilled land, with leaf vegetables growing in them.

A dog began to bark, but there was no other sign of life. They seemed isolated. Even the other bank of the river was invisible, obscured by the last of the drizzle beyond the far end of the marsh.

They came to a halt again.

"I think it's best Asser and I go forward from here." Grunwald spoke in Jutish, a language that Megana understood, but pointedly excluded Thaddeus.

"Very well," she replied. "Thaddeus, you stay here with me, and let Grunwald and Asser investigate the farm. It's a task better left to experts."

While Thaddeus tethered the horses to a stand of willows beside the track, Grunwald drew his sword, and Asser unslung the spear he had carried across his back. The two men advanced silently towards the house. Even the dog had fallen quiet again.

They reached the door, a rectangle of basketwork blocking the entrance, stood still for a moment as if listening, and then ripped it open and charged in. A moment later they emerged with a man in their grasp and called out to Megana that it was safe to come up.

"He's the only adult male, merely a farmer, I would guess," said Grunwald, sticking to Jutish.

The man seems terrified, probably expecting to die at the hands of robbers, Megana thought.

"Your name?" she demanded, using the local patois.

A look of surprise spread over the prisoner's face when he realised the person addressing him was a woman. He did not say anything, however.

"Your name, damn you!" yelled Megana, now only a couple of feet from him. Grunwald tightened his grip on the man's arms.

"Delo," the man muttered at last.

"Well, Delo, do you know who is the master of this land?" Megana asked, filling her voice with aggression.

The farmer shook his head. Probably he had imagined he was the master of the land until a few moments ago, Megana thought.

"Have you heard of a man named Paulinus?"

The farmer shook his head.

"Did you ever pay rent to someone?"

The farmer shook his head again.

"Did you pay tax to the king or the bishop?"

The man did not even bother to shake his head. Megana reckoned the idea of tax was beyond his experience.

"Then you are a squatter on another man's land, and a thief who has stolen what rightly belongs to the king and the bishop."

The man said nothing. Now Megana could see a woman had come out of the house, two children by her side, a small boy and a girl, she judged.

"And do you sell produce from this land in the market?"

The man shook his head.

"E-enough to feed us…my family." He tried to look back towards the woman and children, but Grunwald's grip kept him facing Megana.

"I'm telling you this, so you know your fate, and the judgement I'm going to make. Master Paulinus is dead." Better to keep the explanation simple if not entirely truthful. "This land is now mine. You've been farming my land, without my permission. You've been stealing from me. You've been feeding your family with crops that should have been handed over to me. Do you understand?"

He clearly did not.

"I have every right to take you and hang you from the barn door, and to sell your wife and children as slaves."

"No," groaned the man.

Actually, she did not have the right to hang anybody, or enslave them, but who was going to argue with her in this remote corner? Paulinus might have the right to financial compensation, for the years the man had farmed the land while it had been in his ownership, but given the family's miserable circumstances, and the obvious signs of neglect, even that would be very little. That was Paulinus' problem. Megana had only owned the land since the early spring, and so whatever the miserable inhabitants owed here, it might amount to the value of a pig, or maybe the dog, if it was a good hunter.

The fact was that the property was useless to her without a tenant, and useless to the bishop, too, but now she had seen her plot she was beginning to wonder whether it really made sense to donate it to the church. The fact was that there was potential here, but to realise that potential she needed a farmer, and why not use the one that God had seen fit to put here?

"I'm a merciful woman, Delo, so I won't punish you, not yet." She caught Grunwald's eye, and he immediately understood he could let go of the miserable peasant, whose knees almost gave way as the Jute warrior relaxed his grip. The man staggered, and then cast a fearful and longing glance towards his wife and children.

"Farmer Delo," she said, "now that I've exposed you, you're going to have to pay rent to *me*, otherwise *I* shall send my men to remove you and your family and give this farm to someone more honest."

"I…I'm honest," the man muttered.

"We'll see about that," said Megana. "Do you have any silver to pay me?"

Delo was trembling so hard that Grunwald was forced to catch hold of him again to prevent him collapsing entirely.

"No silver…" said Megana. "Do you have anything of value you can pay as rent?" She forced a smirk across her face. "Apart from your wife and children, of course…your dog, a cow, a pig, maybe?"

A glance from Grunwald told her all she needed to know. The man was living from hand to mouth on the little he managed to grow in the plots around the house.

"Very well," she said finally. "Tonight my men and I will stay here. We'll sleep in one of *my* barns. Find us wood for our fire. Tell your wife to prepare us a meal, and your daughter will bring it to us. I want to see whether she might have value as a servant."

The man nodded, clearly still unsure whether this was really the owner of the land or simply a robbery, and he and his family would end up dead whatever they did.

"What about the horses?" asked Grunwald, tactfully sticking to his native tongue.

"Give them a long enough rein that they can find their own food, but don't let them get in amongst his vegetables."

The warrior nodded.

"In the meanwhile" – Megana switched back to confront the farmer – "my men and I are going to inspect this land to see what would be a suitable rent. Tomorrow I will give you my answer. You may go."

By the time the short day had begun to draw to a close, the unfortunate countryman had gathered together enough dry wood to light a fire in one of the outbuildings, and as darkness began to fall, the nervous form of his daughter, a girl aged perhaps seven or eight summers, appeared with a dish of vegetable stew, with a few meagre samples of rabbit among it, and a basket of unleavened bread, evidently cooked in haste while they had been surveying the land.

"What's your name?" asked Megana, putting on her kindest voice.

"Lilia," said the girl.

"Well, Lilia, would you like to come and live in a big house in the town?"

The girl shook her head, and the inklings of tears appeared in her eyes.

"You can't be serious," said Grunwald, once the girl had left them. "You can't take her to Olive Street against her will. You know that Mistress Signy won't permit slaves in the house."

It was a rule Signy enforced in the house in Olive Street. No one was to be considered a slave. She had once been a slave herself, purchased by her master, albeit a master who came to value her so highly that he had made her his wife, his second, junior wife, but nonetheless his wife. She had almost become a slave again after the Jute raiders had been defeated and she had been captured by the Britons. No one in her household, Signy insisted, was to be owned by another person. The inhabitants of the house in Olive Street might only be servants, provided with food and board in return for their work, but they were no one's property and they were free to leave if they wanted, from Henrik and Victoria to the least maid or stable boy. The fact that the rest of the world did not see things quite the same way was a great incentive for the residents of Olive Street to stay put. Sometimes Signy was a little naive, thought Megana. She raised no objection to Megana and Lanius buying and selling slaves as part of their business, but Grunwald was correct, she would no doubt be upset if the farmer's wife or children were taken.

"The girl's old enough to be useful around the farm," Thaddeus pointed out. "Her father will need her help."

"Then she's old enough to be of use around the house in Olive Street," said Megana firmly, looking from man to man. She was irritated that her own servants were siding with this Delo, little more than a thief, and perhaps worse than that given he was hiding in an abandoned backwater.

"Listen," she said at last. "You've seen this land. Once it must have all been fertile fields and could be again if the ditches were cleared and the water drained away. You saw where the road comes down to the river, and there's a sheltered beach where boats could be launched to transport produce downriver to Aquitania province or the market in Burdigala. It could be like that again. That man, Delo, could become a prosperous tenant, a rich man in the tract, if he put his back into it. I want to make sure that he does, that's all."

"And the girl would be your hostage, you mean?" Grunwald continued staring into the fire. Thaddeus merely grunted. Asser hid his face behind a beaker of the ale they had brought with them.

Megana tried to imagine their thoughts. They admired her, perhaps, were intimidated by her, probably, owed their lives and well-being to her, definitely, but they did not understand her reasoning. A little while ago they had heard her threatening to hang the man, and now she was telling them that he could become rich. That was how the masters were always thinking, they would say to themselves, first one thing and then the complete opposite. No wonder the world is in such a mess. We'll just follow our orders without too much questioning. Except Grunwald had questioned her…She smiled to herself. Maybe the man had a little initiative.

--oo0Ooo--

They were up at dawn. They had a long day ahead of them. They broke their fast on oatcakes and water drawn from the well.

Delo the squatter appeared as Thaddeus and Asser were loading their few supplies and blankets onto the *cisium.*

"Come with me," said Megana. She would have taken hold of the man by the arm of his tunic and drawn him after her, had he not kept his distance. "Come with me, now!" she ordered.

The farmer followed her in silence along the track away from the farm.

She stopped and pointed to the ditches.

"You see these drains…you understand what I mean by drains?"

The man nodded.

"This winter you will clear these drains either side of the track so that the river water flows the entire length and" – she pointed to one of the ditches that stretched from the trackside out into the reed marsh – "you will clear that channel, too, and cut the reeds back on either side. I will return in the spring, and if I'm satisfied with your work, then you may stay, but from now on understand, *I* am your master. *I* own this land, and you obey me, your wife obeys me, your children obey me. If any of you disobey, you and they will face the consequences."

"And my Lilia, you don't take her as your servant?"

"No, Farmer Delo," she said with emphasis. "My men have spoken on your behalf. Your daughter will remain with you for now. But I need help at my home, and a little silver would help you buy more cows or some goats perhaps to eat up this vegetation. I'm a strict master, Delo, that's why you must do as I say, but she'd come to no harm with me, I promise. We'll talk about this again in the spring."

They began to walk back to the farm.

"And, Delo," Megana continued, "in the spring I will come with more men, and if you've done as I asked, we'll turn this entire place into a farmland, as it was once before."

The man gave her a doubtful look and said nothing.

Megana jabbed her finger at his chest. "Listen, I'm not doing this out of the kindness of my heart. This land is my land. I paid for it. I plan to make money from it. If you don't like this, you know where the road is."

The three men said nothing, gathered by the loaded cart, preparing to leave. She caught Grunwald's eye for a moment and thought she saw a twinkle and a hint of a smile. Damnation, she thought, am I so soft that I'll let myself be talked around by my own servants?

"Home," she said sharply, "as quickly as possible."

☙ Chapter 14 ❧ In the Hills Above Aginum

Crossing the hills in the winter was always risky. The weather was not as severe as it was in the northlands, but it was unpredictable, and the new year started cold and wet. However, Signy needed to get out of the house in Olive Street now and then. A visit to the monastery was the best option she had, and worth risking the rain. She made the journey whenever she could, if nothing else to keep company with Ophelia when the cold made writing difficult.

This time Signy's judgement had erred, and she had been caught by a squall and soaked from head to toe. Her clothes had been sent to the kitchen to dry, and she was sitting, wrapped in a blanket, in Sister Hildefrith's private chamber where a cheerful fire was burning, chatting with Ophelia.

"They must be in here," came the sound of Hildefrith from the corridor, and in a moment the door swung open, and she came in, shortly followed by an older man with thinning, shoulder-length grey hair, sinewy with a distinct paunch. Signy recognised him immediately: the Count of Agininum. She had noticed him several times in the town, but they had not been introduced, and she had never had cause to speak to him. The lord of the town, Signy thought, and now, when we meet at last, what's he going to think, seeing me looking like a beggar?

"Ah, yes, too cold and damp in the library, my dears." Hildefrith seemed unbothered by Signy's state of undress. "My cousin, Sismond," she announced.

Ophelia rose to her feet and embraced the count, without much warmth, Signy noted. Signy, herself, was unsure how to greet him, not even daring to get to her feet, anxious in case the blanket would slip. She could only clumsily bow her head, which she hoped would satisfy him as to her humility.

"I hope I'm not disturbing your work," said the count, with a smile to his cousin.

"Not at all," broke in Hildefrith. "Ophelia won't allow a fire in the library, for fear that a stray spark might ignite the books, and poor Mistress Signy was caught in the rain."

"The adventurous Mistress Signy," said the count, a faint smile on his lips. "You seem quite an explorer. Hildefrith was telling me about the man who was murdered in the autumn and mentioned that you had followed the trail of his killers."

"I don't know that they actually killed the shepherd, my lord," said Signy, still from her place on the floor. "They may have killed the dog, but the man…"

"But you followed the trail?"

"We followed the old road, over the hills, my lord, a couple of my men and I."

The count furrowed his brow at the term "my men", though Signy knew for a fact that Grunwald and the others had been sharing war stories in the taverns in the town with men from the count's retinue.

"We saw traces of boot prints," she said.

"So Hildefrith told me…imperialist boot prints."

"Yes, my lord, and I, rather foolishly, rode over the river to see if they continued, and there on the other side I was… apprehended."

She glanced at Hildefrith. What had the abbess told her cousin?

"I was taken to a camp, a military camp…of Roman soldiers. They treated me well enough and allowed me to return to my companions on the following day. They provided compensation for the man who died, though they said it must have been an accident. Xeno's dog had attacked them as they crossed the stream close to his hut."

"But this hut," said the count, "it's only a few miles from this monastery. I've ridden past it myself on occasions. Did they explain what they were doing there?"

"Hunting bandits, my lord."

The count once again exchanged glances with his cousin, an expression of suspicion on his face.

"You believed them?" he said, turning once more to Signy and giving her a hard stare.

"I had no reason not to, my lord."

"How long have you lived in this province?"

"Since last summer, my lord."

"And have you heard of any bandits in the area?"

"No, my lord."

"Exactly."

"But then I suppose the Romans have been successful."

"You can suppose *I* have been successful," said the count with emphasis. He frowned, almost angrily. "Now listen to me, if you or your men, as you call them, discover anything more of these imperialists, you must let me know. The king, our king, Theodoric, has given *me* the responsibility for the county of Agininum, and if the imperialists have a problem, they should come to me. I should have dealt with this earlier, spoken to you in the old year instead of waiting until now. For that I apologise, and for disturbing you in your present condition. I confess I've noticed you in the town, and I assumed you were some… frivolous companion…to this merchant woman who just popped up, Megana…what's she called…Fabiana."

"I'm her friend, my lord," said Signy.

"These men you referred to," he continued, "they're the ones the merchant woman employs as escorts, correct?"

"Rightly speaking, my lord, they are Mistress Megana's servants," she said.

"Mistress Signy is a very fine medicine woman and midwife," said Hildefrith quickly, in an attempt to divert the count's attention, "and your neighbour, too. You might do well to employ her services."

"I certainly won't be needing her…services," said the count, gazing down at Signy's crouching, blanket-wrapped figure, "but my servants, perhaps." He turned to Hildefrith. "I've lived long enough not to underestimate a person just because she's young and pretty."

"You wouldn't be the first if you did," answered his cousin.

"Hm," he grunted, and turned back to Signy. "Come by my workroom in the next couple of days…when your clothes have dried," he added, with a glance towards Hildefrith, "and my clerk will write you out a pass, permission to exercise your profession in Agininum. But follow my advice, Mistress Signy. You're a newcomer to this province. Be careful what you get mixed up in. It would be easy to make a mistake, a misjudgement. You've been lucky, very lucky to come away unscathed from that camp. It was just as well that they were regular soldiers and not a bunch of barbarian auxiliaries. Then you might not be here to share your story."

He turned his back on her and gestured to his cousin that he was leaving.

Signy remained crouching by the fire as they departed, briefly outlined in the door opening. No one, no one, she thought, better corresponded to the image of a barbarian than the Count of Agininum. And as for herself, what was she, a barbarian too, a mere farm girl from beyond the frontier.

☙ Chapter 15 ❧ Agininum

Trading was suspended during the worst months of the year, when the roads and rivers were treacherous. The men were idle, with too much time on their hands, sitting around drinking and playing dice. The count's man, Jorid, who they had befriended, suggested a little outing. Grunwald and Henrik gathered a few of them together: Hrasmus, Asser and a couple of others. They were not looking for trouble, but it seemed like a good idea at the time. They took the road over the hills, crossed the bridge by the men's monastery and made a long circuit on the other bank. They approached the site of the soldiers' camp from the far, supposedly friendly, side. There was no need for caution, it turned out. The camp was empty, the tents packed up and the gates wide open, the rankers and their officers comfortable in winter quarters.

They burned down the storehouse and the cookhouse. They unhinged the gates, dragged them down to the river and watched with satisfaction as they were borne away by the stream. They dragged the boat from its hiding place. The vessel was stoutly built, and resisted their effort to smash it with rocks, so they slid it down to the edge of the water and, with the help of a fallen branch, pushed it out into the river. There the craft spun slowly in the swirling water until the bow fastened on a rock. The force tipped the boat, and one edge of the stern dipped beneath the surface. The water slopped over, filling the hull until all that remained visible was the stranded prow.

The Romans had crossed into the count's territory, and now they were paying the price. The Jutes and the count's men had this in common: no one messed with their chiefs and got away with it, no one, never. The weather turned nasty and an icy rain began to fall, so, quietly satisfied with their achievement, the men rode on to Cadurci, where they got profoundly drunk.

☙ Chapter 16 ❧
Agininum in the Spring

Signy unfurled the scroll, the message that had arrived late the previous day, and read it through again. *If you or your men discover anything more of these Romans*, the count had said, *you must let me know.* But this wasn't anything about Romans, it was about Junius. And, if she did not meet him, then how would she know if there was anything more to discover?

She ordered the bath fired. She unpacked her favourite dress, the one she had been given when she had first arrived in Britannia, of fine grey wool with a coloured band around the edge. Then she slipped away from her maid, avoiding questions by sneaking through the garden and out of the side gate onto The Hill, the main east–west street of the town, which led down from the Christian church, the bishop's residence and the count's house, past Olive Street, beside the marketplace, until it reached the merchants' warehouses along the river. She said a silent prayer that she would not meet the count, before she remembered that he had been called away suddenly to deal with a problem in Tolosa. He had left yesterday, according to his housekeeper, and would not be back for a week.

She should really have let someone know where she was going, she reflected, but Megana was away. In any case, she had never fully recounted what had taken place in the camp with Captain Junius, not even to Megana. Nor had she mentioned a breath of their meeting in Agininum. She could not tell the men, Henrik or Grunwald, either. They would be angry, betrayed, even, and she feared they would try to stop her assignation with the Roman. Besides, it was nobody's business but her own who she went to bed with, and there was something exciting about a clandestine romance.

You could pass him on the street and not realise he's a soldier, a captain of the Roman army, she thought. This time he was dressed simply, a trim beard covering his face, a floppy hat pulled well down. Perhaps she had already passed him in the marketplace, earlier that day, without recognising him. That's just as well, she thought. If someone sees us together, I can tell them he's a patient recovering from an illness, out on a supervised walk.

They ambled along Baker Street to the forum in the warm sunshine of the spring afternoon, and then turned up The Hill. For a moment, she was worried he wanted her to show him her home, take him in, even, but when they reached the far side of the square, instead of turning left under the arcade to North Street and up towards Olive Street, he turned off into an alley.

"If I let you lead, we'll be lost in a moment," she said. "Where are we going?"

He hesitated, frowning.

"Isn't the Christian church at the top of the town? Could we walk up and see it?"

"We can do that," she said, and with a sense of relief, took him by the hand and drew him on through the maze of small streets and passages that she had begun to recognise from visiting patients.

Suddenly, they emerged at the far end of Church Square. She peered out, fearing for a moment she might spot Aija, the count's housekeeper, on her way to the market, or Tygon, his chamberlain. There was no one in the square, only a cat which lazily gazed at them and then proceeded about its own business.

"Impressive," said Junius, surveying the church. "Built on the foundation of a temple, I presume."

"Yes," answered Signy. "There was a processional way which led from the theatre and the temple we visited last time you were here, up the hill past my home and into this square on the far side. I think there must have been more than one temple here in the old days, perhaps under the bishop's palace, and even the count's house."

"Which house is that?" he asked. "I still haven't had a chance to meet him."

"Over on the far side, with the fine portico for the public entrance."

"Excellent," he said, "now I know exactly where to come."

"He's out of town now," she said, "called away again."

"That's unfortunate. It's so difficult to coordinate with busy people."

They had crossed the square. Ahead was the Christian cemetery, where believers could be interred alongside the church, close to the saints and holy men, instead of outside the city gates as pagans had been buried.

They passed under an archway into the shade of some trees.

"Perhaps this was a sacred grove, before the Christians took it over," said Junius, stooping to examine one of the graves.

"It's so quiet. I sometimes come here to read," Signy said. "No one has ever disturbed me, not even the bishop or his assistants."

"A perfect place to hide away," he said with a smile, drawing her towards him. She was not slow to answer, wrapping her arms around him and kissing him. They held each other for a moment, and then he drew back.

"I've missed you…a long and lonely winter."

Me, too, she thought, friends are one thing but…

He took her arm and led her back under the arch and out into the square.

"If the Christians are buried here," he asked, "where were the Romans buried? I don't recall seeing any graves along the river when I was here last time."

"Perhaps that was because I was distracting you," she laughed. "But no, the mausoleums of the Romans are up here on this hill, but outside the walls, outside the north gate of the town." She had ridden past the remains numerous times on the way to the monastery.

"An old and rich town like this, there must have been some splendid tombs," he said.

"Not much to be seen now, unfortunately," she replied.

They passed out of the gate, which stood open to allow the villagers from the north a shortcut to enter and leave on their visits to the town, via the track that ultimately led to the road over the hills to Petrocorti. On either side were scatterings of stones, mounds of turf and heaps of rocks covered with scrubby vegetation.

"Most of the stones were taken to build the church," Signy said. "You can see them if you go inside. This is all that's left, except for one or two undamaged tombs, further away."

"Over there," said Junius, pointing down the road. Signy nodded reluctantly. This was not the direction she wanted to take, but she would humour him.

They walked along the road until it swung to the east. A more or less intact tomb stood at the corner. "Gaius Optimus Gracchus, magistrate of the town and benefactor to its works" was inscribed on the pedestal. Who remembers him now? thought Signy. Did he help build the temple? Did he contribute to the excavation of the theatre or lay out the forum, or just pay for parades on feast days?

Junius gazed out over the landscape one more time and then turned.

"Thank you, Signy, now I think it's time we turned back. I can imagine better places to be with you than a grave-yard."

"Me too," she said, putting her arm round his waist.

They returned the way that they had come, threading in and out of the back streets, until they arrived at West Street again.

Signy wondered whether they would stop to buy food, but he led her on, past the shops and taverns and back to the house in Baker Street.

When they arrived, there was food and wine laid out on a low table, a dish of meat, bread and some fruit.

"I ordered it to be delivered," he said, "from the cookshop. I don't want to show myself too much. You know how some people are hostile to Romans – not the plebs, of course, but the leaders amongst the Goths."

"Count Sismond was irritated that you were here, hunting for bandits."

"That's most unfortunate. We had no intention of annoying him. I plan to come here more often during this summer season. Then you and I'll be able to spend more time together. I might have to bring some of my men with me, if we're going to collaborate with Count Sismond. And that's going to be necessary. Centurion Maxus was most upset that some miscreants had set fire to the camp during the winter. Luckily the centurion's an industrious man, and soon had our quarters in order again."

"I hope I will see more of you," she said. "I would like that, but until then I'll be glad to make good use of the few opportunities I do get."

She slipped off her cloak and shook out her hair. Whatever he thought of her, a loose woman and easy lay, it had not stopped him from wanting to see her again. There was no need to be shy.

"That's an interesting dress," he said, obviously admiring her figure.

"A friend of mine made it for me, in Britannia. I'm glad I still fit in."

"It fits you like a second skin," he said.

But it feels even better when it is off, she thought, undoing the brooch that held it in place.

The sun was coming up when she left him. Most of the way she only thought of her lover, his body, his smell, how she felt when he touched her, the little jokes they had shared, but, just as she turned into Olive Street, she caught sight of the count's house across Church Square. Was it realistic that Junius and his men, Centurion Maxus, even, could collaborate with the count? She would certainly classify Sismond as one of the Goths who were hostile to the Romans. And, which was more troubling, though no one had mentioned anything out loud, she was fairly sure it was the count's men who had burned down Maxus' camp, and her own followers had been with them. She was definitely in an awkward situation, looking forward to being with Junius, excited to have her little secret, but at the same time, if either Junius or Sismond found out…She would have to be on her guard, but that would add an extra thrill to the encounters…for now.

ଓ Chapter 17 ଡ
Agininum

There was a soft call from outside the room. Signy was hiding. Not from any person, but from the chill wind that had suddenly interrupted the spring. The house in Olive Street was poorly designed for cold weather. Unlike the houses in Britannia, there was no hypocaust, and unlike the houses in Juteland or her childhood home across the *limes*, there was no hearth in the centre of the room and nowhere for the smoke to escape if you were to be such a barbarian as to ruin the mosaics and build a fire. On the coldest days, the inhabitants huddled in the kitchen, impeding the work of the cooks.

A brazier in each room, like the poor folks used in Corinium, would help, she thought, but then you would need ventilation. There was only one room where she had succeeded in installing a fire and a chimney, and that was the one she had adapted for preparing her medicines. A metal pan, filled with charcoal, and a clay pipe which led up and out under the roof tiles. There was a double reason for hiding: the warmth and the need to supervise the gently boiling pot into which she had just dumped a couple of fistfuls of chopped foliage. Water dripped from one bowl of her clepsydra into the second, a monotonous plop. Thankfully, in a little while, that would no longer disturb her – until the moment it stopped. Two cycles of the timer, and the herbs would be sufficiently boiled.

"Come in," she answered.

"Mistress!" It was Victoria, the housekeeper.

"What is it, Victoria?" she answered, still watching the boiling liquid.

"There's a girl, Mistress, run down from the count's, says they would have need of you, an injured man, I understood. The girl wasn't very clear."

"Is it urgent?" asked Signy, slightly irritated. If she was forced to stop, then the whole mixture would have to be discarded, and that would mean another journey up to the monastery and another round of begging Sister Agatha. Of course, Agatha would give her what she needed, but still…

"Not urgent, I think," replied Victoria, quickly detecting the tone in her mistress's voice.

"Then tell them I'll come in the evening, while this medication is cooling."

Hopefully the wind will have dropped by then and the nasty drizzle passed over, she thought.

The door closed softly behind her. She had been distracted, and once again the rhythmic plop…plop…plop of the clepsydra penetrated her thoughts until suddenly the sound faded away.

It was later, two cycles of the water clock later, when she sieved the contents of the pot into a second and covered it with a cloth to cool. The remains of the boiled leaves were dumped into a small tub to be taken to the garden to return to nature. Boiled they might have been, but she certainly did not want them to fall into the mouths of the house animals in the yard, who usually consumed the waste, let alone into the overeager hands of her son or young Sophia, or those children from the town who had learned that a friendly welcome and a treat might be available at the house in Olive Street.

She took up a basket containing her most commonly used medications, her knives and needles, and carefully locked the door of the medicine room behind her. Victoria was the only other member of the household to have a key, and the housekeeper had been strongly forbidden to enter unless Signy called for help or was unaccountably missing. In the outer chamber, her bedroom, she found a warm cloak. She passed through the kitchen to announce where she was going, crossed the yard, slipped out of the postern into Olive Street and then up the hill towards the count's house.

The wind had died down, but the air was unusually clear and cold, almost as if it had mistaken its way from its home in the north and ended up in the southlands, rather as she had done. She crossed the small square in front of the church and the two "palaces", as the townspeople called them, the bishop's on the right and the count's to the left, and made her way along the path which led to the yard gate of the count's residence. She now knew her way to the kitchen, where she found Aija, the count's housekeeper, bustling around supervising the girls who were preparing the evening meal.

"Oh, Mistress Signy, I'm so glad you could come," said Aija. "I put him to bed with a poultice, but I'm sure it'll be all for the best that you take a look at him."

"Is there something wrong with the count?"

The housekeeper looked confused.

"No…didn't that girl tell you? It's Brother Wilbert, rode over from the men's monastery during the night in this dreadful weather. It'll be the death of him."

She was not wholly exaggerating, Signy knew that. Too many good people sickened after travelling in poor weather and never recovered, although a cold night in the south bore little resemblance to a blizzard or the piercing frosts of the north.

"Take me to him, Aija, though he'll probably want to help me more by giving me a blessing than I need to take care of him."

"I wouldn't be so sure, Mistress. He was very upset when he arrived. Wanted to speak to the count, at once, but the count was called away again, and won't be back until tomorrow."

There was a young woman sitting by the monk's bed when Signy entered the chamber. She stood up quickly, bowed her head of dark hair and hurried away without speaking before Signy could get a good look at her.

"The count's new…girlfriend," whispered Aija.

She was obviously good-hearted enough to come and try to comfort the monk, thought Signy, unlike the last one, who, according to Aija, had become unjustifiably demanding and arrogant.

"Good evening, Brother Wilbert, how are you feeling?" Signy asked.

"Much better, now that Mistress Aija has wrapped me up in these warm blankets, but I have to speak to the count. It's urgent."

"Wilbert, don't get worked up!" said Aija sharply. "You know the count isn't here."

"You would get worked up, too, if you'd seen what I've seen and heard."

"I don't want to hear. You keep it for the count," said Aija.

"You tell me, Wilbert, and get whatever is worrying you off your chest," said Signy, firmly. "You'll sleep better then, and I'll give you a little potion to help you."

"Oh, Mistress Signy, it's terrible. Robbers and thieves... came in the dark...along the road, and down into the valley. They've burned three farms, taken away the women and children, and driven the cattle and sheep back to their hideout."

"Bandits, you mean?"

"Bandits of the worst kind, come down from the hills."

"But I thought...I thought the Roman soldiers were taking care of them. The officer, Captain Junius, assured me they had."

"I don't know where those Romans are, Mistress, but Brother Michael and I rode after the robbers to try to persuade them to leave the little ones and their mothers, but all we got for our pains was a beating."

"Are you beaten? Why didn't you say?"

"It was nothing, Mistress, compared to what I've had before, compared to what Our Lord suffered, but I have to confess, it made my ride uncomfortable."

"Now don't you speak nonsense, Wilbert. Let me look!"

There was no way that the monk could disobey, so he rolled over on his stomach, while Signy, doing her best to respect his modesty, lifted his gown to examine his back.

"Brother Wilbert, you've been very foolish not to tell us about this. There are bruises up and down your back and rump and the skin is broken in places. And it hasn't helped sitting on a horse all the way from the monastery."

She opened her basket and took out a salve. This wasn't the first battered back she had fixed. There were frequent fights in the town. Even her own men took a beating and needed patching up on occasion, but they only had a short walk home, not a long ride in atrocious weather.

"Now, Wilbert, you must lie on your stomach and let your back heal. Aija, give him these drops in some wine, and make sure he stays this way round. I'll come back in the morning with some vinegar in case there's corruption."

She gathered her things and left the room. From the corner of her eye, she noticed a small figure, half-hidden in the shadows, a pair of dark eyes, who turned and quickly hurried away towards the count's private quarters. The count's new girl again, she supposed.

☙ Chapter 18 ❧
Agininum

"What's this, Wilbert?"

By the time Signy had an opportunity to return to the count's house, Sismond himself had returned from his errand. He had reached the monk before she did. Despite her instructions, Wilbert was sitting up in bed, leaning against the wall. Signy understood he could not leave a man of the count's status staring at his rear, but she winced to think of his damaged back.

"Ah, the witch doctor," said the count, noticing Signy enter. "Can you get him on his feet again?"

"There's nothing wrong with his feet, my lord. It's his back and his lungs that concern me."

"The lungs seem to be working fine," said the count, "fine enough to tell me that a bunch of thugs has laid waste to half the monastery lands and ridden off with their retainers."

"Only the women and children, my lord. The men they killed on the spot."

"You think that makes things better?"

The monk started muttering something about heaven and the afterlife, but the look on the count's face gave him second thoughts. The dead men might have achieved their purpose on earth, but that would not get the fields tilled and the animals taken care of, nor provide manpower for the count's various needs.

"Damnation, monk, this is a serious matter!" said the count, and turned to Signy. "I thought these imperialist pals of yours were taking care of the bandits. Well, they're doing a damned bad job and, as usual, I'll have to take care of matters."

Signy was about to protest that the Romans, in general anyway, were not her friends, and that destroying their camp had certainly impeded their effort, but she made the same calculation as the priest. Quibbling with the count in his present mood would be counterproductive.

“Not only that,” continued the angry notable, “I was called away on some fool errand on the road to Burdigala. A drunken idiot had fallen into the river and drowned. Served the bastard right, if you ask me. And we took all day to fish his body out to make sure he got a decent Christian burial. I don’t know why people bother me with such trivia when hordes of thieves are riding unchallenged through the kingdom.”

The count’s anger suddenly seemed to evaporate, but his features hardened into an icy stare.

“Well, these sons of bitches have messed with the wrong man. On your feet, Brother, as soon as you can. We’re going to need every able body who can carry a sword, and we’re going to put an end to this nonsense, and once we’ve done that, I’m going to tell those bloody imperialists to piss off and mind their own business.”

Signy kept her thoughts to herself, adopting her most humble tone to ask the count’s permission to take care of the patient.

☙ Chapter 19 ❧ Agininum

Sismond, Count of Agininum, was looking thoughtful, an expression that Signy had not seen him adopt previously in their short acquaintance. She was sitting in the room he used for his official duties, at the front of his residence, together with his right-hand man, Jorid.

"I can't get any help from Cousin Thormond," the count grumbled. "He's been called away down to the coast to guard against pirates, so they say."

"And Ludiger, the duke, what support has he offered?" Jorid asked.

"Jorid, Jorid, do you think I'm going to go crawling to Ludiger for help? He's just looking for an opportunity to kick me out, as too old, as incompetent. Do you think I'm going to offer him the chance? No, if the worst comes to the worst I'll go and ask Altaar for assistance. After all, these bandits must be living in his backyard. He should be motivated to do something about them."

"And what do you want from me?" asked Signy, surprised almost beyond measure to be participating in this meeting. If he had invited Henrik and Grunwald, she would have accepted the decision. They had ridden with Jorid during the winter. But they were waiting in Olive Street, their expectations on hold, while she was at the count's palace.

"I would have asked that merchant…what's she called…the Fabiana woman…but she never seems to be here and you, my dear, are. So, you're here to listen to my request. Your men, Henrik and Grunwald and the others, are good men, Jorid says. Know how to handle a weapon. I need their help and as many others as your trader friends can spare. They're going to benefit as much as anyone from eliminating these bandits."

It was a little strange, Signy thought, that, despite his accusations of her being friends with the Romans, the count seemed to have taken a liking to her. Perhaps she was just a pretty Saxon girl who appealed to an old Goth. Perhaps the comments about the Romans were just his way of teasing her. But what he said about Megana made sense.

"I'm sure Master Lanius and Mistress Megana will do what they can to help," Signy assured him. "My friend has a small piece of land quite close to the men's monastery. In fact, she's just now in Burdigala fetching some slaves to put to work there. We haven't heard anything from the farmer. His name is Delo, I think. Suppose the whole farm's now in ruins, the farmer and his family kidnapped or dead."

"They were mainly stealing, looting stuff, that's what I heard, unless people resisted," the count muttered, "as if that's supposed to make us think better of them."

"There'll be no shortage of volunteers among the merchant's retainers, I'm sure." Jorid spoke up. "A fight with bandits has got to be infinitely preferable to trotting up and down the highway between Aginnum and Burdigala escorting carts and pack-horses."

He should know, thought Signy, and where there are bandits, there's always the possibility of looting the looters, if the original owners of the bandits' plunder were no longer around to claim the goods and, often, even if they were.

"And we don't want the bandits getting any ideas about disturbing our trade," Sismond added with a grimace. "That would upset Theo, and my life wouldn't be worth living. Might not last long in my seat, in the worst case."

"We'll help you however we can," said Signy quickly, though she had begun to suspect that Jorid had already secured the assistance he needed before she had ever received the count's invitation. Grunwald and Henrik and the others were free men, and they did not need her permission to join the count, though perhaps Sismond was sufficiently old-school that he did not realise that.

"Excellent. Jorid and I are going to call out the militia, heads of households and young men on all the farms in the valley of the Oltis and the Middle Garunna. If you can pass on the word to your trader friends to loan me as many of their hands, their drivers and carters as they can spare, we'll make short work of the bandits, to everyone's benefit."

☙ Chapter 20 ❧ In the Hills Above Agininum

Count Sismond was sitting on a stone. No doubt, he thought, somewhere behind his legs, the cube of rock was carved with the distance in miles from Agininum, but he did not need to look at the inscription to know how long it took to ride up the road from that city. Jorid was standing at his shoulder.

"I'm glad they've got here," he said, watching the contingent offered by Megana trot up to the meeting point.

"Good men," Jorid confirmed, "experienced fighters, unlike the militia we've rounded up ourselves."

Sismond laughed.

"If you believe the tales they've told you in the taverns."

"You've heard them yourself," retorted Sismond's sidekick.

"I didn't say I believed them, though."

Jorid frowned suddenly. "Isn't that that damn girl of hers, the witch doctor?"

The count glanced over and saw Signy sliding off her horse.

"She's a fine rider, so I've heard from Hildefrith."

"She would know, but the girl…" muttered the warrior.

"That's enough, Jorid," said the count, with a laugh. "You might be very glad to get into Mistress Signy's hands if you are ever on the wrong end of a bandit's spear. She certainly fixed that monk up, and you've heard the stories the Jutes have told. I'd keep on the right side of her, if I were you."

"She already sewed up my ear," Jorid muttered.

"Yes, when you got in that knife fight with the pedlar," said the count, rising to his feet as Signy walked up. "I didn't expect to see you here, my dear," he began by way of a greeting.

"Our men were asked to come, and I've ridden with warriors in the past," Signy said. "I've brought my medicines and my instruments," she continued, pointing to the bags slung over her horse. "You'll find me useful, I'm sure, my lord."

"Grunwald and your boys have told me how you've patched them up after fights!" he said with a smile. "And now you're here, I can hardly send you home. Probably come to regret it if I did. Just stay at the back with the cooks and the baggage, out of harm's way." He turned to Jorid. "We'd better get going. Where's the man with the horn?"

An eerie wail echoed over the hills, as Jorid shook his horse into motion.

"The scouts have traced the bandits to the hills beyond Cadurci," he said.

"I wonder they weren't intercepted by that prick Altaar as they passed through his territories," Sismond observed, "though maybe I shouldn't waste my time trying to guess why."

Perhaps there was a reasonable explanation, the count concluded. Perhaps nothing more than a calculation by the bandits that they should not provoke their local lord, but carry out their thievery in another's lands. Maybe they were just dodging these imperial troops he'd heard were still lurking about on the other bank of the river despite the little accident to their camp.

"Even so," he said aloud, "that lazy bastard should have known what they were doing, sent me a warning, cut off their retreat. Wasn't that why he was made Count of Cadurci, or was it just because he's Duke Ludiger's nephew?"

It was Jorid's turn to laugh.

The count sighed, turned his head and glanced back along his column. They were untried forces, and a lot of men he didn't know. A hundred or more riders though, he thought, that should be enough to see off a bunch of raiders if they could catch them. But how much use would they be in a battle? he wondered.

He could just see Signy riding alongside Brother Michael, the *medicus* from the men's monastery, and two tavern owners from Agininum he had roped in to take care of the provisions. At least she's done as I said, he thought, and kept to the rear. Unattached, so they said. If I was a little younger, I might have made a pass at her myself. On the other hand, the look in her eye…women like that have ideas of their own. Just like Xancha, he reflected, with a twinge of regret. She was another who had ideas of her own, and when I got moved out of Tolosa, she stayed put, even though the kid was on the way. And then Cousin Thormond moved in, took my place, before the bed was cold. The count rubbed his eye. A mote of dust kicked up from the road, he excused himself.

Better to stick to women who do as you tell them, he said to himself, the younger and dumber the better, that's a good motto, and if they begin to get ideas of their own then there's nothing more to do but boot them out and get another. I should have stuck to being a warrior, like that Grunwald and his pals. Easy come, easy go, pulling up on a foreign shore, slaughtering and burning, riding from land to land, filling your bags with loot and having adventures. I'd have been better suited to that kind of life, he thought with a sniff. Maybe I should have been a bandit myself, come to that. Too late now, of course. We've all got to settle down and be civilised.

By evening they had reached the point where the route they were following in the direction of Cadurci crossed the old green road. The count let his eyes wander down the track towards the river. It was here, he thought, that the woman and her friends had come riding over the hills, and she had crossed the ford to the imperialist camp. What the hell're those soldiers up to, claiming they're hunting bandits, when all they're doing is sitting inside their comfy fort, assuming they've managed to patch it up by now, or else riding over my lands. Now's not the time to confront that issue, he concluded, but it'll have to be confronted, sooner or later.

"We'll ride on a little further, Jorid," he said, "until we're well past the junction. No need to stir up a wasps' nest."

☙ Chapter 21 ❧
In the Hills Above Cadurci

Signy was glad they hurried past. She had still not revealed that Junius had rented a house in Agininum and she had been with him on several occasions, and she was beginning to feel she had not done right. What had begun as a delicious secret was starting to feel more like a dangerous snare. How had the bandits passed unscathed so close to the Romans' camp, with stolen animals and women and children as captives, if the Romans were mounting effective patrols? It almost seemed that the soldiers might have avoided confronting the intruders, as Junius had always missed meeting the count. To be fair, Sismond had often been called away just when Junius came visiting, but if he had asked, she could have acted as a well-intentioned go-between.

In the morning of the following day, the column reached a crossroads. Ahead lay the route into the hills, to the right the road to Tolosa, and to the left to Cadurci. The raiders could have come along this road, Signy understood from talk among the men, without attracting the attention of Count Altaar, but the efforts of the scouts suggested that they had probably returned by one of the numerous tracks over the hills. A herd of beasts and captives would have been hard to keep from the eyes of Altaar's sentries, unless, again according to the judgement of Sismond's men, they had been looking another way. Sismond had no high opinion of the Count of Cadurci, Signy recalled, so it was probably his views that were circulating among his troops.

She kept a low profile, at the rear of the column, with the monk and the cooks. Partly, she was glad to be away from the count. He had a bad reputation regarding women, and she had interpreted his greeting when she joined them as sarcastic rather than genuine. However, another part of her was curious and a little irritated at being placed with the civilians. In her earlier life, she had shared the confidences of her late husband, Thorgill, the Jute chief, as well as his bed, and he wasn't the only man who had taken her advice seriously. She did not expect to be included in the decision-making, but when the count announced he would ride into Cadurci to request assistance from Count Altaar, she would have liked to have accompanied him to listen to what was said. Count Sismond took Jorid and a troop of his own men. This was a matter of one count negotiating with another. Obviously, women would not be welcome, even in disguise.

In any case, she received a full report from Grunwald in the evening.

"He was furious," said the Jute, "according to Jorid, cursing Altaar with every other word. Altaar had welcomed him friendly enough, all smiles, offered food and drink according to the custom, but he had said with a shrug that he couldn't do anything about the bandits, didn't have the means, the forces, to take on such well-entrenched troublemakers."

"Troublemakers? They're more than just troublemakers!" said Signy. "They're murderers!"

"It's the term Count Altaar used, apparently."

"So we're to get no help?"

"At least he isn't going to hinder us. Jorid was relieved by that."

Signy could barely believe her ears.

"But how can he allow men who raided our farms and carried off our women and children to take refuge on his lands? Aren't we all in one kingdom here? Won't the king be angry that his lands are lawless?"

Grunwald shrugged.

"Apparently, these are Altaar's lands. They fall under the County of Cadurci, and Sismond has no real right to be here. He could even be criticised for riding into another count's territory with a band of armed men." Signy was about to say something when Grunwald held up his hand. "Altaar isn't going to help us, but he isn't going to stop us. It seems to suit him just fine that Sismond is engaged in a conflict with outlaws. Jorid said it saves him having to get involved with a situation that could turn out badly. And he's under the protection of Duke Ludiger, married to some relative so it seems, so Sismond can't touch him."

☙ Chapter 22 ❧
In the Hills

The scouts led them up a narrow valley cutting into the hills above the Oltis. A path ran along the side of a small river, threading around bushes and rocks. Signy, still at the rear, followed along, until the men riding in front of her came to a halt. A whisper spread down the chain that Sismond had received a fresh report, that the bandits were waiting further along the path, hiding behind some boulders which blocked the track. Curious, Signy dismounted, handed Brother Michael the reins of her horse and began to squeeze up the column of waiting men.

Even without reaching the head of the line, she could see that the bandits had selected a good position to defend their camp. A heap of large rocks had fallen from the hillside and come to rest on the flat area alongside the river. The space in front of the rocks had been cleared of vegetation, and anyone approaching the bandits' hideout would have no cover.

Sismond's force gathered on the edge of the clearing. From the far side came the sounds of jeering, from men carrying spears and waving swords.

"Raise your shields and run," ordered the count. The men set off in a rush across the clearing. They had reached about halfway before the first javelin came flying, embedding itself in the shield of one of the men in the leading rank. Then, the javelin-throwers vanished into cover, and two other figures emerged. With eerie precision they raised bows, and arrow after arrow began to fly towards the onrushing warriors. First one dropped, and then a second. The rush wavered, then came to a halt.

"Keep your shields up!"

"Keep moving! There's only two of them!"

The line edged forward. Another man fell. The line stopped again. Then the archers changed their direction and began to shoot arrows into the air, so they sailed in a high arc, down onto the standing men. Their heads were protected, but not their shoulders and arms.

"Pull back! Pull back!"

"They must have Huns amongst them, with bows like that."

"We'll never get across that open space. Even if we reached the far side, they'd outnumber us."

"We can always block the path down the valley and hope to starve them out."

"But they've just gathered a whole herd of cattle and sheep into their camp. That would take months."

But how? thought Signy. There's no way for even a scrawny cow to squeeze past the barrier formed by the rocks. She stared up at the towering cliffs which closed off the valley. Any cattle coming that way would be mincemeat by the time they reached the valley floor, and even if there was a passage at the far end, it would have taken the thieves an age to drive the herd over the hills, far too long for their own force to make the same trek. By then the bandits would be waiting for them.

She slipped away, leaving the men to their discussion. They wouldn't want her opinion even if she had one, and she didn't.

When she returned to the rear of the group, the horses had already been gathered together in a riverside meadow. The tavern owners had begun to search for a dry area to unload the stores and set up fires. A couple of injured men had been sent back for patching up, and that kept Signy and Brother Michael busy for a while. There was nothing they could do for the men who had fallen in the failed assault. Even trying to drag them back to safety would be suicidal, seeing the enemy archers were such excellent shots.

"Hey, hey, what's going on!" cried one of the boys taking care of the horses. Several of the animals, disturbed by the kindling of the fires to prepare the evening meal, had begun to splash their way across the river. The boys ran after the horses, paddling into the rushing water, and Henrik followed to help them fetch the animals back.

Signy heard the stablemaster call out. "Hoy, Grunwald, I think there's some sort of trail on this side and the tracks of beasts heading up the valley."

Signy watched as Grunwald waded across the stream to join him, and in a moment the two men had clearly forgotten the runaway horses and were scurrying along until they vanished out of sight among the bushes on the far bank.

In a little while they returned, waded back across the river and were immediately intercepted by Signy and Brother Michael.

"What did you find?" asked the monk.

"Well, we could see Sismond and his men milling about in confusion," said Henrik.

"This trail we've been following seems to continue along the river towards the head of the valley," said Grunwald, "and beyond the barrier there's another flat area. That's where the bandits have gathered their defence."

"And beyond that a series of enclosures along the valley wall," added Henrik.

"But were there any signs of the stolen cattle?" asked Signy.

"No, that's what was curious. The tracks of the beasts led off to one side, down towards the river."

"Maybe there's another shallow area," suggested Asser, who had now joined them, along with several of Megana's men, "like there is here."

"And if sheep and cows could wade cross, then so could we," said Signy, who grew up along a river, and understood them.

"Unless they made the animals swim," said Hrasmus. "I wouldn't like to have to swim the river with those Huns shooting at me."

"No," said Henrik, "from the way the water played, rippling and glinting in the sunlight, I think there might be a crossing."

"I agree," said Grunwald, "but the question remains, how to get across alive."

The area around the cooking fires had begun to resemble a camp, and just then Jorid came hurrying along the track towards them.

"Good smell," he said, clapping one of the tavern owners on the shoulder, and then he turned to Henrik. "I hear you waded over to the other side. Find anything interesting?"

"We think we may have found a back entrance," Henrik said, "a way around the rocks. It looks like they drove the cattle over the river to get around the rocks, and then back again further upstream. The water isn't so deep. We could do the same."

Jorid stood thoughtful for a moment, and then shook his head.

"That wouldn't help much. We'd still have to wade across the river in the open," he pointed out. "It would be slow going, and those Huns would have easy targets. I'm not convinced we'd make it."

"Under the cover of darkness?" suggested Asser.

"Do you want to try to get across that river in the dark, with the enemy waiting on the other side? Forget it," said Jorid, "we can't do it," and turned to investigate the progress of the evening meal.

Henrik exchanged a look with Grunwald.

"Well, what are we going to do then? March back to Agininum having achieved precisely nothing?"

--oo0Ooo--

"These hills make me nervous," said Signy, looking up at the slopes above them while she pulled apart a chunk of meat and stuffed the pieces into her mouth. No fine dining in a military camp, she thought.

Brother Michael chuckled.

"It reminds me of home, but our mountains were way higher. They had snow on the top, even at the warmest times of the year. When I was young, we boys used to take cows and sheep and goats up into the hills at the start of summer, and not come back until autumn. You can't imagine what fun we had, especially when the girls came up to do the milking and make cheese and butter. That was before I was called by the Lord, of course," he added hastily.

"It reminds me of my home, too," came a second voice, "up in the northlands."

Heads turned in surprise. The man speaking was Svein, one of Megana's retainers, formerly a masterless wanderer from the lands of the far north, and a man who rarely uttered a word.

"We also used to take the animals up on the mountains." He was staring into the fire. "It was a dangerous job sometimes, especially when the weather got bad. You wouldn't think how many times we had to clamber down the slopes to rescue fallen sheep." He looked up at the circle of faces staring back at him.

Brother Michael chuckled again.

"I remember, too," the monk responded. "Th-they used to lower us youngsters down on a rope," he explained, stuttering with embarrassment.

There was silence for a moment around the fire.

"Could you do that now, climb down the mountain on a rope?" came Grunwald's voice.

"I was only a boy, then," the sturdy monk replied, a look of doubt on his face.

Grunwald stood up, walked around to Svein, took his head in his hands and kissed him on the forehead.

"Svein, you might not talk much, but inside that head of yours, you're a fucking genius. Look, if we could find a path, we could come down the hillside behind them."

"My grandma's from these parts," said another man, one of Sismond's militiamen, who had been sent back to get an injury treated. "There are caves up there, cut into the cliffs. They've probably got their loot stashed, women and children, even."

An air of excitement spread among the group.

"If we came down the hill, we could capture all their stuff."

"And we would occupy the high ground. We could take them out even easier than their archers have been picking us off."

"It would knock them out right away."

The excited tone began to sober up a little as the speakers contemplated the risks.

"Anyone coming down that hillside on a rope would be pretty vulnerable."

"Target shooting for a Hun!"

"Svein, Brother Michael, and you with the grandma, what's your name?" said Grunwald, pointing to the man who had spoken up.

"Tomas," said the man.

"Tomas, you too, come with me to the count and we'll tell him our idea. Maybe Jorid won't listen because he didn't think of it, but Sismond will. And by putting our heads together we can make it better!"

"I'm coming, too," said Henrik.

Signy watched the warriors leave and shivered, not because it was cold, but because of the anxious feeling spreading through her body. Signy might understand rivers, but she was afraid of mountains. There had been no mountains, not the slightest hill even, where she had been a child. Think if Sismond agreed to their plan? Think if Grunwald or one of the others fell from the cliff? Think how many men could be hurt in an assault across the river? Memories of dead bodies lying along a forest road, of the smell of corpses in the dark night, came to her mind and she shivered again.

☙ Chapter 23 ❧ In the Hills

Before dawn, a dozen men set out from the camp, retracing their way along the path, looking for a track up into the hills that would lead them above the bandits' hideout. They had gathered all the rope that had been used on the pack animals. They had taken straps and harness and knotted them together to form anchors or handholds. They carried them slung over their shoulders. They carried their weapons. Count Sismond had approved the plan, though he had his misgivings. The thought of men sliding down the cliffs on ropes seemed far-fetched, but if they were volunteering, who was he to stop them? He wouldn't be joining them. But he would do what he could to help them, by mounting an attack across the river.

"The Huns can't shoot in both directions at once," he had pointed out when Jorid objected. "If they're busy defending their camp from us, they won't be watching their rear…until it's too late."

"Someone's going to end up as their targets," his captain repeated.

"Better you and me than the women and children along the Oltis, Jorid. I didn't accept the honour of becoming count to back out when the going got tough." The count cut further discussion short. "My oath is worth more than that."

Signy watched her friends leave. She watched Brother Michael leave with them. He was a man of peace now, but he was still a man born in the mountains. He was also well-built, portly, even, and might prove a good anchor if none other could be found. This early, there was a genuine chill in the air, but now Signy was not shivering. She knew what her responsibilities would be for the day. There would be nothing she could do to help the men coming down the cliff, but Jorid was right, there would inevitably be casualties among those crossing the river. With Brother Michael away, the responsibility to treat the wounded was all hers. She would need her instruments clean and sharp. She would need her cleansing vinegar to hand, and the herbs that would dull pain. She would need her dagger, too, in case the assault did not go as well as they hoped.

Sismond gathered his men together, and Signy managed to squeeze to the front of the group until she could hear what he was saying.

"Later today, we're going to attack the bandits' camp. I don't want anyone taking any unnecessary risks. We're going to cross the river and sneak up the other side, and then we'll wait in cover until we hear the signal, the sound of an owl, and then we'll advance towards the river."

"How'll we know it's the right owl?" came an anxious voice. There was a nervous laugh among the men.

Sismond closed his eyes for a moment, gathering his strength.

"It'll be a special sort of owl call, a type that isn't heard in these parts. Our friends from the north will recognise it." He looked around and frowned. Most of the men from the north had left with the mountaineers. Who could tell them if it was the signal or just one of the local fauna? His eye fell on Signy, almost with relief.

"You'll recognise the fucking owl call?" he muttered.

"Yes, my lord," she answered, trying not to smile.

"Now men, listen up," the count continued in a brisk voice. "If we try to cross the river right into the bandits' defences, we're going to lose a lot of men. Most of them will be you bastards, dead in other words! And then we're going to lose the fight. That's the rest of us dead. None of us want that, so no one, I repeat no one, is to go beyond the water's edge. You can hesitate, you can look cautious, retreat, even. Until I give the signal to cross! Is that understood?"

There was a chorus of groans and grunts.

"Very well, let's move out!" The count ended his instructions and turned towards the river. The men followed, paddling through the shallows behind their leader. Signy followed the men, a basket on her arm and a bag slung over her shoulder.

Sismond called his forces to a halt while they were still hidden among the bushes. Then he ordered them to spread out upstream and downstream, so that the whole group would appear at once when the signal came. He looked around and found Signy by his side.

"We wait for the signal. Just you stay here by me!"

Signy imagined Grunwald and the others, the tubby Brother Michael, toiling their way into the hills, blown by the winds, peering down the cliffs, searching for holds for the ropes. She felt sick at the thought. She imagined them climbing down the rocks. She imagined the Huns taking aim. She imagined the arrows flying, thudding into their bodies.

There was a soft sound, carried on the breeze, a sound that took her mind away to the forests of her youth, to long winter nights lying awake beside her snoring husband in Juteland.

"It's the owl, my lord, the signal," she whispered.

She peered up at the crest above the bandit camp. Were those the figures of men, dark against the sky?

There was a yell from beside her.

"FORWARD!"

The air was filled with shouts, as men rushed out from every gap in the vegetation. There was no opposition, not at first. The bandits were still clustered by the rocks, expecting another attack from that direction. The first of Sismond's men came to the water's edge, took a step into the river, then remembered the order. But surely if I could only run now, I could reach the other side before the bandits recovered, he obviously thought. The arrow hit him before he was halfway across, and he fell face first into the stream.

The others stopped by the bank, hunched down behind their shields. They no longer needed an order not to try to cross the river. Arrows flew but the distance was too far for spears to reach a target, so the bandits lined up and bravely began to jeer. But that was a mistake. Sismond had several men who were shepherds among his troops, the injured Tomas among them, men who were skilled in the use of slings to drive off beasts from their flocks. The riverbank provided plenty of ammunition, and soon the bandits were forced to retreat in turn. Only the occasional arrow zinged through the air, until even the Huns came to the conclusion they were wasting their ammunition.

There was a stalemate by the river, but one that required constant vigilance from the men engaged in the fight.

Signy strained her eyes on the cliffs. It was so difficult to make out what was happening: dark-clothed men against the rock and vegetation. What if it was impossible? What if they were stuck, like the fallen sheep?

☙ Chapter 24 ❧ In the Hills

Grunwald said a prayer, a prayer to several different gods, and edged himself over the edge of the cliff. Svein had gone first: the Northman knew what he was doing. Now it was Grunwald's turn. Brother Michael, standing by the boulder where they had anchored the rope, waved his hand, giving him a blessing, Grunwald hoped, and took the strain. The rope was wrapped around his back. He took his weight off it for a moment, stepped down, leaned back to tighten it again, moved his feet, moved a hand. *Always keep three against the cliff*, Svein had said, *two hands and a foot, two feet and a hand.* His sword banged against his hip. A stone suddenly loosened, and a little shower of pebbles ran and bounced away. Without thinking, Grunwald glanced down. That was a mistake. He had to close his eyes again, grip the rocks. One foot, the other foot, one hand, the other hand, let out the rope. The cliff rose in front of him. Every foot he climbed down was one less foot to the ledge that Svein had spotted, the very type of ledge where an injured sheep might have been lying in those long-gone days in the northlands.

Suddenly, there was firm ground beneath his feet. He felt Svein's hand on his shoulder. Asser was already on his way down above them. They had to hunch for a moment as pebbles showered past. Tomas, the man who had spoken of the caves, had been left at the camp. He could not have managed the climb with his injured shoulder. But he was right. Just below them, hidden by the overhang, were two caves, and in the area beyond, a cluster of rough huts, some leaning against the cliffs, a fireplace, a wattle fence and a pair of scrawny sheep.

"Time, do you think?" whispered Svein. "I'm worried the falling stones will attract someone's attention."

"Very well," hissed Grunwald in return, and raised his hands to his lips. A soft call, a call from the north woods, spread out over the valley. Grunwald took a deep breath, called again, this time louder, and then a third time as loud as he could. He thought he caught a glint amongst the vegetation on the bank of the river below. Asser plopped down beside him. There was a roar in the distance, a disturbance along the stream, as if the vegetation had suddenly found feet and decided to make a dash for the water. They saw a scurrying of figures below them as the bandits ran from their defences by the rocks to the river side. A small child suddenly ran out from one of the caves, attracted by the sound from the valley below. A woman hurried after him. A shower of earth trickled down the cliff as the fourth man took the last steps to the ledge. The woman felt something against her head. She turned. She looked up. She screamed. Svein leaped. Grunwald leaped. Asser leaped. The fourth man – was it Hrasmus? – with a curse for his own clumsiness, leaped after them. A fifth slid the last yards to the ledge and turned and flung himself into the fray.

Svein hit the woman, flattening her to the ground. Grunwald rolled over, using his legs to absorb the shock, and then got to his feet, tugging his sword free in one movement. A little girl stood staring at him with large eyes.

"Mum…there's a man."

"I told you to stay inside," came a voice from the cave.

A woman appeared, weather-beaten, with hard eyes.

"Stay where you are," said Grunwald, "and no one will come to any harm."

"Who the fuck are you?"

"We're from the authorities, ma'am," said Asser, trying to sound calm. "Just take it easy."

"Are there men up here?" asked Grunwald.

The woman cursed.

"The fuck you think I'm going to tell you!"

He exchanged looks with Asser. The two of them entered the cave, swords drawn. They stood on the threshold, eyes adjusting to the dark.

Asser swore as something flew past.

"Cut that out, or it'll be the worse for you!"

A girl, twelve or thirteen summers at most, glared back at him. Two older women, one clutching a baby, did everything they could to avoid his gaze.

"No men?" muttered Grunwald.

"Only a wannabe man," said Asser, returning the girl's defiant look. There was a call from outside.

"There are people over here, closed up in a hut."

"You," said Asser, waving his sword at the girl, "come with us."

She hesitated. Asser grabbed at her dress.

"Get your hands off me!"

"Then come with me."

The girl shot him a glance that could have killed had it been an arrow but did as she was told.

"Hey, over here…" A man was calling from the far side of the fenced enclosure, standing outside one of the lean-tos.

"Who's in there?" asked Grunwald.

The girl pouted.

"The captives," she said at last, "the ones they brought back from the raid."

"Let them out," shouted Grunwald.

Svein and the other men were standing by the wattle fence, looking down at the open space where the bandits, the male bandits, were facing off against Sismond's men.

Asser had hold of the girl and pushed her towards the fence.

"Call out," he said. "Call out and tell them you've been captured."

She looked at him for a moment.

"Are you nuts? They'll be up here in a moment. There's ten of them to each of you." She snickered.

"Good thinking, love," said Asser, with a smile. "Pity you won't be alive to see the result."

"You wouldn't!"

"Call out…do as I say, and then we'll see!"

The girl turned towards the fence and leaned over. For a moment, she squirmed in Asser's grasp, as if she was making an earnest attempt to escape.

"Hey, Gorm, Ming, there's men up here! They've got us! They've got Marta and Liv! Help, help us!"

"Good girl," whispered Asser with a grin, patting her behind. The girl shot him another sharp look. She got another grin in return.

Grunwald watched as the bandits below turned and began to look up at the slope above.

"We got your women," shouted Asser. He squeezed the girl's buttock hard, and she screamed.

"Get your fucking hands off me!"

He laughed.

Grunwald raised his hands to his lips again and called *hoo, hoo.*

☙ Chapter 25 ❧ In the Hills

"CHARGE!" yelled Sismond.

Signy emerged from the bushes in the wake of disappearing warriors. She made her way down to the edge of the river. The arrows had stopped flying and now the fighting was hand to hand on the far bank.

A couple of men had remained on her side. One sitting with an arrow in his arm, a second knocked out cold. The bandits could use slingshots, too. She bent over the man with the arrow, trying to judge the best way to remove it. She was not used to dealing with arrows. The Jutes seldom used them in warfare, and neither did their enemies. She took out a knife, considering if she would have to open the wound further before trying to draw out the barb. There was a splashing sound behind her, someone crossing the river. They would probably be asking for help in a moment, she thought, but she could only deal with one at a time.

Suddenly, there was a cry and a thud behind her. She spun round. A giant of a man stood over the body of her second patient, the handle of an axe in his hand, the blade buried in the injured man's neck. The giant caught sight of her movement and took a step towards her, wrenching his blade from the dead man's body as he did so. Signy did not even have time to stand up but could only scuttle sideways on her hands and knees. The man lifted his axe. Just as it reached the top of the swing and he was committed to the blow, she rolled. The axe came slashing down to the spot where she had just been lying and sank into the earth. She took a dive forward, towards her attacker, and slashed out with her knife. She felt a tug as the razor-sharp metal cut into flesh. The man took the strain to drag his axe free for the next blow, but as he did so there was a *pop*, a snapping sound. He stood for a moment, looking uncertain, and then heaved again, almost losing his footing as he tugged the axe free. His hesitation had given Signy time to crawl backward, just out of range. He lifted the axe above his head again and took a step forward to reach her, or at least he tried to. Instead, he lurched sideways, unbalanced, flailing with his arms and dropping his weapon. Signy sprang at him, thrusting all her weight into his body. The man, shocked as much by his own clumsiness as by her attack, fell backwards, spreadeagled on the ground. She was on his chest in an instant, her knife against his throat.

"One more move and you're dead," she hissed, her face inches from his.

The man looked puzzled.

"What happened?"

She sat back, her legs either side of him, looking down at him.

"You know the story of Achilles?"

The man tried to shake his head, not easy lying against the earth.

"He had one weak point, on the back of his heel. Just like you."

The man struggled again, trying to wriggle free. She placed the blade again to his neck.

"Don't think I wouldn't kill you, just because I'm a woman. I can kill as well as I can heal. You slaughtered a defenceless man. Do you think you deserve any mercy?"

A flash of anger passed across the man's face.

"Your friends were no more honourable, attacking the women and children."

She laughed at him.

"Did you expect honour, bandit? The only honour you'll get is a mercifully quick death, if you're lucky."

"Then go ahead, woman. I'm not afraid."

"Not afraid to die at the hands of a woman?" she asked. There was something about this man, his way of speaking, that intrigued her. In her childhood, she would have thought of someone from the next village as a stranger, but now, among the people of the wide world, a man who spoke with the same lilt as she did could be a fellow countryman, even if he had just tried to kill her.

"It was a fair fight," he replied. "That's all the gods care about."

Signy responded in Saxon.

"What's your name, giant, and what brings you here?"

The man looked perplexed, suddenly hearing his own tongue. For a moment, he had a look of terror.

"You're not…not…?"

"No, I'm not one of the Valkyries, if that's what you're worrying, come to carry you to Hel. Just a normal, mortal woman, who recognises a man from her own country. Now tell me your name, man, so if I have to kill you, I can at least hold a memory of you."

"Ragvald," he said, "Ragvald the Saxon."

She eased her weight back.

"Roll over, Ragvald, and let me tie your hands. And just remember that this knife can cut your throat or your tongue or your eye just as it cut your Achilles heel."

"What sort of creature is this?" Ragvald muttered. "She's bewitched my foot. There's no pain, yet when I try to use it, it won't move. It must be a curse, just the sort of curse that might be put on a man in battle to freeze his limbs, and so seal his fate. There's nothing I can do but accept my destiny."

He acquiesced.

"Whatever my doom is, it's already been decided," he murmured to himself. "I've been picked out, for Valhalla or Hel. The demon sitting on my chest will decide. There's nothing more I can do."

"Don't try to run," the demon said, making no attempt to tie his hands. "You'll only stumble, and a child of five could catch you. Then I would have to kill you. Get up on your knees and come here instead and hold this man's arm still, while I take out the arrow. Perhaps you can save a life in return for the one you took."

The giant rose to his knees, looking around. Signy read his thoughts in a moment and took hold of the axe. It was heavy. There was no way she could swing the blade, even if just to threaten him. Instead, she carried the axe away a few paces and let it drop well out of his reach.

"Come, Ragvald," she said, pulling at his collar. "You have begun a new life as an assistant to a surgeon. I had hoped Brother Michael would be here to help me, but the holy brother is doing the Lord's work elsewhere."

With the arm steadied by the giant bandit, she was able to extract the arrow. Then another injured man appeared, flopping to the earth beside her, a wound in his side, and then another was carried by a friend, and soon time flew by. It seemed so natural to order Ragvald to place his hands here and there, lift the patient on his side when they shared the same words. She even forgot herself for a moment and handed him her knife to hold while she stitched. Ragvald took it, still looking confused. But a man couldn't use a knife against a spirit, and then she reached out, and he gave it back to her.

Grunwald appeared, kneeling beside her, taking her face in his hands.

"Signy, I'm so glad to see you again. There were moments when I thought I was a dead man."

She looked up at him, happiness in her own eyes, delight in her voice.

"The gods have been with us, Brother," she said in Jutish. The word brother sparked a thought. "My God, Grunwald, we mustn't forget Brother Michael. Isn't he alone up on the hill?"

"Brother Michael is never alone, so he told me," laughed Grunwald, "but nonetheless I'll find Asser, and when we locate the brother's horse, we will ride up and collect him."

He scrambled to his feet and shouted in the direction of the river.

"Don't hurt him! You can't hurt him! He's my dad!" came a sudden cry.

There was a shout, Asser's voice, and a girl came running, throwing her arms around the crouching giant.

"Ferona, my darling, have they harmed you?"

"No, Dad, but why're you here? Why've you got blood on your hands?"

The giant sat back, his useless foot squashed beneath him.

"I'm to die, my dear, it's my judgement. The gods have sent a messenger for me. Soon I'll be with them, and with your mother."

"No, Dad, no, you're alive. You're to stay here with me. Please don't say such things."

Asser's hand came down and reached for the girl, dragging her to her feet.

"No, no, don't take me," she screamed. "If he's going to die, then I want to die, too."

"Hold on, Asser," said Signy. "I don't understand what's going on. Who's this girl?"

"I found her, up in the caves."

"Is this your girl?" asked Signy to the still-crouching Ragvald.

"My daughter, my only child. Is she taken?"

"Everyone's taken who isn't dead," said Asser.

"Asser," Grunwald's voice came from behind them, "I need you to come with me to fetch Brother Michael. Leave the girl with Signy."

Asser looked doubtful.

"I'll tie her hands and feet first. I don't trust her a thumb."

"Do that then and get a move on. It'll be dusk before we get back up there, and then we could fall over the edge ourselves, and we would look pretty stupid if Svein had to climb down and rescue us."

Asser undid the belt from around his waist and pulled it tight around the girl's wrists, but he had nothing to tie her feet with.

"Sit with me, Ferona," said Ragvald. "At least we can be together for these last moments."

"What will happen to him, Miss?" The girl caught Signy with her eyes.

"He killed a man…"

"He killed several men, I saw him," said the girl with a note of pride.

"That's as maybe…but the man I saw him kill was defenceless and under my care. For that he deserves death along with the rest of the bandits."

The girl thrust her face into her hands. Signy reached out and took her by the shoulder.

"But he helped me, too…for every man he killed he has helped me save the life of another," she continued. An exaggeration, perhaps, she thought, but the whole world seemed to be an exaggeration just at this moment. "Maybe, maybe I can persuade the count to save him."

"I'd rather die with honour than be a cripple," said the man, regaining a little courage, the shock of his defeat at the hands of a woman half his size beginning to wear off.

"You needn't be a cripple, if you do as I tell you. Our bodies have a wonderful way of healing if you follow the right path."

The man looked at her blankly.

"And me," said the girl, "what will happen to me?"

Signy shrugged. The girl would not die, but her fate might be just as bad. Signy had once faced such a fate herself, only to escape by a miracle.

By a miracle, she thought. There was always an opportunity for miracles.

"You will be taken down the river, to Burdigala, probably sold as a slave," she said.

The man held his gaze on Signy. She saw he understood exactly what she was not saying, what kind of slave his daughter would become.

"No," he said, "no, spare her that."

Once, years ago, a man had shown mercy on her, Signy reflected. The gods weighed these matters when they judged a person's life. Two people's fates, two people's lives lay in her hands. Some would see them as murderous bandits, only deserving death. She had been seen that way once. But the gods had favoured her and had guided a man to show her mercy.

She leaned towards the giant bandit.

"Ragvald, do you know this sign?" She drew back the edge of her tunic, exposing the lynx head tattooed on her shoulder.

The expression on the man's face told all. An expression of fear almost as great as that he had shown when he thought she was the agent of death.

"The lynx," he said. "You're a healer as you say, but also…the bringer of an easy death."

The girl, Ferona, looked back and forth from Signy and her father.

"Wh-what do you mean?"

Ragvald only shook his head.

"Give me an easy death, your honour, but spare my daughter. Take her as one of your own. The gods have spared her for you."

"Father, please?"

"What a fight, what a victory, though at the cost of half a dozen men!" Sismond's voice came from behind, and Signy turned towards him.

"It would have been more, without the assistance of this man."

"It would have been fewer, too, Signy. I saw him fell Nuntius and Gabor myself, and he had a swing at me." Sismond frowned, seeing the brutal killer seated placidly by Signy. "We can decide his fate later. There are injured men on the other bank who need caring for, and there are women and children among the captives who need something stronger than only wine."

"I can use these two," said Signy, indicating Ragvald and his daughter.

"You can use whoever you like, but just remember" – he continued looking at the giant – "you touch one hair of her head, and I'll smash each of your limbs personally and stake you out for the crows and vultures to pick at. And as for you" – he turned to the girl, appraised her for a moment – "there won't be much left of you either by the time I've finished with you."

☙ Chapter 26 ❧
Agininum

A smell of incense filled the church, more powerful than the perfume in her own bedchamber, thought Megana, as she slipped stealthily along the wall, keeping out of the way of the huddle of congregants standing in the nave. She was unsure what tack to take with the Bishop of Agininum, when she had no idea what kind of man he was. She was unwilling to be subjected to the same humiliation as she had by Bartolomeus of Burdigala, but then everyone, Lanius, his mother, so he said, and even Xancha, had only compliments for Anastasius of Agininum. Perhaps he was as good as they said: learned and kind, thoughtful and sincere. If so, he would be a wonder, but she was not willing to accept others' judgements. If she could see him in action by participating in the service, she might gain some insight of her own.

The liturgy was in progress at the front of the church. From a distance, the scene was merely a blur to Megana, due to the contrast between the dark nave and the candlelit hemicycle where the priests and church dignitaries were going through their rites. Every now and then, the congregation chanted out a response, though Megana wondered how they knew what was required, since the whole ritual was conducted in classical Latin. Habit, probably, she reflected.

To Megana, her relationship with the deities was a private matter. She had visited the modest church by the market square of Agininum several times to light a candle before starting the journey to Burdigala. She had also placed small sums of money now and then on a side altar dedicated to St Laurentius. She would have been embarrassed to have to admit to Lanius that she had even placed a few oatcakes and a bowl of milk in a niche of the shattered altar in the wrecked pagan temple a few streets over from the warehouse, but as far as she knew, no one had ever spotted her there and she wasn't planning to admit what she had done. In trading, however much you trusted yourself, in the end you also needed good luck and to keep on the good side of gods. And you never knew when they might send you a vision or a dream, an invaluable glimpse into the future.

She took a few steps forward, trying to get a better view of the practicants in the apse. Which one was the bishop? she wondered.

She had introduced herself to Count Sismond quite soon after arriving in Aginnum. That had been a practical matter. The civil authorities frowned on merchants coming and going without their oversight, and there was the matter of taxes. She had written a brief note, and been invited to meet the count's clerk and then the count himself. The haggard-looking old fighter, with lank grey hair and watery eyes, had welcomed her to the town. After that she had kept out of his way. In her experience, civil administrators had a sharp nose and an endless need for silver. In Aginnum, she could not rely on the long-standing relationships her family had enjoyed in Britannia to keep the authorities at bay. Her forefathers had been mayors of the city on and off for generations and trusted advisors to the rulers going back to the times of the Empire. In Aginnum, even Vipso had been a minor player and Lanius' warehouse by the Garunna more of an overnight halt than a trading entrepôt. She aimed to change that, but if she wasn't careful, she would end up as a fat cow to be milked to fill the count's coffers. She was already apprehensive that his request for help with his expedition to fight the bandits was only the beginning.

She had almost reached the front of the church. The crowd was pressing against the carved wooden rail that separated the religious from the lay people. She was reluctantly forced to conclude she probably could not approach further. At least she could distinguish the figures at work in the bright candlelight. The tall, clean-shaven man, with the finest cloak and the fanciest headgear must be the bishop, she concluded. She still had difficulty in making out his features, but he seemed to be in his middle age, not an old man, but not a young one, either. That would fit with what Lanius had told her. Bishop Anastasius had long been a friend of Lanius' mother. He admired her work as a book copyist, apparently. So did Signy, Megana reflected. Her friend's hand script had improved greatly since she had started visiting the monastery.

The crowd surged again, and Megana was pushed back, back into a dimly lit side chapel. She propped herself against a pillar and caught her breath, glanced around and noticed an altar against the far wall. She could not make out the dedication, but this alcove would serve her purpose. She owed God a little thanks. The bandits had stolen a cow and three pigs from Delo, as well as the child, Lilia, who had been watching them. She would have to replace the cow and one of the pigs, but the girl…who knew what horrors she was suffering at the hands of the robbers. It was a pity that the child had not come to Agininum when she had the chance. Megana placed a small bag of coins on the altar and kneeled for a moment, head bowed. Tomorrow she would ride over to the Oltis with half a dozen slaves, newly arrived from Hibernia, who could clear the dikes and cut the overgrown vegetation. From what she knew of Hibernia, they should be ideally suited to that type of work. If Delo wasn't in a fit state to supervise them, then she would have to find someone else, and that would be a nuisance.

The crowd had begun to thin. Apparently, the holy ritual was over. The majority of the priests filed out, the one she imagined was the bishop bringing up the rear, waving an ornamented staff, the whole group singing as they went. Her effort had been almost entirely worthless. She had no better idea of what type of man this local bishop was. He had been merely a player in the formalities, a man going through the same routine as he must have done hundreds of times before. She emerged from her side chapel and was immediately apprehended by an older cleric, a priest or deacon or something similar.

"I haven't disturbed your prayer, Mistress?" he asked in a humble tone.

In an instant, Megana assumed that it must be throwing out time, as in a tavern when the landlord had decided to retire for the night. Perhaps the old deacon's tone would not have been quite so humble had the clothes she was wearing not signalled her wealth and social status.

"Not at all," she replied, "I was just making a small offering."

"We have much to be grateful for," said the deacon, "and many sins for which to atone."

And which of those are you implying is my problem? thought Megana.

"Perhaps, Father, I could ask your advice. I'm new to the town and would like to introduce myself to the bishop."

"Bishop Anastasius?" said the man, as if there could be more than one. "I'm afraid he'll be leaving tomorrow, for a meeting in Narbonna. The archbishop…you know…"

What I don't know, I can easily guess, she thought.

"All the bishops in the province will be attending," the man added.

"And when will he return?"

"Ah," said the deacon. "You'll have to consult his clerk, Father Barnabas. The father will remain in town while the bishop is away if you care to visit the episcopal office."

"Thank you most kindly," Megana said, sighing, "I shall make sure that I do."

She passed out of the church, blinking in the daylight. Several groups of churchgoers were standing and chatting in the square. A pair of shopkeepers bowed their heads when they spotted her, their wives giving her a keen examination. The count's clerk smiled as they crossed paths. So she had been seen at the cathedral after all. The visit hadn't been a complete waste of time, though she would still keep up her own prayers in the little church by the market.

She crossed the square, walked the short distance down The Hill and then turned into Olive Street. The yard gate was about halfway along the street and stood open to a silent and deserted yard. Most of the men and horses were away on the count's expedition. She felt a twinge of loneliness when she realised that

Signy would not be there to welcome her, and to be her sounding board after the visit to the church. She thought of the offering she had left. She wished she knew the name of the saint on whose altar she had left it.

"Keep them safe," she said to herself, looking up to the sky.

She walked through the passageway to the inner court and on to her room to discard her cloak. The bishop was unreachable, out of town in Narbonna. In the peace of the house, she would have a little more time to think, to formulate her plan, she reflected. She was quite determined now that she was not going to donate that small plot of Paulinus' land to the church, but could she persuade the bishop to accept another deal, one that would benefit them both in this world, and hopefully also in the next?

☙ Chapter 27 ❧
By Cadurci

Before they could leave, there were dead to be buried and barely living to be prepared for the journey home. When they did set off, the pace was a good deal slower than the journey out. Not only were the injured to be considered, but there were also the women and children they had freed, and the women and children, companions and offspring of the bandits, captives now themselves. There were cattle and sheep – less those that had been slaughtered for the victory feast – ducks and geese, even half a dozen pigs, to be driven out of the valley and along the Oltis back to Agininum County. Of the bandits themselves, they had suffered the same fate as the men from the farms that had been raided. Only one had been spared, Ragvald, because, much to the annoyance of Grunwald and Henrik, he was under Signy's protection. He could not walk, so he had been placed on a donkey. His feet almost reached the ground, which made them all the easier to bind together. That suited Signy, too, as she had wrapped his ankle as tightly as she could, immobilising it. Asser had his reservations about Ragvald, too, but his eyes scarcely left Ferona, as light as a feather when he had lifted her, seated behind Signy, her arms around the mistress's waist.

They took the track over the hills rather than the paved road to find better feeding for the beasts, and as the thieves had amply demonstrated, to draw less attention from the authorities. Sismond was keen to avoid any intervention from Count Altaar now that he was the one with booty. He was not going to share his success with his rival when the man had not offered any help. Only when they reached the point where their track crossed the green road leading to the ford did the count call a halt and bring his advisors together.

"Tell Mistress Signy I wish her to be present, and she should bring her tame bandit with her."

Ragvald came limping after, supported by Brother Michael and leaning on a forked stick that served as a crutch, as Signy made her way through the camp to the place where Sismond was waiting.

The count eyed the bandit up and down.

"You're a lucky fucker," was the first thing he said. "Now tell me…did you and your buddies see anything of any imperialists, and by that I mean people who call themselves Romans?"

Ragvald's face was one great question.

"I don't understand, my lord, why would the Romans have anything to do with us? We never strayed into imperial territory. It wouldn't make sense for us to stir them up."

"Because there are so-called Romans, not half a mile from this place, who claim they've been hunting bandits. You're the only bandits who've made significant trouble in this area, I mean real, organised bandits, the only ones who've bothered my lands in recent years, as opposed to the usual dross of thieves and murderers. Who else would these imperialists be after – on my land – if not you?"

"My lord, we've seen nothing of any Romans. They've left us in peace. Even the count, begging your pardon, I mean the Count of Cadurci, left us alone."

"You're not bullshitting me, are you?" He glanced across at Ferona, who was crouching, almost invisible, beside Signy. The count had already reckoned that the way to put pressure on the bandit was through his daughter, through making sure the man believed he would do as he said. Well, perhaps he wouldn't rip her heart out, that would be a waste. She wasn't entirely to his taste, a bit too skinny, but once he had exercised her sufficiently, she could be sent down the river, or perhaps up to Tolosa. Xancha would find a use for her.

Ragvald noticed his glance.

"I promise you, my lord, on my life, the Romans never hunted us. I've never set eyes on a Roman since I deserted the auxiliaries, and that was almost twenty years ago." Then his brows creased. "Yes…well…except for one."

"What do you mean?" growled Sismond.

"He wasn't a soldier, but he was a Roman, I'm certain. He spoke to Gorm and Ming. He had half a dozen other men with him. Could have been a trader and his followers."

"And when was this?" Sismond's voice was like a glacier scraping rocks.

"A…About a month ago, I reckon, a few days before we set out on the raid."

"And you don't know what they discussed?"

The big man said nothing.

"Very well," said Sismond, "shove off, and take your daughter with you. Not you, Mistress Signy, you stay here."

--oo00oo--

There were six of them altogether, Sismond and Jorid, Grunwald and Svein, Signy and Brother Michael. Sismond had taken a liking to the quiet man from the north after the coup against the bandits. A man like that, a man who knew how to keep his mouth shut until he had something worthwhile saying, was a man he could use. And it was always handy to have a religious person available.

Six of them was enough for a respectable delegation, but not so many as to be provoking. They rode down the green way, across the paved road to Cadurci, and continued until they reached the banks of the Oltis. There they crossed the ford with little difficulty, since the water was low, it being summer. Safe on the other bank, they began to make their way cautiously up the slope through the trees, expecting at any moment to be challenged by pickets as Signy had been. There was no challenge, no pickets, and eventually they came out of the wood and mounted the rise. Spread out before them was the bank and ditch of the Roman camp, but the gates, the replacements for those that Jorid and the Jutes had floated down the river, were firmly closed. A pair of figures appeared over the parapet to one side of the gate. Sismond brought his group to a halt at a safe distance.

"Who's there?"

"Sismond, Count of Agininum, of the Kingdom of Tolosa. I wish to speak to the garrison commander."

The two figures leaned towards one another, apparently discussing the request.

"This is imperial territory, Count. You've no authority here."

Sismond caught himself before he began to quibble. Better to stick to the one simple point with a couple of fools like the men on the parapet, he reckoned.

"Simply a neighbourly visit…to discuss matters of mutual interest."

The figures above appeared to engage in another conversation. There was a certain hesitancy in the voice when the reply came.

"You'll have to come back next week."

"Don't you think you would be wiser to ask your commander first?" Jorid stepped in on behalf of Sismond. The informal tone of the soldier's reply was not worthy of an answer from the count.

Grunwald tapped Svein on the shoulder, and with a signal to Jorid, they rode off, following the ditch round the corner and vanishing from sight.

"In case we weren't clear, he's not here. He's away. That's why you have to come back next week."

"And where has he gone, might I ask?" asked Jorid.

"Um…that's a secret, on business."

Another pair of figures appeared above the parapet, moved along towards the first two, and a heated discussion seemed to take place.

"This is *Decanus* Oltifer," came a self-important voice. "My commander is absent on military duties. If you wish to speak to him, you should send a written request."

The *decanus* fell suddenly silent and toppled backwards out of view. The other three soldiers turned in alarm.

"What the hell's going on?" said Sismond, aloud, but evidently to himself.

In response, the three men on the parapet also vanished from view, one by one. A moment later, the gate began to open, and first a stumbling Roman soldier appeared, shortly followed by Grunwald. The other two soldiers walked behind, their hands on their heads, and the group was brought up by Svein.

"There was no one guarding the other gate. These are the only rankers here, apart from a cook and his assistant and a couple of veterans."

"But there's room for at least a hundred," said Signy without thinking.

"They're not here, they're away, like the man said," replied Grunwald, pushing his captive towards the count.

Sismond dismounted and advanced towards the soldier. Without saying a word, he drove his fist into the man's guts.

"You mess with me, you're messing with the wrong person, chummy."

The count waited patiently while the soldier gasped for breath.

"Where's your commander?"

"I…I told you…it's a secret."

Sismond's fist hit home again. The soldier almost doubled up and would have fallen if Grunwald had not had a firm hold on him.

"Anyone else want to offer some information?" asked Sismond, looking around. The other two soldiers remained silent.

The man in Grunwald's grasp straightened himself up, still gasping.

"I asked you where your commander is?"

"I…I…"

The soldier glanced down and saw Sismond's hand forming once more into a fist.

"He…he…rode south, across the river, and took the century with him. I don't know where to, honest, my lord."

Sismond took a deep breath, as if setting up for another blow.

"My lord, my lord, please, I'm only on guard duty. I have a gippy knee. I can't march."

"You'll have two gippy fucking knees in a moment," said Sismond. "Tell me, now you're being so helpful, did the captain who deals with the locals, the spy, what's his name, Captain…" He turned for a moment and glanced at Signy.

"Junius," she answered quietly.

"Did Captain Junius go with him?"

The soldier looked desperate.

Sismond glanced down, kneewards.

"The captain…the captain's been away a lot. They don't tell me where, my lord, but this time word was he had to ride into the town…the one further up the river…Cadurci, I think it's called, my lord."

"You couldn't make it up, could you, soldier," said Sismond with a sneer. "Let him go, Grunwald, and the other two, Svein."

Before the soldier had a chance to turn, Sismond grabbed him by the collar.

"If I ever set eyes on you again, if I ever find you on my side of the river…" He shook his head sadly and turned to remount his horse.

--oo00oo--

When Signy remounted her horse, though with unaccustomed difficulty, her stomach felt like a lump of lead, and her legs barely able to carry her. Sismond had said nothing to her – of course, he had no reason to – but she could see that he had drawn the conclusion that the "Roman" who had visited the bandits was Junius. Why else would he have asked about him? And that had been the conclusion she had drawn herself. And she had had a chance to quiz Ragvald more closely after his revelation. And now Junius was in Cadurci, and the Count of Cadurci had refused to help them, claiming the bandits were Sismond's problem, but the bandits had been living in his territory, not Sismond's, so they were Count Altaar's problem after all, and Count Altaar had done nothing. And Junius was mixed up in this somehow, and he had said nothing to her, and he had said that the Romans were hunting the bandits, but they had set off in completely the opposite direction, straight into Count Sismond's lands while he was away. And Junius had been away a lot. He had been in

Agininum. And she had been sleeping with him, not that what they had been doing involved much sleeping.

She needed to think. To get things straight in her mind. She had done nothing wrong. There was nothing wrong with going to bed with a handsome man who paid you compliments. She wasn't married. She didn't owe anyone anything in that regard. When she first slept with Junius, she had known no one, had no friends in Agininum, had no understanding of the political situation in the Kingdom of Tolosa. But she did not have that excuse now. And Junius had admitted being involved in the death of the shepherd, and now he seemed to be involved in this business with the bandits. And no matter how you put the matter, however handsome he was, however much she liked what she did with him, that thought was troubling.

☙ Chapter 28 ❧
In the Hills Above Aginінum

The monastery library was a refuge, and an escape from emotions that were beginning to trouble Signy. The books and manuscripts provided a host of safe topics for discussions, abstractions which did not become personal. That day, Signy had come to help Ophelia with her copying. The morning had been fine when she had ridden up from the town, but around midday the skies had clouded over, and rain seemed to have set in. The two women made as much use as they could of the remaining light, but eventually, as the clouds piled high and dark, they were forced to put down their pens. They were just discussing whether Signy should take one of the guest rooms and stay overnight, when they heard an unusual sound, that of men's voices approaching the library.

"Ah, yes," said Ophelia, "Hildefrith's brother. He has come on an inspection, to make sure the money the family has donated to the monastery is being put to good use."

Hildefrith had once recounted to Signy that she had been sent to the monastery because she had refused to marry the husband her family had chosen for her, had refused, in fact, to marry any man. Her father had angrily cried that if she preferred the company of women, then he would send her to a monastery. It had been the happiest day of her life.

"That sounds like more than one voice," observed Signy, as the door swung open. Hildefrith entered, followed by three men. The first was older, heavily built, short greying hair, bright blue eyes. The second was a younger version of the first, though his hair was still dark, and his look slightly uncertain. The third man came in a couple of steps behind them, taking in the library and the two women in a single quick, keen glance.

"My brother, General Thormond," said Hildefrith, "my nephew, Wiseric, and my…cousin, Geseric."

The general held out his hand, his signet ring to the fore. The women understood they were to kiss it. He cast an eye around the library.

"I once read a book," he said, "written by man named Caesar." He turned to his son. "Wasn't that the fellow?" The younger version nodded in agreement.

"The king was very keen," he added, as if to excuse himself, "something about conquering the Gauls."

The general cast another glance around the room.

"Very good, carry on," he stated, as if addressing his troops, and turned to leave. As he did so, Geseric whispered into Hildefrith's ear, and Signy could hear her saying, "Of course."

The abbess held the door open, and the general strode out, followed by his son, but the abbess's "cousin" remained. A backward glance from the general conveyed a faint sense of disapproval, as if the youngster did not quite meet the mark of a man in his eyes.

"I hope I'm not disturbing," Geseric said, "but I would like to learn a bit more about your collection."

Ophelia and Signy exchanged glances, not quite knowing what to do next. Men who were interested in the library were few and far between. The two women were given no help from Hildefrith, who followed her brother and his son through the door, which closed behind them. The young man walked over to the desk where Ophelia had been working and began to scan the manuscript.

"Bishop Augustine's *City of God*," said Ophelia. Signy watched as he ran his finger along the lines of text while mouthing the words.

Geseric turned to her.

"Do you think our grace is pre-determined, Sister?" he asked.

Ophelia stood still for a moment, silent, clearly having difficulty in composing a reply.

"It's rather an impractical view," the young man continued. "Why should anyone strive to do good, if it doesn't make any difference?"

"Perhaps because that's the way God is working out his plan for us," suggested Signy. "Don't you sometimes feel that things happen to you that are out of your control, that you just have to go along with them and see where they lead?"

Geseric looked up from the manuscript, and his eyes met hers. The expression on his face suggested he was about to say *no, he did not*, but the words seemed to stick in his throat.

"So you don't believe in free will?" was what he did say.

"I just said life sometimes feels that way, that some higher power has a plan that you are compelled to follow," replied Signy, holding his gaze.

Ophelia looked from one to the other, a faint smile playing at her mouth corners.

"You put your words in a strange way for an inhabitant of a monastery, Sister," said the man.

"My name is Signy," said Signy, "and I'm not an inhabitant of the monastery, just a visitor, helping my friend, Sister Ophelia, with the copying."

"I'm sorry, I didn't mean to offend you," said Geseric, tearing his eyes away and turning towards the window. "You sound like an educated woman. Do you know the classics or just Christian literature?

"*I went to the house of Circe, with dark thoughts in my mind,*" he quoted.

"*I stood at the gates of the fair Goddess Circe with her braided hair.*

She opened the doors and asked me in, seated me on a silver studded chair,

Beautifully made, with a stool for my feet," he continued.

Signy smiled and interrupted him, and he turned towards her, as if drawn by her voice.

"*She prepared a potion, in a golden cup, for me to drink,*

And in it she put a drug, hoping to do me harm."

How had he chosen these words? she wondered. Had Hildefrith mentioned her before she came into the room, or had the words been planted in his mind by some other source of inspiration?

"But the drug didn't work," said Geseric, crossing towards her. "Odysseus wasn't bewitched."

"Perhaps he was," said Signy, "but he didn't realise it." Perhaps Circe had bewitched herself, she thought.

"He tried to kill her with his sword," said Geseric. It wasn't his sword he was trying to kill her with, thought Signy, but his look. Even a fair goddess could fall for a pair of handsome eyes who met her own as if they were trying to seek her innermost thoughts.

She continued.

"*Who are you, what is your city, your parent?*
I am amazed you could drink my potion and yet not be bewitched.
No man has ever withstood this magic."

"Let me answer your questions first, fair stranger," Geseric said, his tone still playful. "My father was Raymond, a young cousin of the general and your hostess, the abbess Hildefrith. But my father died when I was just a child. Uncle Thormond has been my guardian since then."

"I'm sorry to hear it," she replied. "It's a great misfortune to lose your parents when you are still young."

"You say that with a certain amount of feeling. Are you an orphan yourself, or a mystic, or both perhaps?"

"I've been called a witch by men who know no better," she said. "That's a fate that many wise women suffer, and not only in the classics."

She thought he recognised the discomfort she felt discussing her parentage.

"Can you turn men into swine?" he asked with a smile, turning back to the safety of Homer.

"I would hardly need to," she replied. "They're quite capable of acting like swine without my help."

"I hope you don't think I might metamorphose in that way."

"I think it's better we don't continue this line of conversation," she said, smiling and turning away from him. "There's no knowing where our words might lead." She caught sight of Ophelia laughing silently behind his back.

"My Lord Geseric," the older woman said. "Before you came in, Mistress Signy and I were just discussing whether she should stay for the night or if it would be possible for her to return to Agininum this evening. You're a fine gentleman, and a master at quoting Homer but, while you were staring out of the window, did you notice by chance if the rain has stopped?"

"My uncle will be continuing to Agininum when he has finished his business here, regardless of the weather," Geseric replied. "We'll dine with the count, my uncle, this evening. I'm sure the general would be delighted if you joined our party for the ride back to town," he went on, turning to Signy, "though I must warn you he likes to hold a fast pace."

Signy was not so sure that the general would welcome her company, but Ophelia took a deep breath.

"Let's go and see if we can find Sister Hildefrith," she said, opening the door and ushering the two young people outside. As Signy passed, she felt Ophelia pat her rear, and glanced back to see the older woman give her a wry smile.

Once out of the library, they were pleased to see that the rain had indeed stopped. A rainbow arched over the hills behind the monastery. They found the others in the yard. Three well-built horses, just being led from the stables where they had been sheltering from the downpour, were waiting for their riders.

The general watched his nephew approaching accompanied by the two women, his face wrinkled by a frown. Geseric spoke up.

"My lord, I offered us as an escort to Mistress Signy. She needs to return to Agininum this evening."

The general looked a bit doubtful. He's hoping to make more speed than would be possible with a wagon or cart, thought Signy, but he's reluctant to refuse the request and appear inhospitable in front of the abbess, his sister.

"I don't see why not," he grudgingly acquiesced. His look of surprise could hardly have been greater, when he saw the stable boy lead out Signy's horse, perhaps only equalled by his astonished appearance when she swung herself up into the saddle and took the reins. Signy noticed the pair of mounted warriors, who made up the party, exchange amused looks. Geseric had been too busy mounting his own horse to notice, and was surprised himself when he looked around and found Signy alongside him, and not on a demure pony, but on a creature quite equivalent to his own.

The general gave the signal and led the way out of the gate, his son beside him, Geseric and Signy close behind, and the warriors making up the rear. When the six riders reached the road, the general raised the pace to a trot. It was evident that he was rather irritated by having the woman in the group, especially one who had the impudence to ride such a horse. He kicked his mount again to increase the speed. Signy followed him, pace for pace, until the road began to descend the hill towards the Garunna, and the general was forced to slow down since the paving stones were still slippery after the rain.

As they trotted down the hill, Geseric looked across to Signy. His eyes seemed full of admiration. She tried to read his thoughts. She knew enough of Hildefrith's history, enough of Sismond's past, to know that their ancestors were proud warriors who had crossed the plains and mountains on galloping horses and crushed the might of Rome. Geseric's grandfather, his father before that, might have been such a rough barbarian, but she had the impression that the young man was not considered much of a warrior. The attitudes of his Uncle Thormond and Cousin Wiseric showed how they rated him. She guessed that in their minds he had spent too much time in the schoolroom. Old Goths like Thormond and Count Sismond were rough and ready people, little different from Chief Thorgill, her deceased husband, more likely to come to blows than exchange quotations from Homer. What about their womenfolk? Signy wondered. Did they manage to keep up, sword in hand, or had the warriors just left their women behind on the trail? Signy felt her hair streaming behind her in the wind, and she knew the answer. She could ride a horse as well as any woman she had come across, and she had just proven she could also quote the blind bard from heart and match wits with classical allusions, even though she had been born in a farmer's cottage. A real woman could keep up with her man whatever his inclinations. What do you think, General Thormond, she wondered, of a woman like that? What do you think, Geseric? A woman like me could be an inspiration. Could a woman like me inspire you to do things you never would have believed you could do yourself?

They trotted along the river and into town, turning up past the forum in the direction of Count Sismond's palace. The general looked back. His expression revealed that even he was begrudgingly admiring the way Signy had held the pace. He pointed up the hill to indicate the route he planned to take to Sismond's residence. She saw his sign and called out, "The Street of the Olive Sellers, on the same way."

He nodded in reply, shook his reins and set off again.

As they passed the villa, and Signy drew up, Geseric slowed too and leaned over.

"My lady," he said. "Your husband will be glad to see you safely home."

"Oh, my lord," she whispered, "I have no husband." She could not avoid seeing the sudden flash in the young man's eyes, and wondered if he saw the jump of her own heart when she noticed his look.

"Extraordinary young woman," she heard the general mutter to himself as he rode off, the two young men following. As they parted, Geseric turned back, his eyes meeting hers over his shoulder.

Signy watched them make their way up the hill, and once they were out of sight, she turned her horse into Olive Street. Well inside the yard, she dismounted, a little unsteadily. She had taken a liking to Count Sismond, wondered to herself what type of man he had been in his younger days, a ruffian like her lost husband, probably. She had moved on since her years in Juteland, learned to read and write, learned Latin and Greek, and to study poems and to quote their words herself, not just listen to some bard reciting at a feast. Any man who would be a real companion to her would also have to master those skills. Then, in her loneliness, she had fallen for Junius, the first smooth-talking, good-looking male who had crossed her path. She felt herself turning in the direction of the count's house as if, by thinking hard, she could see through the wall into Olive Street and through the house beyond, and across Church Square and into Sismond's dining hall. Were Sismond and the general teasing their nephew about spending time in the library with the women? Was Geseric embarrassed about crossing wits with a silly Saxon girl or had he already forgotten her? She spun on her heel. What a fool I am! I should at least extract myself from Junius' arms before imagining throwing myself into someone else's. And I would do well to remember that there are tricksters among the gods who delight most in duping people who think they are cleverer than others.

☙ Chapter 29 ❧
Tolosa

At the rear of her former Roman townhouse was a room that Xancha customarily used for confidential conversation. There were two people in the room: Xancha, herself, and General Thormond, dressed casually, old friends and long-time lovers having a tête-à-tête.

"My nephew, that book-reading fool, has fallen in love with some strange woman he ran into at Hildefrith's monastery," said the general, taking a hefty gulp from his wine glass. In this room, with Xancha, he did not have to maintain a façade. They had known one another for years, since a couple of days after he had ridden into town with his cousin, Sismond, two young men on the make, with a bag of gold, ready to buy land, ready to hire men, ready for fun. Xancha had not become Thormond's lover right away. She had been Sismond's girl to begin with. That had made things easier for Thormond. He could enjoy her company, listen to her chatter, use her as a sounding board, without having to perform himself. Then Sismond had been nominated Count of Agininum.

Xancha's chatter had never been mere idle gossip. Any man in Tolosa worth his manhood was caught in her net sooner or later. And the women who sought the dancer's assistance to enhance their looks couldn't help but disclose their husbands' or lovers' sayings and doings as they chattered idly within her earshot. Her network of contacts increased her value as a listener, since her comments were coloured by the tittle-tattle she heard. Thormond sometimes wondered how far his own musings spread through the society of Tolosa, through the court. To the ears of Theodoric, the king, certainly. He reckoned with that, which was why he was still so careful about what he said in Xancha's presence.

"Is that so bad?" asked his companion.

The general sighed.

"If he merely sang her praises, like any other young fool, I could put up with the love and romance, but instead he's going around in silence, thinking."

"So you fear that he's serious." Xancha could not help laughing.

"You know the story, Xancha. Young men fall in love, as if they're in a damned dream, and they start to consider marriage to the girl in their fantasies. They never stop to think that marriage is a business proposition, politics, war by other means!"

"And you had planned to employ Geseric as a fighter in that war?"

The general took another mouthful of wine.

"A very minor foot soldier. After all, his father died when we were young, before Theodoric really managed to secure power, and never reaped the gains in land and position that Sismond and I have."

"I remember," said Xancha. "Raymond was a sweet boy, and Geseric is, too."

The general shot her a suspicious glance. One could never be too careful with these older women. Xancha was renowned to be very choosy who she slept with, but she might have taken a sudden fancy to a younger man.

"But poor and with no position," he emphasised hastily.

"So you would never have been able to attract a wife from one of the major families then, one of Ludiger's daughters, for example."

Thormond laughed.

"I don't think I could get one of those stuffed dolls for my own son, for Wiseric, unless Ludiger had ordered her to poison him in the marriage bed."

"That's been known to happen," said Xancha.

"Perhaps, but it won't happen to my family."

"Then what had you thought?"

"I don't know, someone with a bit of land near the frontier, where there might be a possibility to expand in the right circumstances."

Xancha laughed.

"Do you want me to ask around? Geseric's just the type of boy the girls would fall for…good-looking, can recite poetry, plays music as well, I hear."

The general grunted. Those were not attributes *he* rated highly.

"He can use his sword, too?" enquired Xancha, with a cheeky smile.

Thormond shot her another glance. He had heard enough of her double entendres over the years to know that there was always a hint of truth behind them.

"He can fight, I grant you that. That's why I thought a posting on the frontier would suit him, drive some of the poetry out of his head."

"But he's messed things up for you by falling in love. Is she really so very unsuitable?"

"Some protégé of Hildefrith, a no-name Saxon girl, from what Sismond said. We ran into her in the library cosied up with Hildefrith's…" He hesitated for a moment, seeking the right word. "…friend."

"Lover?" suggested Xancha. "Face it, Thormond, your sister shares her life and her bed with another women. She always did, and she has found a very suitable one in Ophelia."

"Hildefrith should have been married off as Father ordered, whether she liked it or not, and not allowed to do as she wished and hide away in that monastery."

"Signy Wealda…isn't that what she's called? Megana Fabiana's companion?" Xancha interjected.

The general snorted.

"What…do you know her?"

"Thormond. Megana's a friend of mine, you know that. I do believe you're just being sour, jealous that your nephew has found a pretty woman without your help."

"What do you mean? That's what makes it worse. The whole mess *is* my responsibility. He was with me when we came across her! When we went to inspect that house of idle women that the old man insisted on funding."

"To secure his place in heaven, Thormond. Don't forget that. And you didn't know she would be there, did you, this mysterious no-name Saxon girl? Thormond, I wonder if you would really like to get her into your own bed if she's cute enough to snare Geseric."

"Nonsense!"

"My friend, the pretty merchantess, then…?"

"Never set eyes on her!" retorted the general, perplexed. "Nothing of the sort. I'm just suspicious of these foreigners. They come here, nestle in amongst us, help themselves to our hard-won gold, and then seduce our men."

"We were foreigners once, dear, not so long ago, and you can't accuse the ladies of preferring each other's company and seducing our men at the same time. It doesn't make sense."

"Well, I don't know what their game is."

"Assuming they have one. From all I've heard, this Signy's an attractive and intelligent young woman. She would probably be quite a suitable match for Geseric."

"She can ride a horse well enough," admitted the general, recalling the canter from the monastery.

"Well, there you are," laughed Xancha. "The most important characteristic in a woman. She can ride a horse. That's one up on me, though I've never heard you complain. Does she speak Latin at all?"

"Perfectly…reciting poetry like a senator. That's what got Geseric hooked. And Greek, too, apparently." The general sounded disapproving.

"Oh, really! She seems quite interesting. I should have her round for dinner if I can lure her to Tolosa."

Thormond gave his lover a grateful smile.

"Could you do that, my darling, give her a look over, see which way she bends…"

How much easier with men, he thought. An evening at the Fox Tavern and you had them in your pocket.

"And find out if she has any money hidden away in the cold north," suggested Xancha, "under a mound perhaps, like a dragon? Isn't that the custom?"

"It wouldn't harm, since Geseric has none," grunted the general.

"Those merchants always have tons of loot stashed away, gold and silver and ivory, piled in secret rooms."

"You should know," muttered Thormond, "but I don't think Geseric's lady love is any type of merchant. Sismond swears the woman's a magician."

"All the better then," laughed Xancha. "She doesn't need a stash of gold. She can transform lead into gold any time she likes."

Thormond shook his head.

"This is all beyond me…this magic business. A sharp sword and a good horse, that's how a man can make an honest living, if Fortuna is on his side."

"That option isn't open to women, my dear. We have to use our charms. But, very well, I'll take it upon myself to interpret the auspices and determine Fortuna's intentions with regard to Geseric's love life."

The general put down his goblet and kissed her lips to seal the deal.

"This will be an opportunity for another get together with Megana," Xancha muttered to herself, "and it sounds like this other newcomer, this girl Signy, might also become a valuable asset."

"By the way," she continued, blowing out the lamp, "did I hear you'll soon be sent east again, with the army?"

"That's news to me," said Thormond.

"Your dear wife will be delighted to see you…You will call in as you pass by your estate on the road to Carcasso?"

The general did not deign to reply.

☙ Chapter 30 ❧ Agininum

Megana was not intimidated by many people, but Lanius' mother was one of them. The feeling was entirely illogical. The woman wasn't threatening in the slightest. No, the cause, Megana was compelled to admit to herself, was her accent, the trace of the articulation of a British aristocrat, one of the cream of the cream, and the implications played on her inferiority complex. Megana had been born too late to experience Roman Britannia. The legions had gone before she was aware that they had existed and, she had learned, the decline had set in long before that. Nevertheless, the old families, the few that remained, had set a stamp on her childhood. It was Megana herself who had constructed the proposition that in Ophelia's eyes she was a mere merchant's daughter, and an illegitimate one at that. On the couple of occasions when their paths had crossed Ophelia had never said anything untoward, never implied anything critical. And she had shown nothing but kindness to Signy, and Megana was grateful for that.

On the other hand, there was something strange about Lanius' mother. Who exactly was she, and how had she ended up at an obscure monastery in the south of Gaul? Perhaps there was something embarrassing in their past that Lanius did not want to mention. Megana would have liked to ask straight out and settle the matter, but she knew if she upset Ophelia, Signy would be annoyed, and she would risk disturbing her relationship with Lanius. She would have to suffer from unstilled curiosity and presumed inferiority.

It was fortunate that she did not allow these feelings much room for play, because now she needed Ophelia as an ally. The monastery owned land, starting with a donation from when it was established back in the dim and distant past. Hildefrith had brought more property when her family had sent her into seclusion, and over the years, wealthy individuals had made additional bequests, hoping to upgrade their final destination. Ophelia, as the daughter of an influential Roman citizen, had been well educated. That had earned her the role as librarian to the monastery, but also, eventually, that of its treasurer. Lanius had pointed out that his mother had as good an overview of the lands around Agininum as anyone, and had several times suggested Megana should consult her.

"Mistress Megana, I didn't expect to see you here…alone. Have you left our friend Signy in Agininum?" Ophelia's voice sounded hesitant, tense. Megana had to admit to herself that her own greeting had scarcely been warm. She had to try better.

"I'm sorry to disturb you. Lanius suggested I should come to speak to you."

"Oh, you are not disturbing me, I assure you," said Ophelia, though her tone suggested otherwise. "Lanius…is he with you?"

Megana had been accompanied by Lanius on a previous occasion when she had visited the monastery to make a formal introduction. That she had now come on her own seemed to make Ophelia nervous.

"No, he is in Burdigala," replied Megana.

"He is well, I hope."

"Very well."

"I expect he will come before autumn."

"I expect so," said Megana.

Ophelia looked around, as if there might be another person in the room who could take over the conversation, to permit her to abandon the exchange.

"I…I…came to speak to you, Mistress Ophelia, because I wanted to ask your advice."

"My advice…" Ophelia sounded like that was a most unlikely contribution she could offer.

What is it about *me*? Megana wondered. Signy speaks so lovingly of her, and yet she seems like she could shatter into pieces at any moment.

"I have come into some good fortune," said Megana, "a piece of land by the Oltis. It lies adjacent to the monastery lands."

Ophelia took a step back, noticed a stool just behind her and sat down, clasping her hands in her lap.

"I heard that Lanius has been buying land along the Oltis, close to our farm. A man came, from the *notarius*'s office, wanting to know the landmarks so he could confirm the boundary."

"Lanius was acting on my behalf, Mistress Ophelia. You know how the law is framed, and it is always possible the current owner would not sell if he knew who the purchaser was."

Ophelia said nothing.

The monastery's land is not her land, thought Megana, so she doesn't have to worry about the place of women in society, and no doubt the usual sinners are only too pleased to sell their property to God's house.

"I have been considering," she said, "that I could donate the land to the church, but I have begun to have second thoughts."

Megana instantly regretted what she had just said, expecting a look of disapproval, but it never came.

"The monastery's land on the south bank of the Oltis has been neglected," she went on, and the expression on Ophelia's face now seemed to suggest she took the words as a personal affront.

"I mean," Megana stumbled on, "if the land could be cleared, the wood could be floated down the river, to Burdigala or one of the richer estates. They're always short of timber for building, and even firewood. The property could be planted with fruit trees or vines. In a short while, there would be enough produce to justify constructing a press, for wine or fruit. With the example from the monastery, other landholders in the area could increase their acreage of vines, and you could offer a service to the neighbouring farms."

Megana was aware she was letting her words run away from her, spilling out her ideas impulsively. She had thought the business through on the journey to the monastery. The strategy was obvious when you considered matters.

"There's a market for wine in Tolosa. It could be carried on riverboats, part of the way at least, when the conditions are right."

She kept prattling on, but she slowly discerned reason in her babble. Ophelia's posture was relaxing, the tension in her body dissolving. The tight, forced smile, like a gash across her face, was slowly melting into a more revealing expression.

"You remind me of your father, Mistress," she said at last. "I can still hear his voice echoing round Verdaris, trying to persuade my father into some investment or enterprise. He was a young man then, younger than you are now, I suppose. I didn't understand what he wanted from Father, but there was no mistaking his enthusiasm."

Megana felt a clutch in her stomach, as if her entrails had been grabbed by an unseen hand.

Ophelia rose to her feet, the silky-smooth movement of a woman who had gained control of herself.

"Let me call for some of the wine we *do* have, Megana Fabiansdaughter, and in the meanwhile I'll find the description of our farm. It must be close at hand because I had to retrieve it for the clerk."

"You knew my father?" said Megana.

"One moment…"

Ophelia disappeared from the room. Megana could hear an exchange of voices in the passage outside, and then she returned.

"I can't say that I did, really. What had I, a child, and a girl-child at that, to do with the affairs of men, especially men as important as my father. You know as well as I do, my dear, that I was raised to be a wife, not an agent of my own destiny."

"I don't understand," said Megana, "my father, your father? Did you once live near Corinium?"

A shadow passed across Ophelia's face.

"That was another life, a life I've tried to put behind me. Only now and then a memory revives. Your enthusiastic voice brought back one of them, a happy memory. Now let me find that charter."

She turned and disappeared among the shelves, only to return a moment later with a roll of parchment.

"Come here to my lectern, Mistress Megana, and examine this."

A girl appeared, one of the novices, carrying flasks and two glasses, placed them on a low table, and with a nod to her superior, left again.

"I don't often drink wine during the day," said Ophelia, crossing to the table. She poured her guest and herself small portions of wine and added water to her glass. "I find it impairs the quality of my writing, and it is difficult enough to keep the words straight these days. Thank goodness I now have some assistance from your young friend, Signy."

Megana added a conspicuous helping of water to her own wine. While she did so, Ophelia returned to the document and began to run her finger along the description of the marks setting out the boundary of the monastery's farm, reading the text aloud.

"As I remembered." She suddenly stopped. "There has been bad work done here. Our lands do not in fact lie adjacent. There is a strip which was not included when the farm was granted to the monastery, a strip that lies between your land and ours."

"And who is the holder of that strip?"

Ophelia smiled.

"Anastasius, of course, though I don't blame him for the error. It was done before his time."

"Anastasius?"

"The bishop, the Bishop of Agininum. That farm belonged to the bishopric before it was transferred to us, and some careless clerk mixed up the boundary markers…the wrong stream here to the south, I believe."

"The bishop," said Megana, her voice betraying her disappointment. "That's an awkward complication."

"Whyever do you say that?" asked Ophelia. "I'm sure we can work something out. He's been a friend of mine for years, ever since he first came to Agininum. To tell you the truth, I might have transferred my allegiance to the diocese had a new leader been appointed to this monastery who didn't approve of me.

Anastasius has invited me plenty of times. It was my fortune and his misfortune that Hildefrith had so offended her father that he banished her here. But that's another matter. You should call in and see Anastasius yourself. He's practically your neighbour, after all. If you don't ask, you'll never know whether he's interested in your proposal. If you were to make the donation to the bishopric, then it would solve the boundary problem, since the two plots could be joined. In return you could be granted a long-term lease. Then you could still build your wine press and collect the tithe. Donate and lease back…it's a handy way to boost your moral capital and your treasury at the same time, and I don't suppose God cares who is actually doing the work so long as it benefits the church and feeds His people."

She began to roll the parchment up.

"In fact," she continued, "perhaps you could administer the monastery's share of the project as well. The land is far from our house, and you're certainly a more competent *negotiatiores* than either Anastasius or me. If Lanius hadn't already told me so, I would have drawn the conclusion from your family history."

"Perhaps you're right, Mistress Ophelia." Megana was almost lost for words.

"Should I send the bishop a note, mentioning you have my support, when he returns from his synod?"

"Oh, no," replied Megana, suddenly the nervous one, "thank you, but I don't want to get ahead of myself."

"Go and speak to the bishop," said Ophelia, laying her hand on Megana's shoulder. "I know you'll be welcome. You will join us for the evening meal, won't you, and travel home tomorrow?"

It was ever thus, Megana thought. There was no misinterpreting the kind offer and the soft tone. She would do as she was bidden. She was, after all, merely a trader.

☙ Chapter 31 ❧
Agininum

Signy had just returned from a trip to the men's monastery with the horse and cart from Megana's warehouse. Ragvald and Ferona had joined her. They had filled the cart with plants and a small tree from Brother Wilbert's orchard to add to Signy's growing collection. Now she was in the garden of the house in Olive Street, setting out the plants with the assistance of the former bandit and that of her young son, Einar.

She suddenly heard Henrik calling from the house.

"Mistress, do you have a moment? I've heard some alarming news."

She rose to her feet, looking around for Maria to take care of Einar and prevent him pulling up the plants they had just set out. Not seeing the nurse, she picked up the boy herself and hurried up the garden to the portico where Henrik was waiting.

"What is it, Henrik, not bandits again?"

Einar gave her a kick in the midriff and demanded to be put down.

"Farmer Elemus and his wife, they've both been found dead, murdered apparently."

"Farmer Elemus…haven't we bought vegetables from him? Who would want to harm Elemus? He's a decent honest man."

"That's why I called you. Victoria's quite upset, and Grunwald suggested we ride over to show our respects."

"I'll come with you," said Signy. Grunwald is undoubtedly curious, she thought, and I'm no better myself. "Get the horse ready. I'll just leave Einar with Maria and find my boots."

"Don't want," said Einar, giving her another kick. "Want garden."

Too bad, she thought. "You can help Uncle Ragvald another day. Now it's time for your nap."

"Don't want," repeated the boy, but by then Signy had reached the nursery where he was quickly deposited with Maria.

A short while later, she and the men clattered up the hill, past the bishop's residence, the church, round the graveyard and out through the north gate towards Elemus' farm. When they arrived, they found Count Sismond and Jorid already present, talking and pointing. Several other members of Sismond's retinue were standing around chatting and doing nothing in particular.

The count and his master-of-arms turned as Signy and her followers rode up. A frown creased Sismond's brow.

"What the hell are you doing here? This is a murder scene, too late for your skills, unless they stretch to resurrection."

"I'm sorry that they don't. Farmer Elemus was a good man with many friends," she replied, dismounting.

"Including us in Olive Street, my lord," added Henrik.

"Cut down like a butchered hog," said Sismond, evidently satisfied that Signy and her men had some interest in the farmer's fate, "and his wife, too. Who could have done this, do you think?"

There was something in his tone which suggested he already had suspicions.

"I can't imagine," Signy replied. "You dealt with the bandits, and Elemus was not a wealthy man who might attract thieves." Then a cold shiver passed down her back at the memory of another poor man who died in mysterious circumstances. Without waiting for Sismond to speak again, she hurried past the two men and round the farmyard, not giving even a glance at the corpse of the farmer, still lying where he had been slain. Grunwald and Henrik hurried after her.

"Where are you going?" called Henrik, but received no reply until they had reached the far end of the in-field.

"Look," said Signy, finally, pointing into the distance.

"The green way…it passes by Elemus' farm."

"And joins the road to Tolosa a couple of miles further on," said Jorid, who had followed them.

Signy started to walk on, towards the place where the way ran along the boundary of Elemus' land.

"We already looked," said Jorid. She spun around.

"And what did you find?"

"Tracks, plenty of them, though the surface is quite hard and dry."

"Where? Show me!"

"The evidence is quite clear," said Jorid. "The imperialist intruders have been using the track. Why, we don't know, and there's nothing to link them to the murder…not directly."

"Show me the tracks," Signy insisted.

"Show her the tracks," Grunwald echoed, with a sharp look at Jorid.

Signy and the count's man set off along the path through the fields, both in silence. What Jorid was thinking was impossible to tell from the expression on his face, but Signy's mind was in turmoil.

"When did this happen?" she asked.

"In the last day or two…Jeanna, Elemus' wife, didn't come to the market yesterday as she'd promised, so a pair of her friends walked out to the farm this morning and found…you saw what they found."

"While I was away," said Signy vaguely.

They came to the edge of the field, where the path met the way.

"See," said Jorid, "there are the marks of horses and boots. The same marks we've seen elsewhere. The imperialists were here. What were they doing here, so close to Agininum?"

"But we can't be sure they killed Elemus, you said so yourself."

Jorid shrugged. "Do we need to?"

"Wait," Signy said, suddenly squatting. "Stand out of the light."

Jorid gave her an irritated glance but took a step to the side.

"Careful, you'll disturb the prints!"

"Boot prints," said Jorid. "Only the regulars wear boots that would make those prints. It doesn't take an expert…"

"That's not what I'm looking for," said Signy. "Get down here and see, just where the light strikes the prints and raises a shadow."

Jorid crouched down beside her, perplexed.

"There…can you see something strange about that particular print?"

He shook his head.

"The man has had his boot repaired, a repair to the heel." She ran her finger along one of the prints.

"So?"

"I've seen this print before," she said, standing slowly. "I've seen the boots that made them," she added.

"Who? Where?"

Signy did not reply, but set off back towards the farm buildings, eyes on the ground. Sismond was coming towards them.

"Stop, my lord, don't take one further step."

The count came to a halt, looking puzzled. She came up beside him.

"We've nearly destroyed the evidence with our clumsiness. Pray, my lord, that the women who found the bodies and your own men haven't trampled around the farm too thoroughly."

Without saying more, she set off again, leaving the count and Jorid to follow. When she reached the farmyard she stopped, shaking her head.

"Too many feet, too many people," she muttered to herself, and then looked up. "Where's the farmer's wife?"

"Jeanna…in the kitchen," said Jorid, taking a step in the direction of the house.

"Stay where you are, all of you," she said, "please."

Then she began to walk slowly towards the open door, placing her feet with great care and precision. She walked into the kitchen. The woman lay over by the fireplace. She must have been cooking when the murderers walked in. She must have turned, thinking her husband was behind her and then…Signy dropped to her knees. There were marks on the floor, outlines where boots had trampled on the blood that had splashed from the woman's head as they beat her down, unconscious and finally to death.

Signy stood again, called out.

"You can come now, my lord, and Master Jorid, but slowly and carefully."

The room darkened momentarily as the two men pushed through the doorway.

"What is it?" asked the count, almost leaning over her in curiosity.

"Jorid, come forward. Crouch down. Tell me what you see."

Jorid crouched, bending forward.

"It's a boot print, Mistress, a hobnailed boot. Oh, now I understand what you mean. There's a repair to the heel, on the left." He stood up slowly, looking from Signy to the count. "It's the same print you showed me by the green way."

"Yes," she said, "and I could follow them, just, here and there, along the path across the fields. If I looked carefully, perhaps I could have seen them going back, towards the way, but now we have walked so much on the path that I'm afraid we've destroyed the traces."

"That's all very well," said the count, "so now we know the murderer came from the path. I had reckoned that already. I had reckoned he must've been one of the gang of interfering bastards that had assembled there."

"But which exact…bastard, my lord?"

"You said you had seen this print before?" said Jorid.

"I have." She paused, looking at Sismond. "I saw prints like these in the camp. The boot that made them sits on the foot of an *optio*…Captain Junius' *optio*. The captain's man is responsible for this murder. He led me from the captain's tent to the place where I was held prisoner, after Junius questioned me. I saw his boots had been repaired. I saw the trace they made, and I remembered it, because I had seen the same print in the mud by the body of the dog, Xeno the shepherd's dog. Junius told me it had attacked his men, and they had been forced to kill it in self-defence."

"Elemus never attacked anyone," growled the count.

"Nor Jeanna," said Signy. "The man who did this came out of his way to the farm."

"So there's no doubt?" asked the count.

"None at all," said Signy. She felt she was about to be sick, not because of the bodies, but because her stomach was as tight as a ball. Junius' *optio* had been on the track. Junius' *optio* had walked to the farm. Junius' *optio* had trampled in the blood flowing from Jeanna the farmer's wife. Junius' *optio* had killed the dog. Junius had never denied that. She closed her eyes and took a deep breath. Just because the *optio* had come this way, done this horrible deed, didn't mean Junius was responsible. The farm was out of sight of the green way. Junius might have ordered his man to go and tell Elemus what the soldiers were doing, to advise the farmer to keep out of the way. If Junius had stayed at the track, he would have had no idea what the *optio* had done, that the *optio* had ensured that Elemus and Jeanna would be certain to keep out of the way, certain to say nothing. And yet the farmer and his wife were saying something, even though they were dead. Jeanna's own blood had told her that Junius' man had been there in the room as she lay dying. But Jeanna's blood could not tell Signy or Jorid or Sismond who had given the order to murder, if any such order had been given.

Sismond's voice broke into her thoughts.

"The imperialist intruders have gone too far this time, killing an honest farmer, and on the doorstep of Agininum." The count spoke quietly. "And this Junius is involved somehow. I'll get to the bottom of this, and when I do, the guilty people are going to get what's coming to them. Jorid, back to town."

Signy watched him depart. There was a menace in his voice that was more threatening than his usual shouting and cursing. Sooner or later he would catch up to Junius, she thought, and when he did, he would discover…and suppose he concluded that Junius was one of the guilty people? Where would that leave her?

ℭ Chapter 32 ℭ
Agininum

A shadow in the doorway broke Megana's concentration. She was in the middle of counting a stack of baskets, each one filled with onions. The vegetables would have to be loaded onto a wagon or packhorses in the next couple of days and shipped out to Tolosa. She bit into one of the yellow globes to check the quality, and then flipped the remainder in the direction of the warehouse door. There was a yelp, and she turned around to see the figure of a youth, standing on the threshold of the storehouse.

"What the hell do you want?" A young man, clean shaven, shoulder-length dark hair held in place by a thin band, with an expensive-looking tunic ending a good way above the knee, occupied the rectangle of daylight. "I said, what the hell do you want?" Megana repeated.

"I assume I am addressing the merchant, Megana Fabiana."

He had clearly attended elocution lessons.

"You are," said Megana. "Now tell me who you are and what you want, or else clear off. You're disturbing my work."

"It's your work to which my message refers," said the youth, glancing with distaste towards the onion piece that had rolled out into the yard, attracting the attention of a loose pig. He took another, cautious step into the storehouse.

Megana took a couple of quick steps towards him, and the youth hastily retreated, but not quickly enough to prevent Megana seizing the arm of his tunic.

"Citizen Nice Talk, I've already asked you three times what you're doing here. That's twice more than I normally need to get an answer. I won't ask another time."

"It's already unwise to lay hands on the king's messenger," said the youth, since Megana still had hold of his tunic.

Megana sighed to herself. Of all the unwelcome pests!

Now she could see his badge of office on his shoulder. She let go of his garment. He straightened himself.

"I have been dispatched with a communication of utmost urgency."

He hesitated, apparently expecting Megana to show some sign of surprise or respect. She did neither. Every dispatch from the royal household was at least of utmost urgency. Otherwise they wouldn't bother sending it. Usually that meant there was a feast coming up, and some important component was in short supply. Xancha, she knew, was responsible for providing the entertainment, but the food and drink…She wasn't the only merchant charged with that task, but when a panic set in they all received the same message, with the result that Tolosa was often drowning in stale beer or rotting fruit for weeks after.

"The king and his council have decreed," the messenger began, "that all supplies of comestibles previously destined for the Royal Palace in Tolosa are to be remitted with immediate effect to the field army in…" He stopped again, frowning. "In…"

"Don't tell me…" said Megana, "…Carcasso?"

"Oh, no," said the youth, suddenly bright, "the army's on the march. The supplies must be sent to Luteva."

It was Megana's turn to frown.

"Duke Ludiger has been sent to Luteva?"

"Oh, no, you seem to be badly misinformed! The duke is required at court. General Thormond is leading the field army."

"Probably better that he is," said Megana, eyeing the young man carefully.

The youth gave her a cautious smile.

"Mistress, I wonder…I tried to deliver the message to Merchant Tazzius, but he was not in his warehouse. Perhaps you could inform him."

"You have a similar instruction for my colleague next door, Merchant Tazzius?" said Megana.

"I do," said the youth with an eager smile, "and for the other gentleman…Caiphas."

Tazzius, so far as Megana knew, had no business in Tolosa. His niche among the merchants of Aginінum was supplying small lead decorations, glass beads, ribbons and similar knick-knacks to the peddlers who visited the villages and farmsteads round about. He had a stall of his own in the marketplace.

"And Merchant Caiphas?" The youth looked uncertain. "They said he wasn't at home."

Megana's frown deepened. Why would Caiphas need this message of utmost urgency? Caiphas Africanus, as his name suggested, specialised, or rather had inherited, a trade in exotic goods from Africa, dates and ostrich eggs and such like, but he hadn't been seen in Aginnum for years. His warehouse had been occupied by a pair of his slaves and their families, who had salvaged what little of the business they could by journeying down and picking up a few goods in Narbonna now and then.

"And you say the king gave you this message?"

"No, no." The youth shook his head vigorously.

"His steward, then?"

"No, no. Duke Ludiger, himself."

"What the…" – she suppressed her curse – "does the duke have to do with provisioning the army?"

"He's commanding the army. I just told you that," said the youth.

"You just told me General Thormond is leading the army." And Thormond would know that it was cheaper, more convenient and more reliable to requisition provisions from Narbonna, from Agatha, or from the local farms in the east, his own estate included. None of this makes sense, she thought. The duke had never shown the slightest interest in the provision of supplies to the court or to the city. On the other hand, the king's steward was a sensible man, so long as there wasn't a panic on. She received his instructions on a regular basis, and there had been no word from him concerning the army.

"I can't just break my word," she said, "not until I've received clearance from the royal steward."

The youth smiled once again and reached into a bag slung across his back.

"Here, Mistress Merchant, is your order."

He passed Megana a roll of papyrus, which she untied and straightened. The order was unambiguous and stamped with the royal seal: for the next six weeks all foodstuffs were to bypass Tolosa and be delivered directly to the army in Luteva.

Megana shook her head again. The logistics were ridiculous, that was one thing. And Tazzius' and Caiphas' names were written alongside her own, and they did not supply foodstuffs to Tolosa. That was another.

ꟽ Chapter 33 ꟾ
Aginínum

"A typical royal mess!" Megana was describing the incident with the messenger to Signy during the evening meal. "I don't know where they get their information from," she continued. "An order concerning supplying food to the army, and addressed to me, of course, as it should be, but to Tazzius and Caiphas as well? Whoever put that list together didn't have a clue about the merchants of Aginínum. I suppose that's to be expected when Duke Ludiger starts meddling in other people's business."

Signy had already been feeling uneasy. The discovery of the bodies of Farmer Elemus and his wife would have been enough to upset her. But the undeniable connection between their killing and Junius' *optio* had left her greatly disturbed. And if the *optio* had killed Elemus and his wife…She had still not told Sismond she had been meeting Junius in the town, and didn't understand why the Roman officer had not yet spoken to the count.

"Well, you told me that Caiphas supplied food to court," she said absent-mindedly.

"He did once upon a time…that's what Lanius told me, but when I got here, I soon found his trade was defunct. And that doesn't explain how Tazzius' name got on the list."

"He has a warehouse next to yours, doesn't he?"

"Yes, but what's that got to do with it? Gaulman, the charcoal burner, has a depot by the river, too. Odd he wasn't included…"

"Gaulman?" Signy was beginning to pay more attention to Megana's tale. "Who's he?"

"We don't use him, Mistress," said Victoria from beside her.

"Caiphas Africanus, Megana Fabiana, Tazzius of Judea, that's what it said. And Tazzius isn't from Judea. He grew up in Agatha."

"I thought you said he was a Hebrew?"

"So he is, but he grew up in Agatha. He's Tazzius of Agatha, if anything."

A cold, miserable feeling began to seep through Signy's body. She developed a sudden difficulty swallowing her food, as if a hand had clutched her throat and was slowly squeezing it. A small piece of meat caught, half-swallowed, and she began to choke, started coughing, her eyes streaming.

Victoria patted her back.

"I'm sorry," she said. "I don't feel well." She jumped up, knocking over her stool, and ran out of the kitchen.

She sat down on the stone ledge that surrounded the fig tree growing in the centre of the court. A moment later, Megana appeared in the glowing rectangle of the kitchen door.

"Are you alright, Signy?" She came out into the darkened yard. "What's the matter?"

Signy felt herself overtaken by tears, tears of shame and tears of worry. Shame that she had so easily gone to bed with Junius. Worry that she had just realised that the names on the messenger's list were exactly those she had given to her lover, innocently, as they had strolled around the city. She had not known the merchants' business, just their names. She had heard Megana mention them and boastfully blurted what little she knew to Junius.

Megana sat down beside her and wrapped her arm around her.

"Are you sick?" Her tone was worried.

"Sick, sick! I'm so sick I should die!"

There was only one cure to this illness, she recognised. She had to speak to Sismond, tell him everything. There was a risk, of course, that the count would lose his temper, or even take rough justice. He was already angry. She had seen that at the farm. He had a right to be angry. Strangers had encroached on his lands, murdered people who were under his protection, and now she was going to tell him that one of their leaders had even been sneaking into his town to spy on him. He had a right to be angry with her, but she felt she understood him. She felt he would understand her. That she had only acted as any young woman might. That she hadn't hidden what she knew to be wrong from him, only what she thought was her private business. She took a deep breath. She had to trust her luck was with her.

ᏨChapter 34 ᏨAgininum

The count was immensely irritated. He had a murder, two murders, on his hands.

"Probably committed by a roving band of imperialist auxiliaries, if you're to be believed," he muttered, pointing at Signy, "and I'm inclined to believe you. You're young and pretty but you can ride a horse and you're handy with a knife. It's far more than a man could normally ask of a woman."

He spun on his heel.

"But that's no reason for you and your friend to interrupt my evening meal." He eyed the two women. "You," he said, now pointing at Megana. "You came to see me once. I remember you, a trader, presenting your documents last spring, but since then I've not set eyes on you. I would have remembered if I had."

"My men assisted you on your expedition against the bandits," said Megana. "We never met."

"So they did, so they did," muttered the count, taking a seat. "I didn't put two and two together immediately. So what the hell do you want now? My meal's getting cold."

"I've done something wrong," said Signy, "terribly wrong. I must tell you and accept your judgement."

The count sat disbelieving as she told her tale, how she had been attracted to the Roman captain, how he had visited the town several more times in disguise, and she had slept with him, quite willingly.

"He examined the city gates, and the approaches from all directions," the count repeated, when the tale was complete.

Signy nodded.

"And he said he's coming back, later in the summer, with more of his men?"

She nodded again.

"And this list of merchants' names…you gave it to him?"

"Yes," Signy said, "I did. Not deliberately, but without thought, as a woman speaking to her lover."

The count scowled, stood up and paced across the room, turned slowly and paced back again.

"Damnation! You do realise that I could string you up, maybe even crucify you, as a traitor to the realm?"

Signy nodded.

Sismond sighed loudly and rubbed his nose with his hand.

"It would be a damned pity to hang you," he said, "especially as my nephew seems to have fallen in love with you, though I wonder what Geseric will think when he finds out his heart's desire has been rolling in the sack with an imperialist spy…because that's what the man obviously is, a dirty, sneaky, treacherous spy."

He cast a final glance at Signy, sat down heavily and turned to Megana.

"Where's this messenger you're talking about?"

"He's staying at the travellers hostel and then returning to Tolosa tomorrow. He said he needed a stamped confirmation he had delivered his message."

"I'll give him a stamped fucking confirmation," growled the count, and then called "Tygon!" and his chamberlain quickly appeared.

"It seems," he said to no one in particular, once the chamberlain had been sent to find the messenger, "that we may have a conspiracy on our hands. I was beginning to suspect so, when that little shit Altaar was so unhelpful about the bandits…"

Silence descended, broken only by occasional growls from the count, until footsteps were heard in the corridor outside and Tygon entered, leading the messenger.

"Show me the order?" The count stuck out his hand, and the youth slowly and reluctantly handed him the scroll. "Why didn't you come to me, you insolent fop?" the count demanded.

"I was told there was no need, my lord, to disturb you."

"Well, now I *am* disturbed, well and truly disturbed." He tapped his finger against the sheet. "Caiphas…that's a name from the past. Where did you get this order?"

"From the king, my lord…I mean, well, from Duke Ludiger's steward, actually."

"But who put the list together?"

The youth opened his mouth to speak but no words came out.

"And not an imperialist in sight?"

The youth looked puzzled.

"A fucking Roman, that's what I mean!"

"No, my lord."

"Ever heard of a Junius, Captain Junius?"

The youth shook his head.

"Perhaps we shouldn't jump to conclusions," said Megana. "Perhaps there's been a misunderstanding. We should check first, just to be on the safe side."

Sismond pursed his lips. What the merchant was saying made sense. These were deep waters he was wading into. One false step, and it wouldn't be the sorceress who was hanging in the forum but…

"With my cousin directly, I think," said the count, now stroking his chin. "Yes…we'll send a messenger of our own… your man, Asser, he's a chap with a bit of initiative. It would make sense a trader would want to check, so better send one of your men than mine. And in any case, I'm going to need all mine to track down these murderers."

He turned to Tygon.

"This young man, find him a comfortable room, with barred windows and a lockable door. Sir," he said, jabbing his finger towards the messenger, "you might have thought you were returning to Tolosa tomorrow, but you're going nowhere. You'll be staying here as my guest until we get to the bottom of this."

--oo0Ooo--

Signy, crossing Church Square beside Megana, was relieved that Sismond's preoccupation with the conspiracy had distracted him from her own contribution. She was relieved, too, that Megana had become involved in the whole miserable business. She no longer felt so alone. No doubt Megana, like Sismond, thought she had been foolish to get involved with Junius, but her friend kept her opinions to herself, at least. Her relief would only be temporary, that Signy understood, not just because she was sure that Sismond would not forget her for long, but also because a greater justice would see to it that she suffered for her ill-judgement. No…she said crossly to herself, I'll get by somehow, because my luck, my *hamingja*, is with me, so long as I keep my courage and face what I've done. I won't escape free, of course. I'll be tested because I have done wrong, and I must face the challenge, whatever it will be, and trust in my *hamingja* that I'll succeed. I did not make a misjudgement. I didn't know what Junius was up to. Yes, I suspected he was involved in some shady business, but every man I have ever been with has been involved in shady business. I've been involved in shady business myself on many occasions. Who am I to condemn him for that, and what right has anyone to condemn me? And then her thoughts took another leap. Might Geseric have a dark side, too? He had been in her thoughts, all too much, but she knew little about him, little more than she could discern from their meeting, that he was educated, well-spoken and charming. But then so was Junius. In any case, what did it matter? After this, what self-respecting man would want to have anything to do with her? Even if the count did not make good on his threat, he would hardly accept her as his nephew's wife. But who had said anything about that anyway? It was all just another stupid fantasy.

☙ Chapter 35 ❧ Tolosa

Xancha turned to her maid, pointing.

"You may wait…the kitchen is across the yard."

Megana and Asser had accompanied the convoy of packhorses carrying food from Agininum to Tolosa. Asser had ridden on to Luteva with the message for General Thormond. Megana had remained in Tolosa, and immediately sent Pythias, the local factor, to the palace to question the royal steward. The reply was both reassuring and disturbing.

"The delivery should proceed as usual, Mistress," Pythias had confirmed.

Megana had only been able frown in response. Whatever the steward reported, the duke or some other courtier might still try to divert the supplies, and she wanted to be in place if that occurred. So far, though, there had been no intervention, and the baskets and bundles had been offloaded in the palace yard and their contents stacked in the palace storehouses.

The announcement that Xancha intended to pay her a visit, rather than waiting to receive her at her own home, and now the appearance of the courtesan in the warehouse yard, might be a sign that there really was trouble brewing in Tolosa.

"So you've been here before," said Megana, watching Xancha's girl depart.

The ex-dancer smiled.

"Years ago. This was Vipso's warehouse in those days. He had the most comfortable mattress in the city." The rest of the explanation was lost in the sound of footsteps, as Xancha followed Megana up the flight of steps to a door in the wall above the entrance arch. Xancha stopped on the threshold and examined the room within: a plain wooden table, a couple of benches, a chest.

"You have kept the hall very spartan. I'm surprised."

What did she want with me, Megana thought, surely not just to comment on the home decoration?

"I'm here so rarely," Megana replied. "It would be a waste to leave good furnishings for the rats and mice to destroy. The bedchamber's sufficiently comfortable, just space for myself, and Delia, of course. I sent her to the cookshop to get us some snacks. She'll be back in a moment. I can ask her to take care of your girl. Then we can talk undisturbed."

There were light footsteps on the stair outside and Megana's maid, Delia, entered carrying a basket. She quickly laid out the pastries, glasses and a jug of wine, nodded and vanished from the room.

"Well-watered at this time of the day, thank you," said Xancha. "You have the girl well trained."

"She's been with me since she was a child," said Megana. "Now to business…you asked to meet me?"

"I did. I confess that I was sent on a fishing expedition to discover more about your friend, Mistress Signy."

Megana felt an involuntary shiver of concern, one she was sure that Xancha would detect. Had the ex-dancer already some inkling of the trouble in Agininum? She tried to disguise her discomfort with a laugh.

"That's very sudden," she said. "I've a similar errand myself. May I ask who sent you?"

If Xancha had noticed Megana's hint of worry, she did not show it.

"The general…Thormond…He sees your friend upsetting his matrimonial plans. His nephew, Geseric, has been singing your friend's praises a little too loudly."

Megana raised her eyebrows in an exaggerated show of wonder.

"Who's talking about getting married? They only just met…Signy has never spoken to me about getting married."

Xancha sniffed.

"I've not heard Thormond mention any specific plans for Geseric. He's thinking more long-term, I suspect."

"He's getting ahead of himself a little," said Megana, "but I suppose that's why Theodoric made him a general."

"And how close are you, you and Signy Wealda, exactly?"

Megana was a little shocked. Signy had adopted the family name Wealda as a necessity when they moved to Gaul – the *notarius* would not accept a blank for the family name – but she rarely used it. How had the ex-dancer found that out?

She held out her hand, turned her thumb towards Xancha.

"Do you see that mark, that scar? We swore to be sisters, to support one another. She doesn't tell me all her business, just as I don't burden her with all of mine, but that oath we made still holds, Xancha. We fight together."

Xancha laughed and raised her glass.

"I wish I could be in such a sisterhood. Unfortunately, I've always had to fight alone. I understand your partner can ride a horse and knows how to use a knife," the ex-dancer continued. "Your man, Hrasmus, was in the Fox Tavern…I sent a particularly attractive young girl to entertain him…"

So that's how she winkled out Signy's family name, thought Megana.

"…quite useful skills in a companion in battle, but has she the land and treasure to make a respectable bride for a man of Geseric's standing?"

"She won't be getting any dowry from her father, if that's what you're wondering. But Geseric's standing? He's a bit of a mystery, himself."

Xancha frowned.

"A mystery?"

"To me," Megana said, smiling, "and to my friend."

"There's nothing to hide," murmured Xancha, evidently a little uncomfortable. "His father was Raymond, cousin to the general and your Count Sismond. His mother died soon after his birth."

"Raymond?"

"It's sad, really. Raymond was younger than his cousins, and arrived in the kingdom after all the best lands were taken. All he had was a small and barren plot in the hills beyond Carcasso. And then he married, and with a child on the way, so he took a risk, rode north into the disputed territories, to win a place for himself. He never came back. No one knows exactly what happened, a skirmish, apparently, but with who, the Empire's men, bandits, or even perhaps some rival for the same territory. Thormond took the child and brought him up."

"And now he would like to find a respectable bride for him, no doubt, not a poor stranger?"

Xancha sighed.

"He's a fine young man, educated, friendly. That's why Theodoric uses him as he does, to charm the farmers into providing supplies for the army. But it's not a role that wins any honour, disdain more like, from those who prefer to ride around waving their swords, though they would soon complain if they went hungry."

"They question him as a man?"

Xancha laughed.

"Listen, my dear, Geseric visits many lonely farms, and he's a handsome young man from the city. It's not only the farmers he charms, I promise you, or at least so my girls tell me."

"Then he might suit Signy very well," Megana laughed in return, and Xancha understood her meaning.

"Your friend has few of the qualities of a respectable wife, but all the attractions of a partner on the twisted road of life. Well, I shan't burden you with more prying…for now. In any case, there's no need for an immediate report, since Thormond and Geseric have been sent east again. Who knows if either of them will come back alive?"

Megana was grateful that the subject had changed, though the turn was hardly for the better.

"So I've heard," she said, trying to give the appearance of being both vague and thoughtful. "My courier reported that the army was gathering by Carcasso. And the message he brought told me that the Romans are gathering, too, around Arelate, requisitioning food and horses, just like old times. Do you think we are in for a battle, or is it just a bluff?"

Xancha remained silent for a moment. Weighing whether I can be trusted, thought Megana. "Bluff would be sufficient," she continued, not waiting for a reply before providing her own analysis. "It's a bad time to be campaigning, with the harvest almost upon us. If they keep our men away long enough, that will interfere with reaping. The city would be hungry by the spring. If we bring our men back, then the Empire can push the frontier forward, and cut up the Visigoth Kingdom like a ham, slice by slice."

"You're misunderstanding warriors, Megana," said Xancha. "Starving out people doesn't bring any glory. Nor does slicing hams."

"Suppose the strategy has not been designed by warriors, but by a philosopher, or worse still, a church man. That type of thinker wouldn't necessarily be seeking personal glory and, in any case, returning the Narbonensis and Aquitania to the Empire would bring enough fame and honours."

"You're quite right," Xancha responded with a sigh. "There are always men who imagine that they might aspire to the highest position, king or emperor, even."

"And now Thormond's away leading the army. And the duke…here in Tolosa with his men. It looks like he's trying to ensure that Thormond is out of the way."

Xancha laughed.

"I'm sure Thormond doesn't see it that way. He has no doubts he's the best leader for the army."

"Then why isn't he the duke?"

"The king chose Ludiger. It's a matter of balance between the families."

Megana took the opportunity to gather her thoughts by carefully selecting a cake, dipping it into her wine and then taking a bite.

"Delicious," she said finally. "You Tolosans do make exceptional pastries."

Xancha gave her an ironic smile.

Megana took another bite of cake. "What then if one of the powerful families were to side with the Romans?" she asked after swallowing.

"That's out of my area," said Xancha. "I'm not a warrior, not even a trader, like you."

"I'm uneasy, Xancha. It's my job to understand men. My life as a trader depends on it. I don't like that Thormond and his allies have been sent away while Ludiger and his men remain here in Tolosa."

"Oh, Ludiger's not in Tolosa. He set off for Cadurci two days ago, and took a dozen men with him," said Xancha, "on his way to visit his relatives in Aquitania, that's what I heard."

"To get out of Tolosa, while the going is good? His lands are in the west, aren't they? So Ludiger, his family and his allies wouldn't be affected by an invasion from the east?" Megana could not prevent tension creeping into her voice.

"Is there something I haven't grasped?" added Xancha with a frown.

Megana shook her head.

"I don't know. I'm not interested in these court rivalries, and I don't want to get involved, but Count Sismond thinks there is, and that Duke Ludiger is involved in some sort of conspiracy. Perhaps it's all supposition, but nothing you've told me suggests he's wrong."

Xancha's frown deepened.

"Sismond can be very suspicious," she said, "for no good reason."

"But supposing he's right?"

"What do you want me to do?"

"Get Thormond back, as soon as possible. If Sismond *is* right, he's needed in Tolosa," Megana replied. She forced a smile onto her face. "And, as for Signy Wealda, when you see General Thormond, you can tell him I've known Signy long enough to learn that she can be very patient when she has a goal in sight. If she wants Geseric, I'm sure she'll get Geseric, even if she has to wait, even if the general is opposed."

Xancha nodded and smiled in return.

"I thought that way myself, once," she said. "I thought if only I waited then…no, it's no use dwelling on the past."

☙ Chapter 36 ❧
Agininum

Signy was gripped, almost by a fever, the result of a sleepless night and too many complicated and contradictory thoughts. The count's threat still hung over her. Her involvement could easily be painted worse than it was, a deliberate act by an enemy, rather than an honest, well, semi-honest, mistake, and she was an outsider, a perfect scapegoat. And Junius had also promised to return, and when he did he would certainly contact her, and what should she do then?

When Jorid appeared at the house in Olive Street with a summons from the count, Signy feared the worst, perhaps to be hauled before the tribunal and condemned. For an instant, she considered running away, but before she could even imagine where she could run, she was surprised to hear that Jorid had orders to escort her to the count's residence at the top of The Hill, instead of reporting to the basilica and the court.

Sismond was alone when she arrived, holding a slip of papyrus. As she entered the room, the count sighed, flipping the message back and forth as if that would rearrange the contents.

"Business as usual," muttered Sismond, looking up at Signy. "A note from your trader friend…came with the convoy."

He scratched his ear for a moment.

"I don't trust these damned imperialists," he said, finally. "I've learned not to. They've broken their word too many times over the years. So I've set a watch on those soldiers. My men have been observing them ever since we got back, ever since we discovered that Centurion Maxus had conveniently vacated his camp while I was away hunting bandits, ever since your man, Ragvald, told us he had seen nothing of them. And what have we discovered?"

Now it was Signy's turn to shake her head. Why is he telling me this? she thought. I'm guilty, obviously guilty, and there's no need. Just get it over with. Without talking so much.

"Maxus and his men have cleared the old road, all the way over the hills and almost to Agininum, not far, in fact, from Elemus' farm. They've been felling trees and clearing bushes to broaden the path through the woods, filling wet stretches, improving fords. I suspect that the reason Farmer Elemus was killed was because he came across them at their work, and maybe said he would report them to me. I think you were lucky you didn't suffer the same fate. Perhaps it was only because Junius took a liking to you."

Signy said nothing.

"Perhaps he liked you," the count continued, "perhaps he just wanted to use you…a cover if he was spotted here in Agininum."

Signy still said nothing. She had come to a similar conclusion, and did not feel comfortable.

"You said he was going to come back," the count continued. "Do you know when?"

"No, but later in the summer, he said."

"Then you must let me know if he gets in contact again."

"I will. I promise."

"And this house he has hired?"

"A house with a red door…in Baker Street. And I'm sure Junius will be in disguise. He looked like a trader last time, a beard and working man's clothes, not an officer."

"That's probably how he's been able to move so freely. We can't have eyes everywhere. But now we know where to watch, along the old track, and this house with the red door."

"You're going to punish me for what I've done," Signy suddenly blurted out, "that I've misled you?"

The count frowned.

"I've thought about it," he said. "I could easily obtain a judgement. Collaboration with the enemy, betrayal of secrets. Death…I'd make it a quick one."

He sighed and shook his head.

"But that would rather give the game away, wouldn't it? If Junius came looking for you and the whole town was buzzing with the news of your execution? He might have second thoughts about the whole operation and the traitors in Tolosa would be left to plot for another day."

He looked at her again.

"So, no. We're going to let them carry out their plan until we're quite ready, and then we're going to strike, against all of them. The challenge is going to be, my dear, that you're going to have to carry your part through to the end, too, just exactly as if we knew nothing."

"You mean meet him again?"

"I mean more than that, Signy."

"But how can I sleep with him? He betrayed me…"

The count sighed once more and got to his feet. "You'll find a way, I'm sure, just as I'll have to find a way of dealing with the traitors. You just make sure you keep Junius at ease and distracted and leave the rest to me and my men. It's not personal anymore, my dear, just a matter of tactics."

Signy rose, too, still with a heavy heart. She might not be going to a public execution, not yet anyhow, but she had been forced into a private humiliation. Long ago, when she was first stolen from her father's home, she had been sold to a brothel. Only through good fortune, or perhaps through an intervention from the gods, had she been rescued before she became a common prostitute. Now, as she left the count's palace, she felt just as if she had become a woman for hire, in other words, a whore.

"And let me make this clear," Sismond added as she stood in the doorway, "if we fail, then all our lives will be at risk, yours and mine."

Mine first, she grimly concluded.

☙ Chapter 37 ❧ Aginnum

Megana trudged up The Hill as if she had the weight of the world on her shoulders, though actually, she ruefully admitted to herself, her burdens were largely of her own making. She had returned from Tolosa the previous day to find a note from the bishop's clerk saying His Grace would be available for a meeting after the morning service. She needed to clear her head and had, as was her habit, paid an early visit to the warehouse by the river. Then she had made a small offering at the church in the marketplace, and now she was hurrying home. Victoria had promised to attend the service in the cathedral and run to her when it was over. After the bizarre episode with the message from Duke Ludiger and the need to hurry to the capital city, her appointment with the bishop had slipped to the back of the mind, and now she found she was going to have to present her proposal at very short notice.

To make matters worse, she could not shift her thoughts from her meeting with Xancha. Not the political discussion – she had long realised that discord, infighting and jealousy were as inescapable in the Visigoth Kingdom as anywhere else. The Roman Church and the old landowners hated the new masters and did all they could to undermine them. In turn, Our Men despised what they saw as relicts from the past and power-grabbing distorters of God's Word and took every opportunity they could to restrict their opponents' influence. And a third group – the opportunists – kept a sharp lookout for which way the wind was blowing, played one side against the other and shifted alliances depending on where they saw their own advantages lay. In her heart, the reception that Megana had received in Burdigala inclined her against the bishops and the landowners, but her head told her that she had to be an opportunist to survive. Romans, Goths, men, women, Christians or unbelievers, they all needed to eat and clothe themselves, help with the home, the farm or the business, or just to look important. There was no sense in picking sides.

What troubled her more was what had happened afterwards. Their talk had diverged into who and what was new in town, gossip and fashion. The maids had been sent for more wine, and dinner from the food stall up the street. Night had fallen, and Xancha had only then begun to make preparations to leave. Before doing so, she had insisted on *trying Vipso's bed for old times' sake*, as she put it. She had lain down, closed her eyes and promptly fallen asleep. Megana had been flabbergasted. There was only one bed in the apartment, except for a rough mattress which Delia customarily occupied, and Megana was certainly not going to spend the night on that.

"Is it your mistress's habit to fall asleep on other people's beds?" Megana had asked Xancha's maid. "And if so, what's the customary solution?" But the girl had simply tittered at the sight of her slumbering employer. Sharing a bed was not unusual when travelling, Megana considered, and she and Delia had huddled together on many occasions over the years. That had been a simple necessity. So, she decided, was the current situation. She had stretched herself out beside her guest and, after a long and uneasy passage, finally fallen asleep herself.

Megana had awoken with a start, feeling a hand softly stroking her belly. She had opened her eyes and found herself looking into Xancha's dark eyes. The ex-dancer must have awoken in the night, because she was as naked as the day she was born, and probably a great deal more comfortable, nestled up against her unsuspecting companion.

"You're really quite a pretty woman," Xancha had whispered. "You're wasting yourself living alone like an anchorite."

For a moment, Megana had lain still, wondering uneasily what she should do.

"You're as stiff as a board," Xancha had said, stretching herself with a movement which had reminded Megana of a snake about to swallow its prey.

It's hardly surprising, she thought, when I open my eyes and find Tolosa's most notorious courtesan tickling my tummy.

"You should awaken your body," Xancha had continued. "You think too much."

Megana, by this time fully awoken, had managed to gather her wits.

"My body is quite awake, Xancha, my dear," she had said, "and it's telling me I need to go and take a piss," and with that she had rolled off the bed and begun a search for the cape that she habitually used to cover herself, then set out to the latrines in the yard.

Xancha had watched her quite unashamedly as she retrieved the cloak, merely commenting, "You're not too old to change."

Megana had more or less fled out into the hall and down the stairs to the yard, where she had found the two maids standing by the well, giggling together like new best friends. Their laughter vanished when they had caught sight of her, and one after the other, they had hurried up the steps which Megana had just descended.

When Megana had returned, to her relief the ex-dancer was up and dressed and waved away the offer of breaking her fast before she departed.

Xancha merely pecked Megana on the cheek and whispered in her ear, "Next time you're in town, come and stay with me for a few days instead of hiding in this uncomfortable place."

Megana had been disturbed. She was still disturbed. She prided herself on her cool and rational thinking. Of course, there were times when she felt lonely, she reflected. She was an exile, had lost her home, her family, trying to make her way in a world of strangers, a woman in a world of men, but you had only to look at Signy to see where "awakening your body" got you. Jumping into bed with strangers without a second thought: it was easy enough to get neck deep in trouble without bringing it upon yourself by letting emotions get out of hand. That she knew from experience. Most of the time she managed to push these feelings aside, but now and then, like after this chat with Xancha, they thrust their way into the forefront of her mind. Xancha's words vexed her reason, just as Xancha's touch had chafed her skin.

No, no, she thought, this is not the state of mind to be in when I have to pay a business visit to the bishop.

A clerk greeted her with a soft smile and led her through an archway and a maze of small rooms to a study overlooking the courtyard where Bishop Anastasius was waiting for her. His Grace stood when she entered, held out his hands, not for her to kiss his ring, but as a simple greeting.

"Merchant Fabiana," he said, "I'm sorry we haven't met earlier."

He spoke with a voice that suggested he was well aware of her hesitation, and understood.

She had only seen him at a distance in the church, and in the flickering light of the candles her poor eyes had provided her no clear impression. Close up, and in his well-lit study, she could see he was a tall man, slender, as if he took his fasting seriously, with dark eyes and thick dark hair, just a tinge of grey revealing his age.

She stood uncertainly until he waved her to a soft padded chair. The bishop himself crossed to a lectern, took up a roll of papyrus, pulled up a high wooden stool and sat down.

"Megana," she said, "my name."

His brow furrowed for a moment, and then he smiled.

"Ah, yes…Anastasius, my name," the bishop replied. There was a brief moment of silence, before he continued. "I've heard so much about you." A faint smile crossed his face. "Even before you arrived."

Megana only felt embarrassed.

"I've known Lanius for years," he went on, "ever since he was a child, and your brother's wife, Icauna. I stop in and see them every time I'm in Agatha. Alexander and I share a passion for new books. Their mother, Mistress Ophelia, has been a great support for me ever since I first came to Agininum."

"He's my half-brother…Alexander…my half-brother."

"Yes, yes…Alexander…a wonderfully cultured man."

"But a hopeless trader," said Megana.

"Perhaps," said the bishop, with a laugh, "and I suppose that brings us to our business."

What's he heard about me, thought Megana, that I'm rude and difficult, and only care about money?

The bishop flicked open the scroll and held the sheet up to catch the light from the window.

"I'm no expert on these old deeds," he said, "but Ophi told me that there was some mistake in the surveying, and that a sliver of land that should have been included in the donation to the monastery has remained in the diocese's hands…if a diocese can have hands," he added with a smile.

"The bulk of your land, Bishop," she said, "lies to the west of my small parcel, and the land to the east was transferred to the monastery, all except the area between two small streams where the boundary was described incorrectly in the donation."

"So your property is entirely surrounded by the bishopric?"

"Essentially, yes." At last she began to feel more in control of the situation. "I have been" – she hesitated for a moment – "considering donating the land to the church…"

The bishop frowned, evidently parsing the grammar.

"It would certainly be practical if what you are saying is true."

"Yes, but I changed my mind. You see, the land beside the river has been neglected. Once it was good farmland, but now the fields are just covered with scrub. If I donated my property to the church, then it would simply remain a wasteland, in fact as most of the church land is now."

Though *her* plot was no longer a wasteland. Thaddeus, after making a delivery of supplies, had reported that the Hibernian slaves had made great progress with the ditching, and she had ordered him to give them her permission to plant their own vegetable gardens on his next visit.

The bishop looked pained.

"I'm a man of the cloth," he said, "of learning, books, philosophy…not a farmer."

"I'm not a farmer, either," said Megana. "I've never ploughed a furrow or sowed a seed in my life, but I know good land when I see it, and I know how to find competent tenants."

"Yes, well…but we have property much nearer to Agininum that needs supervision." There was a certain anxiety in the bishop's voice.

"That's precisely my proposal," said Megana. "Instead of me donating my land to you, you hand over the management of your lands to me." She paused, watching his expression. "It was Sister Ophelia's idea," she said, now with a smile on her part, "that I take on the responsibility on behalf of the monastery too."

"I see," said the bishop, frowning.

Have you heard that I'm bold and determined, thought Megana, and that I know how to make a good deal? Perhaps that doesn't interest Your Grace.

"My plan will bring in a much greater and more consistent income for the church," she added, "than sitting on a corner of swampland. Especially after I've built a winepress and repaired the boat mooring."

The bishop pursed his lips and leaned back on his stool, as if he was examining a slightly threatening animal.

Megana rose to her feet.

"And you and Ophi have already reached an agreement, I assume," the bishop murmured. "I'd have to check, of course, with the church lawyers, make sure everything was laid out clearly and according to the law and customs."

"Of course," said Megana, "I'd expect nothing less. So when can I anticipate an answer?"

The bishop examined the scroll in his hand once again, and then slowly rolled it tight.

"Perhaps we should pay a visit to the property before we close the deal. It would be so much easier to envisage your proposal if we could see the land before us."

"That would be three-days' uncomfortable ride…there… and three days back again."

"The company would undoubtedly make the journey shorter. We could, for example, read the holy word to one another."

Was the man crazy, thought Megana, that she would waste six days, sitting in a *cisium*, studying the damned Bible? Hadn't she spent enough time on that in her youth? By God, if this bishop wasn't fat and corrupt, then he was some sort of a fanatic.

Suddenly, Anastasius laughed out loud.

"You should have seen the expression on your face, Mistress Megana. I'm joking of course. We really should ride over and take a look, but not just now, and I promise you, no Bible. I'm sure I would have a great deal to learn from you about land management, but first I really do have to consult the lawyer. Sometimes these old donations are all tied up with restrictive clauses, and I wouldn't want to fall afoul of the legal profession. They're quite as tiresome as the clergy."

He rose to his feet and held out his hand. She took it in hers, gave him a weak smile, turned and left. The clerk escorted her through the maze of rooms to the entrance and dismissed her onto the street.

She felt herself grinding her teeth. She had made a fool of herself, she reflected, first by being pompous, by needlessly mentioning she had decided not to make a gift of land to the church, then by missing his attempt at humour and thinking he was as pompous as she had been. All that was just another sign she was not on her best form.

But he was interested in her proposal, she considered. The deal was almost in her hands. She would manage the whole lands of the monastery and those of the diocese along the Oltis, and when other landowners saw that, they would be at her door begging her to do the same for them.

And she had been pompous with Xancha, and mean-spirited, too. The dancer had only tried to give her some friendly advice and she had spurned it. Xancha had reached out and touched her, literally, and she had acted like she had been assaulted. Oh, damn! No wonder she felt alone, if she rejected help, if she couldn't see a joke. What was the matter with her?

ଓ Chapter 38 ଛ
Agininum

What shall I do? thought Signy. I'll have to meet Junius again, pretend that nothing is different, pretend that I want to lie with him. I'll have to go through with it all so he doesn't realise his plan has been disclosed. If his suspicions are aroused, there's a good chance he'll think I've betrayed him, and it's not hard to imagine how he'll react. However much he cares for me, and I wonder how much that really is, it wouldn't be worth a grain of sand if he believes he's been uncovered, believes he's isolated in the town of his enemies. There are ways to avoid a meeting, of course, she reckoned. I could be conveniently absent, be called away urgently elsewhere. I could plead sick, my time of the month, but that would be to forsake my role in the affair, to run away when others are putting their lives at stake. And beyond that, if I don't play my part, then Sismond could take that as further evidence that I'm complicit in the whole matter. On the other hand, if I show up acting the innocent lover, maybe Junius won't even be interested in bed. Maybe he'll just be hard-hearted enough to dispose of me as an inconvenient witness, as he seems to have done with Xeno and with Farmer Elemus and Jeanna. However, Signy calculated, whatever option she considered most likely, she could not avoid the conclusion that her life was at stake, and the immediate response of shame, of revulsion at the idea of sleeping with a man she now considered to be a murderous deceiver, passed over into trepidation, apprehension, foreboding, concern about her own anxious reaction. At least she was already one step ahead of Junius, she thought, unlike his other victims, since she had seen through him, since *her* suspicions had been aroused, but that advantage would be lost if she behaved in an unusual manner and gave herself away. The only solution was to ensure that Junius had an enjoyable evening, a pleasurable night, and for that she had to disguise her anxiety, to behave naturally, to continue to appear like a woman meeting her lover.

Signy was always wary about dipping into her own medicine cabinet. She had used potions at times to reduce the risk of becoming pregnant ever since she had first been bedded. They were unpleasant, but then she had had no desire to risk her life by carrying an unwanted child, and she had no wish to be mother to a crowd of screaming infants. She had also taken part in ceremonies with the sisters of Freya, who used potions to gain insight, to see the gods, but those had been a component of the ritual, in sacred moments, bounded by chants, linked to certain acts, not self-medication. And occasionally she sampled her mixtures herself to test the potency, or to know how to describe the effects to her patients. But now she was facing an emergency, and she would have to use whatever means to endure that she could, and that included the contents of her medicine cabinet.

She had a vague memory of one case, back in Juteland, when she was still learning. A woman, Kjer, was her name, a farmer's wife, had come to her guide, the wise woman Irmengaard, complaining that she no longer wanted to lie with her husband.

"It used to be such a pleasure," she had said. "I have five children to prove that. But now, I don't want a sixth, and I feel so tense and worried, and my husband has become fat and clumsy." The farmer's wife had burst into tears. "I'm worried he'll turn to the yard maids for his needs, and then, then…"

Irmengaard had listened to her story and told her to come back in a week. Then the wise woman had sat and thought for a while.

"If Kjer could put aside her worries – we can always help her if she falls pregnant again – and imagine her husband as he once was, a young man full of vigour, then she may be spared the sight of her home filled with little bastards."

"And the whole household will be happier if the serving girls aren't competing for the master's favours," Signy had pointed out.

Irmengaard had merely smiled. Living alone, she had no experience of that problem. Then she had begun to assemble the ingredients to brew. What had she selected? And what had she brewed? Whatever Irmengaard had prepared, Kjer had returned once, accepted the medicine and never come back. Signy had passed her on a field path one day, belly bulging with yet another addition to the family.

Signy stared at her medicine cabinets. How terrible not to remember, she thought. Once I couldn't read or write and everything had to be remembered, but now, when I can make notes or turn to a book, I no longer remember anything.

There was a soft knock at her door. Only one person had learned to knock like that: Ferona.

"Mistress, are you alright?" her new assistant asked.

"Not really," Signy replied, though she did not yet trust Ferona enough to tell her the reason for her worries. "I have to remember the formulation for a medication. The memory must be inside me. The problem is to dredge it up. I have to imagine myself back in Juteland, back to Irmengaard's house, to my teacher's home, and then I can recapture the moment."

She crossed the room and pulled the shutters closed.

"Do you want me to leave you in peace?" the girl asked.

"No, Ferona, you can stay, you can help me. Find me a tablet and a writing point, and then sit quietly on the stool and keep watch over me."

She lay down on her bed and closed her eyes and began to breath slowly. It had been years since she had left Juteland, left Irmengaard. How much she had been through since then! But all that had to be put aside, put aside so she could see the interior of Irmengaard's cottage, to see Irmengaard herself. At first she had sat quietly after the farmer's wife had gone. Kjer she remembered quite clearly, and her husband was Hjorth, Hjorth Duvesson, and his children…their names didn't come to mind, but they were three boys and two girls. And there had been two more, who had died as babies. And they lived up the river a little way. They were Thorgill's vassals. Hjorth must have been with them on the expedition…but that was the wrong line of thought. She opened her eyes for a moment, caught sight of Ferona sitting watching her, exactly as she had sat watching Irmengaard after Kjer had left. Then the wise woman had risen from the stool and gone over to the shelves of pots and baskets which lined one wall of her cottage. She had stood for a moment in front of the shelves, and then she had chosen, selected a pot and taken it down, extracted a couple of dried mushrooms, then a basket and a couple of berries. A thought intruded…the fungi and herbs on her own shelves were not stored in the same order as Irmengaard's. She could not simply remember what her friend had done and do the same. She had to remember exactly what was in those pots.

And then an inspiration came to her: the materials Irmengaard had assembled were the same ones, or very similar at least, to those that the wise women used in the ritual drink, the drink that took you away from the present and into a deeper reality, made you feel at one with the people around you and with the universe. That's what her guide had done, she thought, to allow Kjer to escape from her fears and worries for a moment, and enjoy being with her husband once again, perhaps remembering the old times when they had been young and carefree.

Signy sat up suddenly and opened her eyes. She saw Ferona come to with a start. How long had she been lying there? Had the girl fallen asleep? But she had the answer. The formulation for the ritual drink she could remember. It was well-imprinted on her mind. Irmengaard had warned her many times as to its potency and the correct time and place to use it. There was always a risk if the user was not in the right frame of mind, not encircled in the ritual, that evil spirits could break in, that fear and madness could take over. Irmengaard must have watered down the preparation she had made for Kjer considerably, otherwise who knows what the woman would have seen.

Ferona was observing her, wide-eyed, as she must once have observed Irmengaard.

"I know the answer," Signy said, picking up the wax tablet and writing quickly before the moment was lost. Then she stopped and examined her notes. They were scribbled in Jutish, or at least an approximation to Jutish, since she had learned that tongue before she could read or write. The names of the mushrooms, they made no sense here in Agininum. No one called the herbs by their Jutish names. Now she would have to choose the equivalents, not just the different names for the same plant, but which plants that grew in the south could be used to replace ingredients only found in the north country. There was no way she could create the *mixtura* exactly as it would have been in Juteland. She would have to do her best and hope.

She stood up and went over to her shelves, and almost as if she was in a dream, as if she had become Irmengaard in her vision, began to pick the items she would need. Ferona sat still on her stool, studying Signy as she had once studied her teacher, the wise woman, the *völva*.

☙ Chapter 39 ❧
By the Oltis

Jorid and Svein sat concealed among the trees overlooking the ford across the Oltis leading from the Roman camp. The flow in the river was at its lowest point of the year. They had watched Maxus' men wading back and forth all day. The water did not even reach to their knees. The soldiers had attached a rope to a stout tree on the far bank and dragged it across to a similar anchor on the near side, so that it spanned the ford. Once they had understood what the soldiers were doing, they had sent Tomas, the militiaman, scuttling through the trees to where his horse was hidden, and away with a report to Sismond.

The count and his men had been observing the Romans for ten days. Surveillance was not so easy when most of the hills were covered with bare grassland, but the Romans stayed on the green way and, as keen hunters, Sismond and his men knew many alternative paths and tracks.

"Listen," said Jorid, as a faint sound of cheering was carried across the river by the breeze.

"Lur-horns," said Svein, "I mean trumpets, big ones, war horns."

"The *cornu*, you mean," said Jorid, "signalling the advance."

Svein said nothing more; Jorid had understood him from the start.

Nothing happened. That was the inconvenience of remaining concealed, a man had to wait for the action to come to him, instead of seeking it out.

Still nothing happened.

And then something did happen. Horsemen appeared from among the trees on the opposite bank. So far away they were difficult to recognise, but Jorid smiled to himself. One of them was carrying the banner, not the eagle of the legions of old, but the colours of the unit commanded by Maxus, and there were more banners than just that one. The first of the horsemen splashed into the river. The banner carriers followed. By the time they were halfway across, Jorid identified the centurion, and beside him rode a second commander, more important, judging from Maxus' body language. Sismond's deputy could not resist tapping Svein on the shoulder and pointing.

"Big man!"

The Northman said nothing in reply, merely watching the horsemen complete their journey across the river and up the near bank, only a hundred paces away. His eyes shifted back across the ford. Now there were infantry, tentatively entering the river, using the rope as a guide. One by one they stepped off the bank and into the water, and slowly, slowly waded across.

Svein had been used to counting sheep in his time and began to reckon in a soft chant.

"A lot," he whispered, finally giving up his tally. There were clearly more men advancing across the ford than only Maxus' century.

The first of the infantry reached the near bank and began to climb up the track. There was shouting and calling as the officers began to form them up into ranks, laughing and cursing by men having to deal with wet feet when the officers had ridden.

Jorid cursed, too. There were times when he wished he could write properly. Nonetheless, he would do his best by cutting notches into a stick. It would give his chief some idea of how many men he would be facing.

"Holy shit!" said Svein suddenly.

Jorid looked up from the stick.

"Auxiliaries? Cavalry?" he whispered.

More horsemen were gathering on the far bank as the last of the infantry entered the water.

"Who can they be? Not Romans, surely…Germans maybe, Huns even, mercenaries, or renegade Goths, hoping to gain by collaborating with the Empire."

Svein's only response was a grunt, and then, "Seen enough?"

"You're right. They're on the move at last."

Jorid tapped Svein on the shoulder, jerked with his thumb and nodded. The two men began to crawl slowly backwards, until the bushes obscured them. Only then they stood up and, as experienced trackers, silently threaded their way through the undergrowth until they reached their horses. Without saying another word, they swung themselves up and rode off.

After about half a mile, they left the riverbank vegetation and set course over the grassland. They would be out of sight of the advancing Roman infantry, and the cavalry would only now have come over the river.

"I hope they can maintain discipline," said Jorid, as they urged on their horses. "I would hate to think of those barbarians swarming over these hills."

"They have a plan, I'm sure," said Svein.

"To Agininum," said Jorid. "Maxus and his men didn't spend all summer clearing the track unless they were planning to use it." Then he had second thoughts about what he had just uttered. A host of horse-riding barbarians descending on Agininum was nothing to wish for.

"I hope the walls hold," he muttered under his breath.

␃ Chapter 40 ␄ Agininum

Medicine alone would not solve her problems, thought Signy, but it would at least get her over the threshold, get her into his bed. But she had to consider practical matters, too. Junius had already told her that he would be bringing some of his men with him. He had not said why, but it must have something to do with the operation Sismond feared. Supposing she was met not by her lover, but by his *optio*, the man she was certain had killed the farmer and his wife.

She found Henrik in the yard, and held out her dagger.

"Sharpen this, Henrik. I fear I may need to use it, and I need an edge that will cut through a man's clothes."

The stablemaster took the blade and stroked it against the back of his hand.

"This is already sharp enough I could shave with it," he laughed, but when he caught her eye he stopped laughing. "I'll do what I can," he said. "I've had several similar requests, all urgent."

If she had to, she could take on the *optio* if he was alone. He would not expect her to be armed or know that she had practised using the dagger long before she ever set foot in the Kingdom of Tolosa. She was confident she could take him by surprise, defend herself, but protecting herself against a whole group of men would be impossible. She went in search of Grunwald.

"I'll need your help tonight, yours and Asser's and Hrasmus'."

Grunwald grimaced, as if he was embarrassed.

"I…I…I've been talking to the count," the warrior said. "He's also asked for our help. There's a man come into Agininum, an agent for the Romans, and he's brought with him a small force."

"So you know?" she said.

"Know…I only know what I've been told by the count. He's setting out the defence of the town right now."

I have to tell him, she thought.

"I have a role to play," she said. "The agent…he's the man I met in the camp when I crossed the river. The count didn't tell you, I'm sure, but I've met him again, here…here in Agininum."

She had to force out the admission.

"I've been sleeping with him."

Grunwald's face betrayed his confusion.

"I slept with him because he's a handsome, well-spoken man, and I wanted a fuck, Grunwald." She knew what he was thinking. If all you wanted was a fuck, I would have been willing to do the job. Yes, but Grunwald, she said to herself, we've known each other too long and that would have complicated matters between me and you, between me and all the Jute boys if they thought I had favourites, if they thought that I might be available to sleep with them. You're my team, my loyal team, and I want to keep you all that way.

"It is what it is, Grunwald," she said. "I don't regret lying with him. I got out of it what I wanted. But now I regret walking round the town with him. I imagined his thoughts were on me, and I suppose they were to some extent, though not solely, it seems."

"He's holed up in Baker Street," said Grunwald glumly.

"In the house with the red door. I know the place. When did he arrive?"

"Yesterday."

"He's going to contact me, I'm sure."

"And will you go to him?"

"Yes, I have to. If I don't, he'll suspect something's amiss."

"And you'll stay?" Grunwald's tone held a note of deep gloom; his eyes fixed on the ground.

"I must. It's what I've done before, but I've always left early in the morning, so I got home before anyone was awake.

Grunwald, you must follow me this time. Bring some of the men. Stake out the house…discreetly. I'm worried. If this is the final push, unless he has taken a real fancy to me, he won't need me anymore."

"I'll wait," said Grunwald, "and if that bastard so much as harms a hair of you, I'll kill him. Anyway," he added, shrugging, "that's what the count wants us to do, hang around by the house with the red door in Baker Street, and if they make a move, a move out into the town, we're to follow them, and once we know what they're planning, we're to kill them, all of them."

"Don't leave me there alone, please."

Grunwald looked up and nodded.

"I'd do anything for you, more than I ever would for the count."

"Thank you for saying that, Grunwald," she said with a smile. "We've been through a lot together. You know the Fates have decreed I must follow the path they have laid out for me. Tomorrow night that path probably leads to the house with the red door in Baker Street. If you hear me scream, then I'll need you. But…I may need you anyway. Let's agree a signal…the owl call, the same owl call we used against the bandits."

Grunwald nodded again, wiping the back of his hand across his eye.

"I'll not leave you. I'll be there."

☙ Chapter 41 ❧
By the Oltis

Centurion Maxus watched as the first of his men splashed through the ford. Today they had left behind their spades and axes. Today they were wearing their armour and carrying their swords and shields. He was proud of what he had done, proud of what they had done. They had cleared the old way from the Cadurci road beyond their fort, all across the hills until they had almost reached the road between Agininum and Tolosa, almost to the banks of the Garunna. It would have been a great deal easier if they had been given the task of running a new road straight over the hills like the soldiers of old, but his taskmasters had insisted that the work was to proceed with the greatest possible secrecy, along the historical route, through the forests and across the valleys, well away from habitation. They had left the last hundred paces before the Tolosa road unmodified, a narrow, overgrown track. His taskmasters did not want any travellers up the valley of the Garunna wondering why a broad path had been opened up, seemingly leading nowhere. His taskmasters certainly did not want any especially curious passers-by turning from their familiar route and following his carefully prepared road back to its source, this ford over the Oltis and his neatly laid-out camp on the far bank.

It had been bad enough when some louts had burned down his camp during the winter.

Maxus shook his head.

Some people seemed too clever by half, but he supposed Junius had been right, and the count and his followers needed to be distracted. But it had been an unnecessary risk that the bandits passed so close to the camp on their raid. It was just as well that he had withdrawn his men in time, back towards Cadurci, and ordered the few guards who remained to lie about their whereabouts when the count and his minions showed up.

"Job well done, Centurion," said the man striding towards him, Tribune Pelagius. "If the water was any higher, we wouldn't have been able to cross in order."

Maxus smiled and nodded. Pelagius clapped him on the shoulder, and then turned to stand beside him and watch the advancing troops.

Not like we had to last year and all this spring, thought Maxus, hauling ourselves across a torrent fed by winter snow, a handful at a time. It would have taken days to get the whole battalion over. That's why the task had taken so long, that and the lack of manpower. He smiled to himself. Centurion, they called him, but he'd never had a hundred men to command, at best forty last year, and that included the camp staff. A matter of money, they said, and no doubt the fact that able-bodied men had a better chance of riches by joining one of the groups of auxiliary cavalry like those who had arrived in the last couple of days. It would be them who would get the best of the booty but, he reflected, then the cavalry would be taking the greatest risk.

"Don't worry," Junius had said, when he had told him to leave the last hundred yards of the track uncleared. "The barbarians will have other things on their minds by the time your men reach that bottleneck."

Once they were out on open ground, Junius had told him, the horsemen had been ordered to make for Agininum by the shortest route.

"By the time they get there, my men will have opened the north gate, and our allies will be able to ride in unopposed."

Maxus chuckled to himself. You've got to hand it to him, he thought, that Junius. Finding a woman in Agininum to disguise his visits. Would they have one last night together? he wondered. Did Junius care enough to protect his lover from the cavalry, or would he tidy up loose ends himself? Maxus didn't like massacres on the whole. They were messy, chaotic and left too much room for chance, but he had to admit they were a useful component of military strategy. Burning and looting one town, slaughtering its inhabitants, carrying off the surviving women and children to the slave markets, would persuade the others up and down the valley of the Garunna that it was not worth resisting. Better, their counts would conclude, to remain as humble servants of the Empire than to suffer…what was his name now? Junius had told him…Sismond, that's right…Sismond's fate.

Of course, there will be plenty to be done by a man like me, he reckoned, once the horsemen have finished their task, once the fires have been extinguished and the bodies buried. From Junius' account, a good part of Agininum consisted of filthy alleys and stinking passageways, houses of wood and wattle. Those would undoubtedly burn nicely, and once the charred remains had been cleared away, the alleys could be replaced by straight, paved roads, with a gutter down the middle so that, with every rainstorm, the rubbish was washed efficiently away into the river. And the houses would be rebuilt in stone, and filled by people who appreciated organisation and order, who appreciated the Empire, and the men who ran it.

"Well," said the tribune, suddenly. "It's time we're finding our horses and getting underway. Despite your efforts, we've a long trek ahead of us all day and through the night."

Pity the bastards who have to walk, thought Maxus. He had been one of those bastards once, until his qualities had been recognised. The Empire needed men like him.

☙ Chapter 42 ❧ Aginīnum

Signy selected her clothes carefully: the grey dress with the ribbon of decoration down the front and round the edge, the one Junius had said fitted her like a second skin, because it did, because it had been made that way. Then she took up her belt and fitted it round her waist, checking her dagger. Junius' invitation had been delivered that morning, carried by one of the boys who ran messages for the market traders. The note had been no glad surprise. The note was not even a surprise. She wondered if the Empire's spy knew though he and his men were disguised as a merchant and his labourers, they were being watched.

She was almost ready to leave, just one more thing to do. She took the glass vial containing the *mixtura*, and tipped one, two, three drops into the bowl of a silver spoon. She had no real idea how much would be needed, but three drops were enough to feel the liquid in her mouth, to feel it slide down her throat as she swallowed. She pushed the cork firmly back into the vial, which she then dropped into the soft leather purse that hung from her belt and pulled the strings tight.

Then she took up a mantle, a plain dull brown mantle, which she wrapped round her shoulders. She clipped the brooch then flipped up the hood to cover her head. She could be any woman of the town, coming home from a day in the market, in a cookshop, heading out to visit a friend. But the people who had to know would recognise her.

She left her room on the verge of darkness and crossed the courtyard to pass under the arch and out onto the portico overlooking the garden. Today there was really no need to leave by the garden gate, furtively, as she had done on previous occasions. She was sure that everyone in the house knew where she was going, who she was meeting, what she was intending to do there, or get done to her, and why. Nonetheless, she preferred to avoid their gaze and the knowing looks, so once again she descended the steps into the garden and took the path towards the fountain, sparkling and twinkling in the moonlight.

A sudden instinct took hold of her. She fumbled at the strings of the purse, and pushing the vial aside, felt for a small coin.

"Take care of me," she whispered, as she tossed the coin into the fountain.

She stepped out of the gate, which swung quietly closed. She glanced up and down the street and took a deep breath. She knew there were eyes following her. That man, standing in the shadows, who dodged into an alley as she approached. Was he one of the stable hands? Was he even now running through the passages and back streets to warn the men waiting and watching in Baker Street that she was on the way? As she walked down the hill towards the forum, she started to relax. Let them watch and wait. Let them strain their ears to listen. She felt the strength of Circe, of Diana, of Cartimandua, of Sváva, of Meadh, expanding inside her, and she knew she could endure.

--oo00oo--

Signy turned into Baker Street. The house with the red door was the fourth on her right. As she approached, she was sorely tempted to glance around, to check if there was anyone standing in the shadows of one of the other doorways but, with an effort, she suppressed the desire. She had no idea if Junius was watching, or one of his men. Even then she could not suppress a movement of her hand to check her dagger, hidden beneath her cloak, but after a touch to her waist, she raised her fist to knock. There was no need. The red door swung open before she had touched it. For a moment, she could not help but tense up. Who was waiting for her in the shadow of the entrance?

"My dear Signy," came Junius' voice, "how I've been longing to see you again."

That sound, the smell of his customary perfume, the feel of his arms around her as he drew her into the passageway, drove away what little of her fears remained. For a flash, one clear part of her mind told her that this was stupid, that the man who was holding her was a dangerous enemy, but that flash was extinguished the moment his lips touched hers.

There was food, as always, beakers of wine, the dancing shadows of lamplight. He made no secret that he had been in Cadurci, visiting the count, and described the town. She asked him about Arelate. Yes, he had been there, too.

"I haven't even been as far as Tolosa," she confessed. "Everything is still so new, even after a year! I still have to live through others' stories."

He refilled her glass, popped a small fig into her waiting mouth.

There was another flash of clarity. What a fool I'm being, she thought, like a stupid girl, talking nonsense when there are serious matters at stake.

"What about your men, downstairs?" she said, suddenly aware of the soldiers' voices rising from the room below, loud guffaws and banging of metal objects. "I don't feel comfortable…knowing they are there, eavesdropping on us."

"They'll be going out…on patrol," Junius replied, "along the river."

She gave him an anxious look, wrapped her arms around her knees, as if she was protecting herself. He got to his feet.

"Very well, my love, I'll go down and tell them to leave now."

He turned and went out onto the landing.

"Hey, *optio*! Isn't it time you were on your way!" he yelled down to the floor below.

The raised voices and laughter continued.

"Hey!" Junius stepped out onto the landing and shouted again.

The laughter died away, and there was a sound of scraping of stools or a bench against tiles.

"You want something, sir?" came a voice from below.

"Yes…a bit of peace and quiet. Isn't it time you men got into position?"

There was the unmistakable heavy thump of boots on the staircase, and Junius took a couple of steps back into the room.

A face appeared in the doorway, the face of Junius' *optio*, the man who had escorted her to the storage hut in the Roman camp. For a moment, Signy's heart almost stopped as he turned to her, a frown passing over his face. Junius must have told his men he was seeing his woman, perhaps even laughing with them about his conquest, his clever strategy.

Was the *optio* making a connection, becoming suspicious? Did he recognise her, Signy thought, though the first time he had seen her she had been dressed as a young man, and now she was obviously a woman?

The man scratched his forehead for a moment, and then turned to Junius.

"Sorry to disturb you, sir," he began, with a nod towards Signy, "but the boys still had a few questions about the operation."

"Oh, very well," said Junius with more than a hint of exasperation. He turned towards Signy. "I'll just be a moment, dear, although why a mere patrol can be so complicated, I don't understand."

Once more the *optio* frowned and cast a glimpse in her direction, but he said nothing, merely turning and descending the stairs, heavy footed, once again. No…probably he was just curious what type of desperate female was willing to make herself available to his officer.

As she listened to their fading steps, the realisation she was uneasy about the men worried her. They must have been there all the time, she thought, even as I stepped in through the door. Why didn't I care about them then? Was I so foolishly overwhelmed? Earlier she had heard them talking in the rooms below, but it had not bothered her. Privacy was a luxury, but just now the soldiers had begun to feel intrusive, threatening, even. Was this a sign that her confidence was waning, just when it was most necessary? Had she made a mistake with the *mixtura*? Perhaps, out of caution, she had simply made the potion too weak. Was the effect now wearing off? And the appearance of the *optio* had disturbed her as well, though that was not so surprising. He had clearly annoyed Junius, too. Nevertheless, better to be on the safe side, she decided, quickly standing up and crossing to the chest where she had placed her cloak and her belt. She pulled the vial from her purse and drew out the cork. How much should she take…a couple more drops? Would that be sufficient to get her through the night? Her eye caught Junius' beaker, still half-filled with wine. Suppose, she thought, suppose I add a couple of drops to his drink. He won't notice. She leaned over, tipped the vial, one, two drops. Suddenly, she heard footsteps coming back up the stairs and straightened. She could not possibly let him see the bottle. She hastily she took a swig, jammed the cork back on and slipped it back into the purse.

"They're on their way," he said. "Now, there's no one to disturb us."

"Thank you," she answered, kicking off her sandals.

She returned to the cushions and sat down.

"More wine?" he asked, reaching for the flask and topping up his own beaker.

"Why not," she replied, reaching out.

His eyes met hers as they drank.

It's getting rather warm, she suddenly thought.

"Perhaps I could open the shutters a little, let in some cool air," she said, jumping to her feet. If he thought there was some contradiction in her desire that his men were sent away for the sake of her privacy and allowing the entire street to hear what they would be doing, he did not show it.

She cracked open the shutters, peered out. The street below was empty.

"It's almost as warm outside," she said, turning back. "I just have to cool down." She walked back across the room, feeling every undulation in the rough boards under her feet.

"You don't mind," she said, as she came towards him, fumbling at the brooch which held her dress in place. With a snap, she managed to open it, and the garment fell to the floor.

She was sitting in her undergown, took a sip from her wine, a bite from her pastry. He switched position so that he was next to her, filled his beaker again, put his arm around her, nibbled her ear, and she giggled.

Even the undergown soon began to feel like a burden, so she stood up, shook her shoulders and let it drop to the floor. She could feel the air against her bare skin, and as she snuggled beside him, the cloth of the cushions seemed as rough as a stone, his skin like sand against hers. She took up her glass again and with a tight grip raised it to her mouth. How very peculiar, she thought suddenly. I'm stark naked and sitting eating and drinking and Junius seems to accept the situation as if it is entirely normal.

Junius could not keep his eyes off her, could not keep his hands off her. His lightest touch felt like a jab, like pins being stuck into her. Even so, she began to feel a terrible desire. She wanted him naked, too, and with her.

"Come," she said, "come," and stood up. She crossed to the bed and lay down, watching as he disrobed. She rolled onto her back as he came to her.

Memories began to flood into her mind, memories of Juteland. The last time she had felt this way she had been with Irmengaard, with the sisters of Freya, round the fire, by the lake, before the sacrifice. She remembered the chanting, the singing, the strange feeling of the heat against her skin, the dancing women, tattooed or painted, their bodies shimmering in the leaping flames, almost lost in the play between the light and the shadows. She still could not remember how the rituals ended but she had been so young, so curious, so excited. And she was excited now, excited as his hands explored her body. She opened her legs to let him in, and suddenly a wave of fire exploded through her, ebbing and flowing, not painful but wonderful, ecstatic. She heard a shriek. It took her a moment to realise she had made the sound herself.

He was above her, his face only inches from hers. He was the one who should be moving, but she felt he was still and that it was her who was surging back and forth. She placed her hands beside her, flat on the bed, to steady herself. His face began to dissolve into its elements, brown and black circles and squares, like a poor-quality mosaic, and then the pieces became separated, drifted apart, so there was no longer a face in front of her, just the impression of a face, the impression of a body.

Whirls of colour began to circulate in her mind like waves washing against a shore, sparkles and flashes as if a multicoloured fire was burning inside her head. And someone was playing a trumpet, first low and then high and then jumping from one note to another, and someone else was playing a drum, *thump*, *thump*, *thump*. Was it inside the room or outside? And it felt like someone was whipping her, or she was touching a fire, or walking through nettles or brambles or thistles, all over her body, starting between her legs and surging out to her hands and feet and up to her head, and all in time with the thumping and the waves of light. Then the waves broke up into sparks, and the trumpet became only squeaks and squeals, and the feelings became pokes and pricks. All sense of time and order had vanished, and the sensations mixed together into one enormous roiling chaos.

Then the strange feeling began to ebb away…first the poking and pricking, and then the squealing, and finally the sparks coalesced back into waves, lapping gently against a shore, with a gentle *swish*, *swish*, and the feeling of sand grains brushing against her skin.

Slowly she began to become aware of herself, that her thoughts were beginning to flow in a directional manner, that her body had an outer and an inner, had limits, and there were objects and existences beyond those limits. There was an emptiness, which began to take on the shape of the room, a flatness beneath which began to resemble a bed, a warmth, a soft object beside her which must be another person.

To begin with she simply lay still, allowing the normal feelings to be apprehended, the light in the room, the sensation of the bed beneath her. Then the idea that she could move began to creep into her mind. She tried to move her arm, and it felt like she was dragging it against a rough stone, that her skin was being ripped apart. She tried to move a leg, and she trembled from a shock as if she had been hit across her thighs with a stick. But her arm moved, her leg moved. She could move if she could tolerate being beaten and shocked. Why did she want to move? There was a thought, a voice inside her which said she should move, like another person was telling her to move away from the man, to move away from the bed.

Carefully, carefully, she shifted her position. The ripping and tearing feeling was still present, but weaker and weaker. There were no more blows, more of a prickling and a tingling, not altogether unpleasant, in fact. For a moment, her feet hung in the air, and then fell, slowly, slowly, until they hit the earth, and her body rose, rose, slowly into the air as if she was reaching for the sky. With a tremendous effort she was able to concentrate a tiny spark of reason to tell herself she was standing upright, and she could lift one leg and then the other to move through space. She moved one leg, but it was as if her body wanted to move with the leg, and she lurched to one side, almost falling, and the room whirled round as if it was spinning and she was standing still, and then miraculously it came to a stop. And she could lift the other leg without falling over and then the other again, and again, and the voice inside talked about a window.

"Go to the window, go to the window."

What was a window? Where was the window? The window was the square in the wall on the other side of the room, the square split up by thin silver stripes, which seemed to float in the air as if a necklace had come to life and could fly. A step, and another step, and she reached out and steadied herself against the vertical surface of the wall, and then sank, sank, down into the angle with the floor.

☙ Chapter 43 ❧
In the Hills Above Agininum

It's difficult to keep a marching army hidden while crossing the hills, thought Centurion Maxus. The grass might dampen the sound of hooves and boots, but the jingling of harness, the clank of the shovels and pots strapped to the men's packs, the chatter of men's voices must carry on the wind. They were descending the slope into the stream valley where he had broadened and levelled the wading place, and had removed the bushes, rocks and stumps along the path. The track was almost as good as an imperial road, though there was a steep slope down to the stream and an equally steep climb up the other bank.

Down the slope rode Centurion Maxus, Tribune Pelagius and the other officers.

"Whoa, whoa!" said the tribune, unfamiliar with the route. "I think we should dismount and lead our horses through the stream. We don't want any accidents."

Maxus, who had ridden this way many times before and trusted his horse, said nothing, but dismounted in emulation of his chief. The horses splashed through the ford, the men, too, and together they began to climb the slope. As they did so, the first ranks of the infantry appeared on the path.

"Take it easy, men!" shouted Maxus' *optio*, "and hold ranks. There's plenty of space after all that hard work we've been doing!"

The first rank descended the slope, crossed the stream and began to climb. The second rank was close on their heels, and rank after rank behind them. Maxus and the officers led the way. Once they reached the top, they would let the infantry file past and take up position on the flat land beyond. They could fall out for a while, get something to drink, grab a bite to eat. There was still a long way to march before they reached their goal.

In the meantime, while the soldiers rested, the cavalry would pass them by and set off as fast as they could, cross-country to Aginninum.

Maxus glanced back with a frown as he reached the top of the slope. There was no way for the men climbing to keep the same pace as those descending, and the need to wade the stream broke the rhythm. Soon the men were clustered in the bottom of the valley, pushing and shoving as more of their comrades descended towards them.

"Hold off, hold off," yelled an *optio*, directing operations by the stream, trying to keep some order.

That was the last thing he said. A spear struck him down, and an instant later, the disorganised huddle of men in the valley bottom was assailed on all sides by spears and javelins, axes and swords. The men who had already begun to mount the slope tried to turn to help their comrades, but they only added to the confusion. The men at the rear were pushed on by the mounted auxiliaries following them, oblivious to what was happening, out of sight, in the valley bottom.

Tribune Pelagius and his standard-bearer had already reached the plateau and emerged onto the moonlit grassy plain. They stopped, distracted perhaps by the commotion behind them. Even Maxus, looking back again, could not make out exactly what was happening and, oddly, noticed a herd of horses grazing peacefully a little way off. In all the times that Maxus had passed this way, he had never seen so many horses. Just as Pelagius took hold of his mount to swing himself up into the saddle, a group of strange men, already on horseback, burst out of the edge of the forest. They covered the ground towards the surprised Romans before they could react. The two groups came to a halt, facing one another on the track.

"Get out of the way," yelled the tribune, "in the name of the emperor."

"Fuck the emperor," said a gaunt old man, evidently their leader. "Did you think I was too preoccupied to take care of my responsibilities, to take care of my county?"

"Do you think a scattering of peasants will stop the legionnaires of the Empire?" yelled Pelagius in turn. "Leave the way and let us through, before I lose my patience and use force."

The gaunt old man tapped his horse with his heels, so it took a step towards the enemy.

"Look behind you, whoever you are, and you, Maxus," he said. "You're alone here with me, and your retreat is cut off."

The count, thought Maxus, suddenly, Count Sismond.

Pelagius did not bother to look back, merely swung himself up onto his horse.

"Don't talk nonsense, we're not retreating!"

Maxus could not restrain himself from glancing over his shoulder. Strange men were blocking the track behind them. There was no sight of his infantry. He turned further, and his horse, sensitive to its master's commands, took half a turn, too.

"That's right, Maxus," said the count. "Look carefully, and listen, too." He turned to the tribune. "Your cavalry is still on the other side of the stream, Commander, and they can't reach you. My men are slaughtering your infantry in the valley bottom. It's an old trick, but it never seems to fail. Surrender now, or die on your swords, those are the only options."

"No, no," yelled Pelagius, his plight suddenly sinking in, and spurred his horse towards the count. The men around him followed.

Only Centurion Maxus remained still, bewildered.

"Everything has been planned so well, organised so carefully," he said, as if he was still speaking to his commander, while he watched the officers, outnumbered and outfought, fall one by one. "My men will march down to the Garunna and sever the road to Tolosa. The auxiliaries will make for the north gate of Agininum where Junius and his men are waiting to let them in. We'll take the town, and when it's in our hands, the road between Narbonensis and Aquitania will be closed. Tolosa will be surrounded. The people will starve. The king will have to surrender, and the Empire will be restored."

The last horseman was now reduced to fighting on foot.

"How has it gone wrong?" Maxus whispered to himself.

He was still standing beside his horse when he felt a sword against his throat and heard Sismond's voice in his ear.

"Come now, Maxus, hand over your weapon. I have a comfortable room for you in Agininum and some good wine in my cellar, and I'm sure our king will be interested to hear your story…before he sticks your head on a spike."

☙ Chapter 44 ❧ Agininum

Signy sat slumped against the wall of the room, just by the window, her arms wrapped around her knees, as if she was steadying herself, as if she was holding herself together in one piece. She drifted in and out of a state of confusion, dreaming, awake. When she was awake, she could not remember how she had got to that place, or how long she had been sitting there. Junius, she could see, was still on the bed, apparently sleeping.

Suddenly, there was a soft sound from outside the window. In her mind there was a swirl of colour, of browns and greens, extending, floating in harmony with the undulations of the sound. Then she woke up with a start. The sound had a meaning, not just a form. It came again. The sound of an owl, an owl from the forests of her childhood. An owl that did not live in the south, in Agininum, that only lived in her memory and that of… Grunwald!

The signal, the sound was the signal, the signal that Grunwald and his band were waiting outside. Groping for the wall to steady herself, she got to her feet, one hand on the window ledge. She leaned against the wall and brought both her hands to her mouth. She had practised, had shown Grunwald she could respond, but that was when her mind was clear.

"*Hoo…hoo*," she blew, her eyes on Junius. He did not stir.

"*Hoo…hoo*," came the reply through the shutters. She should go down the stairs, open the door and let them in. She gritted her teeth and took a step away from the wall. There was a strange tingling in the soles of her feet, as if she was walking barefoot in the snow. It was only then the thought struck her that she was naked. She could not go down the stairs and open the door and meet the men in this state. She looked around the room, saw the cloak where she had placed it when she first came in. She took a tentative step, a second, terrified that she would fall and alert the sleeping man.

She reached the chest, breathing heavily, put her arms down to steady herself for a moment, and as she did her hand brushed against an object lying under the cloak, a long, thin object. She lifted the fabric aside and uncovered her dagger – she had undone the belt and then dropped the cloak over it. She took up the scabbard and slid out the blade. There was another hoot from the street. Grunwald must be wondering what was delaying her.

The dagger glinted in the light of the still-flickering lamps. She held it in her hands, the slim length of razor-sharp steel. A feeling came over her, almost as if there was a voice in her head instructing her what to do. She turned towards Junius who was lying sprawled on the bed, one little oil lamp to his left and the other on his right.

"Nothing should delay you for a moment, Signy," came the voice. "What has to be done must be done to fulfil the expectations of our goddess. You must see that it is done. Signy, it's your duty."

She stepped towards the bed. She looked down at the sleeping man. How peaceful he looked! How handsome! What a pity he was who he was! What a pity to end his life!

He stirred, turned in his sleep.

It was now, or else she had to leave the task to Grunwald.

She leaned down, took a firm grip on the dagger and drew the point across his throat. The first touch woke him. His eyes flew open, and he stared up at her for a moment as his life gushed out of the slash in his neck. She could not focus anymore but grasped the dagger again and plunged it into his neck, once, twice. Then she straightened herself up and backed away. Junius' lifeblood was draining out onto the bed.

"Place the knife down, my Signy, and accept the life you have taken." Whose voice was it? Not Irmengaard's but still a woman's and it spoke in Jutish.

"*Hoo…hoo!*"

She placed the knife carefully at the foot of the bed, just by his feet, then she stepped up again and dipped her forefinger into his blood. She drew the bloody finger down her face, across each of her cheeks. She dipped her finger again and drew it down between her breasts, down her stomach.

There were thumps on the door below. A loud voice calling, in Jutish, just as before, but a man's voice this time. More thumps.

Now she must go down. She had completed the act. The sacrifice had been made as the goddess demanded. She crossed back to the chest, suddenly almost sober, picked up her cloak, wrapped it around her shoulders and descended the stairs. There was no sound from the room where Junius' companions had been gathered. She slid back the bolt, pulled at the door and found herself face to face with Grunwald.

His face screwed up in astonishment when he saw her.

"He's dead," she said.

"It's done?" he asked, astonishment in his voice.

"Done," she replied, and pushed past him into the street.

"Oh, by the gods, Signy, what have you done?" he said, horror on his face. The last she heard was the clatter of his footsteps as he mounted the stairs.

What had she done? She had to get home, to safety, to normality.

The air outside was warm and fresh after the room, though it was still dark, the middle of the night. She walked, barefoot, down the street, holding her cloak tightly around her still-naked body.

Somewhere along the route she must have taken a wrong turning, or perhaps she had returned to the half-dreaming state of earlier, because she suddenly realised she hadn't taken the main street that led up the hill to her home. Instead, she was among the stones of the abandoned theatre. Now, away from the houses, the stars and the moonlight were brighter. She could make out the shapes of the fallen stones, the steps rising up the hillside. She could also make out the sticky feeling, the smell of blood. She looked down and saw her hands were discoloured, dirty – blood, Junius' blood covered her hands. She suddenly felt unclean. She suddenly felt the need to wash. Beyond the theatre, beyond the ruins of the old temple, was the stream. She could dip her hands into the clear water. She could splash it on her face. She could clean her body. She could wipe away the clinging defilement. She walked on, out of the theatre and in among the fallen columns of the temple. She could hear the gurgling and splashing of the stream drawing her on. When she reached the far side, she came to a flight of stairs, made of blocks from the temple, that led down to where the stream formed a still pool, a convenient way to reach the water and wash. Without thinking, she threw off the cloak and, leaving it in a heap at the top of the steps, walked down until her feet touched the water. She took another step, and another, until the water was up to her knees and then her thighs, and then she was floating, floating in the sun-warmed stream. She splashed and rubbed her hands together until she felt they were clean. She ran them through her hair, then she ducked under the water and burst up again, blowing out. How wonderful it was, as if she was wrapped in a warm blanket!

Then her feet touched the bottom. She had bumped up against the foot of the steps. She took a pace, and then another. The water dropped back, past her knees, past her ankles, until she stood on the dry shore. There was little breeze down by the stream, but just enough that her wet skin felt a chill. She picked up her cloak and flung it over her shoulders. With a few steps she was back among the ruins of the temple. Up the slope was the start of the abandoned processional way, which led past Olive Street, past her house, up to the top of the hill. She would take that route, go home, lie down on her own bed and go to sleep, but first she just had to rest for a moment. She sat down, her back against a fallen column, staring out at the sky, at the trees, at the ruins.

What had she done? What had she done, for whom and why? Whose was the voice that had told her to pick up the knife and cut his throat? There was no immediate answer, only an immense feeling of tiredness. The potion must have worn off, and my body needs to recover, was the last thought that came into her mind before sleep overtook her.

Her body, perhaps, did need rest, but her mind woke before her body was ready, filling with memories of what she had experienced, as if in a dream. And in half-wake, half-slumbering reasoning, an idea began to coalesce, an idea which filled her with cold dread from which, asleep as she was, she could not escape.

She must have made a mistake, misremembered the recipe Irmengaard had used for the farmer's wife, and prepared the sacred potion by accident, the potion that should only be used in the ceremonies of the sisters of Freya. She'd imagined she'd seen the wise woman assembling the ingredients. That memory must have been false, but where had it sprung from?

And then she had selected the sacrifice, a handsome young man.

She had shared the sacred meal with the victim.

She had lain with the victim, and through that sacred sex she had experienced the structure of the universe, the end, the infinity.

And then, then she had performed the sacrifice. She had slit the victim's throat, and he had bled to death. She had anointed herself with his blood in acknowledgement of his gift of his life.

She had processed to the sacred pool and cleansed herself.

And now while she slept in the sacred precinct, her companions would be completing the final act, she supposed, and the victim had been cast into the river, to sink, sink into the arms of the goddess.

She remembered how Irmengaard had shaken her head, regretfully, saying, "You'll never become a priestess, Signy. You love men too much. You love life and the world too much to perform the sacrifice, to commit yourself."

But now, all alone, far away in a foreign land, she had done it. Though she had not intended to, she had completed the ritual she had always said to herself she would never go through, the ritual that made her a fully fledged priestess.

There had been no one to see her, no one to celebrate with her, no one to complete the marks on her body that would show what she had become, but she knew what she had done. She knew how the acts added up, what they made her: a priestess of Freya in a land of Christians, a land where the old gods had been banished and their servants were condemned to death.

The first fingers of dawn were beginning to extend through the trees. She was shivering, not so much from the emotion of the waking dream she had just had, but because her cloak had become unwrapped during her restless slumber, and she was now lying in the shelter of a fallen column.

Oh, gods, she thought suddenly, suppose someone has seen me like this, naked on the ground, like the proverbial drunkard. She sat up quickly, wrapping the cloak around her. She was alone among the deserted stones. There was not a moment to lose. She struggled to her feet and began to climb the crumbling steps of the old temple, then made her way across the platform to reach the road beyond. She toiled up the slope until she reached Olive Street, and then the postern gate of her house. It swung at her touch, and she stepped inside. So far she had seen no one, and there was no one waiting for her, only the sounds of the horses stirring in the stable and the ever-alert pigs. Even the dogs were curiously silent. With her heart in her mouth, she crossed the yard and tiptoed past the kitchen, out into the passage and as fast as she could to her own room, her place of refuge. Inside, she closed the door, threw off the cloak and lay down on her bed. In an instant, she was asleep again, a dreamless sleep of comfort.

☙ Chapter 45 ❧ Aginınum

There was a hand touching her shoulder. Signy woke with a shock.

"Mistress, are you well?" It took her a moment to recognise the features of Ferona.

She screwed up her eyes, wishing the world would go away.

"Mistress, Grunwald has been asking after you. He sounded worried."

Signy blinked again, lay back, rubbed her hand across her eyes.

"Mistress, are you really alright?" Ferona's anxious voice brought her back to her senses, to where she was, to the fact she was stretched out on her bed without a stitch on her. She took a deep breath, swung her legs around and swivelled to a sitting position. How awful she felt, like the worst drinking session at a Jutish feast, like she was back on the pitching and tossing boat on the way to Burdigala, heaving over the side.

"I'm not well, Ferona," she said at last. "Give me my cloak… no, not that one."

Ferona had taken up the cloak she had been wearing all night.

"There's blood on it, Mistress. What happened?"

Signy could see the blood. She could see the stains of the soil where she had lain by the rock. She could see such stains on her legs and arms. Her feet were scratched and covered with dried mud. She ran her hand through her hair. It felt tangled and dirty, and her fingers dislodged a cascade of shredded of vegetation. If she had washed herself of Junius' blood in the stream, mother nature had compensated afterwards.

There was little she could do but groan. There was no way she could present herself to the world like this, not even to Grunwald.

"Ferona, my darling, find me a fresh robe, and run to the kitchen for hot water. I must go to the bathhouse and get myself clean." She struggled to her feet, assisted by the anxious girl. Then there was a fresh robe around her shoulders, and sandals for her dirty feet.

Signy hurried through the passage to the bathhouse. There would be no heat in the caldarium, but a place to clean herself, perfumed oil to scrape away the dirt and make her feel more like a civilised woman.

Ferona appeared with a bucket of warm water from the kitchen and with wide eyes splashed her mistress all over.

"Leave me a while, Ferona, please. Go and find me clean clothes, and I'll come back to my room in a moment. And tell Grunwald that I'm fine and I'll come to hear his story when I'm properly dressed."

The girl hurried away, taking the empty bucket with her, and Signy sat on one of the stone benches to dry, her robe wrapped around her. She wished that Megana was there to talk to, instead of only having the same thoughts going round in her head.

She had difficulty recapturing the feeling of the night in that room in Baker Street in the stone surroundings of the bathhouse, in the daylight, and with her mind clear, but she could not avoid recognising she had killed a man as part of a ritual. No one knew, of course, except for her, why she had killed Junius, but she could not deny the deed or the reason to herself. And one aspect still obsessed her. Whose voice, in fact, had urged her to act? Had the voice come from outside, the voice of Gná, perhaps with a message from the goddess, or had it come from inside, the voice of her *hugr*, perhaps dissatisfied with the direction her life had been taking?

Was this the end of her life here, before it had even properly begun? Surely the Christian women, Ophelia and Abbess Hildefrith, could no longer be her friends, nor Brother Michael or Brother Wilbert. If she committed herself to the life of a priestess, she would have to retire to some lonely place, on the edge of the world, as Irmengaard had done, and live alone, feared by those who needed her charms and treatments, and blamed for all that went wrong in the community. What man would contemplate her for a partner in life? At best she could hope that some desperado would come by now and then, curious for the experience of bedding a sorceress. How ironic the words she had exchanged on that first meeting with Geseric now sounded.

If her *hugr* had stimulated her to act then, here in the land of the Christians, it had determined her existence would be a waste.

She sat with her elbows on her knees, her face in her hands.

There was a temptation, of course. A couple of drops of the potion she had concocted would always take away her worries, a spoonful would lift her out of this world into oblivion. Irmengaard had warned her. Potions were powerful medicines, to be used with care, to be used for ritual purposes, as part of the ceremonies, or for helping to see the future. She had never wanted to see the future. She had always refused when Irmengaard had offered to lead her, to watch over her while she explored her own fortune. Perhaps she had seen it now. Perhaps that was the vision she had been offered, a maelstrom of confusion, annihilation, a dissolution into a meaningless nothing. Of course, there were always other mixtures, poisons, which could put a person to sleep, never to wake up.

She shivered and, standing up, drew her robe tighter, anger displacing her self-pity.

That was a ridiculous thought. There was still a life to be led, here and now.

And, she reflected, there's another way of looking at what happened, always another way. She was far from the lands of the old gods, and perhaps the voice had just been a muddled memory, stirred up by the *mixtura* she had taken, of the stories Irmengaard had told, of the rituals she had celebrated in Juteland. This is a Christian land, she thought. The old gods don't have the same influence, not the gods of the Romans nor the gods of the north, and then she remembered…the steps down to the stream. The Christians had built them. They took new members of their group to such places, so Deacon Baxter had once told her, and immersed them in water, just as he had done on occasions in the river that ran by Corinium. She had read enough of their works, discussed enough with Sister Ophelia and Abbess Hildefrith to know what that meant, to be baptised they called the ceremony…that their old life, the wrongs they had done were washed away. Now she had done the same for herself. Suppose that was the meaning? Had her old life, her wrongs, been washed away? Could she have become a new person, newborn, when she stepped out of the stream?

Signy sighed. The truth was, she wasn't going to find the answers to these questions sitting alone in the bathhouse. In Juteland, Irmengaard had been her mentor, a wise and thoughtful person she could turn to for advice. Should she take her worries to Ophelia and Hildefrith? They were kind and intelligent, but hardly educated in the ways of gods, of their signs and reasons. Who could she turn to here in Agininum? The Christian God Himself, of course, and his son, Jesus the Christ, answered desperate petitioners' prayers, so people said. At least she could try.

Ferona's voice called from the doorway, reminding her that Grunwald was still waiting. She slowly rose to her feet. Whoever she thought she was, whatever role she had taken on, there was a world outside, unaware of her inner turmoil, that had expectations of her.

☙ Chapter 46 ❧
Agininum

Signy found Grunwald in the kitchen. No doubt he had been telling the cook and the kitchen girls what he had anticipated telling her. Let's hope it's the expurgated version, she thought, not that he had opened the door to find the mistress covered with blood, barefooted and half-naked running through the streets like a madwoman, though the truth was she had been, in some strange way, quite mad during the time in Junius' room.

He rose to his feet when he saw her, turned away from his audience and embraced her, a look of relief on his face. To see me whole and healthy, clean and clothed, she thought.

"Come with me," she said, speaking in Jutish, "to my workroom. There are matters I need to discuss which shouldn't be mentioned in the kitchen."

They crossed the inner courtyard to the range of rooms that served her and Megana. As soon as they were inside, Grunwald spoke up.

"Why did you kill him?"

That was a question she was not immediately prepared to answer, and he did not wait for one.

"We'd been told to take him alive if possible, as a witness."

Signy drew a deep breath.

"It would have been helpful if you had told me that," she said, sighing, "though I don't think it would have made a difference. I didn't intend to kill him when I went to him."

"It was self-defence?" suggested Grunwald. "He attacked you?"

"No, he didn't," said Signy quietly. "He was asleep. If anything, I attacked him."

Grunwald stood in silence for a moment, and then his face twisted into a frown.

"The candles, the knife at his feet." He looked into her eyes. "The blood on your face?"

Signy took another deep breath. How could she explain to him when she could barely understand herself? Grunwald must have heard of the rituals when he was young in Juteland. He would just have to draw his own conclusions.

"What did you do with the body?" she asked.

The warrior seemed relieved to return to practical details.

"We wrapped him in a cloth, weighted down with stones, and dumped him in the middle of the river. If he does come to the surface, no one will recognise him by then. No one will know how he died."

"And did you clean the room?"

"We have not had time yet, Mistress." He looked hard at her, as if examining her. "There was blood everywhere. When you came to the door I thought you were the one who was dying. You looked like a walking corpse."

"Enough of that, Grunwald. It cuts too close. And what of the other men, the ones who left on patrol?"

"That's what has kept us occupied, Mistress."

"Tell me, then."

Grunwald took a deep breath.

"We had followed them the day before, the men and Junius. I couldn't tell you. Sismond forbade us. He was worried already that your part would be difficult enough for you. They came past this very house, but he wasn't looking for you. They went up into the church square, and out of the north gate. We couldn't follow them all the way. They would have spotted us. When they came back, they stood a long time looking out along the track that leads to the road over the hills, pointing and gesticulating. Then they returned to Baker Street."

"They didn't visit any of the other gates?"

"No, Mistress. Junius seems to have had a plan already prepared."

He had had plenty of opportunity to formulate a plan, thought Signy, while he was walking around the town with me. And then she remembered she had killed him.

"Yesterday evening," Grunwald continued, "I followed you down to the house, watched you go inside. You didn't see me, I suppose. It was already dark, and I kept to the shadows. When you arrived, Junius' men were still there, in the lower room. Shortly after you went in, they left, to leave their chief in peace, I imagine. They took Baker Street to the Stratego's Tavern and ate dinner, as if there was nothing out of the ordinary. When they had finished, they returned to the forum and made their way up to the churchyard, where they went in amongst the mausoleums and hid. Hrasmus and Asser stayed to watch them, while Henrik and I remained keeping watch over you."

Signy felt uneasy. They had been waiting outside, listening no doubt, while Junius was bedding her, while she was lost in her visions. They would have heard everything through the shutters.

"It didn't take long before Asser appeared and told us the men were making their move. We reached the church square just as they were leaving the graveyard, without a care in the world, it seemed. They thought that victory was theirs, I imagine."

"And what did they do?"

"Hah, of course, we might have guessed! They unbolted the gate, and left it wide open, and then they walked a short distance along the path, as if they were expecting someone."

"And was there anyone?"

"No one. The night was as quiet and still as…well, it was quiet and still, and after a while they came back, and we were waiting for them. I downed one, and Asser felled a second with a boar spear before they knew what was happening. The others took to their heels, out of the gate and down the track. It didn't take long to catch them. Their bodies are down in the ravine."

"And the first two?"

"The same fate as their master. We closed the gate and fastened it, and then we went down and checked with the watch if there'd been problems at the other gates. Not a squeak, they said."

"But there had to be some reason why those men opened the gate. They were planning to let someone into the town."

"We'll find out, I reckon, when Sismond and Jorid get back," he said with a shrug. "Anyway, by then I thought we should get back to Baker Street. Once we were in position, I gave the signal. I hoped you would hear it, but…well, I wouldn't have been surprised if you had been fast asleep. I was so relieved when I heard your reply, but after that, when nothing happened, when you didn't open the door, Henrik was ready to break it down, but I begged him to wait a little longer. And then you appeared, more like a ghost than a human being. Honestly, Mistress, I hardly expected to see you alive again, so at first I thought you were a ghost."

"And you found the body?"

"Henrik and I rushed up the stairs. What a mess, blood everywhere, clothes and sheets drenched, the lamps burning, and your dagger lying on the bed."

He fell silent, examining her again.

"You weren't wounded?"

"Not in my body, Grunwald," she said, "but it's a hard task for a woman to kill a man in cold blood."

"It's hard enough to do it in a fair fight, Mistress, for a warrior."

And you didn't have to let him screw you before you did it, she thought.

"I need a little time to recover," she said, "and perhaps you, too, and the others. You were up all night and did a fine job. The count should be pleased."

Grunwald grunted. "Like I said, the count would have preferred to have the captain alive to question, to make an example of, I suppose."

"I'll explain to him."

"There's no need. I'll tell him it was self-defence. That's the best story. I won't have to lie much. You were covered with blood. We'll have to wait till the count gets back – if he gets back – and until then the watch will have to guard all the gates securely, and every able-bodied man in this town will have to help. Someone was supposed to come, and they still might."

"The centurion and his soldiers?" Signy said.

"We'll see," said Grunwald, "and now, if you'll excuse me, I have to go back and tidy the room, gather any records he might have left, since he can't tell us himself, and then I'll grab something to eat and get a nap, 'cause I'm going to have to stand duty tonight as well."

☙ Chapter 47 ❧
Agininum

No, Signy thought, when Grunwald had left, killing Junius was not what was troubling her. Although that was bad enough, and would probably come back to haunt her later, the deed had been done in a moment. Her mind was more seriously disturbed by her own situation, a situation she could not possibly begin to describe to the warrior, even if he had perhaps grasped something of her worries.

She found a plain cloak and pulled up the hood. Then she walked down the garden and out of the garden gate so that no one would see her leave. She turned up the hill, into Church Square and across to the Christian basilica. She had been to their meetings on a Sunday, once or twice, but had always felt uncomfortable, though Ophelia was friends with the bishop. How did the worship operate on a weekday? She was not even sure the door would open until she pushed and walked tentatively inside. She paused on the threshold. The church was dark, with only a couple of candles burning in the distance. She looked around to see if anyone else was present, but the place seemed deserted. Hesitantly, she crossed the empty nave, the space where she had squeezed with the other worshippers in anonymity those times she had visited. At the far end, candles lit up a rounded space, covered with mosaics, a picture of Jesus Christ, triumphant on the cross, not frightened of what was being done to him, not worrying about his fate, not fearing death, but knowing he was doing his duty to save mankind. She gazed up at the picture, then sank to her knees and bowed her head. She was in this God's land. She would have to trust that he would have a sign for her.

She did not hear any footsteps, only a soft voice.

"Sister?"

She turned and looked up.

"Bishop?"

"Mistress Signy?" There was surprise in his voice. "I…I…I didn't know you were a believer."

"I came here to find out if I am, Bishop."

"That's a very strange way of putting it, Mistress." He was bending over her, looking down at her as an adult looks down at a child, a benevolent and puzzled expression on his face.

She held out her hand, and he took it automatically, helping her to her feet.

"I killed a man today," she said.

"I heard there was trouble in the town. Some bandits, they said, come to open the town gates and let their fellow robbers enter. I couldn't imagine you were involved."

Even now, for a moment, she felt she should defend Junius, explain that he wasn't a robber.

"I knew their leader. It was him who I killed while he slept."

The bishop frowned, as if he was wondering what was the most tactful way to proceed while stilling his curiosity.

"Have you come to repent? To seek forgiveness?" he asked.

"No, not at all. Junius was responsible for the death of several innocent people, and perhaps intended the deaths of more."

"I see," said the bishop, "then what brings you here if you think your actions were justified?"

"Because that wasn't the reason I killed him. Do you know what this means?" she asked, slipping aside the corner of her gown.

The bishop took a quick step back, as if she was suddenly exposing a more intimate part.

"I…Mistress Ophelia told me that you had studied heathen arts, among the barbarians. I…I've heard of such marks…among Our Men."

"I was studying to be a priestess, a sister of Freya, but I never completed the ceremony. It involves…"

"Sacrifice," whispered the bishop, "of sheep, and cattle, and horses."

"You know our rituals?"

"I've read the tales."

"Then you know that the sacrifices are completed by the offering of a human life, a man who has lain with the priestesses and the candidate."

The bishop's eyes were fastened upon her as if she was an apparition from some dark legend.

"And you…this robber…"

"I mixed a potion, one very similar to that used in our ceremony. I lay with the man though I had no visions of the gods. And afterwards I slit his throat and—"

"You didn't drink his blood?" muttered the bishop in a fascinated tone.

"No," she answered, "but I daubed it on my face and body. Really, I should have been more careful to draw the sacred signs as the ritual demands, but Grunwald was banging on the door."

The bishop shook his head as if he had difficulty in believing what he was hearing.

"Bishop Anastasius, please don't be angry," Signy continued. "Mistress Ophelia and Abbess Hildefrith have spoken so kindly of you. A voice told me to kill him, a message from the gods or perhaps from my own soul…I don't know."

The bishop scratched his chin and began to speak. "I'm not sure—"

But Signy broke him off. "After I had finished the ritual, I went to the pool, the pool by the old temple, where your people laid down steps."

"Yes," said Anastasius, "you're right. My predecessors used that place to baptise converts. To wash away their sins. No better example of renouncing the old ways and accepting the Christ."

"There was no one there but me, and I walked down the steps and into the pool, into the water. Does the magic work that way as well? Would washing myself in the Christ's holy water undo what I did?"

"It would certainly be unconventional," said the bishop with relief in his voice. "If you truly wanted to repent but…"

"What do you mean?"

"Come with me, Sister, and I'll show you."

He led her across the church, through an archway and into another high-ceilinged building alongside.

"As I said, once our forebears followed the tradition established by John the Baptist, Christ's cousin, and dipped new believers in the river, but here…here's where we baptise new members of the church today."

In the centre of the eight-sided room was a low stone railing, intricately carved. Through a gap, a flight of steps led down to a still, clear pool.

Signy looked from the pool up at the bishop's kindly face.

"You mean bathing in the river didn't count?" Worse, she thought, I slept by the stones of the pagan temple. Suppose that pool, that water, is holy, but to the wrong gods?

"Not without a priest to offer up the proper prayers," the bishop said, sighing.

Though his words seemed momentarily discouraging, Signy rather felt a surge of relief.

"Yes," she said, "the proper priestess and the proper prayers." There had been no priestess yesterday evening, either, she thought, no chanting, no dancing, no one to invoke the gods, and she'd had no vision of them. Maybe none of what she had done counted.

She still had her doubts, though, still felt tense.

"I'm trapped," she said, looking away. "I don't know what to believe. I came here – to the church – to ask for a sign."

"And did you receive one, or did I interrupt?"

"I'm not sure," she said, "but gods choose their time."

The bishop nodded, evidently well aware that she had not specified from which god she was expecting the sign.

She smiled at him. "Perhaps you did give me a sign when you reminded me that rituals must be done the proper way."

"But ritual is not enough," he said. "We must believe. That's the most important part."

But what did she believe? Perhaps simply that Junius was a bad man, and he met the end he deserved. She was merely an instrument of justice. But wasn't that as presumptuous as thinking she could elevate herself as a priestess through a half-remembered ceremony or that the Christ would forgive her simply because she bathed in a pool once used by the Christians?

The bishop must have seen the doubt on her face.

"We have to do our best," he said, "in this world, not always perfection, but our best."

"I try," she replied, looking up at the mosaic, trying to find something to cling to in her uncertainty. "I can save people, not their souls like you do, but their bodies. That's a skill I learned from my mother."

"And you do it very well, so I've heard from Aija."

"But that skill, those practices, they're mixed up, intertwined with the ways of the old gods."

"You can still be a healer." The bishop tried to sound encouraging. "You could become a healer for Christ if you were willing to accept his blessing, willing to be baptised here, in this pool, by me."

"Do you think so?"

"I promise you so, Mistress Signy. I've heard only good things about you, not just from Aija, but Sister Ophelia, Sister Agatha, Hildefrith, of course, and Brother Wilbert."

"Perhaps you're right," she said with a smile.

"And you'd have my support and blessing," he said, giving her an unbishoply warm embrace. "I'll pray for your soul, and for the man you killed. I suppose he must have been a Christian, even if not a good one, and it would be ill for him to come to the seat of judgement as a heathen sacrifice. And Mistress Signy," he added, raising his finger, "you must remember that sacrifice has been forbidden in the Empire for many years. I can't forget what you've told me, but I promise not to repeat your story to anyone, and you should not do so, either. Not everyone will understand that you meant no harm by what you did."

She returned the way she had come, still unsure, but with a feeling that there was a way out if she chose to take it. But that would mean denying a part of herself. Perhaps that was the sacrifice the Christ expected, a part of herself.

She saw Ferona carrying the dress she had been wearing when she met Junius, now freshly cleaned and folded.

"Thank you," she said. "I think I must put this aside and only use it for very special occasions."

She took the robe and went to her clothes chest, which she emptied entirely. Then she placed it at the bottom, and all the other clothes on top.

☙ Chapter 48 ❧
Agininum

Count Sismond had placed Centurion Maxus in a small room at the rear of his residence. A plain cot with blankets, a simple wooden table and a three-legged stool. The window was closed by shutters, and no doubt the centurion had already tried to open them. They were fastened on the outside, and were the officer to peer through the slats, he would just make out an equally bare, whitewashed courtyard.

Sismond had other, more immediate matters to take care of than the captured officer. There was an enemy cavalry force loose in the hills. There was a heap of corpses to strip and dispose of. There were prisoners to march back to Agininum, to hand over to the traders to be shipped off to the slave markets. There were his own dead and wounded to take care of, to carry back to the town or to their farms and cottages. He could take his time with Maxus. The centurion would not be going anywhere.

As for the injured Romans…well, none of them were actually Romans. They were more trouble than they were worth. He did not like to do it, but the best for them was to help them on the way to their inevitable destination…the same hole as their already-dead comrades. Signy, who had suddenly appeared, cantering up from town, thought otherwise. Sismond had no objection when she arranged to have one of Megana's wagons pick up a dozen men and carry them back to Olive Street, so long as she paid some attention to his own wounded men. He had seen her work after the attack on the bandits. He had even seen Ragvald hobbling around the town, his leg held fast in some wooden contraption.

"You think you can fix them up?" he asked sceptically.

"I'll do my best. They're no worse wounded than Grunwald and Asser were once," she said with a confident tone. "The body has a wonderful capacity to heal if you keep the wounds clean and don't interfere."

He smiled.

"I've heard," he said, "from Jorid...there'll be a lot of grateful men around Agininum."

"And their wives and mothers," she said, "glad to have their menfolk back."

"One wife who won't be getting her man back," he said, "Mistress Maxa. I'm just on my way to speak to him. Will you join me?"

"It's not my business," she said quickly.

"You don't want to find out what Junius was up to?"

"I've been trying to put that behind me. It's one reason I took the injured men, to do something good in this, but why not? I doubt Maxus will recognise me. He thought I was a boy when I came to his camp."

The centurion was seated on the edge of his cot reading when the two entered. Aija had taken pity on him and fetched a couple of books, religious books, from the bishop.

"Comfortable, Maxus?" asked Sismond, brusquely.

The centurion put his book to one side, then glanced up, first at the count, and then, with a puzzled expression, at Signy. The count gestured to her to take the stool, while he paced about the room, two steps this way, three back, all the time looking down at the crouching prisoner.

"Feeding you well, are they?" His voice was one of irritated aggressiveness, as if another person, and not he himself, was responsible for the officer's situation.

"Can't speak now, can you? Well, tell me this, what the fuck were you doing invading my county?"

The centurion swallowed.

"Hunting bandits," he mumbled.

"Hunting fucking bandits! How come I had to take my own men to deal with the bandits? How come you didn't go and stir up that lazy bastard Altaar? The bandits were in his backyard, not mine."

"I just did as I was ordered," replied the centurion.

"Did as you were fucking ordered?"

"I was told to fix up the road…to facilitate anti-bandit activities…that's what the orders said."

"And you had nothing to do with visiting the bandits and encouraging them to raid my lands? It was a complete surprise to you when a couple of hundred mounted auxiliaries showed up and you were ordered to escort them along your beautifully fixed-up road?"

"I never went to speak to the bandits. That was Junius' idea. I never went to Cadurci to talk to Count Altaar. That was Junius as well. I never did trust him. He should never have had the peasants killed. I knew that would raise suspicions, but he said they lived too near to the way, that they would see what we were doing and inform on us."

"They informed on you anyway," said Sismond bitterly, "though mutely."

"I'm an honourable man, Count, a soldier. I only did my duty. Roadbuilding, that's all."

"Hm, but for what purpose, Maxus, for what purpose?" said the count. "And as for your honour, that will be for the king to decide."

"If he survives," said the centurion, suddenly defiant. "I mean, we're not the only ones in this war."

Sismond laughed.

"So now you admit this is a war, and not just so-called anti-bandit activities. Well, tough shit for you, Maxus. You failed. A messenger's already on his way to Tolosa to inform the king and anyone else that's listening, and others to Vasates and Elusa, calling for mobilisation and reinforcements."

"I didn't fail," said the centurion, already deflating. "I did my bit. The ford across the Oltis was built. The track was upgraded. Once Pelagius arrived, I had to do as he commanded. I'm an army man, and I took my orders from my higher officer."

"And Junius, was he this Pelagius' man, too?" said Signy, suddenly butting in.

Maxus turned to her in surprise, as if he had forgotten she was there.

"Junius…I told you. Junius is a spy…nothing to do with the army. He'd already left before Pelagius and his men showed up."

"Who gave him his orders to come to Agininum? Who found the house for him and his men?"

"Who writes his orders? I don't know…someone in Arelate probably, or the senator, Marcellus."

"And did that someone order him to seduce and exploit unsuspecting women?"

Maxus face creased with puzzlement.

"You? You…are you the woman he's been speaking about? The sorceress, he calls her?"

"Were there others?"

"How am I supposed to know? He never discusses his orders with me."

"Well, never mind," said Signy. "He didn't have to try too hard to seduce me, and I had a few good nights with him." She tried to sound hard and callous.

"I suppose he does what he has to do, like the rest of us," said Maxus. "He's a handsome man. I suppose he can use that to his advantage, though he has a wife, so I heard, and two young daughters…in Luca."

"And a girl in every city, no doubt," added Sismond.

"He's dead," Signy said. "Dead and gone." Her voice trailed off.

"Oh," said Maxus.

"And his men," added Sismond.

Signy felt a hand on her shoulder, the count's.

"I've had enough. I've heard enough."

Signy stood up and turned to leave.

"I'll see you at dinner," said Sismond, bowing to Maxus. "We can continue this conversation then. In the meantime, I'll send a servant with water and towels. If you give me your word of honour not to escape, you may use the baths and my library."

"I don't suppose it's worth suggesting I could fix him a girl from the town to keep him company," he muttered as they closed the door, though only speaking to Signy.

"I'm sorry, Count," she said, when they were out of earshot. "I don't know why I let Junius get under my skin. I feel really foolish."

"In my experience," said the count, putting his arm around her shoulders, "the best way of forgetting an ill-chosen lover is to find a new one."

"How long will you keep Maxus here?"

"Why, are you thinking of laying hands on him?"

Signy scowled.

"No, but you *will* send him to Tolosa? When?"

"In a couple of days, once I hear my messenger has had an audience with Theodoric, and what his reception has been."

"Are you worried the king will be annoyed?"

"The king, no, but I don't suppose everyone'll be happy that this plot failed."

"You think there are traitors in the court."

"I don't think there are. I know there are. Didn't you hear what Maxus said? That your Junius had been to Cadurci to speak to Altaar?"

"Count Altaar was the man you went to meet, before we confronted the bandits?"

"Correct – the man who refused to help me. Count Altaar is part of the duke's circle, Duke Ludiger."

"And you think the duke has been in league with the Empire? That's impossible…the king's right-hand man? Part of a conspiracy? I can't believe it!"

"Didn't the duke send Thormond on a wild goose chase with our army? And the messenger, who came to your friend the trader, wasn't he Ludiger's man? I just hope Xancha was able to persuade Thormond to return to court before it's too late."

☙ Chapter 49 ❧ Agininum

A couple of days later, and Signy had been called to the count's palace again. She no longer felt quite the same dread as the first time, but rather a dull acceptance. She remained unsure of the count's attitude towards her, still fearful she might be held accountable, at least in part, for the events that had transpired, and that sooner or later the count would have to decide what to do with her.

"I've been ordered to send Maxus to Tolosa," Sismond said, once she was standing to attention in his private office. "I'll be glad to get that bastard off my hands. He's got no dinner conversation, only the angle of the hypotenuse or some similar rubbish."

Signy said nothing but smiled sympathetically.

"Just yesterday I had a most detailed lecture from the man on which grade of stones to use when paving a road. I told him that he would have been better off using his talents elsewhere…" The count shook his head. "As food for lions," he added.

Signy continued smiling. There was little more that her anxious state allowed her to do. She could hardly explain that Roman roads had always fascinated her. She had walked and ridden them far enough, straight and level, and passable in all weathers. How different from the muddy tracks through the forest where she had grown up!

"Anyhow," said Sismond, pursing his lips. "I've decided to send you to Tolosa with him."

"Oh!" was all she could manage to mutter as her heart sank.

"Exactly," Sismond said with a sigh. "No doubt you'll learn a great deal more than you ever wanted to about roadbuilding on the journey."

"But why?"

Sismond fixed her with his gaze.

"I want the king to hear Maxus' story, but I fear, if our friend the centurion falls into Ludiger's hands…" He drew his finger across his neck.

"I'm not going to be able to prevent that," said Signy.

"No," said Sismond, "and I don't expect you to, but you went and killed the other prime witness. I don't blame you for defending yourself, but I'd told Grunwald and the others to take Junius alive if possible. I might have tortured him a bit myself, just to soften him up."

"He…" No, it was better to let the lie stand than try to explain to the count what had really happened.

Sismond, in any case, cut her off.

"I need a backup plan. You're another witness and I doubt, or at least I hope, that Ludiger knows nothing of your involvement. I'll write a note to Thormond, nothing specific, just telling him he should arrange an interview with the king…in private. You can tell Theo what you did with Junius, not the lurid parts, but the snooping and questioning, and anything he let drop to you about his business while his guard was down."

He looked thoughtful for a moment.

"You're not pregnant, are you?"

"No," said Signy, slightly shocked by his question.

"Pity, it would be firm evidence of what you'd been up to," he said, tapping the table a couple of times. "In any case, I need a few days before you can leave," the count continued, almost as if a pregnancy could be arranged in that time. "I have to arrange an escort. Be ready to travel then."

So this is my punishment, Signy thought as she slowly crossed Church Square towards Olive Street, to travel to the court and admit my part in this misadventure, to be examined by strangers and hostage to their attitudes and expectations. She had feared what Sismond might decide, and now she had a greater fear. Supposing the king considered her as guilty as Maxus. Her interview with him would be short and sharp. And supposing he was curious about her marks, her medicines, a foreigner and a loose woman bearing the signs of pagan belief. Anastasius seemed to be understanding, but other bishops…Megana had repeated her complaint about Bartolomeus of Burdigala on many occasions.

Signy, sitting in the courtyard of the house in Olive Street, repeated her thoughts to her friend. Megana looked thoughtful.

"You'll have to have a cover," she said, apparently ignoring Signy's worries. "Several convoys of carts and packhorses have congregated in the town. The traders are fearful of the fighting, and the risk from the roving auxiliaries, but they can't – we can't – afford to loiter in Agininum. If we pool resources, a score of armed men and a much larger number of tough carters and mule drivers, then that should be enough to dissuade anyone. You and Maxus can travel with the group. It'll be all the better if there are several traders in the convoy. Then you won't look like you are in Sismond's pocket before you even get to Tolosa."

"You make it sound all so straightforward."

"Why not?" answered Megana. "It's a matter of first getting from A to B, but then once you're at B, there's not so much I can do to help you."

"Will you come, too?"

"Sismond forbade me," said Megana.

"Maybe he's right," said Signy. "We still have our children to think of. Einar will need a mother if the king and the duke hold me responsible."

"The count didn't put the matter quite that way," said Megana. "In fact, I think he might just see Einar and I as hostages for your good behaviour, so that you don't ride straight past Tolosa, on to Agatha and out of all our lives."

"Is that what you fear, too?"

"No, of course not. Listen, if I'm not in Tolosa, you can stay in the rooms I use when I'm in the city, above the warehouse gate. They're not very comfortable, but there'd be space for you and Ferona." She frowned for a moment. "And you can make yourself useful by inventorying the warehouse. That'll be a good cover story. I had planned to do it myself, to make sure we have enough space to store the harvest through the winter months."

Megana suddenly laughed. "Do you remember when we cleared out the warehouses in Litorina? It hadn't been done for years. What a lot of junk we found from Grandfather's time!"

Signy remembered only too well: heaps of rotting root vegetables, vermin-filled bales of wool, rats' nests and owls' nests, dust and stink.

"I hope it won't be that bad," she said, "but I'll do what you ask so long as it doesn't annoy your factor, to have a nosey woman poking in his storehouses."

"I'll send Pythias a message. I'll tell him I have delegated the task to you."

Signy still wasn't entirely at ease. Megana leaned across and patted her knee. "Darling, people here are no different from Britannia, and there you had the king round your little finger."

That was different, thought Signy. In Britannia, I had helped the king. He was my friend, long before he became my lover. This Theodoric will only know I'm a foolish heathen girl, who slept with one of his enemies. Megana caught her eye and lifted her glass.

"To our luck, and now that we seem to have got it back, long may it last."

☙ Chapter 50 ❧
Aginінum

Tygon, Sismond's chamberlain, bowed and retreated. The remaining men waited until he had departed before speaking. Only then did the count glance around the table at his friends and fellow counts, Meltris and Rodmer. At least they had shown up in response to his request for assistance; merely to talk, perhaps, but that was a start. That's why I asked you here, he thought, so I'm not seen as acting alone. I need friends, and you're the best at hand, dim and reluctant, maybe, but trustworthy allies, nonetheless.

"This quarrel with Altaar's your fight, Sismond," said Meltris of Vasates, lifting his glass to his mouth.

"And you, Rodmer, what do you think?" asked Sismond, turning to the man beside him.

Rodmer of Elusa thought for a moment, perhaps because he was still savouring Sismond's wine.

"Not bad this, Sismond. You must tell me where you got it from."

"From your own estate, Rodmer," said Sismond. "You sold it to a merchant here in Aginінum, one Megana Fabiana."

Rodmer shook his head.

"I had nothing to do with that. The steward of my vineyard manages the trading. I inherited his father from the previous owner."

Sismond grinned collegially.

"I can guess your steward has a soft spot for pretty women, Rodmer. You should pay more attention to your servants, my friend. Keep them on a tight rein, that's always been my principle." He glanced down the table at Jorid, who was carefully suppressing a grin.

"But you have no vineyards, Sismond, so how can you lecture me on supervising my steward? He knows more than I do. If I annoy him, God knows what vinegar he'll deliver to my cellar."

"It seems," said Meltris, "that he's delivering vinegar already, and selling off the good wine…"

"…and probably keeping the very best for himself," laughed Sismond.

Rodmer took another drink.

"Back to the subject, Brother Sismond. I agree with Meltris that Altaar's your responsibility, but I admit he does seem to have been complicit with the king's enemies."

"We don't know that they are the king's enemies," said Meltris.

"Bandits," growled Sismond, "are the king's enemies by definition!"

"There's a great deal of difference between being complicit and turning a blind eye."

"Not in my book," said Sismond, "when you're on the receiving end. And in any case, that's a minor matter. What about this gang of imperialists camped out in his lands?"

"They're disputed lands, Sismond. Arelate would claim that they have a right to be there, and Theodoric's so anxious not to offend the Empire's men."

"But they marched into my lands, our lands, Theodoric's lands!"

"A misunderstanding, perhaps?"

"It was no misunderstanding. It was a fucking incursion. I've a confession from the centurion. Why would Theodoric cut off his own reinforcements, just when the Empire began to press him in the east? No, Altaar was conspiring, conspiring with his wife's uncle, and I've evidence for that, too."

"Ludiger, the duke, you mean." Rodmer sounded anxious.

"I don't like to set myself up against the duke," murmured Meltris.

"You don't have to. No one's suggesting we confront the duke directly, by sending troops into Tolosa, for example. That would be the best way to hand victory to Ludiger and his cronies. Theodoric wouldn't allow it, in any case. He would turn against us."

"Well, what are you suggesting?" said Rodmer.

Sismond frowned. He wasn't sure what he was suggesting. He was annoyed, angry, furious with Altaar. He was convinced that the Count of Cadurci had encouraged the bandits to attack his lands and done nothing about them. He was convinced Altaar had been working with the Empire's men, looking the other way, at least, while they cooked up their own plan. What was holding him back was concern that the auxiliary cavalry who had retreated from the ambush were still lurking in the hills, and that giving Altaar the bloody nose he deserved was impossible with his men alone. It would be difficult enough with a larger force, since Cadurci was surrounded on three sides by water, and on the fourth by a substantial wall. In any case, since Altaar was one of Ludiger's retainers, so long as the duke retained the king's trust, an attack on the Count of Cadurci would amount to rebellion. In other words, the roles would be reversed compared to what they were in reality. Altaar was sitting secure so long as he stayed where he was. Sismond did not, however, wish to share all his thoughts with the other counts.

"I have to keep men here when there's still the threat from the Empire's cavalry. They've already attacked Agininum once and they could do it again. And of course, if they were successful, you and your men would be next, caught on the wrong side of their blockade."

"I'd be alright," said Rodmer, with a glance at Meltris. "They'd hardly be likely to cross the river, and I could get home via Auscii."

Sismond picked up a walnut, crushed the shell in his hand and popped the meat into his mouth. His gaze spoke for him. If you can cross the river and get home via Auscii, then they can, too, and a lot quicker. He crunched contemplatively for a moment.

"It's exactly what they want me to do, of course," he said, "to gallop heedlessly off to Cadurci, like a damned fool. That's why I've not been pursuing the cavalry, to avoid being drawn into a trap."

"I see your point," said Meltris. "If we don't clear out these mysterious horsemen, then we all risk a stab in the back."

It was the Count of Vasates' turn to look thoughtful.

"I could peel off part of my forces, Sismond, to support you, if Rodmer would do the same. That should even up the numbers. But no assault on Cadurci…"

"I've no intention of assaulting Cadurci," said Sismond with reassurance masking a quiet satisfaction. "Neutralise the auxiliaries and make a show of force against Altaar, that's all. And maybe then Ludiger'll be provoked to show his hand."

"Then you'll be risking an attack in your rear…by half of Aquitania."

"That's where I'm counting on you, my friends, Meltris and Rodmer. I've already sent Thormond a message, but encouragement from two loyal allies like you…that's bound to persuade my cousin that he needs to act against Ludiger before it's too late."

"And you're telling us that Ludiger's in league with the Empire, that Ludiger's encouraged them to move against us."

"I have it on best authority."

"Who…someone in the inner circles of the court?"

Sismond smiled slyly.

"You could say that. Someone who has their own sources very close to Ludiger, that I promise."

"You make Tolosa sound like a nest of vipers," said Meltris. "You make me glad that I spend most of my time in the provinces."

"Eating and drinking and hunting, and none of these intrigues," agreed Rodmer.

"If we can work together," said Sismond, "then the sooner we can all go back to whatever pleasures we enjoy best, and it'll be Ludiger's folks who have to sleep with one eye open, if they sleep at all. More wine, gentlemen, and then the food will be served. I've no dancers tonight, but I promise you, if we pull this off, I'll make sure we have the best girls in the south of Gaul as entertainment at the celebration."

☙ Chapter 51 ❧
Tolosa

There was a voice behind her, a female voice, soft, barely above a whisper. Signy was standing at a market stall, examining fruit displayed for view. She had never visited Tolosa before, knew no one in the town. She had thought she would be merely an anonymous stranger, dressed as she was in a plain but well-cut gown and with a scarf pulled tightly around her head, merely Megana the trader's assistant.

"Don't turn round, don't look at me, just listen. Walk slowly and casually to the Fox Tavern. They'll be looking out for you. Pass the serving area and continue into the kitchen. When you get there, you will receive new instructions. Do as I say, Mistress Signy. I'm your friend, and I wish to help you."

She stood, frozen in place, and then forced herself, forced her hand to reach out and lift up a bunch of grapes, examine them, pick one off and pop it into her mouth.

"Very good," she said. "Put some aside for me, six bunches. I'll send my maid later to collect them."

Only now did she turn, but there was no one to be seen but other marketers, shoppers and sellers, and people with nothing better to do.

She clutched her basket and carefully made her way through the crowd. She had not recognised the voice, but there was something about it that roused a memory, an impossible memory of laughter at dinner, of wine and cakes.

She knew the Fox Tavern by reputation, knew that the inn was a drinking place favoured by soldiers, by men from the king's bodyguard, workshop owners and horse traders, her own men when they were visiting Tolosa. The Fox Tavern was not a place where she had ever considered setting foot, so why had the mystery woman directed her there?

It could be a trap, of course. Sismond had warned her that Ludiger and his cohorts might see her as just as much of a threat as Centurion Maxus. But then Ludiger would not need to lure her. If he knew or cared who she was, Ludiger could saunter into the warehouse and ask her politely to accompany him to the palace, and she would have to obey him. Ludiger could carry her away by force, without suggesting she should walk to her doom of her own free will. Ludiger could simply have his retainers finish her off where she stood in the marketplace.

She tried to control her breathing, stopped once or twice to peer into shops, but that did not prevent her from accidentally barging into a farm woman, spilling the contents of the basket she was carrying. She apologised, bent down to collect the fruit that had rolled onto the street. It was a mistake, a nervous mistake, she realised. A woman dressed like her would never normally stoop to help a countrywoman, no matter if she was at fault. Nonetheless, she placed the fruit carefully back into the woman's basket, smiled reassuringly, though she felt like fleeing from the scene.

She cut through a passage which led to the street running parallel to the market, a narrow passage, with room for just one person, instead of walking all the way across the forum to the basilica square and then making her way back up the hill to her goal. She looked back. No one was following her, but then no one needed to, so long as she was in the passageway. They could watch her. She could turn neither left nor right. An urchin came hurrying towards her, noticing her only at the last moment. He stopped, looked up, took a half-step to one side. An urchin could carry a knife, she thought. An urchin could kick her in a sensitive place, disable her long enough for his master to run down the alley to complete the job. She squeezed against the wall and lifted her basket above the boy's head. He ducked and said, "'Scuse me, ma'am," and continued on his way.

The Fox Tavern was on her right. A counter ran along the street. A couple of men lounged against it in preference to using the seats arranged in front. They watched as she walked up. For a moment, she thought they might intervene, prevent her from entering, but though their eyes followed her, they did not move from their spots. She stepped into the gloom of the tavern's inner room, saw a serving desk ahead of her, several dishes of meat and a stack of bread. A man stood behind the desk, wiping a beaker with a cloth. He said nothing but indicated with his eyes that she should continue into the back of the tavern, not using the passageway and stairs that led to private rooms, but under the arch into the kitchen.

"Stay where you are, Miss," said the cook. He paused in his slicing of the meat, a chopper still in his hand. It made no sense to argue with him. A moment later, a boy ran in from the street, the same boy who had pushed past her in the passage, she saw.

"She's clean, what I could see," he said.

"Clean," she echoed.

"No one following you, Miss," said the cook. "You're to slip out the back…there's an alley. Three doors down, there's the back entrance to a tanner's yard. You're to go in. In front of you's a flight of wooden stairs. Go up the stairs, and you'll find the next set of directions."

"You want me to follow 'er again, Baz?" said the boy.

"You stay here a moment, and let her get on her way, and then go out the front and around by Cow Alley, and keep an eye out that no one else goes into the tanner's yard."

Before Signy had time to move, the boy had darted off. The cook shook his head and waved her on her way.

The rear of the tavern was a place of constructive chaos: stables and storehouses, calls and laughter, a whistle as she emerged. She passed out of the rear gate into the alley and turned to her right. One, two, three doors she counted and then, with a quick glance around, entered the tanner's yard. The stench was unbelievable: urine, traces of rotting flesh, all mixed with smoke and bitter fumes, enough to keep anyone without a purpose well away. Ahead was the staircase. No one stopped her as she slipped across the yard and up the stairs. There was a note pinned to the door, a thin slip of papyrus, with the words: *Turn left, take the door in the far wall, go down the stairs and follow the tunnel. You'll be met at the far end.*

She did as she was instructed. The lofts of the works at this end of the street were interconnected, and at the far end there was a door set in the wall. She opened it and was confronted by a steep flight of stone steps concealed in the end wall of the building and leading down below street level. Once she was at the foot, a passageway stretched out before her, dimly lit by sputtering lamps. The air was foul and suffocating, and she hurried on until she reached another set of steps which she almost ran up. At the top was another door, and when she opened it she stepped into another world, a world of colour, of perfume, a world where a pretty girl in a silk dress called out to her.

"Mistress Signy, please follow me."

Wonderingly, she did as she was told. The girl led her down another passage, lined with painted figures of gods and goddesses frolicking, if that was the right word. They climbed a further set of stairs, and the girl in the silk dress came to a halt and knocked softly on another door, before pushing it open. She beckoned Signy to follow. There was a woman standing in the room, also dressed in silk, with silver bangles on her arms and a chain of jewels around her neck. Her hair was carefully arranged with pins that sparkled in the lamplight and the thin rays that pierced the carved screens covering the windows.

"Welcome, Mistress Signy, I'm sorry I had to arrange our meeting like this, but I didn't want anyone to know we *were* meeting."

Signy recognised the voice that she had heard in the marketplace.

The woman gestured to an array of cushions on the floor, suggesting Signy should sit, at the same time speaking to the girl who had accompanied her in a tongue Signy did not understand, neither Latin nor Greek. Her instructions passed on, the woman lowered herself to the cushion, wrapping her legs around with an elegance Signy could not hope to copy.

"My name is Xancha," she said. "I know you are new to Tolosa, but perhaps you've heard of me."

"My friend, Megana, has spoken of you."

Xancha smiled.

"Then you know I've lived in this city many years. I came alone and impoverished, with nothing but my talents. I've tried to use them well. It's always helped that people, men and women, have taken me for a pretty little dancer, a mere courtesan, if you want to use a polite word."

"Not everyone has underestimated you, I think," said Signy, as Xancha poured her wine, "if Megana is to be believed."

"The vast majority," said Xancha, raising her glass.

The girl reappeared with food, small delicacies to be eaten with the fingers, a bowl of rose water and two towels.

When she had gone, Xancha spoke again, her tone firmer, harder.

"You've become involved in some serious business, Mistress Signy, by accident perhaps, but nonetheless…I keep my ears and eyes open, and so do my friends, and they tell me that Geseric, nephew of General Thormond, has fallen in love with you, is openly talking of marrying you."

Signy could not meet her eyes, instead directing her effort into selecting a delicacy from the plate between them.

She could sense Xancha smiling.

"So it's true, and you reciprocate. You seem to change your favours very quickly."

"Did you ask me here to insult me?" said Signy suddenly, her hand with the food piece frozen in mid-air.

"Not at all. I apologise if my words came off that way. I'm merely trying to confirm what I've heard through rumours. Those rumours said that you were the bed companion of a Roman officer, one Captain Junius."

"Can't a girl get laid around here without everyone hearing about it?" Signy's irritation was evident.

"Not often," Xancha replied, laughing lightly, "especially when your bed partners are mixed up in a conspiracy. That sparked a certain additional curiosity. Some people, for example, think you're a spy, though for who is not clear, others that you're some sort of sorceress, seeking illicit power for yourself…I've been accused of that myself, by the way, so don't take it as an insult."

"And are you?" asked Signy, trying to regain a little initiative.

"What?"

"Seeking power, spying, using your charms, spreading your favours about?"

Xancha laughed out loud this time.

"I'm trying to stay alive, trying to put food in my mouth and have a bed for the night. There was a time when I had neither and death seemed like a tempting solution."

"I was lonely," Signy said. "I found myself in a difficult and strange situation, with a handsome man. I wanted him, and I enjoyed having him. You've been lonely. Have you never felt that way yourself? And then I learned that he had been deceiving me, not in matters of romance, should I say – there was no romance – I had fun with him and he with me. No, he deceived me as to his purpose, as to his involvement in killings, and I realised he was a threat to my friends."

"And he disappeared…on a visit to Agininum…where you happen to live. I'm sure I'm not the only one to suspect that he was lured into a trap."

"But he wasn't. I did nothing to trap him. He came quite voluntarily. In truth, I was the one who had to force myself to meet him that final time."

"But you did meet him?"

"I did, and I killed him – myself."

She waited to see how Xancha would respond, but there was no reaction for a moment until she asked, "How do you want me to use that knowledge, Signy? I doubt a mere impulse led you to tell me that."

"I would prefer you kept the information to yourself for now. It might prejudice men against me, the king, for example, if I'm called to bear witness."

"So a test? To see if I can keep my word?"

"You're a friend of General Thormond, that I know, but I'm not sure who else might listen to your whispered words."

Xancha laughed. "I've retired, I promise you, from whispering in men's ears, least of all Theo's. But you trust me, it seems?"

"Megana trusts you, so I must trust you. We swore an oath, years ago…look here." She held out her hand, allowing the lamplight to fall on her thumb.

"A scar…Megana showed me a similar mark."

"So what is the warning you had for me?"

"Yes, let's get back to that. Sismond sent me a copy of the letter that he wrote to Theodoric. In it he explained how you stumbled across the imperial camp, and made friends with one of their officers, this man, Junius. Junius was important to certain powerful men in Tolosa, the liaison between them and the Roman leadership in Arelate. He was one of the men who planned the attack on our kingdom. He boasted that he had a pretty woman in Agininum, and that visiting her gave him cover to explore the town and design a plan for its capture."

"How do you know this?" Xancha had already mentioned hearing rumours earlier, but this sounded more like firm knowledge, and Signy felt her reputation was ruined before she had even set foot in the city.

The ex-dancer pursed her lips.

"Let's say *I* may not whisper in men's ears, but they have a tendency to whisper in the ears of the girls I employ. Not your Junius, I hasten to add – he was professional enough to keep his belt fastened here in Tolosa – but others, who suspect the woman had something to do with the death of Junius. They know she's somewhere in the city, ready to be called for questioning. Just now they're spreading a rumour that she's a heathen sorceress, come to pollute the Christian Church, to discredit her. They're also implying that Thormond and his family and allies are a part of this plan."

"But it's nonsense. I'm no one, a poor stranger."

"That's all the more convenient for them, Signy. And it's true, you do bear certain marks…"

"I'm a healer, Xancha. They're the marks of my sisterhood of healers."

"The lynx head, Signy…I don't think so, not entirely, anyway. I've had a multitude of women and girls through my hands over the years, from many lands, and I've learned a great deal. You cannot carry the mark of the lynx-sisters without being a priestess, any more than the mark of the bear or the elm."

"I am…was…not a priestess, Xancha, merely a curious girl who wanted to learn, and that doesn't make me a sorceress!"

"You don't need to defend yourself to me, Signy. The words people – I would say men, but I've found women are as bad if not worse – use for me are not exactly complimentary, but they still can't resist my services."

She sipped her wine.

"My mother was a dancer in a temple," she said, finally, "far, far away beyond the Middle Sea, until the Christians came and slaughtered the priests and pulled down the altar, and ended her worship for ever. She taught me to dance, and wherever I danced, wherever I used my body, I did it in honour of our god. If there's one reputation more likely to cause public scandal in a Christian country than being a sorceress, it's being a whore and procuress!"

The ex-dancer was silent for a moment.

"And the young men?" she said. "Can you trust them?"

"The men?"

"The men you brought with you. They're loyal to you because you're their priestess?"

"No, it's because I saved their lives, long ago in Britannia, and I was the wife of their chief."

"It makes a bond, doesn't it, when you save a man's life, when you're the wife of his chief…but they know who you represent, and they obey your orders."

Xancha popped a date into her mouth.

"If my requests are justified. My men are not slaves," said Signy.

"Let's hope they find your requests justified, then, over the next few days. Matters are coming to a head, and we'll need all the men we can find, yours included."

"We?" Did she mean General Thormond and Count Sismond?

Xancha smiled.

"I'm on the side of good, of honesty, of keeping your word. We *are* on the same side, aren't we?"

☙ Chapter 52 ❧ By the Oltis

The monks were not especially joyful. Count Sismond and his retinue had ridden over the hills from Agininum, and the buildings, yards and gardens of the monastery by the Oltis had been taken over by militiamen from the neighbourhood: not just Sismond's men, but contingents from Vasates and Elusa as well. Henrik and Grunwald had ridden with them.

"Only for a few days, only for a few days, and then we'll leave for Cadurci," Sismond assured Abbot Angelus, but the count's words did little to satisfy the monk.

"But you've scores of hungry warriors and their horses to accommodate and feed," the abbot protested. "And if I know the ways of armies, you'll want to take all our remaining food with you, our horses too – unless Brother Wilbert can hide them," he added under his breath.

"You've seen no sign of strange riders in the hills?" asked the count, ignoring his host's complaint. The abbot shook his head. The count considered. "That fits with my own intelligence. They've cleared out, and I don't need to guess where they've gone. I need to smoke out that serpent Altaar," he mused aloud, as if the abbot was one of his military officers.

"We use smoke on our bees," said the abbot, trying to be helpful. "It keeps them quiet when we take their honey."

"Smoke out…smoke out…" continued the count. "I'm not interested in keeping people quiet, Father, but stirring them up. You'll excuse me, I hope…" he added, rising to his feet.

"By all means, by all means," said the abbot, trying not to show his relief as Sismond made a sudden exit. Angelus himself rose from his chair, and checking that the passageway was empty, took off in the opposite direction, not to pray, as might be expected, but to find Brother Wilbert and ensure that some stores would remain hidden until after the count and his men had left.

--oo00oo--

Sismond hurried on between the buildings of the monastery. The men he was looking for were housed in the infirmary. They had visited the monastery on previous occasions and knew the most comfortable quarters.

"Grunwald," he called as he strode into the building.

"My lord," said Grunwald, detaching himself from a group playing dice.

"Hey, don't slide off when you are losing," came a voice from behind the big Jute.

"I've a task for you," said the count. "It's not a very honourable one, but if you want your revenge on Altaar and his gang, you'll do it for me. Smoke them out…literally…rags soaked in oil!"

Grunwald listened in silence, and before the count had finished his explanation, the two men were already on their way to the stable yard. They found Abbot Angelus in conspiratorial conversation with Brother Wilbert.

"How convenient," said the count, with an ironic smile to the abbot. "We can obtain your permission without having to mount a search."

"What do you want?"

"Two of your most broken-down horses and a donkey cart," said Grunwald, "and four sets of shabby clothes."

"Broken-down horses…not our best ones?" mumbled the abbot. "And our cart…but we only have one!"

"It is shabby, though," admitted Brother Wilbert.

"We can take the clothes from your lay brothers," said Grunwald.

"You could dress as monks," suggested Sismond, with a glance at the Jute.

"No, no…please," begged the abbot, "take our cart and our horses but don't ruin our reputation."

Sismond sighed.

"I'll return your horses, Abbot, and your cart, even donate you a new one, but perhaps you're right. I wouldn't want to incur God's wrath by abusing the costumes of His servants. You can manage as regular peasants?"

"I expect so," said Grunwald, sounding relieved.

"Wouldn't want to risk offending a god, eh?" chuckled Sismond. "Even if you don't believe in him."

--oo0Ooo--

The troops rose early and departed a little after dawn. The abbot wasn't sorry to see them leave. By mid-afternoon, Sismond was leading his men down the road so thoughtfully cleared and levelled by Centurion Maxus to the ford over the Oltis and into the disputed territories. Four men remained at the junction to Cadurci. They were dressed in the clothing of a quartet of poor farmers. Two of them held the reins of small, thin horses, the others kept watch on a donkey cart.

"You have tinder and a light, in case we're turned away," said Grunwald.

Svein nodded. Henrik pointed to his pack.

"Two days from now, at the inn where we had supper, that time in the winter, right?" said the stablemaster.

"The Goat and Pipes," said Grunwald.

"It's Pan," said Tomas.

"What's a pan?"

"Pan, the god, on the inn sign."

"It looks like a fucking goat playing a pipe to me," said Grunwald.

"That's the one," said Svein.

"Until then, brothers," said Grunwald.

The four men hugged one another.

Henrik and Svein climbed cautiously onto their horses and prodded them down the track towards the river. Grunwald and Tomas climbed onto the cart. Grunwald pulled down the brim of his tattered straw hat and cracked the whip. The donkey woke out of its slumber and with a reluctant effort began to pull at the cart.

☙ Chapter 53 ❧
Agininum

Megana sighed. She felt worried and isolated. Even Henrik had ridden off with Sismond's men. There were only women and girls in the house in Olive Street, and Ragvald. He still looked menacing but, despite Signy's efforts, he wouldn't be much good in a fight if the renegade auxiliaries managed to slip past the count.

And to make matters worse, a note had come from the bishop. The *notarius* had given his approval. She should come over to the palace and thrash out the remaining details of the deal. Normally work would be a welcome distraction, but just now she only felt an insurmountable resistance to focussing on vines and corn and boat ramps and new field tracks and God knows what else was necessary to bring her plan to fruition. Fruit, of course, apples and plums, apricots, even. She gathered her documents together, tied them in a bundle and began an uncharacteristically weary trudge up the hill to the house by the cathedral.

The bishop was all smiles when she came into his study. His clerk was in the process of laying out a roll of parchment, the charter that would state that Megana Fabiana, widow, of the city of Agininum, would lease the diocesan lands for twenty years, in return for an annual fee, payment of taxes and certain improvements to be listed in an appendix. The names were already written in. All that was needed was for Megana to make her mark and add her seal. Together with the lease of the monastery lands, and her own parcel by the shore, she would become one of the largest land holders in the Oltis valley. She would not own the land, but landownership was a flexible concept in any case, when the king could give what you had always imagined was your property to another man or to the church, or worse, an enemy could make his own adjustments of the frontier, and you suddenly found your hard-won home was under the control of quite another monarch with his own set of cronies to reward. Better to have a nice legally tight lease, and then it did not really matter who imagined they owned the land.

She scrutinised the bishop, his honest eyes, his open face, his light smile. Would this man really try to trick her? she wondered, taking the proffered pen from the clerk. Perhaps not the bishop, who evidently understood little of trading, she sadly thought, but his clerk or the notary, or whoever else had cast an eye over the contract with hope of his own gain. She laid the pen down beside the document and began untying her own bundle.

The charter was written on parchment in elegant calligraphy, pricked out neatly, so the lines were straight and evenly spaced. The clerk had even gone to the trouble to ink in the first letter of each paragraph in red and blue. Megana's notes were scribbled, crossed out, jottings added here and there. She had not had the time nor the energy to produce a neat copy.

The bishop took up one of the sheets and rotated it from left to right to try to read the various additions and revisions.

Megana felt ashamed, felt she had not met his expectation, that, in sum, she had done a bad job.

"What's this?" he said, suddenly pointing.

"Oh, I'm sorry," she said, "that means three carts of crushed rock, but I wrote the words in British. I don't know the equivalent in Latin."

She could see his brow furrow.

"I'm sorry," she said again. She looked around, spotted a bench a little way off, took a step or two and sat down, her head in her hands. "I'm ashamed, too, to show you these scribblings, when you've put so much trust in me…trust that I would do a good job for you."

At the same time, she couldn't help wondering what had come over her. She wasn't usually like this, miserable, self-pitying, almost begging for sympathy and help. She should just pull herself together, harden her heart, put a scowl on her face, get the job done and go home.

"Perhaps a glass of wine would help," said the bishop, with a glance at his clerk and a little gesture with his forefinger.

"Nothing special," she said.

"For you," said the bishop, "it'll have to be special."

He hesitated for a moment, and sat down beside her, his hands on his knees.

She lifted her face and looked at him.

"I feel like a fool," she said. "I'm supposed to be a hard-headed merchant, closing my deal, and instead…I'm so worried. Signy has gone to Tolosa, and I think she's in trouble, and all our men have gone with the count, and my warehouse is full and these marauders could strike at any time."

She felt her eyes becoming damp and was forced to wipe them with her hand.

"These moments come to all of us," said the bishop. "Me too, when I'm alone, facing the problems of the world and seeing how very little I can do about them."

"You have your prayer and your God. I don't think God cares so much about my business deals."

"But I'm sure He cares about your friend. In fact, I know He does."

Seeing Megana's face rumple into a frown, the bishop rubbed his chin, as if considering how much he could tell.

"Let's say Mistress Signy came to me with a spiritual question, seeking a sign, she said, as to which path she should take."

"Path?"

"To continue her old heathen ways or turn to Christ."

"And did you point her in the right direction?"

"I'm not sure I'm competent to do that," said the bishop, sniffing. "I think she answers to an altogether different authority." To Megana's surprise, he seemed quite at ease with the idea. "I wasn't sure I could advise her at all. One has to be so careful choosing one's words in a position like mine. You never know how people might take them."

His eyes met Megana's just as the clerk returned, followed by the bishop's housekeeper bearing a tray with glasses and a pair of jugs. The bishop thanked them, while making it quite clear they did not need to stay. He poured the wine, added water and handed a glass to Megana.

Megana had some experience at recognising the quality of wine, and as she took a sip she realised this was excellent wine.

"It's from my family lands in Italia," the bishop said. "I'm sent three amphorae a year, providing I stay away."

"Stay away?" said Megana. "From your family lands! That sounds terrible." Not that her own situation was much better.

"I thought so too in the first years, to be banished from one's own home. But you see, I'm a third son. There's no place for me on my family estate, so I was destined for the Church before I even knew it. With a most generous settlement, too, not just the wine but an annual allowance, providing, of course, I don't get married, have children and complicate the inheritance. And you know what," he continued, lifting his glass and nodding contemplatively, "God must have seen my predicament, and made me the kind of person who fits right in with the religious life and not only that, He directed my path, step by step, all the way to a new home, new friends, new family, almost, in Agininum."

"I've been banished, too," Megana commented, "forbidden to return to my family home…on pain of death, not just loss of fortune. I can't blame anything or anyone but myself, not an inheritance nor my parents and siblings. Maybe I also have to believe that God directed my steps here to Agininum, though I've never felt Him speaking to me."

The bishop returned to the bench, a little separated from her, and turned towards her without saying anything, as if he was anticipating a continuation of Megana's confession.

She had to lighten her heart, she felt, and she began to talk, to tell her story, and after a while, they went to the evening service together, and when they came back, a meal was waiting for them.

☙ Chapter 54 ❧
Tolosa

Suddenly, Signy felt arms tightly wrapped around her. One moment she had her mind on the offer Xancha had made to use her bath and sample her oriental scents, before her audience with the king, and the next she was being dragged backwards.

"Cover her eyes," growled a voice.

"Hey, what are you doing?" came a second.

"Let go, let go. Help…" Her own voice in her ears. She had taken Xancha's warning sufficiently seriously that she had remained at the warehouse, auditing the contents, since their meeting, and now she had asked Hrasmus and Ferona to accompany her to the ex-dancer's house and from there to the gate of the palace where a message said General Thormond's man would be waiting for her.

"Shut up!"

"Help!"

"Stop that!"

"Let me go!"

She was dragged backwards, the faces and the shapes of the market swirling about her. She could hear Ferona shouting, but there was nothing her pupil could do to stop the men. And Hrasmus, where was he? Lying in the gutter, gasping for breath! She could dimly recognise him from the corner of her eye.

"Cover her eyes!"

"Shut the fuck up, and get her into the alley."

"Help! Stop, you're hurting!"

"Get back, you…you're looking for trouble?"

"Get your hands off me!"

"Let go of the woman!"

"Fuck off, it's none of your business!"

"Who are you?"

Her shawl was suddenly pulled over her face and she could no longer see her surroundings. Though that did not matter. She could feel herself being turned around and propelled forward. She could hear from her footsteps and from those of the men that she was in one of the narrow lanes which led from the marketplace. The friendly voices disappeared and only the panting and gasping of her attackers remained. They pushed her along roughly, and she was forced to take ever more rapid steps to stay on her feet. She tripped against a protruding cobble stone and almost fell. The second of her attackers took her by the legs and lifted her from the ground.

The sound changed. They must have left the alley and now emerged into a broader street, then came alley-echoes again. She could not tell if they were going uphill or downhill. She tried to wriggle, to make things difficult for her kidnappers, but only received curses and a blow for her effort.

"Where are we going?" she asked, half-stifled by her shawl.

"Shut up!" was the reply.

The men began to tire. The pace of their steps to slow. She tried kicking again.

"What the fuck! Cut it out," came the cry from the man who had hold of her feet. "Put her down! She can walk now we're nearly there."

Her soles once more made contact with the pavement.

"Walk, woman," snarled the man who had hold of her. She walked.

"Oh, shit, she caught me in the ribs with her foot," complained the other.

"They warned us she was a tricky bitch," said his companion. "Turn here," he added, yanking her round.

An echo above suggested they had gone under an archway, and then a few moments later, there was a dramatic shift in the light penetrating the shawl. They must be inside a building.

"Where did he want her?"

"Ha, ha, don't ask!"

"No, she's not one of those…he said put her in one of the cellars."

The man holding her came to a halt.

"I'm uncovering you! No fucking shouting or tricks. No one here's going to help you!"

He pulled away the shawl. She saw she was standing in a covered way, plain-plastered, the back part of one of the bigger houses in Tolosa, an inn, a warehouse, even.

She now caught sight of the man, the one who had had her feet. He could have been any run-of-the-mill ruffian in the town. He did not look at her, but instead walked ahead down a side passage until he came to a set of steps and began to descend. The man behind pushed her on.

"Careful…do you want me to fall?"

"Not my fucking business if you do," he replied.

It was only dimly lit at the bottom of the stairs, some slits of light up by the ceiling and a sputtering oil lamp.

"In here," said the man in the lead, and she was pushed roughly into a small empty room.

"Thank God for that," said the man, as she stumbled past him. "We'd've been in trouble if the crowd had turned on us."

"Told you surprise was the only way to do it," said the man who had had hold of her, who now took a step back, swinging the door shut as his companion exited the room.

She was in a cellar space, which smelled slightly damp. The last part of her journey had been downhill, and this cellar must be close to the river, close to the palace, in the palace, possibly. Who was the "he" they had referred to…the king? Hardly! She had been ordered to appear at the palace that afternoon, and she had every intention of showing up. Presumably the men who had kidnapped her knew this, or at least their employer did.

She stood still for a moment. At least she was not tied. Her eyes adjusting to the light. She glanced around. The only objects in the room were a wooden pail, its stink suggesting it was for her needs, should she survive that long, and a rough-looking mattress. There was nothing else she could do but sit on the mattress, her back against the wall, as far away from the door and the stinking pail as possible.

She had been warned. Xancha had warned her that she might be in trouble, that Sismond and his cousin, the general, had enemies, but she had never thought she could be grabbed in the street, in broad daylight on her way to the palace. She would have had no chance even if she had had her dagger with her.

Her mind went for a moment to Hrasmus, hoping that her bodyguard had only been punched and not stabbed.

I suppose, she reflected, that I should be grateful that they carried me off and didn't just kill me right away. It would have been easy enough in the crowd.

Whether she should be grateful would depend on what happened next, she concluded.

What did happen next was boot steps in the passage outside, male voices, the door being opened, and a man stepping into her prison. She struggled to her feet, cramped by sitting. Whoever was with the man had a torch, but her vision took a moment to recover enough to make him out properly: tall and heavily built.

"So…Mistress Signy," said the man, "the notorious sorceress."

She did not reply. She could see the man was well-dressed, in the style of Our Men, but with a neatly trimmed beard and hair. He seemed to be older, the age at least of Count Sismond.

"Do you know who I am?" he asked.

She shook her head. She had never seen him before, but an uncomfortable feeling began to form in her mind.

"Ludiger, master of the armies of the Visigoth Kingdom," he replied, confirming her fears, "popularly known as Duke Ludiger. You have heard of me?" he asked.

"I have," she replied.

"Yes, and probably nothing favourable."

"On the contrary," she said, with a note of bitterness. "Captain Junius spoke very highly of you."

The duke grunted.

"My enemies claim that I cannot add two and two and make four. Well, let me explain to you, whatever they say, I'm perfectly capable of adding one and one and one and one, and making that to four. Let's try. One." He touched the index finger of his right hand against the index finger of his left. "Captain Junius told me that he had a pretty woman who he visited as a cover in Agininum. Two." He shifted his right index finger to the middle finger of the left hand. "My dear friend, General Thormond, requests a private audience with the king for a witness to events which have taken place in Agininum. Three." He continued to count with his fingers. "A pretty woman, never before seen in Tolosa, suddenly appears at the warehouse of a trader from Agininum, and four, the previously mentioned pretty woman pays a visit to Thormond's notorious lover by means of her secret back entrance…Yes, Mistress, the whore isn't the only one to have her spies in Tolosa. Now do you see I'm quite as capable of adding up and drawing conclusions as any logician."

Signy held her tongue.

"So you have nothing to say," the duke continued after a short silence. "Well, I can add one more little fact. Before the captain sadly vanished without trace, he reported that his sweet little friend had the marks of a sorceress on her body." He smiled. "Shall we take a look and check my reasoning?"

He reached out and grabbed at her tunic.

"Bring the torch nearer!"

Signy took a deep breath.

"There is no need…I'll show you." She drew back the shoulder of her tunic, revealing the tattooed lynx head.

"Hah, so you are the woman. Do you know what the punishment is for sorcery?" asked the duke, taking a step back.

"I'm not a sorceress, merely a healer."

"Death," said the duke. He stopped, looking thoughtful. "But not straight away. This mark confirms, at least, that you're the woman Junius mentioned and, if hearsay is correct, you've now ensnared Geseric, Thormond's nephew, with your wily charms. Would you like to try them on me while you have the opportunity?" he continued, though the look on his face did not imply any serious invitation.

He turned to the men behind him.

"No…for now I have another use for this sorceress's charms: to lure my enemies out and expose them, to give me the chance to eliminate them once and for all, now I have their precious witness."

He turned back to Signy.

"And then, Mistress, when this is all over, perhaps you can serve me as witness instead. I'm sure Theodoric will be interested to hear how citizens of Rome were murdered by the Count of Agininum. Do you think upsetting the authorities of the Empire is such a great strategy for keeping the kingdom at peace?"

"No," he said with a snort, "I don't suppose you thought further than satisfying your lusts." He added, shrugging, "Well, if you're not willing to cooperate, I can always hand you over to the churchmen. One look at that mark on your tit, and the other I heard you have on your arse, and the crowd'll be calling for your death, and congratulating me at the same time."

He was exaggerating, surely, she thought, to frighten her. Bishop Anastasius had not reacted that way, nor the other Christians she had met. But, of course, she was in Ludiger's hands now, and in his city. No doubt people would do as he wished.

The duke turned to the guards, saying, "Bring some food for her," and then back to Signy.

"Don't worry, you really won't be poisoned. As I said, I can use you alive just at the moment. But all in good time…When you've eaten, you'll be going on a journey, so make sure you use that bucket before you set off."

Signy watched the door close with a bang, heard their footsteps in the corridor, the change in character of the sound as the men mounted the stairs.

To think I imagined that the interview with the king was my punishment, she reflected. Just now I would be glad to kiss his feet and beg for justice.

The food came, good food, a share, perhaps, of what the duke himself was eating, though with only a wooden spoon as a utensil. Evidently she really did have some value to Ludiger. Her mood hardly lifted, but the feeling of complete hopelessness began to dissipate.

Men came. Whether they were the same men or different men, she could not be sure. They carried a rough woollen cloak with an ample hood. They bound her wrists behind her, tied a scarf over her face, wrapped the cloak around her and then pulled up the hood. She did not struggle. There was no other way out of the cellar than in the company of these men. The duke had said he did not want her dead yet, and so, she reckoned, they would not harm her. So long as he had another plan, so long as she was alive, then she would have an opportunity.

"Walk." The man had the flat tone of someone who did not have to make an effort to ensure he was obeyed.

"Steps," he said, just as she began to worry about the stairway to ground level.

They were outside. It was dark. She could smell and hear horses, hear the jangle of harness and the creaking of a cart.

Suddenly, she was lifted, pulled.

"Lie down, Miss," said a voice. She had no choice. There was a tug at her ankles, and she felt a rope around them. The darkness intensified, and she felt a rough cloth, a cover, being dragged over her. There were more voices, a lurch and the motion of the cart, the scrape of wheels against the stone.

꧁ Chapter 55 ꧂
Agininum

When Megana woke up, she first thought she had died and gone to heaven. She was lying in a room decorated from floor to ceiling with frescos of trees and flowers, dolphins splashing in foaming waves, and nymphs playing under exotic trees, and hovering just visible out of the corner of her eye was the vague outline of a figure dressed in white.

Then she remembered. She was in the bishop's guestroom, and the spectral figure was probably only her maid, Delia.

Anastasius had listened to her story long into the evening, and then she had listened to his, until the late hour compelled them to recognise that they should turn in for the night. The bishop, seeing Megana's anxious state beneath the numbing effects of a second shared jug of wine, suggested rather than Megana returning home in the pitch dark of an uneasy night that he had several comfortable guestrooms available which he would be happy to offer to her. When she accepted, he had sent his steward down to Olive Street to let the household know that their mistress would be staying away.

Megana lay still, not wishing to alert her maid that she had woken. How different this room was to her usual overnight stays in travellers hostels up and down the road between Tolosa and Burdigala! As a respected merchant, she never stayed in the public dormitories, but even the private rooms were plain and rough. She would sleep in her travelling clothes, not just because doing so facilitated an early rise and quick resumption of the journey, but that several layers of dresses and gowns offered a certain protection in the case of something untoward happening. Robbery, murder and rape were thankfully rare, but that did not mean they never occurred, and traders and pilgrims were not necessarily spared. Last night, thankfully, Delia had brought the linen shift she sometimes wore in bed at home, and helped her undress and retire for the night with reasonable decency.

She really wasn't a very civilised woman, she reflected. She had read a great deal in her youth. She could speak and write in five or six tongues, depending on how you defined them. She understood geometry and could keep accounts. She could draft a charter or a bill of sale. She could manage a household, that was true, providing it was run like a trading post. But those were not the characteristics of a civilised woman, she readily acknowledged. She was neither skilled nor interested in making men feel comfortable. She could not dance or sing. She could not even spin or weave or sew. When she mounted a horse, she resembled a peasant riding on an ass, and when she did try, the beast was generally quick to detect her lack of skill and take advantage. She was unsure how good a partner she would be in bed from lack of practice. And she wasn't much good as a mother, either. Not that she didn't love her daughter, Sophia, in her own way, but Megana had to secure their position in the Kingdom of Tolosa, and the infant would have been a terrible impediment if not for the nurse, Maria.

On the other hand, Megana considered, she wasn't scared easily, and she was relatively wealthy. If she could make the deal she had struck with the bishop and the monastery work, she would be even wealthier. The men who had shown an interest in her previously had cared more about the fortune she was supposed to inherit from her father and for that reason were evidently willing to overlook her deficiencies as a civilised woman. Apart from gratification in bed, that was, which had not endeared them to her.

But now she was worried. She had been worried for Signy before she had walked the short way up to the bishop's palace the previous evening. Her friend and companion had got herself into a great deal of trouble through her liaison with this treacherous captain, but then Signy had been in a great deal of trouble at earlier times in her life, and she was cunning and resourceful, and men easily took a liking to her. Her current worry now was of a slightly different nature, Megana reflected. She had enjoyed talking to the bishop. He was a calm and open-minded man, full of sympathy and curiosity about her life and thoughts. She had opened up to him, she half remembered, wondering what she had actually said as the night had gone on. And he had been interesting in return, telling of his childhood in Italia and his studies in Mediolanum. How she wished she had been sent to such a city to complete her education instead of a stinking Jutish trading post, though, she smiled to herself, she had learned plenty there. But not to be civilised, however. No, she was merely an ignorant provincial on the make, and Anastasius was cultured and urbane and charming.

She had always rather fancied older men.

She had begun to stir in her wandering thoughts, and that disturbed her maid, and in a moment Delia was beside the bed.

Dear Delia, she thought, what would I do without you, and proper nightclothes, and the basket of perfumed ointments you came with, too.

The maid bent down and kissed her mistress on the cheek, and then lifted her so she could sit up on the bed.

"The bishop looked in earlier," she said, "before he went to the morning service."

Megana could feel herself blushing. Had she been lying, vulnerable, asleep, and in a short shift, with the bishop examining her?

Without meaning to, she began to adjust her gown to cover herself more securely.

"He only stuck his head in," said the maid, laughing, "and withdrew again quite quickly." She began to fuss about looking for the chamber pot.

Megana had only just made herself comfortable again, when she heard male voices from the corridor outside the room: the bishop and his clerk.

"Filbert, we can continue this discussion later." The bishop laughed briefly. "I must just look in on my guest."

A set of footsteps faded away, shortly followed by a sharp rap on the doorframe.

"Throw me my cloak," hissed Megana, suddenly realising she was still dressed in only her over-revealing shift.

"Come in," she called. The curtain covering the doorway was pulled to one side, and the bishop peered carefully in.

"Mistress Fabiana, you're awake. I fear I was a little intrusive earlier."

"Didn't we agree I was to be Megana," she said, smiling, "or would you prefer that I call you Your Excellency, My Lord Bishop, this morning?"

"No, no, of course not. Will you accept an apology from... Anastasius?"

"With pleasure," she replied as the bishop advanced hesitantly into the room, and she double-checked that her legs were suitably covered.

"Have you slept well?"

"Very well, thank you...so well that I thought I had died and gone to heaven."

"That would have been a great pity, and a terrible vexation for me as a host. I'm sure I would find very few of my invitations accepted if the rumour spread that my guests had a tendency to pass on, and on their first visit at that."

"But I didn't," laughed Megana, "so you don't need to worry! My decease has been postponed until at least my second visit."

The bishop stood still, evidently unsure how to react to Megana's joke and what to do next. Remaining standing seemed unnecessarily formal. The bed was too low to be comfortable for a man of his height, and inappropriately intimate. The only chair in the room stood in the far corner, and the stool was occupied by Delia. If the maid had been more alert she should have got to her feet and relinquished her seat to the bishop, even offered to move it to a suitable distance from the bed. But she sat still, fascinated by the scene being acted out before her eyes.

Megana herself felt a slight clutch in her breast. Had she misjudged the situation? Hadn't they laughed together the evening before, or had that just been the wine talking, and now her host was regretting his – their – behaviour.

"I was thinking," he said at last, "whether we could postpone your second visit..." Her heart jumped again, and not in a nice way. "...by extending the first one."

She must have frowned, because he was forced to expand on his thought.

"In the circumstances, with your friend in trouble, your business interrupted and your retainers away, I wondered whether you might like to stay here...in the palace...for a few more days. I've plenty of room. The cloister is sheltered and quiet. You won't be disturbed."

"But..." was the first thing she said. But what? she thought. He had evidently been listening to her, appeared concerned on her behalf. "I..." she began. "But what about the children? I can't leave them alone, with only a maid."

His brow wrinkled.

"The children, yes. Young Einar must be missing his mother, and little Sophia..."

He had remembered their names, though he had never, to her knowledge, crossed the threshold of the house in Olive Street!

"But," he said, and then brightened, "we've plenty of space for them, too. Let them come...and their nurse..." He turned quickly to Delia, who had to wipe the curiosity from her face and straighten herself in an instant. "...Maria, she must join us."

Delia jumped to her feet, almost as if she was ready to hurry and summon her friend right away.

"You're too generous," said Megana. Delia's exasperated stare from behind the bishop's back startled her so much that she abruptly swung her legs off the bed so she was sitting on the edge. "That's a wonderful idea."

"The children won't be any trouble," Anastasius hastily continued. "My cook and housekeeper will be glad to have small guests. Their grandchildren are in and out of the domestic quarters all the time."

It was probably just the same in Olive Street, thought Megana, though she had never paid much attention.

Anastasius took a step closer to the bed.

"I enjoyed talking to you last evening," he said. "I had hoped we could continue our conversation."

Megana's heart jumped again, though this time in a far pleasanter manner.

"And," the bishop said, "I hope you might consider joining the chapter at the evening meal. I'm afraid we're all men, clerics, religious men at that, but none of us have visited the north countries as you have, and," he added with a smile, "Father Parataxes is from Thessaloniki and Cyrus from Damascus, and Brother Clement has just returned from Constantinople."

"Of course I'll join you," she said.

I could kiss you, flashed across her mind.

I…could…really kiss…him, she suddenly thought, getting to her feet and throwing her arms around him.

☙ Chapter 56 ❧
Tolosa

"They grabbed her off the street. It can't be anyone else." There was a note of panic in Geseric's voice. "Hrasmus and Ferona were right there when they took her."

"Calm down," said his uncle, General Thormond. "There's nothing we can do right now, even if you're correct. If they'd simply wanted to kill her, they'd've done that right away. Anyhow, this is part of a bigger plot. You know that. We have to think calmly and carefully."

The general had ridden up to Tolosa after receiving the message from his cousin, Count Sismond. Now he understood why Xancha had been getting so worked up. She was a fine woman, intelligent and good-looking, but he was not going to let her worries get in the way of military matters. Sismond's note, brief as it was, reporting that he had driven off a force of imperial intruders, had put everything into perspective. It could hardly be a coincidence that the day that the note arrived, the general's scouts had reported that the imperial forces facing his own army were packing up their camp, and the first units were already on the road back to Arelate. Thormond left with a clear conscience and orders to his own troops to disperse to their homes…slowly.

On his ride to Tolosa, he had begun to consider how he was going to challenge Ludiger, how he was going to persuade the king that the whole confrontation during the summer had been set up by a man his ruler trusted. Now his thoughts had been momentarily upset by Geseric's news of the kidnapping of Signy, but he was not going to let one worried young man get in the way of the bigger task. He did not give a damn about the girl as a prospective wife for his nephew. If that was all she was, then he might have wished Ludiger good speed on his way. But he had also promised witnesses, in the plural, to the events around Aginінum. Now the girl had been taken, he had been left with that damned pettifogging centurion, who would impress far less than a glamourous pagan priestess and her love affairs.

"But how can I be calm?" moaned his nephew.

"Because you have to be, Geseric, if you don't want to end up dead along with her." The general took three or four paces and turned on his heels and paced back again. "If they, and by they I mean Ludiger and his gang, have her, then they must have some use for her, and the best use I can think of is to draw us into some foolish action."

Suppose the duke tried to use Signy as a witness for his own purposes, Thormond wondered, such as dragging her in front of the king, semi-naked and in chains. That would be quite a show.

"But we have to save her!"

"Just forget the damned woman for now, nephew. We'll do our best, but not because you have fallen in love with her, like some foolish youth in a poem, but because that bastard Ludiger has got certainly some trick up his sleeve regarding how to use her."

He glanced up, and saw the miserable look on his nephew's face.

"Very well," he said with a shrug. "Sismond says she has helped our cause, has been brave and willing to witness on our behalf. I'll give her that. She's acted like she's one of us, whether she jumps into bed with you or not."

Geseric still looked doubtful, and Thormond growled.

"Nephew, this is a fight to the death between us and that damned Ludiger, a fight for the future of the kingdom. Everyone must be judged whether they are for us or against us. That's the only criterion just at the moment. Be grateful I'm counting her in, and that might not be for much longer now that traitor's got his hands on her."

"So what are you going to do, just wait and see what he does?"

"Wait…yes, as far as your little heartthrob is concerned, until we have more information about where they've taken her, because that will tell us where they want us to go."

"And then we go there and get her back?"

Thormond shook his head.

"Then we do our scouting, and then we make our plan accordingly."

"But I can't just sit around doing nothing."

"You don't have to, nephew," said the general. "It's time we take the initiative back. I have heard that Duke Ludiger will be at a certain house in Cooper Street tomorrow for a late, very late, dinner, and I think we'll go and pay him a visit, do a bit of vigorous information gathering of our own."

--oo0Ooo--

Darkness had long fallen when Geseric and half a dozen of the general's men broke up their noisy public drinking session at the Fox Tavern and made their way through the town in the vague direction of Cooper Street. Hrasmus was not with them but, observing as they left the tavern, followed discreetly behind to see if Geseric's troop was being tailed. Thormond himself strolled out of the palace grounds, accompanied by his bodyguard, as if taking the evening air. The bodyguard, ignorant of the plans, raised his eyebrows when his master passed by Xancha's house without a glance.

Ludiger was in bed when they burst into the room, but not alone. The woman he was with, Alaya, a confidante of Xancha, grabbed a sheet and fled, her naked form pushing through the invaders. Ludiger was not so fast on his feet and his way was blocked.

"Put on your tunic, Ludiger. I can't tolerate a body gone all to flab," Thormond growled.

The duke reached for his tunic and dragged it over his head. There was a scuffle by the door, and another, younger man, was shoved, stumbling into the room.

"My…My Lord…" he stammered.

The duke glanced at him with contempt.

"Your guards have become complacent, Ludiger," said Thormond, drawing a dagger. The younger man retreated into the far corner of the room.

"So what do you want?" asked the duke with a snarl.

"I'm not here to answer your questions," said the general. "Merely to state some facts that should have been acted on long ago. You're a traitor to our king and to our cause, Ludiger. You're in the pocket of the Empire and you were willing to sell us out. What for? Money? An empty title? Haven't you seen how every one of Our Men who has aspired to power in the Empire has ended? For you, that end is only coming sooner than you anticipated."

"You're a fool, Thormond, a naive fool. We swore we would be the allies of the Empire when they gave us this land in trust. It was Wallia and now Theodoric who have broken their word. Do you think you can hold out against the power of the Empire? Sooner or later the legions will return, and there'll be death for all of you. I was only trying to bring about the result in a quicker and more painless manner."

"Where is she?" Geseric burst in suddenly.

"Who?" asked the duke, sounding genuinely confused for a moment.

"The girl, the girl your goons carried off from the market-place, our witness," said Thormond, with an irritated gesture to his nephew to keep quiet.

The duke smiled, and then the smile broke into laughter.

"What makes her so important to you, Thormond? Are you planning to switch your allegiance from Xancha to someone fresher?"

"Cut it out, Ludiger. Now where is she? You know she was on her way to reveal your plot to Theodoric. That's why you picked her off the street."

Ludiger snorted.

"Is it my problem if you can't take care of your so-called witness? Maybe she just got frightened and ran off."

"There were men who carried her off, Ludiger, against her will, against my will, and against the will of the king. He'd agreed to hear her."

Ludiger laughed.

"Do you think I know what they've done with some little girl, a pagan priestess? She should be burned in the marketplace as an example."

"Don't give me that crap, Ludiger. Sismond sent me a rundown. I know that Maxus has been blabbing. The girl was to witness, to corroborate his story, and she never showed up. I know you know where she is," said Thormond, "and I know you want *us* to know, so out with it."

Ludiger shook his head.

"You can't expect me to bargain with you in these circumstances, half-naked, in a brothel. Come tomorrow, to my house, and in the meanwhile, I'll make some enquiries, and see if I can help you."

Thormond took a step towards him.

"If you want to come out of here alive, tell us!"

"I'm not going to be bullied by you, General! Don't you realise what you're doing? Setting yourself up against me is the same as defying the king. You're a dead man, Thormond, and your cousin, and this…lover boy."

"And when Theodoric finds out that you've been collaborating with the Empire?"

"You fool! It's all for the sake of peace."

"Where's Signy?" Geseric could not hold himself silent.

"Suppose I don't know?" said Ludiger, shrugging. "Suppose the witch is already dead?"

"Then you're no use to us, Ludiger, only a flabby, treacherous impediment," said Thormond. "Perhaps you're right after all, and Theodoric would be impressed by your story, just as he was impressed by your peace treaty. Perhaps I have gone too far, imagining that an imperial invasion force tried to take Agininum. All in a good cause, I suppose, and I've misunderstood everything. Then perhaps it would be better that Theo never got to hear your side of the story, only mine…"

For a moment, a look of doubt crossed the duke's face.

"Listen, Thormond, I'll do what I can to find out where she is and make sure your witness speaks to the king. Come to the court tomorrow, and we'll sort this out in the presence of Theodoric. I'll explain the whole plan. As you said, it's just a misunderstanding. There's nothing to hide."

Thormond's dagger was an inch from his face.

"You'll achieve nothing by threatening me, Thormond," the duke continued, but now with a tremble in his voice.

"You're right, Ludiger. It's no use threatening you. You're such a skilled liar. Threats will never make you tell the truth." Thormond glanced back, past Geseric, and caught Hrasmus' eye. "You – this is the man who seized your mistress, or ordered her to be seized. Do as you wish."

Thormond stepped back to give space to Hrasmus, who drew his knife.

"No, no…I'll tell you! I'll tell you! The witch is not here, I promise."

"Then where is our witness?"

"I sent her…somewhere safe…out of town…in case something should happen…to Cadurci…to Altaar. You never know these days. People can't be trusted! Theo would understand. You understand…?"

Geseric could not help letting out a groan, could not prevent himself from taking a step towards Ludiger. He had feared the duke all his life, but now that fear had evaporated, and he only saw a pale, fat man, fearful in his turn. He felt a hand on his arm.

"No," came a soft voice from Thormond. "This is a task for Mistress Signy's man." He turned once again to Ludiger.

"How very convenient," he said. "Cousin Sismond is just on his way to Cadurci, with the entire militia of Aginінum and reinforcements from Vasates and Elusa."

"Yes, of course, that was the whole plan. We could meet up there, and sort everything out…quite peaceably."

Thormond shook his head.

"No, Ludiger, no. You see, everyone has already accepted you're guilty and a formal trial would be so embarrassing to your family. Who knows what would come to the surface? Who knows what foolish things you would say? Even the imperialists might be embarrassed and disappointed if their chosen man was seen squealing and begging."

He nodded almost imperceptibly to Hrasmus, who bent over Ludiger and, with all his strength, drove his knife into the duke's body.

Ludiger's eyes opened wide. He could only mouth a *no*, before he fell back, bleeding, onto the bed.

"No!" came a louder voice…from the young man who had been standing silent in the far corner all the time. He took a step towards Hrasmus, but he had no weapon, and before the Jute could strike again, Thormond spoke up.

"Hold your hand, man! Your duty's done for this evening."

He stepped past the Jute and faced the youngster.

"I'm sparing your life to be a messenger. Go down to the duke's house and tell them to come here and collect his body. Tell them to send a message to Count Altaar to expect a visit, and that if he as much as ruffles a hair on Mistress Signy's head, I'll see that the crows eat his guts while he's still alive. I'm coming for him. Geseric's coming for him. Every man in this room is coming for him. Every man at my command is coming for him."

Alaya was in the hallway outside, shaking.

"You did well," said Thormond. "Return to Xancha now. There's a decent husband and a pension in this for you if you want."

He noticed her eyes flick towards Geseric.

"No, not him, he's spoken for."

☙ Chapter 57 ❧ Cadurci

Count Altaar's townhouse did not have the facilities of Ludiger's residence. There was no cellar where Signy could be imprisoned. Instead, she had been shut up in a storeroom in the yard by the stables. A window, closed off by shutters, let in a little light. It was too high up for easy access, and Signy doubted whether she would fit through, even if she could reach the opening. Nonetheless, the attempt would be worth making if her situation became desperate. Otherwise, the contents of the room consisted of a hay-filled mattress, laid directly on the floor, a three-legged stool and the inevitable bucket. Once upon a time, in her early life, the space would have seemed luxurious. Now, she sighed, she had become used to comfort.

"Good morning, Mistress Magician." A voice from the doorway disturbed her thoughts as she lay on her back on the mattress, her arms behind her head. Count Altaar stood framed in the opening. Signy struggled upright, trying to retain some dignity. She knew little of the count. He was married to one of Duke Ludiger's nieces, Sismond had told her that. That made him an ally of the duke. Sismond had cursed him roundly for his lack of assistance after the fruitless meeting in Cadurci. Maxus had implicated him in the invasion of the count's lands. That made him a conspirator.

"Junius told me all about you," said the count, leaning against the doorframe, studying her. "The beautiful woman who had stumbled into his camp and offered herself to him. The strange marks, and the story of being a pagan priestess…you must have bewitched him thoroughly for him to have neglected his duties to meet you in Agininum."

"I was the one bewitched," she answered, "and he was not neglecting his duties."

Altaar laughed, not an unpleasant laugh, but one of a man who had all the advantages in his hands.

"Junius was a good man," the count said. "He was loyal to the Empire and an ally to the cause. My uncle might have warned him off if he'd known what he knows now, but that's bygones…"

"Why am I here and what's going to happen to me?" asked Signy.

Altaar considered for a moment.

"You are here because my uncle wished you to be sent here."

"But the duke had his reasons, I'm sure."

"Of course. You're bait for your new boyfriend and his uncle, General Thormond, to come riding to your rescue – not because you're such a pretty catch, if that's what you're imagining, but because you're their precious little witness that they want to use to implicate Uncle Ludiger in treason."

"You sound like you're laying a trap."

"On your feet, Mistress," Altaar ordered, though with a smile, "and I'll show you the trap, since there's nothing you can do about it but lie in this room and wait for it to close."

He held out his hand. Signy took it.

"We can, I think, behave in a civilised manner in the town? There's no need to tie you up, I hope."

He continued to hold her hand, but his grip was tight as he pushed the door open.

"Lothar, we will walk to the north gate, and you'll remain with us," he said to a man who had been waiting outside. "Keep your sword in your hand and your eyes on the prisoner…not too difficult a task, I should imagine."

The soldier chuckled.

The three of them walked through the forum and down to the main street. From there they turned towards the north gate. To Signy's eyes, Cadurci seemed a prosperous town with people going about their business in the market, shops and taverns. Under other circumstances, she might have enjoyed the tour, taken the opportunity to explore the stalls to look for herbs which grew only in the mountains and rarely reached Aginnum. She could have sat for a moment watching the country people, trying to spot those with ailments or injuries that would respond to careful treatment.

Instead, she was forced along at Altaar's pace until they reached the north gate. She thought he would lead her out, but instead, he pulled her towards the gate tower and some steps up to the rampart. Easing his grip, he ordered her to climb.

When she reached the top, she could see out across the northern approaches to Cadurci, and her heart sank. Pitched across the peninsular was a camp, a military camp. It was not neat and organised like the camp Centurion Maxus had ruled over, more a jumble of tents and poor huts, but there was no mistaking the occupants: a crowd of auxiliaries, her own people probably, tribesmen from across the frontier, drawn by the pay and the hope of reward and riches, perhaps men from her home village, her own brothers, even.

"We're surrounded on three sides by the river," said Altaar, pointing to the left and right. "There's a bridge to the south, but we can close that off easily. With these soldiers blocking the peninsula to the north, we're impregnable. If Thormond is so stupid as to defy the king's orders about interfering in another count's territory and come galloping up here from Tolosa, then he's lost, and so has everyone with him, mere disloyal traitors. And if he doesn't, then we'll pay him and his family a visit instead. Who's going to stop us? Not even the king, now that the army has been sent back to their homes."

"I'm impressed, Count," Signy said, though, now she did not mean her words entirely. Her own husband, Chief Thorgill, had once led a similar army into the forests of Britannia, as large as the one she saw below, and that had been annihilated, save for a few lucky men, among them Grunwald, Hrasmus and Asser. They had been brave men, proud men, but they had been destroyed by cunning and organisation, by a man who had reasoned out their intentions and lay in wait for them. Sismond couldn't hold a candle to Marcus Ursinus, but she hoped he had enough of those qualities, and not simply bravery and pride.

"And this is the trap?" she asked, trying to sound innocent.

Altaar smiled.

"Set and waiting to be sprung," he answered.

"They make me nervous," Signy said. She hoped that Altaar took her for a foolish, anxious woman rather than realising that she knew more about encampments and their occupants than he might imagine.

He took hold of her hand again and drew her towards the steps, which they descended back to the street.

"Fortunately, you'll be safely locked up in my storehouse until Uncle Ludiger decides what to do with you."

Ludiger, she remembered, had said he wanted to use her as a witness, but had he shared his plan with Altaar?

"And what will that be?"

"That all depends." Altaar smiled. "As a sorceress, you should be put to death publicly to discourage others following your example, but Junius implied that you were fun in bed, so perhaps I'll find a use for you."

She squeezed his hand and smiled at him.

He chuckled softly.

"Oh, no, my temptress, you don't catch me so easily. My grandmother lived to a very old age, and when I was young, I used to sit on her knee and listen to her stories from the old land, of shapeshifters and women who lured men under the surface of lakes, of troll women, who you could only detect when you spotted their tail. Junius never mentioned a tail, Mistress Signy, and I'm not about to take a look."

"You might be pleasantly surprised," she said, shifting from Latin to Saxon. "I was born in those forests. Perhaps your grandmother and my grandmother crossed paths."

"My great-great-grandmother, perhaps, and yours," he replied in a similar tongue, showing he understood her.

They crossed the forum and went in through the gate to his headquarters. He guided her across the yard back to the storehouse.

"Junius told me you have a tattoo on your shoulder, though he was vague on the details, some sort of animal, a wolf, perhaps, he said."

She turned towards him and pushed back the cloth of her dress. She heard him gasp.

"What is it?"

"My grandmother had such a mark," he said, abruptly turning on his heels and slamming the door behind him.

She heard his steps echoing across the yard.

Somebody else barred the door.

☙ Chapter 58 ❧ Tolosa

Theodoric, King of the Visigoths, champion of Our Men, was striding back and forth in his private chamber.

"I don't understand, Thormond. What happened to that 'person with important information for my ears only' that you promised yesterday? It's no good telling tales and then not providing any evidence. That just causes ill-feeling amongst our people, and I don't like it. And what has happened to Ludiger? I expected him to be here long ago. You both owe me an explanation."

The king turned on his heel again and took two paces on his return journey.

"And, in any case, why are you in Tolosa, Thormond? You should be with the troops, watching the frontier."

"The imperial army retired, Your Majesty. I suspect they're in as much need of an explanation for their futile marching as you are for the duke's absence."

The king stopped, staring at Thormond.

"And you think you're in a position to supply one, General?"

"I'm in a better position than the duke, my lord."

"Oh yes, and why?"

"Because he won't be coming."

"And what makes you say that?"

"Because he's dead, my lord."

"Dead…dead…how…of what cause?"

"Natural causes," said Thormond. He shrugged himself a mental shrug. Assassination was a natural cause of death for a treacherous, two-faced bastard like Ludiger.

"This is very distressing. I needed to speak to him. I must say I'm confused…by your cousin, amongst others, Thormond."

"Why is that, my lord?"

"He sent me a message, saying a sizeable force of imperial infantry and auxiliaries had entered his land with the intent of blocking the road to Agininum. And that he had driven them off. I would have said the man had gone mad if he had not sent me a prisoner, a Centurion Maxus, with the most preposterous story."

"That he was engaged in building a road," said Thormond, "or shall we say improving an existing road, to assist us in combating bandits."

"I suppose your so-called witness was supposed to shed light on this."

"Exactly, my lord. Sismond sent me the same message, including the information that he had intercepted the force and defeated it. He also mentioned that he had uncovered a group of infiltrators who were to open the gates of Agininum and allow the imperialists into the city. Fortunately, they were eliminated by courageous townspeople. Our witness would have provided a detailed account of their treachery. With her help, my cousin's men were also able to capture a sheaf of documents and the personal property of their leader, a spy named Junius, which Sismond sent to me, and which I had copied and passed on, *in memoriam*, with my sympathy so to speak, to my opposite number in the imperial army."

"You did what? Communicating with the enemy?"

"They're hardly our enemy, my lord, as you are so fond of saying yourself, now that we've signed a treaty of peace. We have common interests, and I presumed that one of those is not losing our men by being drawn into unnecessary combat. I hope I haven't overstepped my authority?"

"Shouldn't I be the one to make that decision?"

"I would suggest the imperialists have a certain say in the matter, my lord, and this time they seem to have come to the conclusion that discretion is the better part of valour. It seems that the two movements were part of a coordinated plan, to cut off Tolosa."

"But they already tried that a couple of years back, and I almost wiped them out, and signed a peace with that bastard Avitus!"

"Of course, thanks to Duke Ludiger, but that doesn't mean some other man wasn't ready to try again, with a new scheme, and the assistance of traitors in our ranks. Last time you had the whole army at your disposal, but if the host was engaged in the east, and you were cut off from reinforcements from the west…"

"I have my guards, Thormond, don't forget. They're quite capable of defending me."

"Of course, my lord. They would have obeyed their orders, just as I did when Duke Ludiger ordered me to lead the host towards Beterrae."

"I would hope that the guards would also obey the duke."

"That would suppose, my lord, that your interests and the duke's were aligned."

"What are you suggesting, Thormond? That they're not?"

"Were not, my lord, were not. The duke, may I remind you, is dead."

Theodoric swung round, his back to Thormond for a moment, seeming to collect himself, and then turned again.

"Thormond, what you are implying is most serious, and Duke Ludiger is not here to defend himself."

"Call his sons then, to answer for their father."

"I shall do so, Thormond, at once."

"But you won't find them, my lord, because they have fled to Cadurci, the moment they heard of their father's fate."

"Fate…I thought you said he had died of natural causes."

"He may have been helped on his way, my lord, by people who had your best interests at heart."

The king gave Thormond a hard glare.

"I assume you're counting yourself amongst those."

"Most certainly, my lord. I always have your best interests at heart, and you may include my cousin, Count Sismond, and all the other men who are loyal to him and me."

"And what, since you seem so well informed, can be found at Cadurci which makes the town such a tempting place of flight?"

"It's not Tolosa, for a start, and is close to the frontier. There's a good escape route to Aquitania, my lord, and Count Altaar of Cadurci has always been one of the duke's most devoted supporters. He married Ludiger's niece, you might remember. As for any other advantages, I'm waiting for a report from my cousin, but he suspects that the imperialist auxiliaries who survived his ambush retreated in that direction."

"Then we had better wait, both of us, General Thormond, until your cousin has the kindness to send his report. I suggest you remain here at the palace where I can keep an eye on you. I would place you under the care of the guards, but you tell me I can't trust them."

"The guards you can trust, my lord, but certain officers… they were appointed by the duke, and I'm sure they wouldn't wish his name to be dishonoured, however misled they may have been."

"Damnation, Thormond, who can I trust? I'm not sure I trust you entirely."

"On my honour, my lord, I'll not set foot outside the palace grounds."

--oo0Ooo--

Thormond was not as sure of his position as he wished to imply to the king. He was well aware that the royal guard was a powerful force within the city walls, and no doubt they would obey their officers, since there was nothing to suggest they should do otherwise. Once Theodoric learned how Ludiger had died, and if the message from Sismond did not arrive promptly, the king might very well conclude that Thormond, the duke's assassin, was actually the traitor. Well, the general thought, shrugging to himself, if I'm going to finish what I've started, I might as well go all in. He had given his word, however, to remain inside the palace grounds. That did not mean that his deputy was required to remain with him, and so Ramius was sent to the general's townhouse with a brief message.

Around midnight, Ramius returned, a tablet tucked under his arm. The general flicked it open, glanced down the list of names.

"Very well, have we enough men to get this done?"

"Everyone in the household, my lord, except Geseric and a couple I left with him to watch the house."

"Let's move then!"

Thormond strode across the inner courtyard of the palace and down to the river gate. There were two guards, slouched against the wall, putting in yet another night shift.

"Open the gate, men," said the general.

The guard he addressed squinted in the half-light and then, recognising who was speaking to him, sprang to attention, fully awake. The bar was lifted, the gate swung open, and men, armed men, streamed in.

"My lord?" muttered one of the guards, unsure whether this incursion was compatible with his orders.

"Say nothing…close the gate and keep to your posts. If you do that, you'll live to see the morning."

"But the king…?"

"The king's in no danger," said Ramius. Thormond was already halfway across the court, leading the men. They passed through the palace buildings, under the arch cut into the old city walls and into the service area. The guards' barracks were to the left, housing for those men who lived in the palace. The officers and the remaining men who were not on duty would be spread out in the town, in lodgings or their own homes. They could be picked off one by one in the morning.

A single officer greeted the general by the gate.

"My lord," he said, "there's a rumour going round that Duke Ludiger has been assassinated, but no one has been able to confirm if it's true."

"Take it from me, he died of natural causes," said Thormond. "Now go to the barracks and get the men up. I want them on parade in the palace courtyard as soon as possible, every one of the guards who's in the building with no exceptions."

Thormond could hear the duty officers playing dice in the wardroom. Their voices were quiet, their laughter nervous.

Probably they had already heard the rumour that trouble was brewing. Thormond could guess what they would be thinking: *Yet another quarrel among the leadership, which the king would tamp down with an appeal to unity as he usually did. A couple of days of jitteriness, and the routine will return to normal.* Nonetheless, when the general and his followers burst into the room, the four officers jumped to their feet, reaching for their weapons, ready to defend themselves.

"On your knees!" he bellowed. The officers hesitated. "On your knees!" he repeated, in a quieter but more menacing tone.

Three of them sank to their knees. The fourth, a far relative of Duke Ludiger, made a grab for his sword. He was flung back across the room by a javelin before his fist could close on the grip.

"You made a wise decision, my boys," said Thormond, as the remaining trio were bound and led away. Though your next posting won't be so comfortable, he thought, in the mountains, facing the Vascones, if you're lucky!

--oo0Ooo--

The king was not a happy man. He jabbed at Thormond with his forefinger, as his attendant adjusted his cloak.

"*You* have murdered Duke Ludiger…"

Thormond opened his mouth to speak, but the king jabbed harder, now poking him in the chest.

"Don't say anything, Thormond…you murdered the duke, your men executed the commander of my bodyguard and his deputy, and I don't know how many others in the town."

"None, my lord, a few – no more than necessary – to protect the kingdom."

"To protect the kingdom, you say, but how do I know this isn't simply to advance your own interest? Don't think I don't know of the rivalry between you and Ludiger. Neither of you did much to hide your hostility."

"But the conspiracy, my lord…"

"Conspiracy? I only have your word that there's been a conspiracy, yours and your questionable cousin's."

"But you told me yesterday, my lord, that you had a prisoner, a centurion, who confirmed what Sismond had told you."

"He spun a yarn, and the other witness, don't you remember, who was supposed to corroborate his story, never showed up," said the king, looking a little more thoughtful, and then suddenly turned towards Thormond, his finger raised again.

"Where's this messenger, Thormond, the man you told me would bring further information from Sismond? Where is he?"

Thormond was uneasy. He had been confined to the palace grounds, and while Ramius was primed to bring the messenger as soon as he arrived, relying on a deputy was not the same as being there yourself. Worse, it eliminated the possibility of hearing what the man had to say before the king did.

"He's on his way, I'm confident, my lord," said Thormond, though his voice might have betrayed him.

"He'd better be, General," said the king, "because if he's not..."

"I wouldn't have contemplated doing what I've done if I wasn't confident I was acting correctly...for your best, my lord."

The king grunted.

"The public audience is within the hour. Ludiger should be at my side, otherwise there'll be whispers, gossip."

If the news had already reached the king, there would be plenty of whispers and gossip already, Thormond reflected. A public audience without the duke would simply confirm them.

"I...I can step in for him, my lord..."

"You shall do no such thing, General. I think you're getting ahead of yourself, wanting to fit the duke's footwear before the matter's settled."

"I...I...had no intention of implying that, my lord."

Theodoric gave him a hard glare, as if Thormond's thoughts were written on his face.

"Who's that?" he said suddenly, turning towards three men who had entered the room. An attendant crossed towards them, barring their way.

Two of them dropped instantly to one knee, the third stood frozen.

"Captain Ramius, you know, my lord, and my nephew, Geseric."

"And this third?" said the king, eyeing the stranger.

"A messenger, my lord," said Ramius, still on one knee, "from the Count of Agininum."

The king took a step towards the man, who stood stiff and silent as a stock.

"And you, who are you?"

"Asser, my lord, merely an ordinary man." Asser sounded anxious, which made his accent almost incomprehensible.

The king laughed.

"Just a man, are you? Who the hell is he?" Theodoric swivelled towards Ramius, but Geseric quickly spoke up.

"He's one of the merchant Mistress Fabiana's men, my lord, who's serving my uncle, the count."

"Are we now dependent on some merchant's minions to do our work?" The king turned back to Asser.

"What do you have to say for yourself, Asser the Ordinary Man?"

Asser seemed flustered and could only blurt out his story as it come into his mind.

"I rode through the night, my lord, and arrived this morning. I was sent by Count Sismond, my lord, with a message."

The look of incomprehension on Theodoric's face brought his flow to a halt.

"What's he saying? What garbled version of our tongue is this man speaking?" demanded the king.

A dribble of cold sweat trickled down Asser's brow. In his haste he had begun to recite his tale in Jutish.

Geseric cast him a glance, more of exasperation than sympathy.

"My lord," he was forced to interrupt. "This is an honest man, from the north, but he doesn't master our tongue or that of the imperialists. When I was in the camp outside Carcasso I took time to converse with some Saxon recruits – just with such occurrences in mind – and I have been able to grasp a little of what this man recounted when he arrived this morning. Most importantly, he has brought a letter, my lord, from the count." He glared hard at Asser, who suddenly jerked into life and extracted a roll of papyrus from his belt and handed it over.

Theodoric took the roll, and immediately handed it to Thormond. The general had no desire to disclose any weakness in his grasp of the written word. With a smile, he handed the letter to Geseric. Make use of all that time sitting with your nose in books, said the sour look his face.

"*To My Lord King, glorious leader of the Visigoths, master of Aquitania and the Narbonensis, worthy successor of the Emperors of Rome, blessed of—*"

"Get on with it!" grunted the king.

Geseric cleared his throat nervously and glanced down the sheet to try to identify the meat of the message.

"*My scouts have identified several hundred foreign auxiliaries camped to the north of the city…*"

"He's referring to Cadurci," muttered the general. The king gave him a sharp look.

"*…and there is constant traffic between the city and the camp, demonstrating they are not a besieging force but confederates of the city authorities.*"

"He means Count Altaar, my lord," said Thormond.

"I know perfectly well who he means," growled the king. "Is there more?"

Geseric threw his overlord an anxious glance and continued.

"*Given the recent incursion into my territory by foreign invaders and imperial troops, once I have my own men arrayed in an appropriate position, I intend to teach these rogues a lesson which will make them think twice about repeating their actions.*"

"Goddammit!" exclaimed Theodoric. "This kingdom is becoming a nest of anarchy, with everyone thinking they can just go around acting on their own initiative. Am I the fucking king or a tailor's dummy?"

"The king, my lord," said Thormond, hastily.

"Exactly, General, despite all appearances to the contrary." Theodoric glared around the assembled men.

"I'm going to get to the bottom of this. *You*" – he pointed at Thormond – "will get your heart's desire and take the duke's place at the public audience, and *you* will explain that the audience is cancelled because there's treachery afoot…though for the life of me I don't know who are traitors and who are loyal," the king muttered to himself. "When you have done that, you will seal the city gates, and no one will pass in or out, including yourself, your retainers, your family members, the army…anyone, until I order them opened, and there will be no more executions or arrests, or holding men for ransom. You'd better hope I don't die myself, because then you'll be sitting here for ever."

He took a breath.

"You, Captain Ramius, will find the highest officer of the guard who you've not already put to death, and you'll tell him the king orders the guard assembled for the march north immediately. Go!"

He turned to Geseric and Asser.

"And as for you, Geseric the Nephew and Asser the Ordinary Man, you will both ride with me to Cadurci, and if I find any, the least, discrepancy between this report you've given me and what I find when I get there, you'll be dangling above the city gate – alive! And the same goes for any other treacherous witnesses and rumour spreaders mixed up in this. I'll root out every damned one of them, and promptly cutting off their heads will be an act of kindness!"

☙ Chapter 59 ❧ Cadurci

The door to Signy's prison flew open.

"You're coming with me!" Altaar was in the room before she could do anything. The Count of Cadurci had a short sword in his hand, and a desperate look in his eye.

"What's going on? Why?" She struggled to her feet, cramped by her sitting position.

"Don't ask, just do as I say!"

She hesitated, a moment too long for his patience. He reached out and grabbed her arm, pulling her towards him, towards his sword.

"Come, now!" He dragged at her arm, twisting her around so she felt a sudden surge of pain in her shoulder.

"Stop, you're hurting me. I'll do as you wish."

He jerked her again, out into the yard.

"Take hold of her," he ordered to one of the men waiting, expectant.

There was an odd atmosphere in the yard. She could not put her finger on the peculiarity immediately. Then she realised there was a smell of smoke in the air, not the usual smell from ovens, nor cooking fires, but that of a threatening, out-of-control type of fire.

"What's the news from the town, Lothar?" Altaar shouted to the man standing nearest.

"There are blazes in several places…the stables of Pan's Tavern, behind the public *lavatorium*, and several shacks by the north gate."

"Deliberately set?"

The man shrugged.

"There's stories of men setting fires, strangers, but no one actually saw who did it."

Several more men hurried into the yard. Among them Signy recognised the two young men she had seen earlier, the sons of Duke Ludiger.

"It's a complete mess, Altaar," said one of them.

"What is?"

"The camp."

Altaar gave him a glare. Rumours had reached him earlier of a disaster in the auxiliaries' camp, so he had sent the brothers to investigate.

"We spoke to some of them," said the other. "They said men rode in before dawn. Everyone was asleep."

"Except the sentries."

"They were already dead."

"Who rode in?"

"Nobody knows. It was dark. They came from the north."

Altaar looked confused for a moment. "From our own side?" Beyond the disputed land to the north of Cadurci was imperial territory. "I thought we were acting on behalf of the Empire," he muttered, as the sons of Ludiger continued their report.

"They threw burning brands onto the tents, trampled through the campfires and on sleeping men, and they rounded up half the horses and drove them away."

"Many men killed?"

"Some, but it's the confusion, the shock, and the loss of their mounts. They're making ready to leave for imperial lands…on foot!"

"But I paid for them…your father paid for them…they can't leave."

"They say they owe their allegiance to the Empire, Cousin Altaar. They say they were sent to support the army in the east, not to get engaged in this kingdom's private feuds. They say they were promised booty and slaves, and they never got any."

Signy could hear the discussion, see the men, their expressions of alarm, almost panic, as they understood the world that they thought was secure was now collapsing around them.

She began to feel a nagging dread. She was trapped. If she tried to run, it would only provoke them, and in this atmosphere, they would lash out. They could make her a scapegoat, perhaps even accuse her of bringing the calamity on them since they seemed to be convinced she was a sorceress. Even if she sat still, obeyed them, they could still decide to kill her here and now, simply to be rid of a burden.

She had lost track of the argument, but she could see there must be one – men gesticulating, shouting, their faces red, and they were suddenly interrupted as a soldier ran into the yard.

"The king, the king!"

Altaar grabbed at him.

"What are you saying?"

"Theodoric is at the bridge gate, demanding to be let in!"

"You kept the gate closed?"

"I did, my lord, but the people are gathering…demanding to be let out…to escape the fires."

"But they can't, damn it!"

"My men'll not be able to resist, my lord, and the king…is the king."

Altaar jabbed at the man with his sword, and the gatekeeper stepped backward, then tripped, falling flat to the ground. Altaar raised his sword as if he was about to stab the fallen official. Then he lowered the blade and turned to the sons of Ludiger.

"Your father's dead. Junius' plan has failed. Our horsemen are scattered, and the town is on fire. If we remain here when the king gets in, we can expect no mercy. We've failed this time, but if we escape, then there can be another opportunity."

He backed away from them, in Signy's direction, reached out and took hold of her.

"Down to the washerwomen's postern!" he ordered. Ludiger's sons looked from one to another as if they were unsure whether to obey him.

"Do you want to be here when the king arrives?"

"No, Altaar, but how are we going to escape? The king is at the Oltis bridge gate, and the north is in chaos. We can't go through the camp. If the auxiliaries thought we were running away, they would kill us. And beyond them, the mysterious enemy…"

"The mysterious enemy! I know who they are. It's only fucking Sismond and his farmers. We can outsmart them any day. Follow me, anyone who wants to save themselves."

"And why are we taking her?"

That's a reasonable question, thought Signy, the first reasonable thing someone has said this whole time.

"Because I want her!"

"You're mad, Altaar. Just kill the witch and let's get out of here. It's her who has brought all this trouble on us. If Junius hadn't been fucking her, if Father hadn't taken her, if he hadn't sent her here, none of this would have happened."

The young man drew a dagger and stepped towards Signy.

"Let me go, Altaar," she said, trying not to sound pleading.

"No…I'm taking you," said Altaar, waving his sword in the direction of Ludiger's sons. "I'm taking her!" He pushed her towards the gate. The other men began to follow after him. Outside in the street there was complete disorder. People rushing to and fro, carrying oversized piles of belongings, dragging crying children, shouting at no one in particular. A man tried to push through the crowd dragging a cart. They would not give way and he started to yell and wave his arms. Another man cursed him, lashed out with his fist.

"Form up for defence," ordered Altaar, seeing the edgy mob.

"Where are you taking me?" asked Signy.

"Away…with me."

"But why?"

"Because I want you," he replied, half running, half stumbling behind the guards who had taken up position in the front of the group. "I didn't understand what Junius told me. I thought he was just taking advantage of some pretty girl in town. But you, you're more than that, you're one of us."

What did he mean, thought Signy, one of us?

"You're one of my grandmother's people. I need you. I can't leave you here. You belong with me."

"But what about your wife, the duke's niece, and your children? You're leaving them?" Signy was almost tripping over her own feet as she tried to keep alongside Altaar, without the grip he had on her arm hurting her more.

"They'll survive. The king won't harm them. But if he catches me, I'll die, so I'm going to run, and I'm taking you. I can have new children with you, beautiful wise children, new sons with a sister of Freya…just as my father was my grandmother's son. We'll go to Aquitania, to the family estates."

No, Altaar, she was screaming inside, I won't go. But what was the point of screaming inside? And if she screamed aloud, he might change his mind, or one of Ludiger's sons might decide to defy the count and kill her anyway. She did not want to be Altaar's prize or bear his sons, but she wanted to be dead even less.

They were shoving their way through the streets, through the milling populace. At the end of a passageway, she could see a building on fire, men pulling at timbers to stop it spreading, others throwing buckets of water in a feeble effort to extinguish the flames. Altaar hurried her on, down a narrow side street, round a turn, into an alley, out into another side street. Ahead she could see the city wall, and at the end of the street a crowd had gathered. Two guards, swords drawn, were blocking an iron-studded gate.

"Make way, make way!" shouted the men in the lead, and when an old woman did not make way quickly enough, they pushed her, stumbling, tumbling, to the side.

There was a scream; another woman fell. The people by the gate turned towards them, seemingly threatening until they saw the weapons, when they shrank back, fearful.

"Open the gate," yelled the count, "and let's get out of here."

"They'll come after us," said one of the guards.

"Then cut one or two of them down. That'll hold them back long enough," said Altaar.

The men with him pushed back at the crowd. Signy was squeezed against Altaar, and in a moment they were outside the walls, looking down over the river. A narrow path zigzagged down the slope. Altaar let go of Signy's arm but pushed her in front of him. She had no choice but to follow the path. Altaar came after. Down, round a turn, down across the slope again, another turn. She glanced up the hill. Ludiger's sons and the other men who had come with the count were following them down the path. She could just make out the guards, still flailing with their weapons at the gate, and then she was forced to turn her eyes back to the track to avoid falling.

"Straight ahead!" said Altaar, when they reached the bottom, a flat, open space which Signy recognised must be where women from the town could reach the river to do their washing. A narrow path ran alongside the bank, and then Signy understood where they were heading. Two boats were tied up under an overhanging tree, shallow-draft boats like the one Maxus had used downstream by the ford.

"Get in," said Altaar.

What could she do? There was nowhere further to go. The path came to an end by the trees. Several of Altaar's men were already standing beside the other boat, a few yards downstream, blocking any further progress, and others still pushing forward along the path. She clambered over the gunwale, to the far side of the vessel, and sat down on a plank seat. The boat rocked as Altaar boarded, rocked again as the men from his group followed.

"Into the other boat," he yelled, gesticulating to the sons of Ludiger.

"In a moment we'll be free, away," said Altaar, patting her knee with his hand. She did nothing to arouse his suspicions, to alert him to the thoughts rushing through her mind.

"Casting off," came the call from the downstream boat, and at that moment it swung out into the river.

A yell from the slope above caused Signy to look back. Several people were running down the track, and the first had already reached the wash place and was turning onto the path towards the boats.

"Push off," said Altaar quietly, and the last of the guards leaped over the side with the mooring rope in his hand. Those already in the boat slid out oars and began to steer the craft away into the river.

Signy glanced up again, now seeing pillars of smoke rising from the town, rising from the buildings which were burning. More people were rushing, cascading down the bank towards the river. The boat swung and tossed as it was caught by the stream.

In that instant, she rolled and threw herself over the side into the dark surging water. For a moment, she sank beneath the surface, and then bobbed up, spluttering, gasping for breath. She could hear shouting from the boat, Altaar's voice, the splashing of the oars, but it was too late, the vessel had been caught by the current, and there was nothing the men on board, no expert oarsmen, could do to stop the boat being carried away.

She took another breath, forced herself to relax. If she strained or panicked, she would surely drown, but a girl who had grown up by a river knew how to swim, had been taught, had been lectured over and over again, about what she should do if she fell in the water and the river carried her away. She took another breath, and let the river bear her along, and then she took a stroke and another across the stream. Thank the gods – yes, thank Jesus Christ as well – that she was only wearing a light dress which did not weigh her down, did not hinder her. And the water had been warmed by the summer sun. Another stroke, and another, and in a moment she was out of the rushing current and into a stretch of calm. She rolled onto her back, took another deep breath and then tipped herself vertical. She could not feel the bottom, so she stayed for a moment paddling with her arms and feet. She could just make out the shape of Altaar's boat, carried away, bobbing and swaying on the water. She turned again and swam slowly towards the bank. Once she could see stones on the riverbed, she lowered her legs and waded to the shore onto a little rocky beach. She pushed her hair from her eyes, feeling the water trickling down her body. She was panting, shaking. She sat down and looked out, seeing Altaar and his crew vanishing around a curve in the river. She thought of her childhood. How many times she had sat gazing out over the river splitting the forest, passing the cottage where she had grown up.

She had wondered where it led, where the boatmen were travelling, what other places lay round the bend, over the horizon. She had never dreamed her fate would lead here, to a rocky shore beside another river beneath a city in flames. The sun began to warm her and dry her, as it had warmed her and dried her those lazy summer days so long ago. The wall of stone loomed over her, loomed over the little rocky beach, and from above drifted the smell of burning homes and the screams of frightened people as King Theodoric and his men marched into the city.

☙ Chapter 60 ❧ Tolosa

"So you've got what you wanted at last." Xancha was sprawled on her bed, while Thormond sat across the room on a chair. "Now you're 'The Duke', the king's right-hand man, the second most important person in the kingdom."

"There's his wife…and his sons, Theodoric's sons."

"Oh, come now, Thormond, Theo's sons are just young men and have none of your experience."

"One of them will inherit the kingdom, sooner or later."

"But that's not what's bothering you, is it?"

"No," said Thormond, shifting his gaze from empty space to his mistress. "I could see him, almost as soon as he had made the announcement, scanning the audience, looking for a man, men, who he could promote in my place…a new general for the army, a new count for Carcasso, perhaps."

"His famous balance?"

"His famous fear that any man might become powerful enough to threaten him."

"Well then, don't threaten him."

"I don't intend to," said Thormond, rising to his feet. "But I can already see how matters will play out. It won't be long before Ludiger's sons are forgiven and return to court."

"But they're fools."

"And speaking of fools, I wouldn't even be surprised if Altaar is forgiven and reinstated as Count of Cadurci."

"Surely not. I thought I heard that Tyrhest had been given the honour."

"But Tyrhest is not from one of the old families. He's an outsider, a servant, more or less, entirely dependent on the king's favour. It would be easy enough to replace him."

"But won't it happen, Thormond, that the old families will all, eventually, be replaced by newcomers? And they will be replaced in turn?"

"That's what worries me, my dear," said the duke, returning to his seat. "Look at my family…I have only one son, and he's not yet married, and my daughters, very well, I have grandchildren, but they've been taken up by their husbands' families, my…rivals, let's say. And Sismond…he has no children at all…"

Xancha was about to growl that he seemed to have forgotten one, the child she had once been obliged to give up, but he raised a hand.

"…legitimate, recognised children. I'm not forgetting. And I'm not forgetting that Sismond may have had any number of brats with those women he has taken in over the years without telling anyone, but none of them are family."

"And Geseric, he wishes to marry."

"Geseric…to that Saxon witch. You should've seen her when he found her down by the river, soaking wet and semi-naked, like a peasant – worse, like a half-drowned rat."

"I thought he was gallant to have rescued her," said Xancha.

Thormond turned abruptly towards her.

"He didn't. She rescued herself, threw herself off Altaar's boat and swam to the shore, if that story's to be believed. And what the hell was she doing, leaving with Altaar, in the first place?"

"I heard she was compelled, at sword point."

Thormond snorted.

"I don't trust them, none of them." He raised a finger which he wagged at Xancha. "I remember what Mother always said about that clan, that they only masquerade as Christians to keep out of trouble."

"There are many masquerading, Thormond," said Xancha, "and plenty more giving voice to their Christianity and behaving in quite a contrary manner. Don't think I haven't heard enough about The Word, my dear, given some of the men I've entertained over the years. Anyway, that's beside the point.

You're moaning about lack of sons in the family. Signy's already proved she can raise a son. Get Geseric married and let them start work. She seems to be keen enough to jump into a man's bed, that's quite clear. Soon you'll have a whole tribe of little heirs running around."

She raised her finger and wagged it back at her lover.

"Why not, if you're so desperate, offer to adopt the little boy she already has, Einar, isn't he called? A good Germanic name."

"Some northern pirate's offspring…forget it," grumped Thormond.

"Don't get so proud, my dear. You sometimes forget that your forefathers were chopping wood and living in skins when mine were priests and temple dancers in one of the finest cities in the world."

Thormond laughed. This was an old argument between them, and he never failed to reply the same way.

"Xancha, my darling, those priests could never have been your forefathers. They'd all cut their own balls off."

"That was an entirely different temple – the temple of Cybele, Thormond, as I've told you so many times before."

"They've all gone the same way in the end, balls or no balls," noted the freshly minted duke, sourly.

"The girl then, does Geseric get her or not? Otherwise, I'll write a letter to ex-count Altaar and let him know she's still free. If he's as heathen as you say, he might be tempted to take a second wife who shares his primitive tastes."

"Don't you dare!"

"Hah, you see."

"As a matter of fact," the duke muttered, "Sismond has offered to be godfather…you know, stand in for her actual father – whoever he might have been – at the marriage. Was even willing to put up a dowry, but apparently the girl has wealth of her own."

"It was me who told you that," Xancha quickly interjected. "And I've got something more to tell you. That sweet Bishop of Agininum, Anastasius, has offered to bless them in church…make the whole thing look decent."

"Anastasius…what's he got to do with us? He's a bishop of the Nicene church, not ours. He should keep out of this!"

"Darling, you just intimated that Signy isn't even a Christian, so he's doing you a big favour. My dear, now you're being obtuse. Signy's a pretty enough young woman – I'm sure you couldn't keep your eyes off her if she *was* semi-naked."

"Good God," Thormond suddenly muttered, getting to his feet, "that reminds me…I can't stay. They've arranged a feast, in my honour, the new duke, and I have to be there to welcome the guests."

"So you're going, and I'm not invited. What a spoilsport!"

"It's not me," grumbled Thormond. "I've a position, a place in society to uphold. I have to play the part."

She scrambled off the bed and crossed the room towards him.

"I know, my dear, and you can count on me to support you. But you will give your approval to Geseric, won't you?" she said, kissing him tenderly.

--oo0Ooo--

"Thank you," said Megana, as she and Bishop Anastasius descended the steps into the garden of the house in Olive Street, "you're a kind and generous man."

"Oh, you've had the fountain repaired," said the bishop, walking slightly ahead of her down the path.

"I brought a man up from Burdigala to fix it," she said. "Apparently, there's a pipe that leads under the house from the stream that runs behind the count's residence."

The bishop turned towards her.

"Your romantic side?" He smiled. "I knew you had one, and I always thought it was a pity this beautiful house was allowed to fall into disrepair. Soon the garden will look wonderful."

Megana had moved away from the fountain and settled on a stone bench nearby.

"Even *I* think there's more to life than making money," she said, patting the bench with her hand. "Come and sit here. It's warm from the sun."

The bishop stepped over and sat down beside her.

"I followed your advice," she said, "and passed your offer on to Xancha. I received a message from her today that Thormond has given his blessing to the marriage."

"I'm so pleased," said the bishop, "for your friend, for Geseric, for the happy young couple."

He turned and glanced in the direction of the fountain before continuing after a moment.

"It's at times like this I regret my own situation a little."

"Oh, yes?"

"I sometimes think it would have been nice to have gone through life with a companion by my side, children, a family for me to care for and to care for me."

He turned now and looked towards Megana.

"Don't you think you might feel lonely, if Signy moves away to live with her husband?"

"I hadn't planned to be lonely," Megana replied, unable for a moment to look him in the eye.

It was the bishop's turn to say, "Oh, yes?"

"I had hoped…" Megana continued, "I had hoped that I might have found a new friend."

"But, Megana, I can't…you know."

"I understand," she murmured. "I'm not expecting you to marry me, Anastasius."

"Just to be friends?" His voice had a tone of disappointment.

"Well, let me put it this way," she replied. "I had in my mind a slightly different arrangement."

The bishop looked slightly perplexed.

"All the benefits of marriage, but without the practical trouble of the legal state."

"Well, I…I'm not a young man…" he muttered, his focus on her large brown eyes, "…and you're so…"

"Companionship, love, a female touch, children, a family, isn't that what you said you're missing?" she whispered.

He reached out his arms, and for a moment, as she half stood up, they clutched a little clumsily in an embrace. Then she shifted around and sat down on his lap, her arms around him.

"Do we have a deal?" she asked in a businesslike tone, and seeing tears in his eyes, before he could answer, she pressed her lips against his.

♋ Character List ♌

Family and Friends

Signy (Wealda)	Saxon healer and midwife
Einar	Signy's son (infant)
Megana (Fabiana)	Merchant from Britain, Signy's best friend
Sophia	Megana's daughter (baby)
Lanius of Burdigala	Megana's business companion
Vespa	Lanius' wife
Alexander of Agatha	Megana's half-brother
Icauna	Alexander's wife, Lanius' sister
Thorgill	Jutish chief, Signy's dead husband (memory)

Court Circles

Altaar	Count of Cadurci, Ludiger's "nephew"
Geseric	Thormond's nephew, his adopted child
Ludiger	Duke of the Kingdom of Tolosa
Meltris	Count of Vasates
Ramius	Thormond's aide-de-camp
Raymond	Geseric's father (dead)
Rodmer	Count of Elusa
Sismond	Count of Aginnum
Theodoric (the elder)	King of the Visigoths (historical person)
Thormond	General, Count of Carcasso, Sismond's cousin
Wiseric	Thormond's son
Xancha	Former dancer, courtesan and businesswoman, Thormond's mistress

Servants and Countrypeople

Aija	Count Sismond's housekeeper
Alaya	Courtesan of Tolosa
Delia	Megana's personal maid
Delo, Lilia	A farmer and his daughter
Elemus, Jeanna	Farmer and his wife
Ferona	Ragvald's daughter and Signy's assistant
Filbert	Bishop Anastasius' clerk
Grunwald, Hrasmus, Asser	Signy's retainers from Juteland
Henrik	Megana's stablemaster in Aginnum
Jorid	Count Sismond's master-at-arms
Lothar	Count Altaar's servant
Maria	Nursemaid to the children
Pythias	Megana's factor in Tolosa
Ragvald	A robber, and gardener at the house in Olive Street

Svein	A silent Northman
Thaddeus, Tomas	Local men, servants of Megana and Signy
Tygon	Count Sismond's chamberlain
Victoria	Housekeeper, of Olive Street, Agininum

Religious People

Agatha	Herbalist of the Monastery of Mons Agininum
Anastasius	Bishop of Agininum
Angelus	Abbot of the monastery by the River Oltis
Barnabas	Bishop Anastasius' secretary
Bartolomeus	Bishop of Burdigala
Hildefrith	Abbess of the women's Monastery of Mons Agininum, Thormond's sister
Irmengaard	Pagan priestess, Signy's mentor in Juteland (memory)
Ophelia	Librarian of the Monastery of Mons Agininum, Lanius' and Icauna's mother
Parataxes, Cyrus, Clement	The chapter of Agininum
Petrus	Stablemaster of the Monastery of Mons Agininum
Wilbert, Michael	Monks from the monastery by the River Oltis
Xeno	Shepherd

Traders and Merchants

Osmo	Boat captain in Lanius' fleet
Tazzius, Caiphas, Gaulman	Merchants of Agininum
Vipso of Burdigala	Lanius' father-in-law

Romans

Aetius	*Magister militum* of the Roman Empire (historical person)
Avitus	Senior Roman official (historical person)
Junius	Roman officer and spy
Maxus	Centurion
Paulinus	Former landowner (historical person)

☙ Acknowledgements ❧

Many thanks to Kahina Necaise, Rachael Mortimer, and Cecily Blench for their comments and suggestions during the preparation of this manuscript, coordinated once againm by the folks at The History Quill (thehistoryquill.com). Thank you, too, to my wife, Marja, and to my mother, for their enthusiastic support.

☙ By the Same Author ❧

I
Memories of a Fading Empire

In the year 407 CE the influence of the Roman Empire on the province of Britannia is ebbing away. The imperial administrators and the legions have left, but thousands of people must continue their everyday lives as best they can. The departing governor of Britannia Prima suddenly appoints Marcus Lucullus Silvanus, the son of a regional landowner, as his delegate while he travels to Rome. When the governor disappears without trace, Marcus, his wife, Hypatia, the daughter of the missing governor, his friends and colleagues, struggle to preserve the bankrupt province, opposed by the jealous and determined Astrebanus brothers. The Romans have gone for ever, and a new era has begun, an era of chaos and decay, the era we know as the Dark Ages.

II
Journeys Through a Fading Empire

412 CE: From a dinner party in Verulamium, two journeys begin through the chaos and confusion of the late Roman Empire from Britannia, through Gaul and on to Rome. Ophelia Ursina, daughter of the governor of Britannia Prima, is seeking freedom and security. Drusus Astrebanus, son of the governor's arch enemy, is seeking vengeance for the death of his brother and the return of his family's property and status. In the wake of the failed uprising of General Flavius Claudius Constantinus, the usurper and co-Emperor Constantine III, the risks have only become greater as barbarians from the east infest the fading state. The rule of law no longer applies, and violence becomes the only defence. This is a dangerous world for men and even more so for women.

III
In the Shadow of a Fading Empire

430 CE: In the shadow of the fading empire of Rome, Marcus Lucullus Ursinus is toiling to maintain the peace and prosperity of the former province of Britannia Prima. Raiders from over the eastern sea may be the most obvious threat he faces, but the most dangerous challenge comes from growing tensions within the province, amplified by his deadly enemies, the Astrebani. The progress Marcus has worked for, securing the frontiers, forging alliances with neighbours, providing schooling for girls and boys, building a Christian church to appeal to pagans, employing taxes for the good of the public, and supporting competent and resourceful merchants, all appear to kindle disorder and strife. The cycle of history is turning, civilisation is in retreat and, despite Marcus' efforts, the future seems ever darker.

IV
On the Frontier of a Fading Empire

435 CE, in the Saxon lands. A girl, the daughter of the village midwife and herbalist, dreams of the lands which lie down the river which flows past her home, beyond the forest that fills the horizon. One day she is torn from her family by a band of passing boatmen and sold as a slave. Beyond the horizon, on the frontier of the fading empire, she discovers fear and pleasure, hatred and love, people she thought only existed in tales, and lands she could never have imagined, follow one another as the Fates decide. But each twist in the thread of her life provides an opportunity to learn, an opportunity to develop into a woman who can offer health and happiness, life or death.

Printed in the USA
CPSIA information can be obtained
at www.ICGtesting.com
LVHW021959231024
794641LV00009B/134

9 798218 524937